KU-262-782

SEDUCED BY SECOND CHANCES

REESE RYAN

ONE NIGHT, WHITE LIES

JESSICA LEMMON

MILLS & BOON

First Published in Great Britain 2019
by Mills & Boon, an imprint of HarperCollinsPublishers,
1 London Bridge Street, London, SE1 9GF

Seduced by Second Chances © 2019 Harlequin Books S.A.
One Night, White Lies © 2019 Jessica Lemmon

Special thanks and acknowledgement are given to Reese Ryan for her contribution to the *Dynasties: Secrets of the A-List* series.

ISBN: 978-0-263-27186-7

0719

MIX
Paper from
responsible sources
FSC C007454

Printed and bound in Spain
by CPI, Barcelona

SEDUCED BY SECOND CHANCES

REESE RYAN

For all of the amazing readers who read and
recommend my books, *thank you*!
Your support is invaluable.

For Building Relationships Around Books (BRAB),
Round Table Readers Literary Book Club,
Victorious Ladies Reading Book Club and Sistas'
Thoughts from Coast to Coast (STCC Book Club),
thank you for hosting me for lively book discussions.
I cherish the time spent with you and appreciate
all you do to promote authors.

One

Jessie Humphrey scrolled through her cell phone contacts and located the number she was searching for.

Her dream list of world-famous producers was a short one, but Chase Stratton reigned supreme. He'd worked with the top talent out there. Single-name artists at the pinnacle of their careers and critically acclaimed artists on the rise.

Jessie paced her tiny one-bedroom apartment in SoHo and chewed on her fingernails. Her entire future was riding on making this happen.

She sank onto the living room chair where she did much of her songwriting.

Her record label had offered her a new contract. To her agent's dismay, she'd rejected the offer. The studio wanted her to make cookie-cutter pop music rather than the soulful songs about love and loss that were her forte.

She'd been writing for some of the studio's biggest stars for years. As an artist, she had two albums under her belt and a growing base of die-hard fans. Including wealthy, powerful people like Matt Richmond, who'd paid her a generous fee to perform at his exclusive event in her hometown of Seattle, Washington.

With her current recording contract fulfilled, Jessie was at a stalemate with the label's top exec, Arnold Diesman.

She'd taken Matt Richmond's gig in Seattle because of the lucrative contract. Money she would invest in starting her own independent label where she would retain creative control.

Chase had a long line of artists with household names and the deep pockets of the record labels backing them. But Jessie needed to convince him to take a chance on working on her indie project.

She'd called in every favor she had to track down the phone number of Chase's personal assistant. Jessie dialed the number.

"This is Lita."

"Hi, Lita, this is Jessie Humphrey. I sent a couple of demos to Chase—"

"We received them. Thank you. But Chase's schedule is booked solid right now."

"I'm not surprised. He's the top producer out there right now." Jessie was undeterred by the woman's attempt to blow her off. "I know I'm not one of the single-name artists he usually works with and that I won't have the backing of a big studio for this project—"

"You realize you're making a case *against* me passing your demo on to Chase, right?" Lita laughed.

"Just acknowledging the obvious." Jessie paced the hardwood floors. "But he should consider my growing fan base. They don't care whether a big studio is behind the album. They only care that—"

"Look, honey, not everyone can drop an independent surprise album that'll shoot up the charts. And it's unheard of for an independently produced album to be Grammy-worthy. I know Beyoncé and Chance the Rapper made it look easy, but it isn't. And Chase only deals in top caliber projects. Now, if you have your studio rep contact us…"

"My contract is over and I'm not interested in signing another. I want complete creative control." Jessie continued when the woman didn't respond. "I've written huge radio hits for Top 40 acts. I know what sells."

"Look, Jessie… I'm a huge fan. But Chase has much bigger projects in his sights. And without studio backing…" The woman lowered her voice. "There's a reason Chase commands such an exorbitant payday. He selects his projects carefully. He always wins because he only plays the game when he's holding a royal flush. I listened to your demo. The songs are amazing and so is your voice. But Chase isn't willing to take on the risk of working with you without the backing of the studio."

"I see." Jessie stopped pacing. Tears stung her eyes.

"I'll hold on to your demo. When Chase needs a new songwriter, I'll recommend you. Maybe once he works with you in that capacity, he'll take a chance on your indie project."

"If I could just talk to him myself—"

"Sorry, Jessie. This is the best I can do for you right now. Chase is preparing to work on the West Coast for the next several weeks. But I'll keep you in mind when he needs a new songwriter. Promise."

"Lita, wait—"

The woman had already ended the call. Jessie sat at the piano that took up most of the space in her living room.

She'd have to find another way to get face time with Chase.

Jessie was determined to make authentic music. She

wouldn't be strong-armed by the studio into cranking out forgettable songs.

It wasn't about the money or the fame. Playing the piano while singing songs she'd penned about the pain that had ripped her heart in two alleviated those feelings. It seemed just as cathartic for audience members who sang along with tears in their eyes. That connection with her listeners meant everything.

That was what she wanted to share with the world.

Chase Stratton had name recognition and a string of hits under his belt. He took an artist's raw material and spun it into gold while respecting their unique sound.

She had something different to offer the world, and she needed a team around her discerning enough to recognize that.

She'd find another way to get to Chase. And when she did, she'd be ready.

Jessie grabbed a pen from her little side table, and the pile of magazines on it shifted. She picked up the ones that had fallen to the floor.

The financial magazine bore the image of the incredibly handsome Gideon Johns.

After all these years, sadness still swept over her whenever she thought of Gideon. And she hadn't been able to stop thinking of him since her recent return to Seattle for Matt Richmond's event. She'd been equal parts hopeful and terrified that she'd encounter Gideon for the first time in well over a decade.

Gideon had been the reason she'd written her very first song. A song of heartbreak and unrequited love. It had been one of the songs on the demo that earned Jessie her first songwriting gig with a small record company. So rather than resenting Gideon's rejection, she should thank him for breaking her heart.

Nothing had really happened between them back then. And nothing would happen between them in the future. So why couldn't she let thoughts of Gideon go?

Jessie tossed the magazines back onto the pile and returned to the piano, pen in hand.

She hated that she was still so affected by a man to whom she clearly hadn't meant anything. But berating herself over it wasn't productive. Instead, she would allow those frustrations to fuel her creativity so she could write the next song.

Jessie scribbled a few notes that had been playing in her head all day on the blank staff paper. Then she played the corresponding notes on her piano and started to sing.

Gideon Johns sat on the front edge of his large cherrywood desk. He folded his arms as he sized up his assistant, Landon Farmer. He had something to say, and whatever it was, he was fully aware that Gideon wasn't going to like it.

"Look, Landon, whatever it is you're dancing around here…just say it. We're both busy people."

"Our top two investors just pulled out of the United Arab Emirates deal." The words rushed out of his mouth.

"What?" Gideon's voice boomed, filling the room. He hadn't intended to shout, and since the man looked like he wanted to flee the room, he felt bad for doing so. Still, it was a natural reaction to discovering that he'd lost half of the capital he was counting on for a two-billion-dollar building project.

"What the hell happened? The last time I spoke with them, they were champing at the bit to get in on this deal. In fact, I didn't solicit either of them. They came to me."

"Both cited the recent volatility in their own industries, Mr. Johns." The man reverted to addressing him formally whenever Gideon was displeased.

"Do they have any idea how much I have riding on this deal? This is our first project in Dubai. If word gets out that the deal is collapsing—"

"Then we don't let it collapse." Landon sat a bit straighter.

"And where do you propose we get nearly a billion dollars in the next two months?" Gideon raised an eyebrow.

"The company has considerable assets, sir. You already know that—"

"No." It was a single, nonnegotiable sentence.

"But, sir—"

"Investing in the project isn't an option." Gideon returned to his seat. His chest felt tight and his head was beginning to throb.

"But you just said what a disaster it would be if the project fails—"

"It won't fail. I'll find the money." Gideon looked at him pointedly.

"I have no doubt that you will, Mr. Johns." Landon straightened his tie. "But what if you can't secure the funds? Wouldn't it be better for our company to invest in the project than to have to admit we couldn't raise the capital?"

"Making real estate deals using other people's money has been my policy for the past ten years. If investors discover that I needed to liquidate assets and sink that kind of cash into my own project, it'll wreck the brand I've spent a decade building."

"We could do it discreetly," Landon suggested.

"I believe in being transparent with my investors." Gideon frowned. "Besides, liquidating that kind of cash will inevitably attract attention."

"All valid points." Landon stood and massaged the nape of his neck. "I'll scour our database of potential investors and see who might be right for the Dubai project."

"Go for the big fish. And focus on those who have liquid assets readily available. We need to stick to our original timeline or the remaining investors will start to worry." Gideon made a mental note of the effects this sudden change might have on the project.

"There is one potential investor who comes to mind right away."

"I know." Gideon tapped the table. "Matt Richmond."

Matt was a friend who'd mused about investing in one of Gideon's projects, but had yet to pull the trigger.

Gideon made it a point not to pressure investors to join his projects. He simply laid out the opportunity and return on investment to be had, and allowed his track record and reputation to do the rest. The timing wasn't great, but he'd need to prod Matt and see if he was serious about investing.

This project had the potential to make all of them a shitload of money. He'd never take the project on if he didn't wholeheartedly believe that. Nor would he ever try to rope his friend, or any investor, into a shaky deal. But he needed to be a bit more direct with his friend.

"I've got Matt. I'll try to meet with him within the next week." Gideon woke his computer screen to send an email to his friend. Another email captured his interest.

It was the Google alert he'd set up on singer/songwriter Jessie Humphrey. She was beautiful, brilliant, talented—and the little sister of his ex, Geneva Humphrey. The woman he'd planned to marry a lifetime ago. Right up until the moment she'd broken his heart.

He'd gotten over the break with Geneva. Had even come to realize she'd been right to end things between them. But his relationship with Jessie was more complicated.

Two years after his breakup with Geneva, Jessie had shown up at his door wanting more than just friendship. She was his ex's sister, so he'd promptly sent her packing. But he hadn't ever been able to forget that day. Or get thoughts of Jessie out of his head.

The first time he heard Jessie Humphrey's voice flowing from the speakers of his Aston Martin Vanquish Volante he'd been over the moon with happiness for her.

She'd walked around wearing headphones and singing her heart out for as long as he'd known her. And despite her parents' insistence that she pursue a "real" career, Jessie had always wanted to share her gift with the world.

Now she was and he couldn't be more proud of her.

Gideon had carefully followed her career ever since.

"Is that all, boss?" Landon furrowed his brow.

"Yes, thank you." Gideon waited for the man to leave, closing the door behind him.

Gideon clicked the link in the email. It took him to a video of Jessie performing at a small club, seated at a piano.

She was stunning. Who knew that she'd turn into such a beautiful, confident young woman and a rising artist?

Jessie had such a powerful voice and a unique sound, even back when he'd known her. Geneva had teased Jessie about her incessant singing and starry-eyed dreams, but Gideon had loved to hear her sing. He'd told her that one day she'd be famous. And he'd been right.

When the performance ended, he listened to it twice more. Despite following Jessie's career, he'd decided against reaching out to her. After the way they'd left things, he doubted Jessie would welcome seeing him again. And he didn't need the heartbreak of falling for another Humphrey sister.

It was safer to admire Jessie from a distance.

Which was a shame, because he'd love to see her again.

Two

Teresa St. Claire had spent most of the week hiding out in her office. Once she arrived in the morning, she'd only peeked her head out when it had been absolutely necessary.

Yes, she was the boss. But she felt like the screwup employee who'd put the entire company in jeopardy.

Every time she closed her eyes, she could see the ugly headline that had been running for the past week.

Mogul's Torrid Affair with Father's Mistress Ends after Her Surprise Inheritance Revealed.

She'd been pegged as a home-wrecking gold digger who'd had an affair with the late Linus Christopher and now had her sights set on his heir Liam. The ugly rumors, complete with uncomplimentary videos and photos, lit up the airwaves and seemed to follow her everywhere online.

Teresa had been hounded by gossip columnists and bloggers. Even a woman she'd always considered a reputable reporter had shown up at her home, inquiring about the nature of Teresa's relationship with both Christopher men.

The effect the rumors were having on her business was bad enough. But the additional tension it had created between her and Liam was unbearable. She could only imagine the embarrassment the rumors were causing him.

Teresa wiped away warm tears when she recalled the expression on Liam's face when he'd confronted her about the rumors. He'd even had the audacity to imply that she might've been behind them. Still, her brain was flooded with the warmth and passion that had been growing steadily between them, despite his constant mistrust of her.

She sighed. The outer office was uncharacteristically quiet. Other than calls from gossip reporters, the phones barely rang. Her employees spoke in hushed tones with their heads together rather than with the jovial, energetic nature she was accustomed to.

At this rate, the doors of Limitless Events would be shuttered for good in a few weeks, and it would be her fault.

A knock at the door startled her from her thoughts.

Teresa sat ramrod straight in the chair behind her desk. "Come in."

Corinne, her personal assistant, stepped inside. The woman dragged a hand through her headful of red corkscrew curls with an exasperated frown.

"We've had another cancellation, haven't we?" Teresa practically held her breath. That made three this week already. Not to mention the three or four clients who'd gotten nervous about having her plan their parties. It had been all she could do to calm them down so they wouldn't jump ship. But she realized that any one of them might change their minds at any time.

Corinne nodded. "Maggie Ellington called to say that she's sorry, but she just can't take a chance that the scandal won't have died down by the time of her daughter's wedding."

"That's understandable." Teresa tried to sound unaffected by the latest news. "She wants to make sure her daughter and son-in-law are the center of attention, not me."

"You mean she wants to make sure that *she's* the center of attention, and she won't be upstaged by anyone. Not even the bride." Corinne folded her arms.

"True." Teresa laughed and gave her assistant a reassuring smile. "But we'd both do the same if we were in her shoes. I can't blame her. In fact, I don't blame any of them for canceling."

"Well, I do." Corinne dropped into the chair in front of Teresa's desk. "They're all a bunch of hypocrites. Most of them have done more scandalous things on an average Tuesday than you're being accused of. Not to mention that the whole story is just a crock of—"

"I get it, Corinne." Teresa held up a hand to calm her assistant.

Corinne was fiercely loyal and feisty as hell. She knew how to get things done and she wasn't easily deterred. It made her an invaluable assistant. But it also meant that this situation wasn't sitting well with her.

"That may be true." Teresa shrugged. "But we can't force them to work with us."

"So what do we do in the meantime? The phones are barely ringing. If clients keep jumping ship…" Corinne's cheeks flushed.

"We won't let it get to that," Teresa said firmly. "I'm trying to drum up business with some new clients. The kind who don't run scared at the first hint of scandal."

"Reality stars?" Corinne asked, then rolled her eyes when Teresa confirmed with the nod of her head. "God, they're the worst." She heaved a sigh. "But hey, I get it. We have to do what we have to do. For now."

"The other key element of weathering this storm is

that we hold on to as many current clients as we can. Keep reassuring them that this has all been a big misunderstanding and it'll blow over soon. Speaking of holding on to the clients we have now, have you heard from Matt Richmond?"

Limitless Events had planned an elaborate business retreat on behalf of Matt Richmond—the incredibly handsome and fabulously wealthy CEO of Richmond Industries—at The Opulence last week. The hotel was extravagant and luxurious, the food was going to be delectable, and the guest list was to include the rich and powerful. The event was the talk of the town, but for all the wrong reasons.

Torrential rains caused a mudslide that had knocked out the power and damaged the hotel before the retreat could take place. Matt Richmond's event should've been Limitless Event's pièce de résistance. Instead, it descended into a chaotic catastrophe for the dozen or so guests who'd arrived early. Though she obviously didn't control the weather, Teresa felt responsible for the calamitous party.

Thankfully, Matt Richmond hadn't blamed her for the disastrous nonevent. Undeterred by the incredible fail, he'd been determined to reschedule the retreat. Yet he hadn't called, as he'd promised, to initiate the planning.

Had he not returned her calls because of the scandal hitting the airwaves? Or had Liam, Matt's best friend, discouraged him from working with her?

"I haven't heard from him and whenever I've called, his assistant can't get a hold of him." Corinne shrugged apologetically. "Maybe we should call Nadia. After all, she does work for you."

"As an independent contractor," Teresa clarified. "And I don't like the idea of leveraging her marriage to Matt. That isn't why I asked her to work with me."

"Then maybe I should visit his office."

"No…don't." Teresa waved off the suggestion. She could imagine Corinne's friendly visit to Matt going wrong six ways to Sunday. "I'll try him again later. How is the search for a new venue going?"

Corinne's frown deepened and she blew a puff of air between her plump lips. "Not well. Not if Richmond is determined to schedule the retreat anytime soon. The venues with openings in the next couple of months don't meet our standards of elegance and luxury."

"I was afraid of that." Teresa heaved a sigh. "I know it's a tall order, but keep trying. Ask our top choices to call us first, in the event of a cancellation."

"Will do." Corinne popped up from her seat, her red curls bouncing. "Anything else, chief?"

"No." Teresa riffled through papers on her desk, knocking over a small four-by-six photo of her and her brother, Joshua, on a trip to Mexico together a few years ago. She picked up the photo. "Have you heard from my brother? He left me several messages when my phone went dead last week, but I haven't been able to contact him since then."

"I haven't taken any calls from him." Worry lined Corinne's forehead. "Should I try to raise him for you?"

"No, you have enough on your plate." Teresa set the photo back in place. "It's probably just Joshua being Joshua. I've left him several messages. He'll resurface when he's ready."

Corinne nodded, closing the door behind her.

Teresa relaxed in the comfy leather executive chair she'd splurged on when they'd opened the office. Now she only hoped she wouldn't be forced to shutter her doors and sell it along with everything else.

She was trying hard to keep it together, but it was a lot to ask when her entire world was imploding. The ill-fated weekend extravaganza, the false rumors, her brother's disappearance. But the thing that made her heart ache was Liam's rejection.

Amid the craziness of bad weather and a tree falling through the hotel that had nearly taken her out were moments that had taken her breath away. Her cheeks flushed and her entire body filled with heat whenever she thought of their steamy encounter in that spa room. And her heart stirred when she recalled the worry in his eyes when he'd rescued her from beneath that tree and tended to her ankle.

Without thought, Teresa rotated her ankle, still a little sore.

She'd been grateful he'd confided in her that night, explaining to her why he had such difficulty trusting people. But after all they'd been through and the moments they'd shared...how could he still not trust her?

Her desk phone rang and she picked it up. "Yes?"

"I tried Richmond's office again. His assistant was out and he answered," Corinne said triumphantly. "I have him on the line now."

Teresa smoothed a hand down her pant leg. "Thank you, Corinne. Please put him through."

"Hello, Matt, I know you're busy, so I'll only take a moment of your time," Teresa said cheerfully. "Last week, you indicated that you'd like to reschedule the retreat as soon as possible. I wanted to touch base so we can move forward with the plans."

There was a moment of uncomfortable silence. Teresa's pulse raced.

Oh no. He's going to cancel, too.

"When will The Opulence be available again?" he asked finally. "I know Shane Adams has people working around the clock, but..."

"Not anytime soon, I'm afraid. And once they do re-open, they're booked solid for several months. Would you like to wait until then?"

"No. It's for our fifth anniversary, so I'd like to keep the event as close to the anniversary date as possible. I realize not all of the people who were originally invited will be available if we reschedule with such a short timeline. So we'll need to expand the guest list based on how many from the original list will be able to attend."

"Just have your assistant pass those additional names on to Corinne and we'll take care of the rest."

"So then you have a venue in mind?" His tone was doubtful.

"Not yet," she admitted. "But my staff is working tirelessly to find a venue that's available on short notice and meets our standards and yours. I'll be in touch as soon as I have a few good options."

"And what about a headliner? Would Jessie Humphrey be willing to perform at the rescheduled event?"

Embroiled in a scandal and bleeding clients, Teresa hadn't considered whether Jessie would be willing to fly across the country again for the rescheduled event. Not to mention that she might have a conflict in her schedule.

"I'll do my very best to book her. Same deal?"

"Yes. I'll look forward to hearing from you once you've worked the details out."

Her phone pinged with a text message.

"I just sent you the two weekends that are most ideal for this event."

Teresa strained the panic from her voice. Both options were only a few weeks away. "I'll get right on it."

"Anything else?" he asked.

Teresa gripped the receiver tightly and nibbled her lower lip. She wanted desperately to ask Matt how his best friend was holding up under the glare of the rumors and innuendo about them. But this was business. Besides, she didn't want to drag Matt into this.

"No, but I wanted to say thank you for not giving up on my company or me despite everything that's happened. I can't tell you how much I appreciate it."

"You're welcome, Teresa," Matt said after a long pause. "Call me when you've got a venue and Jessie has confirmed."

Teresa hung up, grateful she still had Matt Richmond's confidence. She was more determined than ever to reward it.

"You can't just walk in there." She could hear Corinne's voice through the closed door.

Suddenly the door opened. Liam stood glaring at her.

"It's all right, Corinne." Teresa held up a hand. "I'll take it from here."

Corinne narrowed her eyes at him, then walked off in a huff.

"Have a seat." She gestured toward the chair when he closed the door behind him.

"I won't be staying long. I just came to remind you that, according to my father's will, your presence is required at Christopher Corporation's board meeting." He folded his arms.

His icy glare chilled her. He regarded her as if she were an untrustworthy stranger.

Had he forgotten that he'd shared his deepest vulnerabilities with her just a week ago? Brought her incredible pleasure on several occasions before that? Rescued her when she'd needed him desperately? They should be working together to clear their names, currently being dragged through the mud.

But the hardened look that distorted Liam's handsome

face indicated that it would be a wasted argument. He was back to treating her as his enemy.

"In light of the rumors swirling about us, I didn't think you'd want me there." She raked her manicured fingernails through her shoulder-length blond hair.

"Pity my father's will didn't make allowances for bad press," he said dryly.

She folded her arms on the desk in front of her rather than raising the single digit that would best convey how she felt. "My assistant has access to my calendar. On your way out, stop by her desk and make an appointment."

Three

Liam's face and ears burned with heat in response to Teresa's brush-off. She'd summarily dismissed him and had returned her attention to the sheet of paper on her desk.

He clenched his jaw as he surveyed her. She was beautiful in a royal-blue silk blouse and white linen pantsuit. Teresa looked hurt and angry. She obviously just wanted him to be gone.

Liam couldn't blame her.

He'd blown into her office, behaving like an ass. But he was furious with her for putting his family and business in this position. *Again.* And he was furious with himself because he still wanted her…desperately. Despite everything that had happened. Despite the rumors swirling around about them. Despite the fact that he wasn't sure he could trust her.

Shit.

He must seriously be out of his mind because he wanted to trust her. And he cared for her. But he wouldn't allow anyone to make a fool of him. And there was still a strong possibility that was Teresa's endgame.

So why did he feel such a strong pull toward her? And why did he want her more than he'd ever wanted any woman?

Teresa insisted that her relationship with his late father had been strictly that of a mentor and his mentee. But the man he'd known his entire life would never have given a quarter of his company to anyone out of the mere goodness of his heart. Hell, he'd often wondered if Linus Christopher had possessed even an ounce of selflessness.

Was he really supposed to believe that the man who couldn't be bothered to show his own son warmth and compassion would've left this woman 25 percent of the company's shares unless there'd been something more to their relationship than either one of them had been willing to admit?

Teresa leaned back in her chair, narrowing her blue eyes at him. "Are you going to stand there all day brooding? This is my place of business. I have work to do."

Liam sighed. "Look, I know I came off like a complete ass just now. I'm sorry. But you need to face the fact that if you want to liquidate that stock, you'll need to comply with the stipulations of my father's will. That means we have to work together, and you need to be at the meeting this afternoon."

Teresa checked her calendar begrudgingly. "Fine. What time should I be there?"

"Actually, my car service is waiting. I thought we could ride over together so I could bring you up to speed on the meeting." Liam gestured toward the door.

"The sooner we leave, the sooner I can get back here." She pursed her lips in a sensual pout that made him want to take her in his arms and kiss her.

His hands balled into fists at his side.

She's the enemy. Why can't you remember that?

"It's best if we aren't seen leaving the building together," he mused aloud, more to himself than her.

"Then why are you here in my place of business? Or didn't you notice the stalkerazzi parked across the street?"

Liam straightened his tie. "I came in through the back entrance."

"Well, you can leave the same way you came in."

The hurt in her eyes and the pained tone of her voice made him feel as awful as his father. The last thing he wanted was to mimic Linus Christopher's cruelty. After his talk with Teresa, he'd thought a lot about his relationship with his father. And his relationship with her.

"If you need to bring me up to speed on the meeting, call me from your car. In fact, you could've done that in the first place rather than showing up here and *demanding* that I drop everything and come with you."

Liam squeezed the bridge of his nose. The situation was snowballing and he was the one to blame. "I'd like to go over a few documents in the car. It'll be much easier if we ride together in the limousine."

He shoved both his hands in his pockets and leaned against a tall wooden filing cabinet. Hoping she'd say yes. Because while every word he'd said about them needing to work together was true, the deeper truth was that he'd missed Teresa.

He missed the scent and feel of her skin, the way her sparkling blue eyes danced when she laughed and the sweet taste of her pouty lips. And he missed the incomparable ecstasy of watching Teresa St. Claire fall apart in his arms.

Teresa stood in the nude Stuart Weitzman block-heel sandals she'd worn in deference to her still-sore ankle. She retrieved her matching nude clutch from her desk drawer and walked to the door, only slightly favoring her injured leg.

"Your ankle…" He furrowed his brow. "Is it okay?"

"It's fine. Just a little sore." Teresa didn't want to think of Liam as the man who'd rushed to her rescue that night. Nor did she want to forget that he'd come charging into her office like an entitled ass who thought the world revolved around him. Still, she wouldn't behave like an ogre, even if he had. "Thank you again for what you did that night."

"I'm just glad you weren't seriously hurt. When I think of what could've happened…" He seemed genuinely distressed by the near miss. "I'm just glad it didn't."

Don't be swayed by a few kind words.

She walked out to Corinne's desk, not acknowledging the evil eye her assistant was giving Liam.

"We're a go for the retreat." Teresa forwarded Matt's text to Corinne. "I just sent the dates Matt Richmond is interested in. Pull a couple of staff members in to call the entire guest list. Find out if either date is tenable. With such a short turnaround, we should get a feel for whether either date will work before we put too much time and effort into it."

"Got it." Corinne scribbled notes on a sheet of paper.

"I need a list of viable venues as soon as you can come up with them. I'll work on a few possibilities from my end, too. There has to be something available in Seattle that fits the bill for an event of this magnitude. Don't call Jessie Humphrey. I'll call her. A bit of persuading might be required after the nightmare we put her through last time."

Corinne nodded her agreement. She eyed Liam again, then shifted her gaze to Teresa. "Will you be returning to the office?"

Teresa cast a glance over her shoulder at Liam. He was especially handsome in a navy suit that hugged his strong frame and reminded her of all the reasons she loved the feel of his toned body pressed to hers.

But he'd rejected her after their unbelievably hot encounter at the spa. And again after the rumors about her being a scheming gold digger surfaced, despite the poignant moments they'd shared the night before.

Teresa's spine tensed. She gripped the clutch under her arm and reminded herself to hold on to that anger. So she'd never end up in Liam's bed again.

"I have every intention of returning here as soon as I can." Teresa turned and made her way toward the door, aware that every pair of eyes in the office was focused on her and Liam Christopher.

They left the building by the back entrance, where Liam's driver was waiting. Her cheeks stung at the thought of being shuttled away under cover because he was embarrassed to be seen with her. She slid across the leather seat, putting as much space as possible between them.

Liam had the audacity to look hurt.

"I know you have things you'd like to go over, but I need to make a call first. If there's any chance Jessie Humphrey isn't already obligated on the dates I have available, I don't want to miss my window of opportunity."

"Of course." He picked up a black leather portfolio and shuffled through its contents.

Teresa pulled up Jessie Humphrey's number and hoped things would finally go her way.

Four

Jessie closed her eyes and settled into eagle pose, her left leg wound around her right and her right arm wrapped around her left. Unable to keep her mind still long enough to formally meditate, she enjoyed the moving meditation of yoga.

The ring of her cell phone disturbed her peaceful solitude.

She unraveled her arms and legs and peeked at the caller ID.

"Teresa St. Claire." She muttered the name under her breath, then considered ignoring it until she'd finished her yoga practice.

But Teresa had indicated that Matt Richmond wanted to reschedule his event. Despite the chaos of the heavy rains, power outage, and a tree falling into the hotel which nearly took Teresa out... Matt Richmond had generously paid her the full agreed-upon amount of her contract without quibbling.

If she was going to do this project independently, without the backing of her label or the blessing of her agent, she needed an infusion of cold, hard cash.

Jessie answered the call just before it went to voice mail. "Hello."

"Jessie, it's Teresa. I'm glad I caught you. Matt Richmond has decided to reschedule his retreat. The only bright spot to the entire ordeal at The Opulence was your impromptu concert in the lobby. I swear, it's probably the only thing that kept the guests from rioting." Teresa's words were rushed and her voice seemed tense. "So, of course, he'd like you to perform at the rescheduled event."

Not wanting to sound too eager, Jessie hesitated before responding. "That's nice of you to say, Teresa. The situation got pretty intense, so I'm glad I was able to help. The event isn't going to be held there again, is it? It was a lovely hotel, but after the mudslide I'm not in love with hotels situated on a cliff."

"Understood. It'll be a while before The Opulence is up and running again anyway. And Matt would really like to get this retreat done soon—"

"How soon?"

"He's considering two weekends this month." Teresa's tone was tentative. "I'm hoping you'll be available on one of them."

Jessie grimaced. She'd planned to spend the month writing songs for her next album and securing the producers and musicians she wanted to work with on her dream project. "Actually, I cleared my calendar to work on my next album."

"I can appreciate how busy you must be, Jessie, but if you have any flexibility at all, you know Matt Richmond will make it worth your while. We'd do the same generous deal as last time. In addition to your booking fee, we'll pay for your flight via private jet, and all of your room service expenses at the hotel."

Jessie chewed on her lower lip and paced the floor. "I don't know. This album is really important to me. I didn't tell you before, but I've decided not to re-sign with my current label. I plan to start my own, so I'll have the freedom to make songs like the ones I performed that day in the lobby."

"I applaud your decision, Jessie. I did the same when I broke away from MSM Events and started my own company. So I know how rewarding it can be, but I also know that you need money and connections when you're breaking out on your own. And at Richmond Industries' fifth anniversary gala, you'll have an opportunity to nab both."

"What do you mean?" Jessie sat on the edge of her sofa. "Who's going to be at the retreat?"

"Since not all of the invited guests will be able to attend on such short notice, Matt instructed me to expand the list. If there's a producer or music exec you're eyeing for your new project, I could try to have them added to the guest list. I can't promise you they'll attend, but I'll do my best to get them there. I'll even seat you at the same table."

Jessie sat on the piano bench. As much as she'd like to spend the next several weeks immersed in this project, if she was going to make it a reality, she needed the money she'd get from this gig. And if Teresa St. Claire could get her at a table with Chase Stratton or Dixon Benedict and allow her to showcase some of the new material she was working on for the album, all the better.

"And if you're looking for wealthy music lovers who might be willing to help bankroll your project, there'll be a few in attendance, I'm sure. Also, we might be able to increase your exposure by broadcasting your performance live this time. If that's something you want, I'll talk to Nicolette Ryan about it."

There were too many benefits to this deal to ignore. "You've got a deal. Send the contract over to my agent."

Sinking onto the mat, Jessie tried to resume her yoga practice.

She'd managed to avoid Gideon Johns the last time she'd returned to Seattle. Maybe she could again. The money and exposure were worth the risk.

If she did cross paths with him, things didn't need to be awkward. She couldn't stop thinking of him, but he probably hadn't given her another thought. So she'd hold her head high, greet him politely and move on with her life.

Jessie allowed her eyes to drift closed as she inhaled a deep breath. Everything would be fine. In fact, it might be good to see Gideon again. Perhaps it would prompt her to relinquish the silly fantasy she still held on to. Then she could finally let go of the past and any thoughts of what might've been.

"Good news." Landon knocked on the partially open door of Gideon's office. "You won't have to pin Matt Richmond down for a meeting after all."

"Why not?" Gideon looked up from his laptop where he'd been writing an email, trying to close the deal with a potential investor in the Dubai project. "Have we gotten all the capital we need?"

"Not yet." Landon frowned as he took a few steps inside Gideon's office. "But we're close. And I think we might've gotten even closer. I just confirmed that you'll be available to attend the rescheduled Richmond Industries anniversary retreat."

Gideon leaned back in his seat and rubbed his chin.

"Matt is hosting the event, so it'll be hard to pin him down for a one-on-one presentation."

"I'll put together a quick video presentation with all of the basic facts. Something eye-catching that'll grab his attention." Landon slid into the chair in front of Gideon's desk. "You can hand him a copy of the prospectus as well as email it to him so he can review it at length."

"Good work, Landon."

"Thanks." He grinned, settling in the chair.

Gideon raised an eyebrow. "Guess that means you'd better get to work."

"Right." Landon hopped up quickly and headed for the door. "Oh, and I sent you over that list of prospective investors."

"I'm working on it now," Gideon confirmed. He peered through his thumb and forefinger. "I'm this close to securing another hundred million."

Landon's phone rang. But rather than a traditional ringer, it played a familiar song.

"That song…"

"Sorry, I usually turn my ringer off in the office, but I just came back from lunch and—"

"That's a Jessie Humphrey song, isn't it?" He'd recognize Jessie's soulful, heart-wrenching voice anywhere.

"Yeah, it's one of the more obscure songs on her recent album. It doesn't get any radio play, but if you ask me, it's one of the best songs on the album." Landon seemed impressed that he knew who Jessie Humphrey was. "My girlfriend loves the song, too. That's why I chose it as her ringtone."

"Well, you'd better call her back, huh?" Gideon went back to typing out his email.

"Right. But I'll send you the tentative dates for the retreat first. And I'll get to work on that presentation just as soon as I can."

Gideon hit Send on the email. Then he pulled out his phone and searched for Jessie's recent album. He'd purchased every album she'd made and the songs she wrote for other artists over the years.

Despite the debacle of the kiss, Jessie had been a friend. Someone he truly cared for. He wanted only the best for her.

He stared at the album cover where Jessie sat in a leather chair wearing a short, flirty dress and a sexy smile. He often wondered if things would've turned out differently between them if more time had passed after his breakup with Geneva before Jessie had kissed him. Would he still have reacted negatively? Or would he have kissed her back?

Gideon shook the thought from his brain. They'd both gone on to fulfill their dreams. Wasn't that proof enough that things had happened just as they should?

He scrolled through the song list. Most of the songs on this album had an upbeat pop sound. But the song Landon had chosen as his girlfriend's ringtone was more like the soulful performance Jessie had given in that intimate little club. It was the kind of song that made her unique vocals shine.

Gideon shut the door to his office and played the song on repeat, losing himself in the mellow sound of Jessie's voice and her heartbreaking lyrics.

Five

Teresa ended the call with Jessie Humphrey, holding back a squeal of glee. In an otherwise crappy day, this was a victory worth celebrating.

She tapped out a quick email to Corinne confirming that Jessie Humphrey would perform. She asked her assistant to make sure the contract was ready to send the moment they selected a date and secured the venue.

Teresa checked the shared spreadsheet updating which guests were available on either of the possible weekends.

"Shit," Teresa mumbled under her breath.

"What's wrong?" Liam stopped scanning the documents in his folder. His smoldering blue eyes seemed to slice right through her. "You just secured your headliner. I'd think you'd be ecstatic."

"I'm thrilled that Jessie confirmed." Teresa ignored the fluttering in her belly and the electricity that danced along her spine when he stared at her that way. "But I'm not happy that most of the guests are selecting the earlier date. That gives us just two weeks to find a venue and get everything in motion. So far, every suitable venue in Seattle is booked. I'm going to have to venture outside the area."

"Have you considered Napa Valley?" Liam returned his attention to the documents.

"That's at least six hundred miles from Seattle."

"Seven, but who's counting?" Liam's eyes danced when they met hers and a sexy little smirk curved one corner of his mouth. It reminded her of the look he'd given her when he'd…

Teresa shut her eyes and tried to push thoughts of their amazing nights together from her brain.

"That would considerably increase the cost of the event."

"True. But it might also lure more people there. Especially those who are still unhappy about what happened at the previous event in Seattle. The beauty of the vineyards and an endless supply of wine will earn you a lot of forgiveness with this crowd. Besides, it's the company's fifth anniversary. Matt needs to make a big splash with this event so everyone will forget what happened at The Opulence."

"All good points, but I can't book a venue without seeing it for myself. I need to make sure there's adequate event space, suitable accommodations and trained, professional staff. I'd need to sample the food and attest to the cleanliness of the rooms. I'd want to talk to people who've used the venue before to make sure their level of customer service is on par with what my clients expect."

"So find a few possible venues and fly there and check them out." Liam shrugged.

Teresa gritted her teeth. Was he being intentionally flippant about something that could make or break her?

"I would, but my private plane is in the shop." She dropped her phone in her clutch and snapped it shut.

Liam chuckled, his eyes twinkling. "Then by all means, take mine."

"Now you're just being cruel." She folded her arms and pursed her lips. "I know this doesn't mean anything to you, but this event is important to me. With everything that's going on right now, this might be my only chance to keep my company from going under."

"I wasn't being facetious." His tone and expression seemed genuinely apologetic. "I'm being sincere."

Teresa stared at him, blinking. "I don't get it. Not an hour ago you could barely stand to be in the same room with me. Now you're offering to let me use your private plane to plan your friend's event?"

"That's just it," he said quickly. "Matt's my best friend and this event is important to him. I want to ensure his retreat succeeds. Besides, Matt and I will be making the announcement about our joint venture, the Sasha Project, so I'm invested in the success of this event, too. That's why I'd like to accompany you on this scouting trip."

Teresa stared at him blankly, still waiting for him to pull the rug from beneath her. She sifted her fingers through her hair. "I'll have to check with Matt first. If he's good with relocating the event to Napa Valley, I'll gladly accept your offer. Thank you."

"Anything for a friend," Liam said calmly, though his heart danced in his chest. He could barely keep from smiling at the thought of spending time alone with Teresa in Napa Valley.

She's supposed to be the enemy.

Yet he wanted to haul her onto his lap and kiss her like it was the only kiss he'd ever need. The way he'd kissed her when last she'd been in his arms.

His eyes drifted to her momentarily, scanning the royal-blue silk blouse that was a welcome pop of color against her stark white linen pantsuit.

Teresa always managed to look so buttoned up and proper. It was a calm facade that gave no indication of the raging heat and unbridled passion that lay beneath her cool exterior.

Liam's face and chest flushed with heat and his heart thumped so hard in his chest he wondered if she could hear it, too.

Being in such close proximity to Teresa made it difficult to remain aloof and pretend he didn't want her as much now as he ever had. That he didn't think of her constantly.

It would be a painfully long twelve months.

According to his father's will, that was how long Teresa had to take a role in the company before she could divest herself of the shares he'd left her. That meant twelve months of working closely while rumors swirled around them and this palpable heat raged between them.

He honestly didn't know if he could take it.

Teresa had been tapping out a text message on her phone, presumably floating the idea of moving the event to Napa Valley past Matt.

"There." She put her phone on the seat between them. "We'll see what he says."

"Great. Now about this meeting." He handed a portfolio to her. "Here's the basic information you'll need to know this afternoon. We'll be meeting with the board to—"

Teresa's phone dinged and she picked it up. She grinned, turning the screen toward him. "Matt loves the idea. Now I just hope I can find a venue for our preferred date."

Liam flipped his wrist and looked at his watch. It was clear Teresa wouldn't be able to focus on anything else until she had some peace of mind about finding a venue.

Liam placed a call to his assistant.

"Duncan, please email Teresa St. Claire our list of pre-ferred hotel venues in Napa Valley. Preferably those near a vineyard. And be sure to copy her assistant Corinne on it. Thanks."

Liam ended the call and put his phone away. "Let Corinne know she should call off the search for Seattle venues. Then maybe we can get to the business at hand."

Teresa stared at him. "Why would you—?"

"Same reason. I'm doing this for Matt and for myself. I need you to focus on Christopher Corporation right now, and until that was resolved, it was apparent you wouldn't be able to."

He opened his portfolio after she'd sent her text mes-sage. "Now let's get started."

Six

Gideon had been working in his office all morning with the door closed and Jessie's first album playing. She'd hit the music charts with one or two of the songs from her most recent album. But the songs on this older EP were far better. Her voice had a raw edge that reminded him of Alicia Keys's first album. And the songs all seemed so personal and heartrending.

He couldn't help thinking of her older sister Geneva and how heartsick he'd been when she'd broken it off with him. But he was also reminded of the day two years later when Jessie had shown up at his place.

Gideon couldn't help cringing at the memory.

He didn't regret rejecting Jessie's advances then. It was the right thing to do. But he did regret *how* he'd handled the encounter. He would never forget the heartbreak and pain in those dark brown eyes. It haunted him still.

Gideon paused as he listened to the song.

"I was so young. Did you have to be so cruel? All I ever really wanted was you."

He rubbed his jaw.

Was the song about their encounter that day?

Maybe it made him arrogant to speculate whether the incident between him and Jessie had been the inspiration for the song. But it'd been fifteen years, and he hadn't been able to get that day out of his mind. Was it really so implausible that it'd had a lasting impact on her, too?

Gideon massaged the base of his skull, where tension always gathered.

The Humphrey sisters.

Painful memories of both Geneva and Jessie were inextricable parts of his past. As were the happy memories of them that he'd always treasure. So he could never regret the rainy Saturday afternoon he'd first encountered the pair at a local movie theater. Or the ways in which that encounter had shaped his life.

As painful as it'd been, the dissolution of his relationship with Geneva had been the best thing for both of them. He wouldn't be the man he was today if not for his drive to prove Geneva and her snobby, elitist parents wrong.

It had taken a while for him to get over the sting of her rejection, but Gideon harbored no regrets about Geneva. But Jessie... He groaned.

Jessie was another matter altogether.

He'd considered contacting her, if for no other reason than to apologize for handling the situation so badly. But he'd decided against it.

He would welcome the chance to make peace with Jessie. But he wouldn't reopen an old wound just to absolve himself of guilt.

There was no point in revisiting old hurts. What was done was done.

So despite his desire to make it up to Jessie for hurting her, some relationships were better left in the past.

Seven

Liam lagged a bit behind Teresa and Evelyn Montague, the manager of The Goblet Hotel and Vineyards in Napa Valley, as the woman offered them a tour of the facility.

The vineyards and the grounds of the hotel were lovely. The hotel itself had loads of charm, something he knew both Matt and Teresa would appreciate. The art deco style hotel featured lots of chrome, silver, black and red. The furniture and wallpaper sported bold geometric shapes. The lighting, the mirrors, and much of the furniture and finishes exuded an iconic elegance of days past. Yet the hotel was tastefully modern and chic. The Goblet offered style and luxury without being pretentious.

It was the reason he'd fallen in love with the place when he'd visited it several years ago.

"I can't believe that you can accommodate our event on such short notice. A hotel this beautiful… I was sure you'd be booked." Teresa's eyes roamed the sumptuous space as they entered one of the ballrooms.

"Yes, well…" Evelyn glanced back at him, then cleared her throat. "We had some cancellations."

"I'm sorry to hear that." Teresa stared at the woman, following her gaze. She looked at Liam quizzically, the wheels turning in that pretty head of hers. She returned her gaze to Evelyn. "But it certainly worked out to my advantage, for which I'm appreciative."

Her thank-you seemed to be addressed to both him and Evelyn.

Teresa flipped her blond hair over her shoulder and straightened her suit jacket. "I've seen all I need to see. I'm prepared to sign the paperwork as soon as it's ready."

"Very good." Evelyn nodded. "I have a couple of items to handle first. So please, enjoy lunch and cocktails on the house. The covered patio overlooking the vineyard is quite lovely."

"That would be wonderful. Thank you." Teresa's blue eyes glinted in the sunlight spilling through the windows.

They followed the woman to the dining space, then she whispered something to their server before excusing herself.

There was an awkward lull of silence between them as they reviewed their menus. Finally, Teresa spoke.

"I honestly can't thank you enough, Liam."

"For?" He raised a brow, still surveying his menu. The offerings had changed since last he was there.

"For recommending Napa Valley and The Goblet." She put her menu down and leaned forward. "More importantly, thank you for whatever you did to convince them to make space for our event."

"Me?" He feigned ignorance.

"Please don't pretend you don't know what I'm talking about. I saw the look Evelyn exchanged with you. There was no cancellation, was there?"

Liam put his menu down and straightened his tie without response. He avoided her mesmerizing blue eyes, for fear his would reveal anything more.

He said instead, "What looks good to you?"

You.

Teresa bit back the automatic response perched on the edge of her tongue.

He was wearing a lightweight gray gabardine suit that fit him to perfection. His baby-blue shirt nicely complemented the icy blue eyes that calmly assessed her.

"You didn't answer my question." She sipped her water. "You must've gone to a lot of trouble to make this happen. As grateful as I am for what you've done, I'm completely perplexed. Why would you go to such lengths to help me?"

"Matt's my best friend, and I try to help my friends whenever I can. They'd do the same for me."

"You're a bit of a fixer yourself."

Liam chuckled. "Never thought of it that way before."

She hadn't heard the sound of his laugh in so long. It was nice to hear it again.

"Well, even if you did this for Matt, I want you to know how much I appreciate it. With everything that's been going on lately…" Her shoulders tensed as the weight of the rumors and lost business settled on her again. "Limitless Events won't survive if I don't pull this off. So thank you."

"You're welcome." He furrowed his brow. "And I'm sorry I accused you of leaking information about us to the media. Someone is obviously trying to damage your business and reputation."

"Do you have any idea who might've done it? Not many people knew about us. And I don't believe any of them would ever do something like this."

"Isn't it more likely it was one of the reporters you invited to your events?"

"Are you suggesting this is my fault because I invited the media?"

"No. But you can't blame me for being wary of them until we get to the bottom of this."

That she could understand.

What she couldn't understand was why Liam insisted on accompanying her on the trip and touring the hotel with her.

Did he really expect her to believe he'd done all of that because he and Matt were best friends or because of their collaboration on the Sasha Project?

"Are you sure it's a good idea for us to stay overnight at the same hotel with all of the rumors already out there about us?" She glanced at the server, who seemed to be staring at them whenever she looked up.

"We're both part of Christopher Corporation for now. This is a working trip. Duncan is still trying to get me an early-morning meeting with the CEO of a local medical technology company I've been eyeing. It'd make an excellent acquisition for our portfolio, but the owner isn't very enthusiastic about the possibility."

"I didn't realize Christopher Corporation dabbled in the medical field."

"Our interests are quite diverse. Real estate, technology, entertainment…any solid investment that piques my interest and will provide a good return.

"If you'd read the company material I had sent over, you'd know this."

She ignored the jab. "So maybe this medical tech company just isn't interested in selling."

"I have it on good authority they are. I get the sense they just don't want to sell to me."

Liam thanked the sommelier when he brought out the

bottle of four-year-old cabernet sauvignon Evelyn had rec-
ommended and decanted it. Then the server brought their
appetizers. Artisanal cheeses with a charcuterie tray and
crackers, both house-made.

"Why wouldn't they want to sell to you?" Teresa sipped
her cabernet. The savory, full-bodied liquid, bursting with
the flavor of plums and berries, rolled over her tongue.

Liam's cheeks and forehead flushed as he studied her
intently. He loosened his tie. "I'd say it has everything to
do with the kind of person my father was."

"Linus shouldn't be an issue for them anymore." Teresa
hoped she didn't sound insensitive.

"The culture and philosophy of a company often survive its founder. Especially when a family member takes
over." Liam swirled the dark liquid in his glass, then took
a sip. "They probably suspect I'll run the company the
same way."

"Show them that isn't true." Teresa piled duck prosciutto
and Fourme d'Ambert onto a cracker and took a bite. "Oh
my God. That's good," she muttered, one hand shielding
her full mouth.

Liam's eyes darkened and his Adam's apple bobbed as
he swallowed hard. He spread duck rillettes and a savory
goat cheese on a toasted baguette. "If they'd returned any of
the calls Duncan made to them, I'd happily reassure them
I'm nothing like my father."

She took another sip of wine and spread foie gras on a
cracker. "Call the CEO yourself and request an informal
meeting. Don't dance around the issue. Go at it head-on.
Let him know that while you respected your father, you
didn't always agree with his methods. You have a different vision for Christopher Corporation. One you'd like his
company to have a starring role in."

Liam rubbed his chin, his head tilted thoughtfully. "My

father might've been an asshole, but people respected him. I can't go into this deal with him thinking we're coming from a weakened position."

"Sometimes a softer touch makes a stronger impact. Besides, it'll give you a common enemy and a chance to bond because of it."

Liam put prosciutto on a cracker and popped it into his mouth.

"What I've been doing clearly isn't working," he conceded. "Maybe it's time to try something new."

"To new beginnings, then." She lifted her glass.

"To new beginnings." Liam clinked his glass against hers.

They both seemed to relax into an easy, comfortable conversation that reminded her of the nights they'd spent talking and making love. Before the will was revealed. Before those rumors had started flying, wrecking the fragile relationship they'd been building.

Teresa's mind whirred with unsettling thoughts. About her turbulent, off-and-on relationship with Liam. Her unpredictable brother, who still hadn't returned any of her calls. The rumors that were causing her to hemorrhage clients and whoever might be behind them.

"Teresa." Liam's large, warm hand covered hers. "Is everything all right?"

She glanced down at his hand and he quickly withdrew it, pressing it to the table.

"Yes, of course." She bit back the tears that burned her eyes. "I'm fine."

She most definitely was *not* fine.

Teresa was angry. With Liam for the distance he'd put between them when she was given shares of Christopher Corporation. With whoever leaked those ridiculous affair rumors to the press. But most of all, she was angry with herself. Because despite it all, she couldn't help still wanting him.

She longed for the heat that had raged between them during their past toe-curling encounters. But she also longed for the tenderness in his touch the night he'd rescued her from beneath that fallen tree. And the vulnerability he'd displayed later that night when he'd told her about the awful relationship he'd had with his parents.

Teresa drew in a deep breath. It was nice enjoying a delicious meal and incredible wine with Liam as they overlooked the vineyard, with no qualms about who might see them. But it was the exception, not the rule. So she shouldn't read anything into it or expect it again. She should just enjoy it.

She needed to get through the next year quietly, without any more incidents or negative press.

Liam's phone buzzed for the third time. He glanced at his watch. "I can't believe we've been here three hours." He'd forgotten how easy she was to talk to.

"No wonder the staff has been circling us." Her eyes gleamed.

Liam couldn't pull his gaze from her bright smile.

Teresa was beautiful, but there was something much deeper that appealed to him. She was smart and diligent, and she seemed so sincere.

He wanted to believe her interest in him wasn't a calculated ploy to grab a bigger piece of Christopher Corporation. That she genuinely enjoyed his company as much as he enjoyed hers.

"Is everything okay?" She regarded him with concern, her head tilted. "Do you need to take that call?"

"It's nothing pressing." Liam slid his phone into the pocket inside his suit jacket.

Teresa put her phone back in her purse and indicated to the server that they were finally ready to leave. She returned her attention to Liam. "Thank you again. You didn't have to do any of this, but I'm glad you did." She smiled. "Despite all of your posturing, you're a really good guy."

His heart swelled, but then it was seized by guilt over having accused her of running a scheme on his family.

"Let's make that our little secret. Don't want the competition thinking I've gone soft." He winked at her and then left some cash on the table for the server.

They'd spent three hours talking about the mundane. From Matt and Nadia's wedding to how Seattle's sports teams were doing this year. Over a second bottle of cabernet sauvignon, they discussed which Netflix shows were worth binge-watching.

All safe topics.

The server smiled broadly when he spied the additional tip Liam had left on the table. "Can I get you two anything else? A dessert perhaps? I can have it sent to your room."

"*Rooms*," Teresa clarified. "We're work associates."

The way the man's eyes danced made it clear he believed otherwise. "Shall I have something sent to your rooms?" He stressed the *s* at the end of the word. "On the house, too, of course."

"I couldn't eat another bite…until dinner." Teresa rubbed her belly. "But please give our compliments to the chef. The food was spectacular and your service was impeccable."

The man thanked them, then stepped aside, allowing them to exit the table.

When Teresa stood, she teetered slightly. Liam placed his hands on her waist to steady her. Their eyes met for a moment.

"That cabernet sneaks up on you." She pressed a hand to her forehead. "I'd better lie down before dinner."

"I'll walk you to your room." Liam guided her toward the exit, his hand resting on the small of her back. The server gave him a knowing grin.

Just great.

The server didn't believe they were simply business associates and Liam was to blame.

Accompanying Teresa on this trip was a bad idea. Suggesting they stay overnight was an even worse one.

They were in Napa Valley, rather than in Seattle where the rumors about them were swirling. He hoped they'd be safe here. He'd always been impressed by how discreet and respectful of his privacy the staff at The Goblet had been. He had no reason to suspect that this time would be different.

As they rode the elevator up to her room, his hand grazed hers. A rush of pleasure flooded his senses as he recalled the sensation of her soft, bare skin caressing his when last he'd held her in his arms.

He tried to block out the growing desire to back her against the elevator wall and claim her sweet mouth in a demanding kiss. Graze her nipples with his thumbs through the silky material.

Suddenly, the elevator chimed, indicating they'd arrived on her floor.

She exited the elevator. "Will I see you for dinner?"

"I'll walk you to your door." He stepped off, too. She'd seemed slightly tipsy, so he wouldn't rest unless he knew Teresa was safely in her room.

She seemed pleased by his offer.

"Dinner would be nice. I'll pick you up at your door around seven."

"Or I could meet you downstairs."

"It's like you said… I'm a nicer guy than I let on."

They stopped in front of her door and she opened it, stepping inside.

"Thank you again, Liam. The hotel is perfect for Matt's retreat. You have no idea how badly I needed this win." Her lips quirked in a soft, dreamy smile that lit her beautiful eyes. "This has been a really lovely day. After all of the crappy ones I've had this past week, I needed a day like this. So thank you." She looked at him expectantly.

Liam leaned against the doorway, his arms folded as he stood just over the threshold from Teresa. There was barely a foot of space between them. He wanted to lean in, erase the distance between them and take her in his arms. Kiss her until they were both breathless.

The eager look in her eyes and the soft pout of her kissable lips indicated it was what she wanted, too. But he'd promised himself he'd stay strong, so they wouldn't end up tumbling into bed.

There was too much unresolved baggage between them. So as wonderful as the good times they'd shared were, those moments where overshadowed by the pain, distrust and resentment that still bubbled just beneath the surface for both of them.

Liam heaved a long sigh as he pushed off the wall. "I'm going to give that CEO a call, like you suggested. Thank you for a lovely afternoon."

Liam strode toward the waiting elevator before he changed his mind.

Eight

Jessie put down her pen and huffed. She'd written two new songs for her album, but she was still struggling to write the title song. The one that would stand as a metaphor for her ability to rebound from both heartbreak and the disappointment in her mentor, Arnold Diesman, the record label's top exec, turning out to be a lecherous jerk.

She unrolled her yoga mat, sucked in a deep breath and went into her favorite sun salutation. It was the perfect way to alleviate the stress she was feeling, and it got her creative juices flowing.

Jessie bent over into a deep forward fold, her hands pressed to the mat and the blood rushing to her brain.

Her phone rang.

Figures.

Her phone had been silent all day, but the moment she'd gone into moving meditation, not wanting to be disturbed, it rang.

She checked the screen. *Teresa St. Claire.*

Jessie answered. "Hi, Teresa. What's up?"

"Hi, Jessie. Great news. We've nailed down the date and venue. The retreat happens in two weeks and you're going to adore the venue. It's a cute little art deco boutique hotel and vineyard in Napa Valley. I'm here now. The place is incredible. Very Old Hollywood glamour." The woman spoke excitedly.

"Didn't want to take another chance on Seattle rain and calamitous mudslides, huh?" Jessie wasn't sure if she was more relieved by not having to deal with the dreary weather or avoiding an encounter with Gideon.

She'd frittered away too much of the time she should've spent writing this album with imagining what it would be like to see Gideon again.

"With the short notice, we just couldn't find another venue in Seattle that was both available and luxurious enough for this event." Teresa's response brought Jessie out of her temporary, Gideon-induced haze. "Otherwise, I would've loved to keep the event in Seattle where most of the guests are based."

Lucky me.

"I've always wanted to go to Napa Valley, so I'm looking forward to it." Jessie sat on the piano bench with her back to the keys. "Send the updated contract with all of the particulars to my agent. We'll get it executed and return it as soon as possible."

"Corinne will send the contract first thing in the morning," Teresa said. "And more good news… Matt Richmond approved adding Chase Stratton and Dixon Benedict to the guest list. He was thrilled you suggested them. Both men were on his radar for future projects. He'll invite them both personally tomorrow. I can't confirm yet that either man will be there, but as promised, they'll both be invited."

"Keep me posted on whether they RSVP?"

"I will, and one more thing." Jessie could hear the grin

in Teresa's voice. "I told you that wealthy music lovers who might invest in your indie project would be in attendance. Well, I'm reviewing the updated guest list and I just got confirmation that real estate billionaire Gideon Johns will be there as well as—"

"Gideon Johns RSVP'd?" Jessie began pacing the floor, her heart racing. She'd managed to avoid Gideon when the Seattle retreat was canceled. She obviously wouldn't have the same luck in Napa.

"Yes, and I'd be happy to introduce you."

"That won't be necessary," Jessie responded tersely. "We've met."

"I see." Teresa's voice registered worry. She was silent for a moment, then asked tentatively. "Gideon's presence won't be a problem for you, will it?"

Part of her was eager to show Gideon that the girl he'd dismissed was now an in-demand recording artist. But another part of her dreaded the encounter. A man as rich and powerful as Gideon probably barely remembered her, while she'd thought of him often over the years.

But she wouldn't allow the possibility to sidetrack her career. Nor did she need Gideon's help.

"No." Jessie forced herself to smile. "He's my older sister's ex-boyfriend, that's all. He probably doesn't even remember me. Thank you for the call. I'll look for the contract from my agent."

Jessie ended the call and continued to pace the floor.

Why should she care whether Gideon would be at the retreat? She should be over what happened between them fifteen years ago and over him. But her mind was buzzing with memories of the man who'd wanted to marry her sister.

The man she'd had a killer crush on from the first time she'd laid eyes on him when she and her older sister Geneva met him one Saturday afternoon at the movie theater.

Their parents hadn't been thrilled about Geneva getting serious with a poor kid from the wrong side of the tracks. But the more they objected, the more Geneva dug in.

Her sister had truly cared for Gideon, in the beginning. But at some point, it became more about defying their parents than genuine affection for him.

On her sister's birthday, Gideon had presented Geneva with an engagement ring. That's when her sister realized she'd let things go too far.

Geneva was about to embark on a year of traveling in Europe and she wanted the freedom to see other people. So she'd kissed Gideon tenderly and ended it.

Gideon had been devastated, and so was Jessie.

She'd adored him.

Jessie sat on her yoga mat, her legs folded in lotus position. Eyes squeezed shut, she inhaled a deep breath, trying to shut out the heartbreak she'd experienced the day she'd told Gideon how she really felt about him. But as a songwriter, she was in an unenviable position.

She needed to conjure up the raw emotions she'd felt that day. Feelings that compelled her to pen songs about unrequited love, living through the pain of a shattered heart and learning to rebuild it. How else could she convey that pain so palpably that the audience felt it, too?

But that meant that in moments like this, her wounded heart bled afresh. As if it had happened yesterday instead of a decade and a half ago.

She certainly hadn't spent her entire adult life pining away for Gideon. But in moments like this, it was clear she'd never really gotten over him.

"Gideon, we need to talk." Landon stood in the doorway of Gideon's office looking flustered.

The kid was brilliant, but Gideon wondered if he'd ever

have the steely spine it took to deal with the ups and downs of real estate.

Financial and real estate journals had proclaimed that Gideon had the Midas touch. But he never fell for his own hype. He was good at the real estate game and had a gut sense of what deals and which investors were right for a project. But nothing was foolproof.

Gideon nodded toward the seat in front of his desk and leaned back in his executive chair. "What's happened now?"

"Some of the smaller investors in the Dubai deal are nervous because they've learned that our two largest investors pulled out of the deal. No one has jumped ship yet, but I get the sense they're considering it."

"You did the preliminary work on this deal. Are you confident in your research?"

"Yes, of course. I did solid background on everyone involved. I've run comps in the region. It's a hot area. Demand for and the price of hotel rooms continues to climb. New shops and restaurants are going up. Investors from around the world are clamoring to get in on deals in the area." Landon spoke animatedly. He seemed insulted by the insinuation that the preparatory work he'd done was lacking.

"*That* level of confidence…" Gideon pointed to the younger man. "That's what you need to convey to any investor who might be getting cold feet. They wanted to be part of this deal and they understood the inherent risks. So what they really want to hear is that *we're* still completely on board with the deal."

Landon nodded thoughtfully. "I can do that."

"Next time one of them calls, let them hear the fire and bass in your voice that I just heard."

"You can count on me." Landon was infinitely more self-assured than he'd been when he entered the room. "One other thing…we have a limited window of time here. We'll all feel more confident about the deal once the remaining funding has been secured. I know you have meetings lined up with several potential investors, but Matt Richmond isn't among them."

Gideon had hoped to bring up the deal in casual conversation with his friend. But neither man's schedule had permitted for an impromptu lunch or meeting for drinks.

"We've both been busy." Gideon shuffled through a stack of papers on his desk without looking up at his assistant. "I'll give him a call."

"Preferably today."

Gideon narrowed his gaze at his assistant. "How about as soon as you leave my office?"

"You've got it." Landon saluted as he rose to his feet. "Keep me posted."

As soon as Landon was gone, Gideon pulled out his cell phone and dialed his friend.

"Gideon, what's up?" Matt answered, out of breath.

"I didn't catch you in the middle of—"

"No." Matt laughed. "I took a break to work out. I was on the treadmill."

"If this is a bad time—"

"It isn't. I could use the break."

"It's about that deal in Dubai I mentioned to you before. You've been griping about missing out on my last three projects."

"True. They had killer returns. I'm still kicking myself for not getting in on that deal in New York. The price per square foot in that neighborhood is through the roof."

"Precisely," Gideon said. "That's why I'm trying to save you a spot on this Dubai deal. The ROI is going to be even bigger than on the New York project."

"I hear exciting things about the opportunities in Dubai.

But I'm a little nervous about investing in real estate internationally outside of my part-time residences. Investing in the Middle East makes me particularly apprehensive."

"Have you ever been to Abu Dhabi or Dubai?" Gideon prodded.

"Can't say I have."

"Both cities are remarkable. In fact, if you and Nadia are still debating a honeymoon destination, Dubai would be a terrific spot. It's a luxurious oasis."

Matt had recently gotten married to his former assistant, Nadia Gonzalez, but with the anniversary retreat, they'd postponed their honeymoon.

"I was thinking somewhere tropical, like Tahiti." Matt chuckled. "But I get your point. Look, I don't want to be on the outside looking in on your next big deal, but I need to know a little more about what I'd be getting myself into on this one before I'm willing to invest the kind of money you're talking about here."

"Understandable." Gideon drummed his fingers on his desk. "We're working on a fairly tight window here. So why don't we discuss the details over lunch?"

"I'm in the midst of preparing for the retreat I've rescheduled. So I'm pretty tied up," Matt hedged. "You'll be there, right?"

"I look forward to spending time in Napa Valley."

"Come in on Thursday instead of Friday. You and I can sit down over drinks and hash this out then."

Gideon's jaw tensed. The retreat was two weeks away, making the timeline even tighter. But if he squeezed Matt on a deal he was already squirrelly on, it'd scare his friend off.

"Sounds perfect," Gideon said.

"See you in Napa Valley two weeks from now."

Gideon hung up with his friend and sighed.

Nothing worthwhile ever came easy. His entire life had been a testament to that.

Gideon scrolled through his emails and came across the invite to the retreat again. A gorgeous photo of Jessie was plastered across the graphic. He was still a sucker for those big brown eyes and that generous smile. The one that still instantly made him smile, too.

He'd begged off the Seattle retreat at the last minute, deciding it would be better if he and Jessie didn't cross paths. In the end, it didn't matter since it was canceled, but the truth was he feared Jessie hadn't forgiven him. That she wouldn't welcome a reunion. But avoiding the rescheduled retreat in Napa Valley wasn't an option. So it was better that he went in with a plan.

He needed to approach Jessie first. Wipe the slate clean and let bygones be bygones. He only hoped Jessie was inclined to do the same.

Nine

Gideon Johns walked into the lobby of The Goblet Hotel on Thursday a little after one in the afternoon. He'd arrived even earlier than Matt suggested to ensure he got a chance to sit down and chat with his friend well ahead of the start of the festivities.

"Gideon." Teresa grinned as she approached him, a wide smile spread across her face. Her gorgeous blue eyes sparkled as she shook his hand in both of hers. "It's wonderful to see you again. Matt said you would be arriving today."

Gideon leaned in closer and lowered his voice. "I realize I'm here ahead of check-in, but I'm hoping my private cottage is ready."

"I anticipated that you'd arrive prior to check-in." Teresa grinned. "Your room was ready at 10:00 a.m."

"You're amazing." Gideon smiled.

Teresa walked to the front desk with him. "Melva, this is Mr. Gideon Johns. He's the guest I requested early check-in for. He's in one of the private cottages."

Gideon handed the clerk his credit card and identification. He turned toward Teresa, lowering his voice again.

"I'm glad you're in such a good mood." Gideon didn't want to wreck her upbeat disposition by going into the specifics of the ugly rumors circulating around Seattle about her and Liam. But he wanted to assure her he didn't believe them. "You're good people, Teresa."

Her smile deepened and her eyes were filled with gratitude. She placed a hand on the forearm he'd propped on the front desk. "Thank you. That means a lot."

He'd spent most of his adult life honing his ability to read people and decipher their intentions. Nothing about Teresa St. Claire made him believe she was the scheming vixen that the haters and gossipers in his circle would have him believe her to be. But in a business like hers, perception was everything.

It was a dilemma to which he could relate.

Gideon didn't believe for an instant that Teresa had nefarious motives when it came to Liam Christopher and his family's corporation. But as he spotted Liam sitting in a chair across the lobby watching them intently, it was clear that Liam's interest in Teresa wasn't just business.

The hunger in his eyes as his gaze slid over Teresa's body spoke more of the bedroom than the boardroom. The way the man's eyes narrowed and his nostrils flared when Gideon leaned in to speak to Teresa in a hushed tone indicated the slightest hint of possession.

Regardless of what might have gone on between them, Gideon refused to believe the woman he'd gotten to know was capable of the deceit and betrayal of which she'd been accused. But in his experience, many people born of wealth liked to believe that people who came from very humble beginnings, like him and Teresa, didn't belong, regardless of how hard they'd worked or how high they'd risen. They were a social experiment waiting to implode. And when they did, they'd shake their heads and wag their tongues as they mused about their moral defectiveness.

It was the reason he felt a kinship of sorts with Teresa.

"Your business partner over there is giving me the death stare." Gideon indicated Liam's general direction with a shift of his gaze.

Teresa's cheeks flamed and she cleared her throat. "I can't imagine why."

"Can't you?" Gideon gave her a good-natured smile as he returned his credit card and ID to his wallet while the desk clerk prepared his room key. "Relax, Teresa. I don't believe any of the bullshit I've heard. But it's obvious you two care for each other. I know it doesn't seem like it right now, but my gut tells me that everything will work out for the two of you."

"Who knew the great Gideon Johns was a hopeless romantic?"

"Maybe once upon a time, but that time has long…" Gideon turned toward a beautiful brown-skinned woman wearing expensive sunglasses, a chocolate-brown silk dress and a pair of rose gold high-heel sandals with a sexy crystal bow detail. The height of the heels and the thin, barely-there straps across the ankle and toe made the one leg exposed by her dress seem a mile long.

"Jessie Humphrey?" He whispered the name beneath his breath, but Teresa, who'd followed his gaze, clearly heard him.

"I hear you two don't require an introduction." Teresa beamed, clearly amused by how distracted he was by Jessie's arrival. She nodded toward the goddess with miles of creamy skin who approached the desk.

"Jessie, I'm glad you made it. I trust that your trip was less eventful this time around." Teresa stepped past Gideon and clasped Jessie's hands, as if the two of them were old friends.

"Yes, thank you, Teresa. And thank you for arranging everything. My flight was lovely."

"Well, I'm sure you're tired after your cross-country trip. I'll get your registration started so you can check into your room right away." Teresa stepped over to the desk.

"Hello, Gideon." Jessie finally acknowledged his presence, but she didn't remove her shades. "It's been a long time, hasn't it?"

"Fifteen years." He practically whispered the words as they exchanged an awkward hug.

He'd seen her PR photos on her cover and online. He'd even watched some of her performances on video. But nothing could prepare him for how stunning this woman was in person. Her creamy brown skin was flawless and her dark brown hair was pulled back into a sleek bun.

Jessie's high cheekbones and petite nose were reminiscent of her older sister's. Yet the similarities between the two ended there.

Gideon had always thought of Jessie as Geneva's little sister, which was why he'd reacted so poorly to Jessie's unexpected kiss that rainy afternoon nearly two years after Geneva had ended their relationship. He'd hurt her feelings, and they hadn't spoken since.

But that was then.

Gideon wouldn't dare reject a kiss from the woman standing before him now.

"How've you been?" He shoved a hand in his pocket.

"Well, thank you. And you've obviously done quite well for yourself." She gave him a cursory smile before handing her credentials over to another desk clerk.

"Sir...sir..." Melva gave him a knowing smile as she

handed Gideon his room keys. The woman probably thought he was a shameless groupie way past his prime.

He nodded his thanks, then turned back to Jessie. "Your voice is amazing, Jess. But you know I've always thought so."

"Thank you, Gideon," she said quietly.

"How's your family?" He wasn't asking about Geneva because he was interested in her. He asked because inquiring about the health of her family without malice was the polite thing to do. Regardless of Geneva's heartbreaking rejection or her father's cruel remarks that he would never be worthy of his daughter.

"They're fine." Her shoulders tensed and she turned toward the desk clerk. "I hope yours are, too."

Even after Jessie had stepped out of Gideon's embrace, the heat from his body wrapped itself around her like a soft, warm blanket. His subtle, deliciously masculine scent tickled her nose.

However, when Gideon asked about her family, code for her sister Geneva, the warm, fuzzy feelings ceased instantly. Leaving her with the cold, dark memories of their last interaction and how broken it had left her.

Geneva had rejected him, but she was still apparently the only Humphrey sister he was really interested in. His inquiries about her were superficial niceties.

Maybe it made her petty to give him such a cryptic response. But if he wanted to hear all about his ex, he'd have to ask her directly.

"Last I heard, Geneva was living in Europe. Switzerland, maybe?"

Jessie drew in a tight breath, but fought to keep her expression neutral. She accepted her room key from the desk clerk.

"She was for a while, but she's lived in Amsterdam for the past seven or eight years with her husband, Edmond. She's Geneva Torian now." She gave him a manufactured smile designed to protect her suddenly fragile pride. "It was nice seeing you, Gideon."

Jessie turned on her four-and-a-half-inch-tall Aminah Abdul Jillil open-toe sandals and strutted toward the elevator. The bellman, who'd stacked all of her bags onto a luggage cart, moved with her.

"Jessie, wait." Gideon caught her elbow with a gentle grip. "We haven't seen each other in more than a decade. I have an important meeting today, but I'd really like to catch up."

You mean you want to hear more about Geneva.

Jessie bit back the caustic remark that burned her tongue and gnawed at her gut. Why give Gideon the satisfaction of knowing how much his rejection hurt?

She'd be cordial, but aloof.

"I hope to line up a couple of meetings of my own." Jessie tipped her chin so her gaze met his as she slipped her arm from his loose grip. "I'm performing tomorrow and I'm still tweaking some of the material. Maybe we can catch up after my final set on Saturday night."

"Of course." His voice reminded her of the pain she'd heard in it the day her sister ended things between them. "But if you're able to free up some time to grab lunch or perhaps drinks… I'd really like that."

Jessie nodded her acknowledgment, then resumed her trek toward the elevator with the bellman in tow.

They stepped onto the elevator and Gideon stood frozen, staring at her, as the elevator doors closed. As if he'd seen a ghost.

Jessie hated that she was still hurt and angry after all this time. She shouldn't be. If anything, she should be grateful to Gideon. She owed her career to him.

The heartbreak and subsequent longing she experienced drove her to pick up a pen and write poems and eventually songs. After writing songs for small local acts, Jessie had slowly climbed the songwriting ranks and written songs for chart-topping musicians.

She'd fought for the chance to sit center stage at her piano and sing her own songs. After a successful EP, she'd accepted a contract from a big studio, but she would only agree to a single album contract because the studio hadn't been willing to give her full creative control. She'd gambled on demonstrating that she was worthy of that level of oversight before she signed another contract. Hopefully for a multi-album deal. But Jessie hadn't anticipated the cost of that freedom. Nor had she been willing to sacrifice her soul for it.

Her experience with label exec Arnold Diesman taught her not to trust a wealthy, powerful man to do her bidding or have her back. In the end, that man's only real interest was his own selfish desires.

Jessie sucked in a deep breath as the elevator opened on the second floor. She followed the bellman to her luxury balcony suite. A bold silver wallpaper with a black geometric pattern welcomed her to the elegant art deco style space. She tipped the bellman once he'd unloaded her luggage, then locked the door behind him.

Jessie slipped off the flowing brown silk Cushnie designer dress with an asymmetrical hemline that skimmed her ankles in the back but rose thigh-high over her left leg. She kicked off her shoes and slipped into a pair of comfy gray sweat shorts and a white V-neck tee. Then she sank onto the sofa in the suite's well-appointed sitting area.

Seeing Gideon after all this time had been harder than

she'd imagined. Which meant that the next few days would be difficult. It would be especially hard performing in front of the man who'd first inspired her to write songs of love and loss.

Chase Stratton and Dixon Benedict had both RSVP'd for the retreat. This was her best opportunity to get Chase and Dix on board with her project. So she wouldn't allow anything to throw her off course. Least of all handsome, uber-wealthy, aging-like-fine-wine Gideon Johns.

This project had the potential to change everything for her. So she wouldn't let a teenage crush distract her from her dream.

Later that evening, after making a few last-minute adjustments to her song, Jessie pulled out her cell phone in its pink rhinestone-studded case and tapped out a quick message.

You'll never guess who just asked about you. Gideon Johns.

Gideon watched as the elevator doors closed, his pride hurt by Jessie's chilly reception. He realized she wasn't happy about the way they'd left things. But he'd done the right thing. Was Jessie really still angry with him after all these years?

He'd be the first to admit that he'd handled the situation poorly. But what he rarely admitted was why he'd gotten so angry that day. Buried beneath all the practical reasons he'd rejected Jessie's proposition was the fact that he'd been startled by the way she'd made him feel. It was something he hadn't wanted to admit, even to himself.

He'd been attracted to her. Wanted her. Feelings he'd immediately rejected. She was his ex's sister.

The last thing in the world he'd wanted was to fall for another Humphrey sister. It was still the last thing he wanted. And yet, seeing her just now, he realized that he was as susceptible to it today as he'd been back then.

Gideon ordered a glass of wine at the bar.

Jessie had always been such a sweet and gentle soul. She was a ray of sunshine that he'd missed having in his life. But the woman he'd just encountered was unlike the girl he'd once known.

Was she still angry about how he'd rejected her back then? Or had fame and ambition changed Jessie?

Back when he'd known the Humphrey sisters, Jessie and Geneva had been like night and day. Geneva was confident, assured, ambitious and a bit entitled. Jessie was sweet, shy and thoughtful. Geneva always thought of herself first, while Jessie's primary concern was the people she cared about.

It had been Jessie's most endearing quality.

But maybe Jessie was more like her older sister than he remembered.

If Jessie preferred not to revisit their past, all the better.

Besides, rekindling a friendship with Jessie would sidetrack him from his primary goal this weekend. To seal the Dubai deal with Matt Richmond. Then he'd return to Seattle and forget about his encounter with the surprisingly aloof Jessie Humphrey.

Ten

Liam walked into the bar and sat down, leaving a space between him and Gideon Johns.

"Gideon." He nodded toward the man, who could barely hold back a smirk.

"Liam." Gideon took another sip of his wine. "If you've come to give me a back-off-my-woman speech, I can save us both time. My interest in Teresa is strictly professional."

"As is mine." *Now.* That critical detail he kept to himself.

Gideon's laugh made it clear that he wasn't buying it anyway. Not even for a moment.

"Do you make a habit of staring down the men who have close conversations with your business associates?" When Liam didn't answer, Gideon set his glass down. "Didn't think so."

"I thought you were too discriminating a man to believe the gossip mill, Gideon," Liam said after he'd ordered a Manhattan.

"If you mean the rumors disparaging Teresa... I don't

believe a word of them." Gideon's expression grew serious. "But the part about your relationship with her being more than just business...you're the one who told me that."

"What do you mean?" Liam turned toward Gideon.

"You sat in that chair watching the woman's every move. Scowling at any man who dared smile at her." Gideon nodded toward Teresa as she walked past the bar with a male member of the hotel staff. "You can't keep your eyes off her even now. So, a word of advice, if that's the story you're going with, you might want to take it down a notch...or ten."

Liam groaned and raked his fingers through his hair. The man was right. Though it hadn't been intentional, he hadn't been able to keep his eyes off Teresa as she flitted about the hotel. Today she wore a fitted black pantsuit that perfectly complemented her figure. The sheer black blouse beneath it had a deep neckline that had his imagination and memory working overtime. Was it any wonder his eyes had a mind of their own?

"I'm sorry if I seemed—"

"Territorial?" Gideon offered, finishing his glass of wine.

"Something like that," Liam conceded. "It's a complicated situation."

"I'm no stranger to complicated situations." Gideon ordered another glass of wine. "So no judgment here. But if you're really going with the story that it's only business between you two, you might want to rethink your approach."

"Thank you for your honesty." Liam patted the man on the shoulder, then excused himself to go to his guest cottage and return an important call.

Pangs of guilt twisted Liam's gut as he picked up the telephone to return the call to Jeremy Dutton, the man he'd assigned to comb Teresa's background. The man was much more than just a private investigator. In fact, that barely scratched the surface of just what Jeremy Dutton was capable of.

While it was true that he'd come to the conclusion that it didn't make sense for Teresa to have gone to the press, there was still a lot he didn't know about the woman. Had she been honest about the nature of her relationship with his father? Was there a hidden agenda behind her interest in him? Did she have designs on acquiring a controlling interest in Christopher Corporation? Was Dutton able to dig up anything about her father, Nigel St. Claire, working for Christopher Corporation twenty years ago?

When it came to Teresa, there were too many questions and not enough answers. Answers that he needed since, thanks to the terms of his father's will, Teresa now owned 25 percent of the stock in his family's company. They were already dealing with all of the rumors and innuendo about her relationship with his father and now him. Liam needed to ensure that there were no additional skeletons that would come crashing out of this woman's closet to plunge his family and company name into further disrepute.

Anyone in his position would do the same, for the sake of their business. But he had an additional incentive to look into Teresa. He'd been given no choice about bringing her into the company. But the fact that he kept bringing her into his bed…well, that was all on him.

He genuinely liked Teresa St. Claire, but he had millions of reasons to distrust her. Most of which were sitting in local and international banks. Still, he was inexplicably drawn to her in a way he hadn't experienced with anyone else.

Common sense dictated that he leave Teresa alone. Deal with her only as he must. But the time he'd spent with Teresa at The Goblet made him remember just how much he liked her. And she seemed just as enamored with him.

Which made him feel particularly shitty about having her investigated. Despite the fact that any sensible businessman in his position would've done the same. Still, there was a question that kept running through his brain.

What if he chose to pursue a relationship with Teresa? How would she react once she learned of the investigation? Could she ever forgive him?

Despite his initial objections, in the few short weeks since Teresa had been a part of Christopher Corporation, she'd demonstrated that she could be an asset to the organization. But he couldn't sustain any further liabilities where Teresa was concerned.

Liam dialed the private investigator. The man answered right away.

"What've you learned?" Liam asked after exchanging a cursory greeting.

"Straight to the point." The man chuckled. "My type of client."

Liam waited without reply for the man to give him the highlights of his report on Teresa.

It essentially amounted to nada. Zip. Zilch.

What the hell was he paying this guy for? He wasn't sure if he should be extremely pleased or incredibly suspicious about the lack of dirt his investigator was able to dig up after weeks of searching. Dutton was a thorough investigator on whom he frequently relied to vet potential businesses and potential business associates.

The only thing the man could confirm was that Teresa had spent a considerable amount of time with his father.

"Keep digging," Liam said. "Everyone has secrets. If there's something there, I need to know what it is."

"It's your dime, Christopher." Dutton chuckled. "I'll

keep knocking on doors and kicking over rocks for as long as you're paying me to do it."

"Fine, but be subtle about it. Discretion is everything on this one."

Liam ended the call and slipped the phone into his pocket. He was protecting his family's interest and his heart. Still, he couldn't help feeling like he was betraying Teresa by doing so behind her back.

Liam loosened his tie and opened the doors to the patio that overlooked the vineyard. He sat at the little café table, his thoughts immediately returning to the three-hour lunch he and Teresa had enjoyed together on the property just two weeks before. A memory to which his mind often drifted.

Liam could recall nearly everything about the hours they'd spent together. What she was wearing. How she'd worn her hair. Her delectable scent. The sound of her laugh. How much he'd wanted to kiss her. How his body had craved hers as he lay in bed alone that night.

Liam sighed. He was sure Teresa was hiding something. But then, he'd been holding something back, too. A secret he hadn't dared share with anyone.

He had reason to suspect he'd been adopted.

Eleven

Jessie checked her watch after she'd steamed the dress she chose for her performance the next night. It was nearly 10:00 p.m., almost 1:00 a.m. back in New York. She was already feeling the jet lag. If she went to bed now, she could get a decent night's sleep and still work out before breakfast. Her phone rang.

Geneva.

"Hey, big sis." Jessie yawned. A signal that their call wouldn't be long. "What are you doing up this early?"

It wasn't quite 7:00 a.m. in Amsterdam.

"Where did you run into Gideon? Did he recognize you right away?" Her sister completely ignored her question.

"I'm at The Goblet. It's a —"

"Luxury hotel in Napa Valley." Her sister sounded impressed.

"You know it?"

"Who doesn't?" Geneva scoffed. "What are you doing there?"

"That gig I got to perform for billionaire Matt Richmond and a bunch of his business associates—"

"The one that got canceled because of a mudslide?" her sister said incredulously. "What about it?"

"They rescheduled the event and moved it to Napa. I'll be performing the next two nights."

"So Gideon is a friend of Matt Richmond of Richmond Industries?"

"It seems so," Jessie said through an exaggerated yawn. As if it were the least interesting piece of information she'd ever heard. "They both live in Seattle. You know the rich guys there run in the same circle."

"So what did he look like? Did he recognize you right away? After all, he hasn't seen you since I broke up with him."

Not true. But it wasn't a secret she wanted to share with her sister.

"He did recognize me right away. And he looks pretty much the same. Only more mature." *And infinitely more handsome.* A fact she didn't need to mention.

"Do you think he's as rich as the business magazines say he is?"

How the hell was she supposed to know? "I'm not a forensic accountant, Gen."

"I know, smart-ass. Tell me what he was wearing, and don't spare any of the details."

"It's not like I was cataloging his entire outfit."

A slim-cut charcoal-gray Tom Ford suit with subtle pinstripes, a crisp white shirt with a burgundy Tom Ford tie, and a pair of black leather Dolce & Gabbana shoes buffed to a high shine.

Not that she was paying attention.

"Well, what did he ask you about me? You do remember that, don't you?" Geneva said, impatiently.

"I do." How could she forget? For the first time it seemed Gideon saw her as an attractive woman. But then he'd burst any delusions she had about his interest in her by inquiring about her sister. The woman who broke his heart. "He asked how you were doing."

"And?"

Jessie sighed. "And if you were still living overseas."

That was the part that had irked her most. It meant Gideon had been keeping tabs on Geneva. Pining away for her, though her sister clearly hadn't wanted him.

"Why do you care so much, anyway? You're an old married woman, living the life abroad, remember?" Jessie teased.

Geneva suddenly got quiet. "There's something I haven't told you, Jess. Edmond and I…well, we're separated."

Jessie had moved into the bathroom and started unpacking her toiletries, but her sister's admission stopped her in her tracks. "Since when?"

Geneva was slow to respond. "The past three months."

"And you're just telling me?" She and Geneva weren't the kind of sisters who told each other everything. Still, Jess couldn't believe her sister would hold back something like that.

"We've spoken at least a dozen times over the past few months." Jessie returned to the main room of her suite and looked out the window at the surrounding vineyard, lit by strings of lights. Had she been that wrapped up in her own life that she hadn't noticed how unhappy her sister had been?

"Why didn't you say something?"

"I hoped it was only temporary. That I'd never need to worry you or Mom and Dad with this."

Jessie doubted Geneva's reasons for holding back the truth were as altruistic as she made them out to be. Like their mother, Gen had always cared about maintaining appearances.

"But you no longer believe you two will reconcile?" Jessie sank onto one of the comfy chairs in the room. "Or has the news that your old flame, billionaire Gideon Johns, inquired about you prompted that decision?"

"Don't be like that, sis," Geneva pleaded. "I know you think I'm the tough one, but this whole thing with Edmond has done a number on my ego."

"I'm sorry. I didn't mean to be…" Jessie raked her short, trim nails through her hair. "What happened? The last time I visited, you and Edmond seemed very happy."

"I thought we were happy, too. But that didn't stop Edmond from finding a younger, prettier model that made him happier."

"He cheated on you?" *It figured.*

"Don't gloat, Jess. Please. I couldn't take that right now."

"Well, for what it's worth, I'm sorry to hear it." Jessie returned to the bathroom. She needed to strip off her makeup and get ready for bed. "Will you be returning to the States?"

"I haven't given it much thought. I love my life here in Amsterdam, but I hadn't realized how inextricably it's tied to Edmond. Now that the people in our circle are being forced to take sides, it's clear that they're his friends, not mine."

"You should stay with me for a little while, as soon as I get back to New York. Or Mom and Dad would love to see you."

"Thanks. I'll think about it," Geneva said. "I have to get ready for work, and it sounds like you need to hit the sack. Love you."

"Love you, too." Jessie put her phone on the charger and got ready for bed.

Gideon's inquiry about her sister had prompted Jessie's envy, but it seemed to be just the thing her sister needed. She should be grateful to Gideon for that.

It was just as well because Gideon was only interested in Geneva.

Perhaps that was exactly how it should be.

Twelve

Gideon rose early and dressed in his workout gear, determined to get in a session before his meeting with Matt Richmond later that morning. They'd had to cancel their planned meeting over drinks the night before due to an emergency conference call Matt had to take.

Gideon walked over to the main building from his luxury cottage on the property and used his key card to access the workout facility. When he stepped inside, he was greeted by an angelic voice.

Jessie was running on a treadmill wearing a headset. Oblivious to his arrival, she was singing her heart out. Gideon couldn't help smiling. He'd always loved the unique, husky tone of her voice.

He was frozen where he stood as he surveyed her. Jessie looked incredible in her tiny workout shorts and racerback tank.

Long, lean brown legs that seemed to go on for miles. A curvy derriere and generous breasts that bounced slightly with each movement. Her dark brown hair was piled atop her head in a high ponytail.

After Jessie's icy reception the previous afternoon, he'd planned to avoid any further interaction with her. But seeing her now, he just couldn't walk away. Jessie had once meant so much to him. He thought he'd been important to her, too. He needed to understand what had changed.

He stepped onto the treadmill beside Jessie's. She was startled, but grabbed the sides of the treadmill and recovered mid-stride.

"I'm so sorry, I didn't… Gideon. Good morning." Once she recognized him, her demeanor shifted from open and friendly to polite but shuttered. She yanked the key from her machine and it ground to a halt. "I'll leave you to your workout."

Jessie turned to leave, but he caught her elbow as he'd done the day before.

"I know you have to prepare for tonight, but if you could just give me a few minutes."

"Why?" She looked at him defiantly.

"Because I need to know why it is that I couldn't have been more thrilled to see you yesterday, but you obviously don't feel the same."

Jessie tugged her arm free, but her demeanor softened, and he saw a glimpse of the sweet young woman he'd once adored.

A chill swept up his spine as her gaze met his.

Jessie was sexy and gorgeous. She had an incredible voice and a regal presence.

Any man would be attracted to her.

But what worried him most as he stared into those big, beautiful brown eyes was that the feelings he'd tried so hard to ignore came rushing back. Feelings he needed to shut down, for both of their sakes.

* * *

Jessie's gaze swept down Gideon's physique. He was obviously no stranger to workouts. The fitted sleeveless shirt highlighted his strong arms and broad, muscular chest. His athletic shorts showcased a firm ass, strong calves, muscular thighs and the outline of his...

She raised her eyes to his quickly, meeting his dark, penetrating gaze. The image of a young Gideon Johns was permanently burned into her brain. But fifteen years later he was more handsome than ever.

As she surveyed his fit body and handsome facial features what she felt was desire, pure and simple.

But then, her feelings for Gideon had never been as simple as her physical attraction to him.

"The last time we saw each other—" Jessie tipped her chin and folded her arms "—you made it exceedingly clear you wanted nothing to do with me."

She'd gone to Gideon's apartment. Kissed him. Admitted that she wanted him. And he'd flatly rejected her.

"I know I could've handled the situation better, but you surprised me and I overreacted. You were my ex's sister. I didn't want to cause friction between you two. And if I'm being honest, I wasn't willing to take the risk of getting involved with another Humphrey sister. Your father didn't believe I was good enough for one of his daughters. I wasn't interested in going through that again."

Jessie's central memory of that day was how harsh Gideon had been toward her. He'd yelled at her. Something he'd never done before. His eyes had been filled with what she'd perceived as anger. Now she wondered if it'd been fear. "You should've told me how you felt."

Gideon sat on a nearby weight bench. "I knew you well enough to know you would've tried to convince me otherwise. I didn't want to hurt you, Jess. But I didn't want to be hurt again either. It seemed best if we both walked away and didn't look back. I hope you can understand where my head was that day. I realize, in retrospect, that I was an ass about it. I'm sorry for that."

The sincerity in his voice and dark eyes made her chest ache.

"The resentment I've harbored since then wasn't fair to you. So I'm sorry, too, Gideon."

"I'm glad we finally had this conversation." His broad mouth quirked in a half smile. "It's something I've wanted to say to you for a long time."

"Thank you, Gideon. It really was good to see you again." Jessie turned to leave.

"Wait." He sprang to his feet, standing between her and the door. "You're still leaving? Why?"

"I was practically done with my workout anyway." She folded her arms, her gaze not meeting his.

Gideon had glanced at her machine. He folded his arms, too. "You had thirty minutes left."

She smoothed back her hair. "I'm on a tight schedule this morning. I have to grab breakfast and get some practice time in on the piano I'm performing on tonight. Then I hope to wrangle a meeting with a couple of music execs who'll be here this weekend."

"Chase Stratton and Dixon Benedict?"

"Yes. How'd you—"

"I overheard Teresa talking to her assistant about them. Neither of them has arrived. Stratton's studio session got extended another day and Benedict is coming in a day late."

"Oh." Jessie's heart sank. She didn't regret taking the gig. The payday was more than generous and she was grateful for the chance to have this conversation with Gideon.

But this retreat was her best chance of connecting with her two dream producers.

"Look, if meeting them means that much to you, I'll talk to Matt. I'm sure he can arrange some—"

"No." The word came out more harshly than she'd intended. After all, Gideon only wanted to help.

He frowned, confused by her objection.

"I mean…thank you, but no. I prefer to do this on my own."

"I admire your spirit and determination, Jessie. But if I can do this for you—"

"Then I'd owe you."

Jessie hadn't meant to say the words aloud, especially not so bitterly. Her face stung with heat, remembering the day Arnold Diesman had offered to give her complete creative control on her next album, if only she'd play the game.

She'd considered Arnold a friend and mentor until the moment he'd tried to convince her that quid pro quos were the way things were done in the industry. That it wasn't a big deal.

"When I reach the pinnacle in my career, it'll be because I earned it. Not because I knew the right exec or because I'm beholden to a billionaire."

Gideon's thick, neat brows came together. He stepped aside. "I'm sorry I offended you."

Guilt knotted Jessie's gut. Gideon was a good guy who wanted to do a wonderful thing for her. She appreciated that. But doing this on her own was important to her, and she needed to spell that out to Gideon in no uncertain terms.

"You didn't offend me. I just need you to understand my position on this." After a few moments of awkward silence between them, she jerked a thumb over her shoulder toward the door. "I'd better go."

"Wait, Jess." He stalked over to where she stood near

the door. "If you want to do this on your own, I respect that. Hell, I even admire it. But that doesn't mean two old friends can't catch up over breakfast, does it?"

Jessie turned to Gideon.

God, he's handsome.

He seemed eager to absolve himself of any guilt where she was concerned.

"I could meet you at the restaurant in an hour."

He glanced at his watch and frowned. "I have a business meeting then. What about now?"

"I'm not going to the restaurant looking a hot, sweaty mess. I have my public persona to consider." She smoothed her hair back.

Gideon nodded thoughtfully and shoved his hands in his pockets. The move pulled the panel of fabric tight over his crotch and inadvertently drew her eye there. "Room service in my room?"

Oh. My. Gawd.

Her entire body flushed with heat and she resisted the urge to fan herself with her open hand. When Jessie raised her gaze to his, he'd caught her checking him out.

He was more than a little pleased with himself. The smirk on his face reminded her too much of the one on Arnold's face the day he'd invited her up to his suite to strategize the direction of her career.

It was like an icy shower had been turned on over her head.

She wouldn't make the same mistake again.

"I don't think that's a good idea. How about breakfast in the restaurant tomorrow at eight?"

"Sounds good." He pulled out his phone and added their breakfast date to his calendar. He assessed her tentatively. "We should exchange numbers. In case there's a last-minute change of plans for either of us."

Jessie rattled off her cell phone number.

He sent her a text message. "That's me. Call me if there's a change in your plans or…anything." A broad, genuine smile spanned his handsome face.

Jessie's heart danced. She was as drawn to him now as she'd been then.

Thirteen

Gideon folded the burgundy pocket square and placed it in the front pocket of his suit. Tonight's festivities would officially be under way in just a few minutes. He removed a pair of platinum cuff links from their felt jewelry box and pushed one through the hole of his custom-tailored dress shirt. He'd just put the other cuff link in place when his cell phone rang.

He checked the screen.

Landon.

Gideon answered the phone and put it on speaker before returning it to the bathroom counter. "What's up, Land?"

"Mr. Johns…"

Oh shit. This wasn't going to be good.

"I'm sorry to bother you while you're at the retreat," he continued. "But I'm afraid I have a bit of bad news."

"Is another investor considering bailing on the project?"

"No. I think I've done a good job of addressing any concerns they may have had."

"Then what is it?"

"Some issues have come to light regarding the owner of the construction company whose bid we planned to go with. I know his bid was considerably less, but concerns are now being raised about the quality of his work. Complaints that weren't available when we did our preliminary groundwork. Even if it turns out that the information is false—"

"There'll still be the perception that the builder employs shoddy materials and workmanship." Gideon cursed under his breath. "We have no choice but to go with option two."

"Which is nearly ten percent higher than the initial bid. We'll also need a bigger contingency."

Gideon's head was starting to pound. "Of course."

"I don't mean to push, but have you had the opportunity to sit down with Matt Richmond?"

"There's been a lot going on." It was an excuse he'd call bullshit on if one of his employees had offered it. But his breakfast meeting with Matt had been interrupted when his friend's assistant alerted him to a problem at Richmond Industries' Miami office. "We still have a few days, so don't panic, Landon. Besides, we have a bigger issue."

"Even if Matt says yes, I doubt you anticipate getting the full remaining investment from him," Landon said. "And the total amount needed has just escalated." The man was silent for a few minutes. "Mr. Johns… I've been thinking. In light of everything that's been going on with this deal… maybe the timing just isn't right for it."

"It's the nature of the beast, Landon," Gideon said calmly. "It doesn't matter if it's a tiny residential rehab, a towering skyscraper or a commercial complex. Shit happens. Sometimes it's a little. Sometimes it's a lot. And the bigger the risk, the more shit is going to hit the fan. It's as simple as that."

"So you're not worried?"

"It's my job to worry. I do that whether we're behind the eight ball or way ahead of the game." Gideon checked his watch. He needed to get over to the main building for the welcome party. He didn't want to miss Jessie's performance. "Your only worry should be doing your job and doing it well. Everything else will be fine. Now, I've got this under control. Go out and enjoy your weekend. We'll hit the second-tier potential investor list hard on Monday morning."

Landon agreed, sounding more upbeat.

Gideon ended the call, straightened his tie and got ready to join the party.

Gideon stepped onto the patio of The Goblet. The tented space was elegantly decorated. The patio was overflowing with some of the most elite and powerful captains of industry in the fields of technology, information science, entertainment and more. A four-piece live band stood on the stage playing soft jazz.

"Good evening, Gideon." Teresa grinned as she approached him. "What do you think?"

The woman had traded her usual pantsuit for an elegant silver dress with a low-cut back and crystal detailing on the front. Her blond hair fell to her shoulders in soft, beachy waves. She stood beside him and admired her work. It was one of the few times in the past two days that he hadn't seen the woman moving so fast on her designer high heels that she was practically a blur.

"It's quite lovely, Teresa. I'm impressed, especially since you've done this on such short notice." Gideon accepted a glass of red wine from a passing server and took a sip. "And holding the event at a boutique hotel with a working vineyard. That was a stroke of genius."

"It was, but sadly, I can't take credit for the selection of the location. It was Liam Christopher who suggested it."

She nodded toward Liam, who stood on the far side of the patio, eyeing them.

The man acknowledged them with a quick nod. Then he averted his gaze and moved to talk to another partygoer. A beautiful redhead wearing a long, flowing green gown.

The slightest frown furrowed Teresa's brow.

Neither of them is exactly subtle. No wonder rumors are flying about them.

"I'd like to keep this venue on the map for a real estate investor retreat I'm planning next year. I'm focused on another project right now, but give me a call in a few weeks. I'd like to do some preliminary planning. You did such an amazing job at my last party. You are the only event planner I ever want to use."

Teresa beamed. She tapped out a memo on her cell phone. "I'll have Corinne give Landon a call later next week."

She nodded toward her assistant, who spoke animatedly to a member of the hotel staff. The woman wore a long, simple black gown. Her corkscrew red curls were pulled into a low bun.

The mention of his assistant reminded him this wasn't just a social call. He needed to nail down Matt Richmond's investment and identify a handful of smaller investors.

Teresa excused herself to go and speak with one of her staff members.

Gideon finished his drink, then moved toward Matt and Nadia, who stood together near the center of the party. Now wasn't the time to pin Matt down. But he could continue to sow seeds of interest and perhaps reel in other potential investors.

He was embroiled in a lively conversation with Matt, Nadia and two other guests when Jessie Humphrey swept into the space. She was stunning, stealing his breath away in the midst of a conversation about his most recent visit to Dubai and the building explosion there.

The flowing red floor-length gown had a simple but lovely top with a deep vee that showed off the buttery smooth skin of her toned brown shoulders. The bottom portion of the dress boasted intricate beading over a sheer fabric that overlaid the satin skirt beneath it. The dress commanded attention and partygoers gave her a wide berth as she moved about. He'd venture that their reaction was as much because of the incredible beauty of this woman in her stunning ball gown as because of her celebrity status.

"Someone is certainly an admirer." Matt chuckled. "Pretty sure I've never seen you speechless before." He leaned in closer so only Gideon and Nadia could hear him. "I could introduce you."

"Not necessary." Gideon loosened his tie and cleared his throat. Suddenly the space seemed much hotter than it had been before Jessie arrived. "We're already acquainted. In fact, we have a breakfast date tomorrow morning."

Matt's and Nadia's eyes widened.

"There must be a story there." Nadia smiled. "Why don't I take these gentlemen to meet our guest of honor. That should give you a chance to tell it."

Matt gave his wife a quick kiss on the cheek before she ushered the other men toward Jessie.

"Nadia is working with Teresa now, isn't she?" Gideon inquired.

"As a contractor, not an employee. But not at this event. Teresa insisted that she should just enjoy the event with her husband. And I couldn't agree more. But don't change the subject," his friend teased. "You certainly didn't waste any time getting to know Jessie Humphrey."

"Actually, I've known Jessie for many years," he clarified. "I dated her older sister, Geneva, when we were teenagers."

"Well, baby sis is all grown up now." Matt nodded toward her.

Amen to that.

Gideon sighed without response, his eyes trailing Jessie as she flitted about the room meeting partygoers.

She is so damn beautiful.

A partial updo allowed soft spirals to spill down one side of her lovely face. Her makeup was perfect. Naturally luminescent rather than overly done. Her eyes sparkled and her teeth gleamed as she flashed her brilliant smile or launched into the contagious laugh he remembered so fondly.

The woman was mesmerizing and she exuded confidence, which made her sexier still.

He was in serious danger of falling for her.

Jessie smiled and nodded as she mingled with a few of the guests before her performance. It was part of her contract.

Not that she wouldn't have mingled with the partygoers anyway. She'd just prefer to wait until after she'd performed, so that she could remain focused.

Despite being most comfortable onstage in front of an intimate audience, she still tended to get nervous before she performed. But the jitters she felt and the fluttering in her belly had more to do with the tall, dark, handsome man standing on the other side of the room staring at her.

Jessie hadn't met Gideon's gaze, but she'd angled her head so that she could study him. His tasteful black suit, complete with vest, fit his large, muscular frame well. A burgundy tie and pocket square were the perfect choice. And the shoes...gradient burgundy and black oxfords with an elegant style and shape that made her reasonably sure they were a pair of Corthays.

"Will you be performing songs from your current album tonight, Jessie?" a beautiful blonde woman in an elegant white dress asked eagerly.

"A few." Jessie kept a smile plastered on her face. It was a sore point. Of course people wanted to hear her perform the bubbly pop hits that they'd heard on the radio. But that wasn't what she wanted to play. "At an intimate event like this, I try to provide something you can't experience listening to a Top 40 pop station. So I'll also be performing new material."

The woman squealed, gripping the arm of the handsome man accompanying her. "I can't wait to tell all my friends I was one of the first people to hear Jessie Humphrey perform an original song. Would you mind taking a selfie with me?"

"Not at all." Jessie smiled graciously and stood beside the woman.

This part never got old. Sure, there were times when she just wanted to sit in peace and enjoy her dinner or get onto a plane in her sweats and baseball cap without being spotted. But in those inconvenient moments she always reminded herself to remain grateful. And she remembered how badly she'd wanted her name on that marquee, instead of solely in the songwriting credits.

After taking several photos together, the woman thanked her.

"You look absolutely stunning, Jessie."

Her spine stiffened at the sound of the smooth, honeyed voice that washed over her and made her pulse race and her spine tingle.

"Good evening, Gideon." She turned to face him.

The man was even more handsome up close, and he

smelled absolutely divine. Jessie had the urge to lean forward, press a hand to his broad chest and inhale his delectable scent.

He bent toward her and whispered in her ear, "You're the most beautiful woman in this room, and you are incredibly talented. You're going to kill it tonight."

Jessie's face warmed as she inhaled his masculine scent and absorbed the heat radiating from his body. She smoothed down her skirt with trembling hands.

"Thank you, Gideon." Her words were soft, meant only for him. "You saying that…it means a lot to me."

"I'm only stating the obvious." Gideon seemed pleased by her admission. "Look, I know you have to mingle with the crowd, but I'd love to buy you a drink and chat later, if you have time."

"That would be wonderful." Jessie gave him a reserved smile, then watched as he disappeared into the crowd. Her body tingled with desire for this man. That certainly hadn't changed. But getting involved with Gideon was a bad idea.

The sun had just gone down when Jessie sat on the bench in front of the gleaming baby grand piano. Matt Richmond had introduced her and escorted her onto the small stage. She scanned the glamorous, well-dressed crowd of people eagerly anticipating her performance.

She hadn't seen Chase Stratton or Dixon Benedict in attendance at the event yet. It was disappointing, but it wouldn't change how she approached her performance. She would be authentic and give the audience her very best, leaving it all on the stage.

That was her policy for every performance, be it as the opening act on a stadium stage or in a small club that could barely accommodate a baby grand piano.

Jessie started to play the chorus of an older song of hers

that she didn't intend to sing. She leaned into the microphone mounted over the piano.

"How are we doing tonight, beautiful people?" she asked in a soft, intimate rasp that prompted the crowd to shout variations of *good* or *fine.*

"That didn't sound very convincing, now did it?" she teased. The crowd laughed in response. "Why don't we try this one more time. I said, how are you incredibly beautiful people feeling on this amazing starry night?"

The crowd shouted back more enthusiastically.

"Now that's what I'm talking about." She nodded. "And are we having a good time tonight?"

The audience shouted back *yes,* many of them holding their drinks up as they did.

She started the set by playing snippets of a few of the songs she'd written for top acts. Something that always got the crowd going. Then she amped up the party by playing a couple of the songs from her recent album that had made it onto the pop charts.

Jessie played the bluesy intro from her first EP as a bridge to the emotional, deeply sentimental songs she'd play next.

"This next song is one of the first songs I ever wrote." Jessie continued to play the piano as she spoke. "I was a shy teenager and I'd had my heart broken for the first time." The audience *aw*-ed in unison. "I know, right? We've all been there. But it wasn't all bad. Because if it hadn't happened, I don't know if I'd be sitting here with you tonight."

Many people in the audience nodded as if they could relate.

"So I picked up my scented gel pen." The audience laughed. "Hey, I was still a teenager, y'all." She laughed, too. "But I picked up this pen and I decided to write some poetry. I wrote my little heart out and it was…trash." She laughed. "Utter and complete garbage. I filled two waste-baskets trying to get my thoughts on paper in a way that empowered me and healed my broken heart just the tiniest bit. Eventually, I wrote something that felt right, except it didn't quite feel complete."

She dramatically played the chords that made up the chorus of the song she was going to sing, and people cheered and clapped with recognition. Then she returned to playing the intro.

"It needed that little oomph. It needed music. The kind of music that touches people's souls. So I converted my sad little love poem into lyrics, and I wrote the bars of the chorus. The rest worked itself out from there. So if you've ever had your heart broken, if you've ever needed someone to remind you that no matter how bad it feels right now, it's not the end of the world, this song is for you." She scanned the crowd, pleased by their enthusiastic responses.

"The sun will shine again tomorrow. And when you wake up, in all of your fabulousness…" She waved one hand over the crowd. "You'll get the chance to eventually get it right. Whether it be with the same person—" her gaze involuntarily met Gideon's "—or with someone new."

Jessie launched into the opening bars of "Next Time I'll Get It Right," her voice strong and clear. She sang the song with every bit of her heart and soul. Just the way she'd written it. It gutted her every time she told the story of this song. Every time she performed it. But tonight it felt surreal, performing the song that had launched her songwriting and eventually her singing career. Knowing the man who'd inspired it was standing in the crowd, just a few feet away.

Fourteen

Jessie's pulse raced after the extended applause from the audience at the end of her performance. Regardless of how many people were in the crowd or how long she'd been doing this, an enthusiastic response was always exhilarating.

Matt Richmond returned to escort her off the stage. He and Nadia were gracious hosts.

She'd taken official photos with them before she'd gone onstage. Afterward, they both raved over how much they enjoyed her performance. Nadia even confessed that back when she was hopelessly in love with Matt, who also happened to be her boss, she'd taken solace in Jessie's songs.

Jessie returned to the party to mingle and take photos with many of Matt Richmond's business friends. After taking what felt like her hundredth selfie of the night, she was finally standing alone. Gideon, who'd been watching from his perch on a barstool all evening, approached her.

"I've been listening to your albums for the past few weeks, and I have to tell you, I didn't think you could possibly top the recordings. But that live performance was brilliant. It was intimate and gut-wrenching. Yet you left us on a positive note. It was truly outstanding."

"You've listened to my music?" Jessie had never given thought to whether Gideon was out there in the world listening to her music. He'd loved rock and hip-hop. What she sang was neither.

"Absolutely. I'm not stalking you on social media or anything, but I've followed your career enough to know you've written some pretty damn amazing songs for the biggest artists out there. You're unbelievably talented, Jessie. Guess those piano lessons your parents made you take paid off after all." He chuckled softly.

"Guess they did." Jessie couldn't help smiling, remembering how she'd whined and complained because Geneva didn't have to take lessons. "Of course, they're disappointed that I'm not making *real* music." She used air quotes.

Gideon's expression soured. His voice was suddenly tight. "How are Mr. and Mrs. Humphrey?"

He grabbed two glasses of champagne from a passing server and handed her one.

"As pretentious as ever." She accepted the champagne flute with a bitter laugh. "Though my mother isn't above musing to her friends about just how close she came to having a billionaire for a son-in-law."

Gideon frowned. "I doubt your father shares that viewpoint."

Jessie sipped the bubbly liquid. It tickled her nose.

"My father believes that had he not deemed you unsuitable for his daughter, you'd never have developed the drive to become a self-made billionaire." She hated repeating her father's words, but she wouldn't lie to Gideon. Besides, after his history with Milton Humphrey, she couldn't imagine that he'd have expected anything less of him.

"I've often contemplated that very thing." Gideon took a healthy sip of his champagne. He shrugged. "Maybe he's right."

"I don't believe that for a minute. Look at what you've accomplished over the last fifteen years. I refuse to give my father credit for all of that."

"I'm not saying I would be in the same situation I was born into. I know I would've made something of my life, if for no other reason than I loved your sister and would've done anything to give her the life to which she was accustomed. But this…" He took another sip. "I suppose I should thank your father for proclaiming me unworthy of his daughter."

They stood together quietly, drinking champagne and watching the crowd move around them.

Jessie set her empty champagne flute on a passing tray and rearranged the large flowing skirt of her beautiful designer dress. The ballroom gown took up so much space between them. But perhaps that was a good thing. It gave her room to breathe in a space where his close proximity and subtle masculine scent already seemed to overwhelm her.

The band had set back up and started to play again. Couples were filing onto the dance floor.

Gideon set his empty champagne flute on a nearby tray, then extended his large palm to her. "Care to dance?"

Jessie's gaze went from his offered hand to his incredibly handsome face and the dark, penetrating eyes that seemed to look right through her.

She couldn't speak. She nodded, placing her smaller hand in his, and followed him onto the crowded dance floor.

Gideon took Jessie in his arms and they swayed to the music in silence. He still found it hard to believe that the woman he was holding in his arms now was the same sweet, awkward girl with the big smile and beautiful spirit he'd once known.

It'd been one thing to see Jessie in a video or on an album cover. But standing with her now felt surreal.

It felt odd to be swaying with the beautiful woman she'd become and feeling such a deep attraction to her. And she was obviously still attracted to him.

His relationship with Geneva had ended long ago and she'd certainly moved on. He saw no reason he and Jessie couldn't explore their feelings.

"I guess I should thank you for not outing me as the lout who broke your heart back then." His lips grazed her ear as he leaned down and whispered the words in her ear.

"You're assuming you were the impetus for the song." Her back tensed beneath his fingertips. "I never said that."

"True." He nodded. "But I've been listening to the lyrics from that EP. It reminded me of conversations we've had."

"I write songs as a way to tell my story, not as a way to humiliate anyone else." She met his gaze. "I'm not a fan of revenge songs. Mostly because the people who've become famous for them tend to have a thin skin when the tables are turned."

"I agree," he said. "But I'm grateful just the same. I'd hate to become known as the cad that broke Jessie Humphrey's heart. Especially since it's the last thing I ever intended to do."

"I realize that now." Jessie dropped her gaze.

"What happened that day prompted you to become a songwriter. Just like your father's harsh dismissal set me on my path." He smiled faintly. "I guess there's some truth to those clichés."

"Like when one door closes, another opens," Jessie volunteered. "That was my grandmother's favorite."

"Mine, too." He smiled, thinking of the woman who'd

meant so much to him. "We were destined to take separate paths, but I'm grateful they've crossed again."

"So am I." Jessie's eyes glistened with emotion as they danced beneath the stars.

He held her closer and she laid her head on his chest as they moved together.

She smelled like a field of flowers in spring and it felt good to hold her body against his. The attraction he'd felt for Jessie when he'd first seen her yesterday afternoon had only grown stronger.

He was glad they'd cleared the air. Perhaps they'd laid the foundation upon which they could rebuild their friendship. But as he held her in his arms, it was impossible to deny that he wanted more than just friendship with Jessie. If they could manage it without damaging this fragile thing they were rebuilding.

There was something about this beautiful young woman with an old soul who touched people's hearts. He wanted more than just a night or two with Jessie. But he had no reason to believe she wanted the same.

Jessie was thrilled Gideon was happy about their unplanned reunion.

She certainly hadn't felt that way initially. A feeling that was compounded by his inquiry about their family, in what she'd suspected was a sly bid for information about her sister.

But nothing about their conversations since made her believe Gideon was angling for a chance to renew his relationship with Geneva. So perhaps she'd been wrong. Especially since his reaction to her yesterday and tonight made it clear he was attracted to her.

She'd concentrated so much of her energy on her anger toward Gideon. But once that raw, jagged emotion dissipated, her heart was filled with the warmth and affection she'd once had for him.

Jessie had been thinking of him since their encounter in the gym that morning.

How would Gideon react if she kissed him tonight?

She was no longer a teenage girl crushing on her older sister's ex. She was a grown woman fully capable of entering into a consensual fling.

And that's all it would be.

Gideon had his life in Seattle. She had hers back in New York. But the desire to be with him burned strong. He was still the man she compared every other man to in the back of her head.

"You told me that Geneva is married, but you didn't tell me anything about yourself. Is there a special guy waiting for you back home?"

"No." Jessie's spine tingled, hope filling her chest. "What about you? Is there a Mrs. Gideon Johns?"

Gideon laughed, as if it were a ridiculous question. "No," he said finally. "Maybe that's because I've been so focused on chasing the next deal."

"With all the success you've had, I'm surprised you're not thinking of retiring to some tropical island. Maybe starting a family. And you've never been married."

Jessie wanted to take back those last words as soon as she'd uttered them.

"So you've been checking up on me?" Gideon grinned.

"Only after we talked in the gym this morning. And I might have a financial magazine or two at home with your face on them."

"Somehow it makes me feel better that, even when you were angry with me, some part of you still cared enough to wonder what was going on in my life. I've always wondered about yours."

"And Geneva's," she said. It wasn't a question. He'd known her sister had lived in Switzerland. His information just hadn't been up to date.

"And Geneva," he repeated the words. "There was a time ten years ago, after I'd made my first million in real estate, that I wondered if there wasn't still a chance for us. I considered calling her up."

"Did you?" Jessie stared at him intensely.

"No. I flew to Zurich instead, planning to surprise her and sweep her off her feet."

A knot tightened in Jessie's stomach. "What happened?"

"I went to see her with a big bouquet of flowers in hand. But as I approached her flat I saw her with someone else. It was obvious he'd spent the night and she was seeing him off. I felt foolish for making the trip. For assuming that she'd want me."

"So you never really got over her. Is that why you never married? Because you were holding out hope that you and Geneva would eventually get back together?"

"No." The denial wasn't nearly as convincing as his earlier one. "We were never meant to be. I've made peace with that."

Jessie's gaze snapped to his. "What if Geneva weren't married?"

"She is."

"What if she weren't?" Jessie insisted.

"What I felt for Geneva…that was a long time ago. Truthfully, your sister was right. We wanted different things in life, even then."

Jessie gnawed on her lower lip in silence as she stared at the handsome man who held her in his arms.

What if she could finally trade her fantasies and what-ifs for a night in Gideon's arms? In his bed?

It was a thought that had consumed her all afternoon.

But if Gideon still had a thing for Geneva, she'd be setting herself up for heartache, despite her intention to walk away at the end of their weekend.

Besides, she'd spent one evening with Gideon and she was already allowing his presence to distract her from her focus. She was here to convince Chase and Dixon to work on her project. But she'd spent the entire night drowning in Gideon's eyes and fawning over him.

"Thank you for the dance, Gideon. I should mingle with some of the other guests." She pulled out of his embrace. "And I need to check with Teresa to see if Chase or Dixon has arrived."

"Of course." He nodded, shoving a hand in his pocket. "I won't be able to make it for breakfast tomorrow morning due to an important business meeting. Maybe we could have a nightcap later?"

Jessie wanted to accept his offer. To whisper in his ear exactly what she'd imagined so many times. But it would be a mistake. When he learned that Geneva would soon be free, he'd choose her instead.

"It's been a long day and I'm still jet-lagged. Another time maybe?"

"Sure." Gideon smiled, but his eyes revealed his disappointment. He kissed her cheek. "Good night, Jess."

She made her way to the other side of the covered patio, away from Gideon Johns.

Fifteen

Gideon watched Matt's reaction as the man surveyed the prospectus that Landon had put together for him on the Dubai deal. After trying to meet with Matt twice already this weekend, he'd arranged for them to have room service breakfast at his private cottage.

It was the best way for Gideon to minimize the interruptions as he tried to finalize Matt's participation in the deal.

"How much do you have on the line on this one?" Matt asked calmly as he sipped his coffee.

"Everything." Even Gideon was taken aback by his frank response.

He wasn't one to rely on a pitiful song and dance in order to get investors on board. Not even when the potential investor happened to be a friend.

"Not monetarily, of course," Gideon added when Matt regarded him skeptically. "But my reputation and the future of my company are riding on this deal. I won't lie to you, Matt. A couple of major investors pulled out recently.

Not because of anything having to do with the deal itself. This deal is solid. We've done our homework on this and expect to see one of our greatest returns to date."

"Then why'd those two investors pull out of the deal?" Matt folded his arms, his brows knitted.

"Both men were spooked by volatilities in their industry. Teaches me a lesson going forward. Don't rely too heavily on investors from a single business sector. If market changes negatively impact that industry, the deal could go under."

"Makes sense." Matt nodded. "But I'm looking to invest ten million max in this deal. How do you plan to make up the shortfall?"

"Landon and I have been working the phones tirelessly for the past two weeks. We've secured most of the required funding for this deal. Once you're on board, I'll just need a few additional investments."

"And?" Matt looked up from cutting into his omelet.

"I've got phone meetings lined up for those this afternoon." Gideon took a bite of his crepe. He spoke calmly.

No pressure.

Despite the fact that he needed Matt's investment in order to complete this deal, his friend wouldn't be making this commitment as some favor to him. It was an excellent opportunity for Richmond Industries to make an awful lot of money. That's what he'd focused on during his presentation to Matt. The solid return this deal offered with a relatively quick turnaround.

Matt picked up the prospectus and thumbed through it again in silence. Gideon didn't interrupt. He just kept eating his crepe and drinking his orange juice. As if all of this were no big deal.

"Okay." Matt put the folder down and looked squarely at Gideon. "I'm in. Send the paperwork to my office. Our attorneys will review it and then we'll cut you a check. Anything else I need to do?"

"No. We'll make this as convenient for you as we can," Gideon said nonchalantly. "The paper work will be waiting for you when you return to Seattle."

Matt shook his hand. "I look forward to finally doing business with you. It's been a long time coming."

"It has." Gideon kept his voice even, despite wanting to do a victory dance worthy of an end zone. "Welcome aboard."

"Speaking of something being a long time coming, it seems that your reunion with Jessie Humphrey was worth the wait." Matt took the final bite of his omelet.

"It's been great seeing her again. We were able to clear the air. Hopefully we'll rebuild our friendship."

"Friendship?" Matt's eyebrows drew together. "I saw how you were looking at her. Seemed like more than friendship to me. A couple of guys asked if you two were an item. They were hoping to ask her out."

"Who wanted to ask her out?" A knot formed in his gut and his hands clenched into fists.

"See, that face right there—" Matt laughed as he pointed to him "—that's definitely jealousy. You want to tell me again how she's just a friend?"

Gideon cut another piece of his crepe without responding. No need to add fuel to the fire. Matt was already enjoying this way too much.

"It's more serious than I thought." Matt finished his coffee. "You usually have a much better poker face. I should know. I've lost to you enough times because of it. Does Jessie know?"

"Does she know what?" Gideon tried not to be irritated with his friend. After all, the man had probably just saved his Dubai deal. "That I want to be friends again?"

"That you see her as more than a friend or a weekend hookup. I've seen you with both. Neither has ever produced anything nearly as intense as the vibe you're giving off right now or the aura surrounding you two on the dance floor last night."

"Vibes? Auras? Really, Matt?" Gideon teased his friend. "Next you'll be telling me the stars aligned to bring us together this weekend."

"Sounds more like something Nadia would say than me, but I can't disagree. Maybe this was the whole point of that disastrous mudslide at the original event. If that's the case, I've got a pretty hefty bill I'd like to send you." Matt climbed to his feet.

"Ha, ha, ha." Gideon stood, too. "You're a regular comedian."

"Nope. I'm just a guy in love who recognizes it when I see it in another guy. Especially one who still has no clue that he's already in over his head." Matt smiled broadly. "I have to prepare for my presentation with Liam later this morning. So I'd better go. Thanks for breakfast and for bringing me in on this deal. I'm excited about it."

"One more thing." Gideon drew in a deep breath, knowing he shouldn't ask but unable to stop himself. "The two music producers who are here—"

"Dixon Benedict and Chase Stratton. What about them?" Matt frowned. "Looking for more investors?"

"No, it's nothing like that. Do you think you'd be able to arrange a meeting with the two of them?"

Matt smirked knowingly. "You mean do I think I could secure a meeting for Jessie with the two of them?"

If he wanted to prove to Matt that he wasn't into Jessie he was doing a shit job of it. "Yeah."

"I'll see what I can do." Matt shook his hand again and left.

Gideon was as disturbed by Matt's observation about him and Jessie as he was excited to tell Landon they were close to finishing the deal.

Jessie was smart and beautiful and she made him laugh. Of course he was interested in her. He'd thought a lot about what would happen if she tried to kiss him again.

This time, he wouldn't stop her.

The image of Jess lying in his bed beneath him had kept him up, tossing and turning, all night.

Gideon grabbed his phone off the coffee table and dialed Landon. He would focus on the business at hand and let things with Jessie take their natural course.

Whatever that might be.

Jessie sat at the piano playing one of the songs she'd written for her new album. She was still tweaking the key in which she should sing it.

Teresa had confirmed that both Chase Stratton and Dixon Benedict had arrived at The Goblet the previous evening. She didn't think either of them had been there for Jessie's performance. But Teresa expected both men to be at the gala that evening and had promised to get them a table in front of the stage.

Jessie needed to deliver the performance of her life and impress both men. And she needed to stay laser-focused on her primary reason for taking this gig: securing the funding and ideal producers for her independent album.

She'd chosen to bet on herself, rather than accept a soul-sucking record deal. Or trade her integrity for the deal she wanted. *Everything* was riding on this project.

She wanted to create a collection of songs that would become part of the soundtrack of people's lives. If she succeeded, labels would be knocking down the door to offer her a deal. And she would establish her right to retain creative freedom on future projects.

The album needed to be brilliant enough to receive critical nods and outsell her last album, despite limited distribution. It was a skyscraper-tall order. But big-name producers like Chase and Dixon could help her get wider distribution than she could on her own, even with her past success.

She needed to remember what was at stake tonight for her career rather than obsessing over Gideon. What he meant to her then. The mistakes they'd both made fifteen years ago. How he'd react if she proposed a weekend tryst.

Jessie sucked in a deep breath, her head spinning as her hands moved across the keys. She hit the wrong note, then banged on the piano keys in frustration.

She couldn't lose focus, lost in thoughts of Gideon. It was a cruel catch-22, because the song she hoped to wow Chase and Dixon with was one that had been inspired by Gideon's rejection that day. Born of all the pain, hurt and anger she'd felt and the realization that it was time to let it all go and move on.

It was ironic that he'd waltz back into her life after she'd written that song. The universe had one hell of a sense of humor.

"Okay" was the most raw, emotional song she'd written to date. She needed to tap into the pain and loss she'd felt that day. And she had to transport the audience to that place where they could connect to their own experiences of love and loss.

It had been unnerving to perform with Gideon in the audience last night. Especially when she'd introduced the song that had clearly been about her feelings for him. But tonight, most of her planned set featured songs that would force her to relive those intense feelings. She'd be playing them all out in front of the man who'd inspired them.

She couldn't hold back any of those raw emotions. Her authentic sound and poignant delivery were what set her apart from her pop diva peers. So she would lean into whatever feelings arose and ride the wave of those emotions.

A piece of her hoped Gideon didn't show tonight. Then she could lay her heart out on the stage for everyone except him to see.

She doubted she would be that lucky.

The only thing that mattered was that Chase and Dixon would be there for the performance. They needed to understand what she was capable of. If she could manage that, she wouldn't need to convince them. They'd be clamoring to work with her.

"Jessie, is everything all right with the piano?" Teresa approached her with a platter containing a mug of tea and a saucer. "You're certainly deep in thought."

Jessie hadn't realized she'd stopped playing. She was sitting there as if the entire world weighed on her shoulders.

No wonder Teresa was worried.

"Everything is good. Thank you." Jessie took a sip of the warm chamomile tea the woman handed her. "In terms of attention to detail and anticipating the needs of the guests, you're one of the best event planners I've worked with. If you weren't on the West Coast, I'd hire you to plan the album release party once I'm done."

"Thank you, Jessie." Teresa beamed. "And thank you for agreeing to do this event. After the disaster at The Opulence, I wouldn't have blamed you if you'd turned me down."

"Well, you did sweeten the deal." Jessie laughed. "I can't thank you enough for getting Chase and Dixon in the room for tonight's performance."

"I'm glad we could make it happen. If you give them even half of what you gave us last night, they'll both be *begging* to work with you." Teresa looked up when the banquet manager called her name. "I'd better go. Call me if you need anything. We want to build up the drama of your performance tonight, so don't mingle with the guests beforehand this time. Let's save it until after your set. If you could arrive in the staging area about an hour before go time, we'll make sure everything is ready."

Jessie thanked Teresa. Then when she had the space to herself again, she closed her eyes and let her fingers travel over the keys.

Sixteen

Teresa stood at the back of the auditorium late Saturday morning as Matt and Liam sat at the center of the stage concluding their talk on their new joint AI venture, the Sasha Project. The room was nearly filled to capacity. At the end of their presentation, they were greeted by thunderous applause.

The retreat was going better than either she or Matt had expected. More than half of the guests invited to the original retreat were able to attend, despite the short notice. They'd expanded the guest list to tastemakers and change agents in other industries. People like Chase Stratton and Dixon Benedict, both of whom had finally arrived and were seated in the auditorium.

After a quick update from Corinne and two other members of her team, Teresa's next stop was the kitchen. She consulted with the chef on the gala dinner menu. They also reviewed all of the special meal requests of various guests. It seemed that nearly a third of the attendees had dietary restrictions, but the chef and his staff had everything well in hand.

Chef Riad offered to prepare her a lovely pasta and chicken dish so she could have a quick, early lunch. It would probably be her only chance to grab a bite until later that evening.

Since it was such a gorgeous day, he suggested that she enjoy her lunch on the patio beside the pool, where he'd have it delivered.

It was the perfect suggestion. She could get a little sun, enjoy the gardens and inspect the pool to ensure that everything was as it should be. As she approached the large heated outdoor art deco pool, Liam emerged from beneath the water.

She nearly dropped her cell phone at the sight of him.

The man is a ridiculously perfect physical specimen.

He strode in her direction, his lips pressed into a subtle smirk. The black Versace swim trunks he wore were imprinted with a gold Barocco scroll print and the iconic Greek key print at the waist. The length of Liam's swim shorts showed off his strong thighs, while the band at the waist highlighted his firm abs.

Liam ran his fingers through his dark hair, plastered to his head. His light blue eyes beamed in the sunlight.

"Good morning," he said finally, obviously pleased by her reaction to his barely clad body.

A tingle of electricity ran down her spine and she involuntarily sank her teeth into her lower lip. Thoughts of when she'd last seen him wearing that little filled her brain, and her body ached for him.

Damn him.

"Good morning," she stammered. *Get a hold of yourself, girl.* "The Sasha Project announcement went well."

"It was great to finally make it public. But as soon as

we were done I needed to clear my head. So I went for a swim." He accepted two towels from the pool attendant and thanked her.

Liam wrapped one towel around his waist and hung the other around his neck, drying his hair.

"You know Nicolette Ryan, don't you?" Liam nodded toward a beautiful woman stretched out on a lounger beside the pool with her bare legs crossed.

Liam collapsed on the chair beside her and she offered him one of the two drinks that a poolside server had just delivered.

The muscles in Teresa's back and neck tensed. Her free hand clenched in a fist at her side.

Nicolette Ryan. The reporter. What the hell was Liam doing cozying up with her?

Had Liam been the one who'd leaked the photos and information about Teresa to the press? Was he playing some sick game to drive her away before she could liquidate her shares in Christopher Corporation?

"Good morning, Teresa." Nicolette waved cheerily. The woman's brown eyes sparkled and her dark hair was smoothed back into a low bun. Her creamy, light brown skin shone. "Thank you so much for granting me a press pass for this event. The grounds are remarkable and Jessie Humphrey's show last night was one of the best live performances I've ever experienced."

Teresa forced a smile, despite her tense shoulders. "Glad you could make the retreat on such short notice."

Nicolette gave her a knowing smile. "I wouldn't have missed it."

She lay back, stretched out in the warmth of the sun and closed her eyes.

Teresa gritted her teeth. She looked for a patio table that

would allow her to eat in peace without seeing or hearing Liam and his new friend.

She plopped down in one of the wrought iron chairs at a patio table beneath a large umbrella and sulked.

No, she and Liam weren't a couple. And she had no right to dictate what activities he engaged in and with whom. Still, she couldn't help the churning in her gut, thinking of Nicolette and Liam doing God knows what together.

She cast a sideways glance in their direction. Heads together, they were engaged in a private conversation. One to which they obviously didn't want her to be privy. She could barely hear them whispering in hushed tones. For a moment, she regretted selecting a table so far away.

"Here you are, ma'am. Chef Riad's special chicken Alfredo, just for you." The server set down her plate and laid out her silverware. He poured a bottle of sparkling mineral water in her glass.

Teresa wished he'd shift just a little to the right so she could see exactly what Liam and Nicolette were doing.

Spying on Liam wouldn't help her sanity with all that was already going on. What she needed was distance.

"I'm sorry, but would you mind if I moved to the cabana the hotel gave us access to for the weekend?"

The server politely gathered everything up on his tray again before heading over to the cabana.

Once he was gone, Teresa ate her meal in peace, trying hard not to wonder about Liam or his newfound interest in the beautiful reporter.

"I feel terrible about the photos that leaked after the blackout at The Opulence." Nicolette Ryan sipped her piña colada. "And those awful headlines. They weren't fair to you or Teresa." She nodded toward the woman who'd moved to the other end of the pool.

Without turning his head, Liam glanced in Teresa's direction in time to see her get out of her seat and follow the server to one of the more secluded cabanas.

"Liam." Nicolette called his name impatiently, as if it wasn't the first time she'd had to say it.

"Yes, I'm sorry. I was just…thinking." He took a gulp of his Manhattan. He turned to face her fully. "So you think someone has it out for me?"

"At this point, I'm not sure if their grudge is against you personally or against your father's company. It's even possible that Teresa is the real target of this cruel game someone is playing."

Liam frowned, glanced involuntarily over his shoulder at the cabana that Teresa occupied. If someone had it out for her…why? Had she done something questionable in her past that would make someone want revenge? If so, just how far would they go to make her pay?

"Teresa could be in danger."

"I don't know." Nicolette shrugged. "But I'd suggest that you both operate on the side of caution. Someone has definitely been asking around about the two of you and inquiring about her history with your father."

Nicolette adjusted her lounger, sitting upright. "People often discount me because of the topics I cover. Celebrities, fashion, Hollywood and society gossip," she said bitterly. "But I operate with integrity. *Always*. I don't want to see you or Teresa get hurt. Nor do I want to see either of your reputations ruined. Watch out for unscrupulous reporters and paparazzi. They're like sharks, circling in the water, sniffing out blood."

"Who has been asking about me and about my father? If you know that someone is asking, surely you know who it is."

"I don't have all of the details." She shifted her gaze from his and sipped her drink.

"There's something you know, but aren't telling me." Liam studied Nicolette's face.

Her brown eyes wouldn't meet his. "I have to protect my sources. I've already told you too much. In fact, I'd better go and get ready for lunch. Mr. Richmond doesn't want his guests hounded by the press this weekend, but a few have agreed to talk to me. I have some interviews lined up."

"Wait, Nicolette." Liam placed a hand on her arm. "Surely there is something else you can tell me."

Nicolette scanned the space before returning her gaze to his. "I'm not one hundred percent sure who is behind this, but it's quite possible that the source is much closer to you than you think. If I were you, I'd be careful about who I trust."

"I will." Liam ran a hand through his damp hair. "Thank you for sharing what you could."

Nicolette slid on her shades, gathered her things and headed inside the hotel.

A source close to him?

The number of people he could trust not to keep secrets from him steadily decreased, starting with his parents. His father had pulled the rug from underneath him by leaving Teresa 25 percent of Christopher Corporation stock. Then there was the even bigger secret…

When Linus Christopher lay dying in the hospital, Liam had caught a glimpse of his father's medical records. Linus's blood type was listed as AB. He hadn't given it much thought at the time. But later it occurred to him that his own blood type was O. If the information in his father's chart was accurate, there was no way Linus Christopher was his father.

Parents were often hesitant to reveal to their children

that they were adopted. But he wasn't a child. He was a thirty-two-year-old man who needed to know his medical history. So if he was adopted, why hadn't his parents told him the truth?

After his father's funeral, Liam had asked his mother, Catherine, about the discrepancy. She insisted the hospital chart had been mistaken. And she assured him he was their biological son.

Still, he couldn't stop thinking about it.

Maybe his mother was right and the admitting staff had made an egregious error. But then there was the emotional distance he'd always felt between himself and his father. It had never made sense to Liam. But if the medical chart was to be believed, his father's resentment suddenly made sense.

Then his father had gone and left a quarter of the company's shares to Teresa—a virtual stranger. It only fueled his suspicion that he may not be a Christopher after all.

Seventeen

The Richmond Industries fifth anniversary event was going off without a hitch. The accommodations and food were fantastic. The guests were all well-behaved and seemed to really be enjoying the experience. And the hotel staff's customer service was unparalleled. Teresa couldn't have asked for anything more.

Liam had been a genius for suggesting this venue and a saint for using his pull to secure the hotel for her on such short notice.

Teresa closed her eyes against the memory of Liam and Nicolette whispering together beside the pool. Despite her growing affection for the man, he didn't trust her, and without that, they had no future.

She needed to get her head in the game and focus on her work at Limitless Events and the Christopher Corporation. That should be enough to keep her busy so she didn't think about Liam or how incredible his body had looked dripping wet.

Her phone buzzed. She lifted it and checked the new text message.

Speak of the devil.

Urgent. Meet me in my cottage in ten minutes. Need to speak with you in private.

Teresa frowned. Why couldn't Liam have asked her to meet him at the bar or even beside the pool?

Because none of those areas offered true privacy. And from the sound of his urgent text, the issue was sensitive and meant only for her ears. Still, going to see Liam Christopher in his cottage was a profoundly bad idea.

Teresa dialed Liam's phone, but the call rang until it went to his voice mail. She called it twice more and got the same.

Teresa frowned and tucked her hair behind her ear as she made another sweep of the lobby to ensure everything was fine. She gave a few quick instructions to the staff setting up lunch in the banquet hall and followed up with Corinne and Evelyn Montague. Then she made her way across the property to Liam's cottage.

She knocked on the door, but there was no answer. Teresa knocked again, miffed that Liam had sent her such a cryptic text but now wasn't answering his phone or the door. She was just about to turn and leave when Liam answered.

"Sorry, I was in the shower. Got sidetracked by an unexpected call." He answered the door with a towel slung low on his waist. Droplets of water from the shower still covered his body. "Come in."

Liam stepped aside to allow her into the room, then he glanced around the courtyard.

"Liam, what's going on?" Teresa demanded, her arms folded. "Were you checking to see if I was being followed?"

"Yes." He took the towel draped around his neck and dried his hair.

"By whom?"

"That's what I'd like to know." He went into the kitchen and pulled out a bottle of water, offering her one.

"No, thank you." Teresa went to the window and peeked outside. She pulled the curtains closed once she was convinced no one was there.

The man was seriously making her paranoid.

"Then why would you think someone is following me? And what's up with the cryptic text? I have a million things going on right now. So spare me the drama and tell me what's happening."

Liam excused himself to go into the bathroom and change, leaving her to pace in the living space, which opened to the bedroom. She found herself staring at the bed. Thoughts of the nights they'd shared filled her brain. For one happy moment she had truly believed that they could have something more. Something real.

But there was so much baggage between them. Her history with his father. Liam's inability to trust people, ingrained in him by his mother. The terms of his father's will and the suspicion and animosity that had created between them. The rumors that threatened both of their reputations and her livelihood.

"Is everything all right?" Liam placed a gentle hand on her arm, startling her. She hadn't even realized that he'd emerged from the bathroom. "I called you a couple of times but you were in a daze."

"I'm just running everything about tonight's gala through my head. Trying to make sure I didn't forget anything." There were enough secrets between them. She hated adding an inconsequential lie to the mix. "So you were going to explain the text."

"Right." He stepped away, creating space between them. As if he needed it as much as she did. "You might've noticed that I had a chance to chat with Nicolette Ryan, the lifestyle reporter for—"

"I know who Nicolette Ryan is, Liam." She folded her arms, her jaw tight. "I issued her press pass."

"Yes, of course," he conceded with a little smirk. He seemed to be getting a kick out of her spurned-lover routine. "The reason Nicolette wanted to speak to me so urgently was because she wanted to warn me...*us*, really."

"About?" Teresa raised an eyebrow.

"Nicolette doesn't believe that the leaking of those photos and videos of us was just some random act by someone trying to make a buck." Liam sat on the white sofa. "She thinks that someone has a calculated agenda to destroy one of us."

"Or perhaps both." Teresa sank onto the other end of the sofa and turned to him. "But who and why?"

"That's what we need to put our heads together and figure out," he said. "And soon. Preferably before they strike again and do more damage to our reputations and organizations. Christopher Corporation can easily ride out the current scandal, but if something else like this happens..."

"Limitless Events will be dead in the water." Teresa raised her eyes to his. "What do we do? I've invested everything I own in this company. I can't afford for it to fail. Too many people are counting on me. My staff, my family..."

"I know." Liam placed his large hand over hers, resting on the sofa between them. "And I'll do everything in my power to help keep that from happening. I hope you believe that."

Teresa nodded. "I do. You've already done so much. Getting Jessie Humphrey to The Opulence despite the weather.

Getting this place for us on such short notice. You didn't have to do any of that."

Liam gave her a reluctant nod. He stood, pacing the floor. "We both need to be aware that there are unethical reporters out there who'd do anything to get a big story and some of them don't give a damn about the facts. They just want a juicy, salacious story, regardless of how fictitious it might be. I'm sure that people like that would think nothing of employing spies to get dirt on us or our companies. Perhaps even people we know and trust." He stared at her pointedly.

"You think there's a spy in my camp? Like one of my employees?" Teresa was incensed by Liam's suggestion. "I handpicked each and every member of my team. I'd vouch for any of them."

"I get it. They're good people. Seemingly trustworthy. But people aren't always who they seem."

"Like the fact that I'm not the home-wrecking gold digger you believed me to be?" She folded her arms, one brow raised. "Or that you're not the ogre I once thought you were?"

"Yes, people can surprise you for the better," Liam admitted. "But they can also stun you in truly terrible ways. We can't discount the probability of that."

Teresa stood, too. "Why do you automatically assume it's someone from my company? It could just as easily be someone from Christopher Corporation."

"True." He nodded sagely. "But aside from Duncan, I don't have a relationship with my employees that's quite as familiar as the one you have with yours. There's some truth to the saying that familiarity breeds contempt." He rubbed his jaw.

Teresa shook her head vehemently. "I still don't believe it. Besides, why would they do something that's jeopardizing their livelihood? I can see the fear in their eyes, Liam. They're all just as concerned as I am about the impact these rumors will have on the future of the company. I'm telling you, no one at Limitless Events would've done this. *No one*," she said again for emphasis.

Liam didn't try to hide his exasperation over her unwillingness to believe one of her employees had sold her out for a quick payday.

"Maybe they are really honest, loyal, hardworking individuals." Liam focused his gaze on hers. "But if someone has an agenda against one of us, it's possible they'd stop at nothing to achieve their end. Even if it meant blackmailing someone close to us. Perhaps even threatening to harm a member of their family."

"Joshua…" Teresa pressed a hand to her forehead.

"You think your brother might've been compromised?" Liam asked. "Could that be why he went missing when you got that crank call about him?"

When she'd gotten a mysterious call implying that her brother may have been kidnapped, she'd confided that to Liam. He'd offered to have his investigator check into it and it turned out to be a hoax.

"Josh would never do anything to hurt me. Certainly nothing like this." Teresa didn't believe for a minute that her brother would be party to destroying her career. "Besides, he doesn't know about us. We haven't spoken in a while, and I certainly wouldn't tell my little brother that you and I…" Her eyes darted involuntarily to the bed in the other room. "It just couldn't be him, that's all."

Teresa paced the floor, her back to him. As soon as she left Liam's cottage, she needed to call her brother.

"Okay, if we can't figure out who, let's approach the other side of this."

"Which is?" Teresa turned back to Liam, studying his face.

He ran his hands through his dark hair and his expression offered an unspoken apology. "I need you to be completely honest with me, Teresa. Is there more to the story about what happened between you and my father? Are there any more stories that are likely to come out?"

It hurt that Liam felt the need to ask the question again. That he still didn't fully believe her though she'd told him the unvarnished truth. She was never romantically involved with his father. Linus Christopher had been nothing more than a friend and mentor to her.

"How many times and how many ways do I have to say it?" she seethed. "I did *not* have an affair with your father. I wouldn't. And I never saw him as anything other than a mentor. I hadn't seen Linus in years. I'm as shocked as you are that he'd leave me twenty-five percent of the company."

Liam grimaced when she mentioned the portion of the company she held. "I believe you about my father," he said quietly. He didn't want to ask about her father's connection to Christopher Corporation until Dutton gave him more to go on. "But is there anything else you might have to worry about? Anything that might cause a problem for your company or mine? Because, as you indicated, you now own a quarter of the company. So it's not just Limitless that's in jeopardy."

"I do have secrets." She shrugged. "Doesn't everyone?"

Liam stepped closer. "But is there anything that could be damaging to the reputation of Christopher Corporation?"

"I already told you about my brother and his problems. That he got in trouble with some dangerous people in Vegas and owed them a lot of money."

"The trouble that the Fixer helped you get him out of." Liam folded his arms and frowned. "It isn't ideal, of course.

But we could probably find a way to spin the story. Everyone loves the story of a person who would go to bat for their family, at all costs."

"It isn't a story, Liam. It's the truth. Maybe this is all just about bad press to you, but this is my life." Her voice broke and tears burned her eyes. She swiped a finger beneath one eye, trying not to ruin her makeup. "Not that you'd understand."

"Teresa, wait..."

Before he could stop himself, Liam had caught her hand in his. She turned back to look at him. Hurt and disappointment filled the lovely blue eyes he'd found himself drowning in just a few short weeks ago.

"I realize how difficult this must all be for you. I didn't intend to come off as an insensitive, self-centered boor." He rubbed his thumb over the soft skin on the back of her hand. "I've been groomed my entire life to think of Christopher Corporation first and everything second...including the people in my life. I never much liked being on the receiving end of that treatment. That's something I need to remember going forward."

Teresa nodded, looking at him thoughtfully. The night the tree crashed on top of her, he'd told her about the rocky relationship he'd had with his parents. Had admitted how painful it was for him growing up. So he knew she understood what he meant. He appreciated the compassion in her eyes.

"There is one other thing I should tell you." She dropped her gaze from his momentarily. "The only reason I didn't reject your father's gift of shares in the company is because the man who made the threatening phone call about my brother implied that Joshua owed someone money. A lot of it."

"How much?"

"The caller said seven million dollars. I knew Joshua owed some money a long time ago, but I thought when the Fixer bailed Josh out, those debts were settled, too."

It was all starting to become clear to Liam. "So you'd like to have the money on hand, just in case."

"Yes." More tears rolled down her face and her cheeks turned crimson, as if she was embarrassed by showing emotion in front of him. She swiped at the tears angrily with her free hand.

"You didn't have to tell me that." Liam couldn't help staring at her firm, kissable lips. "Why did you?"

She looked at him squarely again. "Because I don't want there to be any secrets between us."

Liam cradled her cheek, wiping away her tears with his thumb. He stepped closer to this beautiful woman who had an uncanny gift for making him feel an array of emotions. Anger, frustration, lust, jealousy, pain and a deep, growing affection that seemed to squeeze his chest whenever he thought of her.

He leaned in so slowly it felt as if he could hear the seconds ticking in his head. Teresa didn't object. Instead, she leaned closer, too. Her eyes drifted closed.

Liam pressed his mouth to hers and kissed her.

Teresa let go of his hand and relaxed into him, her hands pressed to his chest as she angled her head, giving him better access. He trailed kisses across her salty, tearstained cheeks. Then he pressed a soft kiss to her ear.

"Why is it that I can never resist kissing you?" he whispered.

"Maybe it's the same reason I can't help wanting you to kiss me." Her breathy reply did things to him. "Or stop thinking about the nights we spent together."

He kissed her again, and she parted her lips to him, inviting him to deepen the kiss. He obliged, his tongue gliding against hers. He reveled in the sweet, minty taste of her warm mouth.

The kiss that had started off slow and tentative escalated. The hunger in his kiss was matched by the eagerness in hers.

Her arms snaked around his waist, and her fingers pressed into his back, pulling their bodies closer. He wanted her. Hadn't been able to stop thinking about her. And he'd used nearly every excuse he could manufacture to spend time with her.

Everything he'd been taught from the time he was a boy told him he shouldn't trust her. That he should resent her intrusion into his life and the way she'd insinuated herself into his family's business.

But another part of him found Teresa to be a breath of fresh air in a world filled with self-important blowhards whose bank accounts were the most interesting thing about them.

She made him feel things he hadn't felt before. Things he wanted to feel again. So despite the promise he'd made to himself, he wanted to taste her skin. To experience the passion they'd shared as they brought each other mind-blowing pleasure.

Liam broke their kiss, his eyes searching hers for permission. Teresa sank her teeth into her bottom lip, her breathing ragged as she removed her suit jacket and tossed it over the chair. She turned her back to him, giving him access to the zipper of her bustier.

He leaned in and pressed a soft kiss to her neck and shoulder as he unzipped the fabric, threaded with a metallic silver. He tossed it on top of her suit jacket in the chair. His hands glided up her belly as he kissed her shoulders. He palmed her breasts.

Teresa whimpered. Her knees buckled slightly and her curvy bottom pressed against him. He slid the zipper down the side of her slim gray pants. She kicked off her heels, standing in her bare feet and a silvery gray lace thong.

He turned her around, pressing another kiss to her mouth as he lifted her. She wrapped her lean legs around him as he carried her to the bed.

Liam stripped off his clothing, thankful the boutique hotel provided a welcome kit that included a handful of little foil packets. He sheathed himself, then tugged off the little scrap of lace and dropped it to the floor.

He kissed her. Savored the sensation as her body welcomed his. Her fingers dug into his back as he drove deep inside her. Their bodies moved together. Their murmurs of pleasure growing more intense as they each hurtled closer to their edge.

Teresa froze, her fingernails scraping his skin as she called his name. The contraction of the muscles deep in her core sent ripples of pleasure up his spine that brought him over the edge.

He cursed, his body trembling as he collapsed on the bed beside her, struggling to catch his breath.

Neither of them spoke.

Finally, he rolled over and propped his fist beneath his head as he lay facing her. He trailed a hand down her stomach. "That was…" He blew out a breath, words escaping him.

A smile lit her eyes. "It was, wasn't it?"

"It always is between us."

Teresa's phone rang. She glanced at the clock on the wall, then cursed beneath her breath and climbed out of bed.

"I have to get back." She gathered her clothing.

"Of course, but do you have to go this instant?" He hoped for an encore as soon as he recovered.

"Yes." She rushed into the bathroom, but smiled over her shoulder at him. "But I'll take a rain check for later tonight."

He grinned, already counting the minutes.

Eighteen

Teresa smoothed the gorgeous blue floor-length Zac Posen fishtail gown she'd gotten for a steal down over her hips. She took one last look in the mirror as she carefully applied her matte red Dior lipstick. Then she dropped the tube in her clutch.

Today had been hectic. She'd handled several last-minute preparations, headed off potential problems and resolved a few unusual guest requests. But there were two events that had shaken her the most during the course of the day. Learning that someone may be acting on a calculated vendetta against her and…

Teresa's body tingled with electricity as it seemed to relive the trail that Liam's strong hand had taken as it moved across her skin. She'd allowed herself to be pulled under again by her attraction to him.

Not just because he was an incredibly sexy man. Though her eyes drifted closed briefly at the memory of Liam emerging from the pool in those swim shorts. She was attracted to him because, despite the distrust and bravado, at his core he was a sweet and thoughtful man. He'd come to her aid in countless ways in the past few months. Many of which he hadn't even wanted her to know about. He'd done it simply because she needed the help.

Still, were their physical attraction, similar interests and the fact that they enjoyed spending time together enough to overcome Liam's issues with trust and the nasty rumors out there about her?

Teresa pushed the disquieting thoughts from her mind. She had a gala to manage. And tonight would go off without a hitch.

She'd do whatever was necessary to ensure it.

"Teresa."

Matt approached with Nadia on his arm.

Teresa had brought Nadia on at Limitless Events as a contractor when it became evident that she wouldn't be able to keep her job as Matt's assistant once they became involved. She was smart, resourceful, hardworking and trustworthy. Which made her the perfect fit. But this was her husband's event, so Nadia was a client, too, serving as Matt's official cohost.

Nadia looked gorgeous in a strapless red gown with her blonde hair twisted in an elaborate updo. And despite his disdain for suits, the man wore an athletic-fit tuxedo that highlighted his muscular physique.

"This weekend has been fabulous. A wonderful way to celebrate Richmond Industries' fifth anniversary. It was a great call having the retreat here. Almost makes the disaster we endured last month worthwhile." He chuckled, his arm wrapped around Nadia's waist.

"It truly has been a wonderful weekend." Nadia's gaze met Matt's.

Her brown eyes glinted in the light and her cheeks

flushed as her husband drank her in. As if he were seeing her for the very first time.

"You've honestly outdone yourself, Teresa." Nadia finally turned to meet her gaze. "Thank you for all of your hard work. With such short notice for the rescheduled event, I know it wasn't easy. Quite frankly, this was something of a miracle. Far more than we expected, given the timeline."

She nudged Matt, who was looking at Nadia dreamily once again.

"You've done outstanding work, Teresa. We'll be in touch to discuss the plans for our next retreat."

Matt excused himself and he and Nadia walked away to greet their guests.

Teresa was thrilled that Matt was so pleased. Just a few more hours and she could put this event in the books as a phenomenal success.

"Teresa St. Claire, I'm Brooks Abbingdon." A tall, handsome man with curly hair approached her. His wide smile gleamed. "We don't know each other, but—"

"Of course I know who you are, Mr. Abbingdon." Teresa smiled. "You're the CEO of Abbingdon Airlines, one of the fastest-growing private airline companies in the country." She shook the hand he'd extended.

"And you're the woman who put this incredible event together in just two weeks." Brooks grinned.

He was handsome with creamy, light brown skin. His dark hair had a natural curl and he towered over her at well over six feet in height. His liquid brown eyes and gleaming broad smile were simply mesmerizing. No wonder the man had a reputation as something of a playboy.

"I didn't do it alone, of course. I have an incredible staff." Teresa could barely contain her smile. After what she'd been through these past few months, it felt good to have everything going so smoothly and to receive such heartfelt acknowledgment from Matt Richmond and now Brooks Abbingdon, one of his high-powered guests.

"I'm sure you still have lots to do tonight, Ms. St. Claire, so I won't take up too much of your time." Brooks stepped closer and lowered his voice. "I'd like to discuss the possibility of engaging your services for an upcoming event."

"Call me Teresa." Her belly fluttered with excitement. A new, high-profile client like Brooks Abbingdon was *exactly* what Limitless Events needed right now. The success of the Richmond retreat and being tasked with planning an event for the popular bachelor could be just the thing to pull her company out of the sharp decline that began because of the recent scandal. "Thank you for considering Limitless Events. May I ask what kind of event you're planning?"

He grinned and his eyes, the color of dark, rich coffee, twinkled. "My wedding."

"Congratulations! I didn't realize you were engaged."

Teresa liked to keep up with the latest on the wealthy and powerful of Seattle. Especially when the news meant that they might need her services.

"I'd be honored to work with you to plan your wedding. If you give me the basics—your fiancée's name, the time of year you'd like to get married, the date, if you've set one, and any ideas you have about your ideal wedding—my assistant will work up some preliminary ideas to present to you when we get together."

Teresa pulled out her phone and started typing an email to Corinne.

"I appreciate your enthusiasm," Brooks said. "But I realize how busy your team must be. This is Matt's event, so I won't impose on his time, but I'll definitely be in touch."

Brooks flashed his megawatt smile and walked away before she could object. He was headed right for Nicolette Ryan, who had set up in a lovely area of the hotel lobby to

interview some of the guests as background for her cover-
age of the retreat.

Not surprising.

The man could teach a master class on how to manipu-
late the press to one's advantage and have them love you
for it.

Besides, he was right. She had a million things to keep
watch over, beginning with making sure that Jessie had
arrived in the staging area and would be ready to perform
in less than an hour.

Liam stood by the bar and watched couples swaying on
the dance floor to a big band song the musicians were playing. The retreat had been outstanding, and the announce-
ment of the Sasha Project that morning had gone well, but
the Saturday night gala was simply phenomenal.

The decor was modern glitz and glamour that played
upon the Old Hollywood feel of the hotel's art deco style.
And hiring a group to play big band songs and Rat Pack
standards was a stroke of genius.

The food Chef Riad prepared had surpassed his expectations and The Goblet's private-label wine produced at the
on-site vineyard was one of the best cabernets he'd ever
had. It was so good that he'd forgone his usual Manhattan
for the evening.

Liam caught a glimpse of Teresa as she darted through
the crowd in search of the next fire to be put out. He wasn't
sure how, but the woman seemed to get more gorgeous each
time he laid eyes on her.

The stunning blue dress she wore complemented the
color of her eyes and fit her body like a glove. It was sleeveless with a low neckline, so it showcased her strong arms
and provided just enough cleavage to make his imagination go wild.

Only he didn't need imagination. He'd seen the full show and it was spectacular. Memories of that body haunted him in the middle of the night when he lay in bed alone, wishing she were there beside him.

Satisfaction washed over him when his gaze met Teresa's from across the room. Her eyes danced and a soft, sexy grin curved one corner of her mouth.

It took every bit of self-control he could manage to stay rooted in place when what he wanted more than anything was to pull her into his arms and kiss her. To remind her of what they'd shared earlier in the day when he'd made love to her in his cottage.

In fact, as wonderful as the event had been, he couldn't wait until it was over so he could take her back to his room and have her again.

"She looks amazing in that dress, doesn't she?" Nadia stood beside Liam. They both stared at Teresa as she dealt with one of the other guests.

"She does." Liam sipped from his wineglass and kept his response even. "As do you in yours." He nodded toward his friend's wife. "And nearly every other woman in this room, for that matter."

"Yes, but you are not staring at me or any other woman in this room." Nadia gave him a knowing grin. "You're staring at one woman in particular. And it seems that she is quite taken with you, too." Nadia cocked her head, watching Teresa for a moment. Suddenly the woman's eyes lit up. "Why don't you ask her to dance?"

"She's working and I—"

"The party is pretty much under control, and I know for a fact Matt wouldn't mind. So ask her." Nadia nudged him. "If you don't, I have the feeling you're going to regret it."

The woman sashayed off in her strapless red gown with

her blond hair twisted up. Nadia was a beautiful woman and his best friend was a lucky man.

Perhaps she was onto something with her suggestion.

Liam finished the last of his wine and made his way to where Teresa stood near the back of the room monitoring the gala.

"You look stunning." He stood beside her, both of them watching the band on the stage. Liam placed a discreet hand low on her back and whispered in her ear. "But I happen to know for a fact that you'd look even better out of it."

Her cheeks flushed and she grinned. "You look pretty good yourself." She gave him a quick, sideways glance. Her grin deepened. "In or out of the tux."

Teresa surveyed the crowd, as if she was worried about who might be watching the two of them together.

Liam hated that it had come to this between them. They both needed to protect their business interests and their reputations. He realized that. But by allowing some shadowy figure to control their actions, they were giving the person power over them. Emboldening him to do who knew what next.

On the other hand, if they behaved as if the rumors had no effect on them, perhaps the culprit would realize he hadn't succeeded and just move on.

"I'd better go," Teresa said, pulling away from him.

He tightened his grip on her waist. "Don't. At least, not yet."

"Why not?" She turned to face him, a look of panic in her eyes.

The band played the opening chords of Frank Sinatra's "The Way You Look Tonight" and Liam smiled.

Perfect.

He removed his hand from her waist and extended it to her. "Dance with me."

"What?" She looked at him as if he'd lost his mind. "You want me to dance with you? Here? Where everyone can see us?"

"Yes to all of the above." He smiled. "This is my favorite song, and I can't think of anyone I'd rather dance to it with tonight."

"That's sweet, Liam." Her expression softened into a dreamy smile for a moment, but then she glanced over to the spot where Matt and Nadia stood. "But aside from all of the other reasons it isn't good for us to be seen dancing together, I'm working, remember?"

"Let me worry about Matt, okay?" He nodded toward the dance floor. "Come on. Just one dance. That's all I'm asking."

"One dance." She slipped her hand in his. "But don't expect me to kiss you in the middle of the dance floor this time."

Liam burst into laughter, remembering when Teresa kissed him for the first time on the dance floor at Gideon John's party. It had been completely unexpected, but not unwelcome. He'd gladly kissed her back.

"Well, you never know. Maybe I'll kiss you this time."

They found a place on the dance floor not far from where they'd been standing. He took her in his arms and swayed to the music, singing along softly so only she could hear.

It felt right to hold her like this. To stop hiding and pretending that he didn't care for this woman as much as he did. It was obvious that they couldn't stay away from each other, no matter how hard either of them tried. So maybe they should stop fighting the growing feeling between them.

What was the worst that could happen if they just admitted that what they felt for each other was more than either of them had expected? That it was powerful and intense and worth exploring more fully, rumors be damned?

"This is one of my favorite songs, too." She tipped her chin to look up at him. There was a mixture of happiness and sorrow in her glistening eyes. "My mother listened to it when I was a kid. She and my dad danced to this song the first night they met. She plays it often, particularly when she's really missing my father."

"I'm sorry, sweetheart." He stopped singing and swaying to the music. "I didn't mean to make you sad."

"You didn't." She widened her smile and swiped the dampness from her eyes. "I hadn't heard the song in a long time. And I've never been serenaded with it before. It just struck me because…well, my mother always told the story of how my dad did the same thing the night they met. It just made me a little nostalgic."

"Happy memories, then?" Liam stared into her eyes, fighting the overwhelming desire to kiss her.

He wanted to articulate all of the feelings for her he'd been struggling with. But Teresa was here in a professional capacity, and he needed to respect that. Even if his body didn't.

"Happy-ish." She forced a smile.

"You haven't said much about your father," Liam noted, taking her in his arms again and slowly swaying.

"I guess I haven't. It's not something I talk about very—" Her phone rang and she gave him an apologetic frown. "I'm sorry, Liam, but I need to take this."

"Of course. You're working." He released her from his grip and shoved a hand in his pocket. "I understand."

She pulled the phone from her purse and read the screen. "It's Evelyn Montague. I'd better see what she wants. Besides, there are a few things I need to confirm about the farewell breakfast tomorrow morning. I have to go, but we're still on for later, right?"

"Nothing could possibly keep me away." Liam grinned. "I'll see you then."

Liam hated that Teresa had to go, but he thoroughly enjoyed the view as she sashayed across the room in that fitted blue gown, the fishtail hem swishing in her wake.

His body ached for this vibrant, brilliant, beautiful woman. In his head, they were already back in that cottage where his biggest problem would be finding the zipper so he could strip her out of that dress.

Liam went to the bar to order himself a Manhattan. As he sipped his cocktail, he silently assessed the crowd.

He felt secure in his decision not to allow the coward hiding in the shadows to dictate his life. But a small part of him hoped like hell he hadn't just thrown gasoline on the fire by pissing off whoever had an ax to grind with either him or Teresa.

Nineteen

Jessie paced the greenroom as she warmed up her voice and reviewed the final changes she'd made to both the lyrics and the musical arrangement of the song she'd be singing for the audience. Tonight's performance had to be absolutely perfect.

Teresa had confirmed that both Chase Stratton and Dixon Benedict were out in the crowd mingling. Dixon had even mentioned to Teresa that he was eager to hear Jessie perform live. In addition to the two dream producers for her project being in the audience, Teresa had informed her that entertainment reporter Nicolette Ryan would be broadcasting her performance live from her show's website and social media pages.

The live broadcast meant that tonight's performance had the potential to either be a viral sensation or a hot, flaming mess that could spawn a dozen memes and make her an industry joke.

Jessie preferred to believe it would be the former, not

the latter. She just needed to showcase her songwriting and voice together in a way the syrupy pop album hadn't permitted her to.

Even if Chase and Dix passed on her project, maybe the live broadcast would capture the interest of another producer on her top ten list.

No. Don't think that way.

Jessie released a deep breath to drain the tension from her body. Tension in her jaw, chest and throat would make her voice tight and strained. In the bigger moments of the song, she'd sound like she was trying too hard instead of singing from deep down in the bottom of her soul. So she had to relax. Let go of all of her anxiety about the big moment ahead.

She smoothed her hands down the ethereal one-shoulder floor-length Laylahni Couture gown. Jessie had fallen in love with the dress the moment she'd laid eyes on it. She loved the contrast of the pale pink silk chiffon against her warm brown skin. And there was something so Old Hollywood about the twisted tulle overlay, embroidered skirt and bodice, and short but elegant train.

The gown made her feel beautiful, but also strong. She was a woman who was completely in control of her destiny. All she had to do was give an honest, raw performance. Leave it all out there on that stage for everyone to see.

Jessie continued her vocal exercises and warmed up her wrists and fingers.

With her entire future riding on this performance, Jessie tried not to think about Gideon being in the audience. Nearly impossible since her brain had been flooded with thoughts of Gideon all day. She couldn't help wondering how he felt about her and whether he was truly over her sister.

A mood which matched the raw, personal song she was unveiling tonight. "Okay" explored the pain of being in love with a person who loves someone else.

She wasn't a starry-eyed teen anymore and she now had a renewed understanding of their past. So why did this song still sum up exactly how she was feeling? And how would she react to singing those words with Gideon just a few yards away?

Lean into it. Use it as fuel.

Jessie drilled the words in her head again and again. She tried to release the apprehension rising in her stomach. To ignore the lingering feelings for the man who clearly still wasn't over her sister.

No matter how deeply she'd buried her feelings for Gideon over the years, they kept resurfacing. Maybe it was the same for Gideon where Geneva was concerned.

Even if he did have feelings for her, what did she expect to come of it? He had his life back in Seattle and she had hers in New York. She'd seen what happened to other female artists when they'd gotten serious about a rich and powerful man. It meant the death of their careers. And when the relationship was over, and it inevitably was, the woman was left to resurrect her career from the smoldering ashes.

That wasn't the fate Jessie wanted for herself.

Choosing Gideon meant *not* choosing her career. A career she'd worked for her entire adult life. One she wouldn't walk away from just because she'd reunited with her old crush.

Gideon had moved from his table near the stage and taken a seat at the bar at the back of the room. He didn't want to be a distraction to Jessie. He understood how much was at stake.

He sipped the whiskey he'd ordered neat. Gideon welcomed the heat building in his chest as the smooth liquor with a fiery bite washed down his throat. It'd been fifteen years since that incident with Jessie, and the shock of her kissing him felt as fresh now as it had then. But now he found himself in a completely new dilemma.

He felt something for Jessie. Something deeper than friendship or physical attraction. Something he wanted to explore. Yet the prospect of getting involved with his ex's sister gave him pause.

How would Geneva react to him and Jessie being together?

The last thing he wanted to do was cause animosity between the sisters. Nor did he want anyone to think this was some sick attempt to get back at his ex.

And what if things did work out between him and Jessie? He'd have to find a way to let go of his resentment of her parents.

Gideon took another swig of his whiskey. He should be celebrating right now, not agonizing over his feelings for Jessie.

Despite all of the drama, they'd secured the remaining funding for the project in Dubai and managed to pull the deal off. Construction would begin on time.

This was when he normally celebrated with a perfectly aged bottle of bourbon and the warmth and comfort of a beautiful stranger. But he hadn't looked at another woman since he'd laid eyes on Jessie.

It had driven him crazy to watch the men here fawning all over her last night. Most of them had no real interest in her other than the bragging rights of having slept with a celebrity.

He'd wanted to tell her last night that the tables had turned. That it was him who desperately wanted her. For a moment when they'd danced together, he believed she wanted the same thing. That she would be open to spending the evening with him, even if all they did was catch up on each other's lives.

But then Jessie had started asking questions about Geneva. Fishing to see if he had any lingering feelings for her sister. He'd answered her questions honestly. That included admitting he'd gone to Zurich ten years ago with hopes of rekindling what he'd thought they once had.

The evening had quickly gone off the rails from there.

After Jessie's performance, he would tell her the truth. Geneva had been his first love, so he'd held on to a romanticized view of their relationship. But they'd been too different from the start, and those differences had expanded over the course of their relationship. He'd tried to hold on to her by asking her to marry him.

It would've been a mistake.

One that would've left them both miserable and resentful. Altered the course of his life in ways he didn't want to imagine. He and Geneva were both exactly where they should be. And he was convinced that Jessie's reappearing at this point in his life was meant to be, too.

It would be a mistake to dismiss what he and Jessie were feeling just to spare Geneva's feelings when she was more than five thousand miles away.

Now if only he could convince Jessie of the same.

They announced Jessie's name and she emerged onstage to the sound of thunderous applause, aided by the fabulous acoustics in the room.

The sight of this woman, more beautiful than he could have ever imagined, stole his breath away.

Jessie wore an exquisite rose-colored gown worthy of anyone's red carpet. The goddess-style gown had a sheer overlay that covered one shoulder and added an elegant dimension to the dress. The fabric hugged her hips and dropped straight to the floor, but formed a short, graceful train behind her. And the dusty pink color popped nicely against Jessie's flawless brown skin.

She wore her dark brown natural hair in loose ringlets that dusted her shoulders. She'd captured the attention of everyone in the room and she hadn't even opened her mouth.

Jessie took a seat at the piano, adjusted the microphone and greeted the crowd. She went right into one of the songs from her recent pop album. But not one of the ones that got frequent airplay. It was a soulful tune about the highs and lows of being in love called "Nobody But You." As she sang about a love that, even in the tough times, was better than the best times with someone else, he couldn't help wondering who'd inspired that song.

Whomever it had been, Gideon couldn't help feeling a twinge of jealousy. For the first time in a very long time, he yearned for that kind of relationship. The kind that made you eager to return home at the end of a long, busy day because the person you loved was there waiting for you.

Jessie played the crescendo of the song, and the pounding of the keys brought him out of the daze he'd gone into. If he was looking for someone who'd be waiting for him at the end of a long, hard day, he'd set his sights on the wrong woman. He was in Seattle and she was in New York.

Gideon owned properties in New York, Miami and Los Angeles and on the beach in Costa Rica. Place wasn't the biggest challenge to exploring a relationship with Jessie. It was their careers.

He'd be making frequent trips to Dubai to oversee the deal and when the album was done, Jessie would undoubtedly spend several months out on tour.

How could they expect to make a life together when they wouldn't be on the same continent?

He was in a very different place in his life now. This weekend, he'd been quietly observing the joy and contentment of men like Matt Richmond. No longer moving from one conquest to the next, Matt seemed genuinely happy.

And for the first time in his life, as he watched the men around him on the hunt, he recognized the faint emptiness in their pursuits. Something he'd long felt deep down inside, though he'd always ignored it.

He'd focused on the high of the next big deal and the solitude at the bottom of a well-earned glass of whiskey. The temporary comfort and fleeting company offered by a pretty face.

He didn't want to live that way anymore.

Maybe it was because of Jessie. Or maybe it was a realization that had been a long time coming. Either way, he wouldn't let Jessie walk out of his life without telling her how he felt.

Gideon was mesmerized by her soulful performance. Her melodic voice had range. She was capable of going low with a voice that was gritty and raw. But she could also hit notes in her upper range that were simply angelic. Her lyrics touched him in a way no performance ever had.

He watched her onstage, completely rapt by her performance, like nearly every other person in that room, including the two producers she was so eager to meet with.

"Thank you so much." Jessie seemed genuinely shocked by the enthusiastic applause that just wouldn't die down after her last song. "You all have been such a wonderful audience. So I'd like to show you my appreciation by sharing a new song with you that I haven't performed for anyone else. It's called 'Okay,' and I hope you like it."

Gideon finished the last of his whiskey and set the glass

down on the bar as he turned back to the stage. For the first time that night, Jessie's eyes met his as she sang the opening lines of the song.

"You were the only one I ever wanted. Your heart was the only one that spoke to mine. But it was never me that you wanted. You loved the one I stood behind."

Her words and the pain in her voice and in her eyes as she said them felt like a punch to the throat. But he couldn't look away, no matter how deeply the words cut.

She turned her attention to Chase and Dixon, who seemed just as rapt by Jessie's performance.

Jessie's voice was raw and powerful. You could almost hear a pin drop in the space as she performed the song.

Her eyes met his again as she sang the chorus. "You deserve to be happy, for that I'll be glad in time. Right now my heart is still aching, but just know I'm gonna be fine. Because I'm okay, okay. Even though my heart is still breaking. I'll be okay, okay. So for that, love, one day I'll thank you. Because I made it to the other side...okay."

He'd wanted to stand up at the back of the room and tell her right there in front of everyone how damn sorry he was things worked out the way they did between them. That he hated that it took fifteen years for them to find each other again. That the time was right for a second chance for them.

Instead, he placed his hand over his heart, then blew her a kiss.

Her eyes widened and she acknowledged his gesture with a quick smile, the emotion in her voice intensifying. When she was done, the entire room erupted with applause and Dixon Benedict jumped to his feet. The rest of his table and the rest of the room quickly followed.

Tears glistened in Jessie's eyes. "Thank you all so much. This has been such a tremendous night and I just want to say..."

Suddenly Jessie froze, her eyes filled with fear as a man babbling incoherently made his way to the front. He hopped on the stage, swiped the microphone from Jessie's hand and started to yell into it, his speech slurred.

Gideon sprinted toward the stage as quickly as his legs would carry him.

Twenty

It felt like everything was moving in slow motion. Liam had been lost in thought as he listened to Jessie Humphrey sing about loving someone you wanted to be with, but couldn't. He didn't see the man until he'd already climbed onto the stage.

Next, he saw Gideon Johns rushing toward the stage, leaping over a chair or two to do so. Liam was closer, so he jumped into action. He climbed onto the stage and tackled the man, who was still mumbling incoherently about rich liars and losers.

The man thrashed wildly. His elbow nearly caught Liam in the chin. Liam punched the man, knocking him out cold.

Liam shook his throbbing right hand and tried to catch his breath. "Jessie, are you all right?"

"I'm fine." She nodded. "How about you?"

"Jessie!" Gideon rushed onto the stage and gripped her arms. "He didn't hurt you, did he?"

"No, not physically." She turned to watch as the crowd

was escorted from the room by members of the security team Matt had hired for the event.

"Where the hell were you guys *before* this drunk party-crasher leaped onto the stage?" Liam barked at the men, who lowered their eyes and continued to evacuate the room.

Gideon pulled Jessie against him as he stared at the man lying unconscious on the floor. It was as if he was waiting for him to climb to his feet so he could land his own punch.

Two members of the security team climbed onto the stage to assess the crazed man.

Another approached Jessie. "Miss Humphrey, I need to escort you to your room until we've assessed the threat."

Jessie turned away from the man and stared up at Gideon, her eyes wide. The poor woman looked trauma-tized.

"No." Gideon hugged her against him tightly. "She's staying with me. I'll see that she's okay."

Jessie gave him a grateful half-smile, then confirmed to the man that she was staying with Gideon.

The security man walked away reluctantly, then noticed Nicolette Ryan's cameraman with his camera still propped on his shoulder. "Are you still filming?"

Nicolette, who'd been staring at the stage in horror, was shaken from her daze. She rushed over to her cameraman and placed her hand over the lens. "Cut it. Now!"

He shut off the camera and the two made their way toward the exit. Nicolette turned back and mouthed "Sorry" to Jessie.

"Get me out of here, please." Jessie clutched Gideon's chest as she turned her head away from where other guests were filming the ruckus on stage as they filed out of the room. "Now," she pleaded.

"Have you got this under control?" Gideon asked Liam as he clutched Jessie, who'd buried her face in his chest.

"We're fine. Just take care of her." Liam wiggled his fingers, making sure none were broken.

"Thank you, Liam." Gideon shook his left hand, then escorted Jessie from the stage.

"I can't believe this." Teresa hurried toward the stage, going against the flow of the crowd. "I was in the kitchen speaking to Chef Riad when we heard screaming and people running. What on earth happened?"

"This dude crashed the party, climbed onto the stage and ripped the microphone out of Jessie's hand." Liam hopped down to the floor and pointed over his shoulder to the man still facedown on the stage. Liam shook his aching hand. "I had to sucker punch the guy before he hurt someone. He was behaving erratically, like he's on something major."

"Your hand is swelling." Teresa took his hand in hers gingerly and examined it. "We should get you to a doctor."

"I'll be fine." Liam shrugged. "I just need to submerge my hand in an ice bucket. Is there one around here somewhere?"

"At the bar, I'm sure. I'll take you back there and—" Teresa pressed a hand to her mouth and hurried onto the stage.

"Teresa, what's wrong?" Liam turned back to look at her.

She rushed toward the man the security guys had flipped onto his back. She dropped to her knees in her beautiful dress and hovered over him. Her hands were pressed to the floor on either side of the man's head.

"Josh, honey. It's me, Teresa. Are you okay?"

"Josh? As in your brother, Joshua St. Claire?" Liam stood in front of the stage.

"Yes." Teresa patted her brother's cheek, attempting to wake him. "I don't know what he's doing here or how he even knew where I'd be. We haven't spoken in weeks."

"Well, someone obviously told him where to find you." Matt Richmond approached them. He was clearly furious with Teresa. "How did this happen? You assured me that your personal issues wouldn't impact my event."

"It didn't, I mean I couldn't have known—" She stammered, her face red and her eyes brimming with tears. "I'm so sorry, Matt. I don't know how this happened, but I promise I'll find out."

"A lot of damn good that'll do me," he said bitterly.

"Take it easy, Matt." Liam held up his open palms. "I realize you're upset, but so is she." He gestured toward Teresa. "Your security team can sort out what happened later. I'll take care of this. Why don't you and Nadia go and try to calm the guests. Hopefully, everything will be back up and running soon."

"That's a good idea, Matt." Nadia squeezed his hand. "The guests need to see that you're calm and that this is just a minor inconvenience."

"Fine, but we will get to the bottom of this." Matt huffed, wrapping an arm around Nadia. "Your mother tried to warn me against using Limitless Events. I should've listened," he groused.

"My mother contacted you?" Liam turned to his friend.

Matt nodded. "Too bad I didn't listen."

Liam's mother still believed Teresa had had an affair with his father back when he mentored her as a college student. She hadn't been pleased that Liam no longer believed it. Still, he didn't think his mother would go out of her way to bash Teresa's business and hamper her ability to make a living.

"Will you be pressing charges against my brother?" Teresa asked quietly as she knelt beside Joshua. He was breathing normally, but still unconscious.

"I honestly don't know yet." Matt dragged a hand

through his close-cropped hair in frustration. "Do you think Corinne and the rest of your staff can manage the remainder of the retreat without you?"

"Yes," Teresa stammered, her eyes wide.

"Good, because I want you and your brother out of here as soon as possible," Matt said.

Teresa nodded, tears streaming down her face.

Her career was over and her brother was in deep trouble. Even if Liam hadn't given him a serious concussion and Matt didn't press trespassing or assault charges against Josh, he had another problem. If anyone was looking for him, they might've seen him on the live internet broadcast. That meant they knew where he was.

She hadn't talked to him in weeks. Who knew what kind of trouble he might've gotten himself into this time?

Perhaps it was a good thing Matt wanted them to leave.

"Joshua," Teresa whispered, running her hands through her brother's dark hair to check for a bump. "What've you done now?"

"Teresa, I didn't realize this was your brother. Obviously, I wouldn't have hit the guy so hard if I'd known." Liam stood on the floor in front of the stage. A frown furrowed his brow.

She wasn't sure if it was because of the shitshow Joshua had just put on or because his hand was still throbbing.

"Your hand." Teresa scrambled to her feet with the help of one of the security guys who was watching Josh closely. "I completely forgot. Come on, we'll get you that ice."

Teresa walked to the back of the room and asked the bartender to put some ice in an ice bucket for her. The man obliged.

They sat at a table at the back of the room, which was

now empty, aside from the security team members and a bomb-sniffing dog they'd brought in.

She carefully set the vintage glass art deco style ice bucket on the table, shifted the ice around, then put his hand inside it.

He winced momentarily. "So about your brother...why do you think he showed up here severely impaired after dropping off the map?" Liam asked the question gingerly. "And since you two haven't talked, how did he know where you were?"

She was grateful for the kindness in Liam's tone. After her conversation with Matt, it was the lifeline she needed.

"Those are excellent questions, Liam. I only wish I had answers. And in Joshua's current condition, I don't expect we'll get coherent answers anytime soon."

"Does he drink a lot?"

"He did for a time in college, when he fell in with the wrong crowd. But what he's been up to of late, I'm ashamed to say I don't know." She shifted her gaze to where Joshua still lay on the stage. "I've been too consumed with my own issues. Trying to keep my business afloat and my name off the front page of the paper."

Teresa sighed, her hand resting on his wrist. "I haven't been a very good sister, have I?"

"Don't blame yourself for this. Josh is a grown man, capable of making his own choices. You can't babysit him for the rest of his life."

"Maybe." Teresa sounded unconvinced. "In the meantime, I need to find transportation home for us."

"You and Josh can ride back to Seattle on my plane." Liam clamped a gentle hand on her arm before she could get up from the table.

"That's sweet of you, Liam. But what happened tonight makes it abundantly clear that I need to stay away from you. If I don't, I'll end up bringing Christopher Corporation down, too."

"Teresa—"

"I have to go before Matt changes his mind about pressing charges. He might even consider suing me. I wasn't to blame for the mudslide, but the same can't be said tonight."

"Don't worry about Matt. He's angry now, but he'll get over it."

"Like your mother has?" she asked, then shook her head. "I'm sorry. I shouldn't have said that."

"No, you shouldn't have. Given what my mother still believes about you, you can understand why she's holding a grudge." Liam hated what his mother had done and that she wasn't willing to reconsider her position. But he understood her resentment. In fact, he'd shared her righteous anger just a few weeks ago.

"That's all the more reason I need to stay away from you and from your company. I couldn't forgive myself if something happened to you or to your father's legacy because of his generosity to me." She stood.

"I can help you, Teresa. You said it yourself, I'm a fixer, of sorts. If we work together, I know we can—"

"Josh is my brother, and this is my problem, Liam. I won't bring you into this any more than I already have." Her chest ached at the thought of not being able to keep their planned date later that evening. "This is something Joshua and I need to figure out."

"So what are you going to do? You don't honestly expect to get a commercial flight back to Seattle tonight, do you?" Liam removed his hand from the bucket and dried it on a towel.

"Looking for a ride back to Seattle tonight?" Brooks Abbingdon approached their table and picked up his cell phone, which he'd apparently left behind when he was forced to exit the ballroom. "Since the festivities ended earlier than expected, I'm flying back tonight. Leaving in a little over an hour if you'd like to come along."

Liam tensed. If even half of the rumors about what a playboy Brooks Abbingdon were true, he didn't want Teresa flying back to Seattle on the man's private jet.

"It isn't just me. My brother would be coming, too." Teresa pointed to Joshua, who was just starting to stir as the men stood watch over him.

"That's your brother?" Brooks gave a long, low whistle. "Is he gonna be a problem?"

"No, he won't. I promise," Teresa said. "But if you don't feel comfortable having him on the plane, I can understand that."

"As long as you can keep him on a short leash, I'm fine with it. Truth is, we all have family like that, now don't we?" Brooks winked. "My car will be downstairs in a little over a half an hour. I'll see you then." He nodded at Liam and then walked away.

"Teresa, you don't need to go with him. You can go with me tomorrow morning. You can both stay in my cottage tonight, if you need to."

"No," she whispered, her eyes filled with tears. "I won't get you any more mixed up in this. But thank you for offering and for being a listening ear."

She leaned down to kiss his cheek, but he turned and pressed his lips to hers instead. A kiss that sent electricity down her spine and filled her body with heat as she remembered what had happened between them earlier. And that it would never happen again.

She slipped out of Liam's embrace and walked to the stage to collect her brother before Matt Richmond returned.

The security guy agreed to help her brother to the concierge's office, right by the hotel entrance, where they

would wait out of sight for Brooks's car service to arrive.
And he promised to stay with him until she and Josh left
the property. It was less of a favor to her and more of an
order from Matt Richmond, she was sure. But she appreciated it just the same.

She would need to coordinate with her remaining staff,
go back to her room and pack all of her things and meet
Brooks at the front door of the hotel in twenty minutes flat.

"Melva, I'll be checking out tonight." Teresa approached
the front desk in a hurry. She apologized to the beautiful
woman standing at the desk for interrupting.

"I'm so sorry, Teresa." Melva frowned. "Under the circumstances, I hate to ask, but this woman is—"

"You're Jessie Humphrey's sister. Jennifer?" Teresa had
seen photos of the two women together on Jessie's Insta-
gram account.

"Geneva." The woman smiled warmly as she slipped
her hand in Teresa's. "It's a pleasure to meet you. I flew
all the way in from Amsterdam to surprise my little sister,
but both of my flights were delayed. It seems I missed both
of her performances."

"You did, I'm sorry. They were both brilliant." Teresa
nodded impatiently. She had no doubt Brooks would pull
off with or without her. "What can I do for you, Geneva?"

"I wanted to surprise my sister, but she isn't in her room
and she isn't answering her phone. Do you know where I
can find her?"

"I don't." Teresa thought better of telling the woman that
she'd last seen her sister leaving the ballroom with her ex,
Gideon Johns.

"And I can't allow her to enter Ms. Humphrey's room
without her express permission," Melva piped. "I'm not
really sure what to do with her until her sister pops up."

"Right. Of course. And the hotel is completely booked."

Teresa thought for a minute. "I'll tell you what…my room is paid for through Monday. You'll just need to leave a card on file for incidentals and we can switch the room over to Mrs.…"

"*Ms.* Humphrey." A pained look dimmed the light in the woman's eyes momentarily before her easy smile slid back into place. "That would be wonderful. Thank you, Teresa."

"Give her my room number and a key," Teresa instructed Melva. "Just give me thirty minutes and I'll be gone. Perhaps you'll even run into Jessie in the bar while you wait."

Teresa said her goodbyes to both women and hurried to her room to pack as quickly as she could.

Twenty-One

Jessie collected her makeup and changed out of her Lay-lahni Couture ball gown in the greenroom while Gideon waited.

Her head was still spinning with all of the chaos that had ensued once the man made his way onto the stage.

She was in the midst of saying her thank-yous and had one encore song left to perform. Why couldn't the drunk party crasher have waited until then to jump onstage?

Jessie stared in the mirror. Her eyes were puffy and red from the tears that wouldn't seem to stop flowing once they'd started. She'd held them back until she'd entered the bathroom alone. But Gideon would know she'd been cry-ing the moment he saw her eyes. Unless…

She dug into her leather Gregory Sylvia hobo bag and pulled out her black Bôhten shades and slid them on. She hated doing the obnoxious sunglasses-at-night celebrity thing, but right now it was more important to protect her pride.

Jessie put a satin-lined slouch hat on her head and tucked her curls beneath it. Then she emerged from the bathroom wearing a pair of GRLFRND high-waist, ripped skinny jeans, a T-shirt and kitten heels. She carried the beautiful Laylahni Couture gown over one arm in a garment bag.

"You came out just in the nick of time." Gideon smiled softly, taking all of her bags except her purse from her. "I was just about to come in after you to make sure you were okay."

"If that's a pun because of the song I sang tonight…it's too soon."

Jessie exited through the exterior door rather than going through the lobby of the hotel. Party guests still milled around and Nicolette Ryan and her cameraman were camped out there.

Nicolette had texted her and asked her for an exclusive interview about the incident as she and Gideon made their escape to the greenroom.

She declined.

Nicolette seemed understanding and sympathetic. But Jessie had no desire to relive her performance going up in flames. All because some guy who couldn't hold his liquor decided to be a complete ass during the biggest moment of her career.

"I wasn't trying to be cute," Gideon said. "What happened was no laughing matter. The guy turned out to be harmless this time. But what if he hadn't been?" Gideon seemed especially perturbed at the possibility that something could've happened to her. "And I know how important that performance was to you. But, Jessie, you nailed it. Your set last night was terrific. But what you did tonight… it was brilliant. You should be damned proud of yourself."

"Thanks." She came to a halt at the fork in the path and

turned to face him. "And thank you for not being an ass about me writing these songs about you."

Gideon gave her a half grin. "Not everyone can say that they inspired someone to write a song. Let alone several. Especially one as good as 'Okay.'"

"Did you really like the song or are you just being unbelievably gracious about the whole thing?" She practically held her breath waiting for his response.

"Of course I really loved the song. Every damn person in that room loved it. Everything about it was perfect. The lyrics. The music. The way you sang the song…you poured your heart out on that stage."

"Until random drunk guy came and stomped on it." She took a deep breath and reminded herself there was no crying in record deals. This was a tough business. If she was going to break down in tears every time things didn't go her way, she needed to find another dream to chase.

"I know you're bummed about what happened, but let me tell you something, Jessie. Anyone who saw that performance tonight, anyone who experienced it as deeply as I did…they will never, ever forget it. I can assure you of that."

"Thanks." Jessie's mouth quirked involuntarily in the slightest twinge of a smile. Her cheeks heated, and her body tingled with electricity from his nearness.

"So, am I walking you back to your room?" Gideon asked.

Neither of them had moved beyond the fork in the path. Either they could take the route back to the hotel where her room was located or they could take the path that led to his cottage.

"Actually, if the invitation still stands, I could really use that nightcap you offered." Her heart raced as she anticipated his response.

He studied her for a moment, as if he was debating the

wisdom of taking her back to his cottage. "Of course it still stands."

They turned up the path toward the private cottages.

"Chase and Dixon seemed blown away by your performance," he noted. "I wouldn't be surprised if both of them contact your agent, eager to work with you. You knocked them off their feet."

"They seemed really into it when I was performing. Dixon was right there with me the whole time. He even started a standing ovation."

"That was pretty incredible."

"It was." She couldn't help smiling. "Chase didn't really seem to get on board until I performed 'Okay.' But their table was among the first to be ushered out of the room." The disappointment of not securing a meeting with either Chase or Dixon weighed on her.

Then there was the matter of Gideon.

She glanced over at him. He was handsome and tall with broad shoulders and such an incredible smile. He was still the smart, funny, determined guy she'd known back then. But he was also a successful businessman who employed members of his community and gave generously to important causes.

She'd always admired Gideon and expected great things of him, regardless of what her father and sister believed. But he'd exceeded her wildest expectations.

And she wanted to be with him more than ever. Not because of the schoolgirl crush she'd once harbored for him. But because he was exactly the kind of man she wanted in her life.

If she told Gideon that, he'd think she was still a silly, immature girl with a crush. After all, how could she know in just a few days that she wanted to be with him?

She just did.

That day when she'd shown up at Gideon's door, she told him that he was the only person who really understood her. That he got her in a way her parents, sister and even friends didn't. She was sure that Gideon was her soul mate. And it was her that he was meant to be with.

He'd probably thought she was a melodramatic teenager who didn't know what she was talking about. But here they were fifteen years later and the more she got reacquainted with Gideon, the more she believed she'd been right all along.

All of her fears about her career aside, what if they really were meant to be together? Shouldn't she at least be brave enough to give it a try?

"You're awfully quiet, Jess." Gideon set her bags down on the doorstep of his cottage, but he didn't open the door. "If you'd rather I walk you back to your room, I understand. You've had an exhausting day. You're probably ready to call it a night after everything that's— "

Jessie drew in a deep breath, clutched Gideon's tuxedo shirt and lifted onto her toes, pressing her mouth to his in a tentative kiss that built slowly. Gideon slipped his arms around her waist and hauled her body against his, the intensity of their kiss building.

Finally, she forced herself to pull away, her eyes fluttering open as they met his. "Does that answer your question?"

Gideon poured a glass of sauvignon blanc and handed it to Jessie.

She took a sip and made a purring sound that sent a shiver up his spine and made him want to cut the formalities and tell her exactly what he'd been feeling these past few days.

That he hadn't stopped thinking about her since she'd

walked through the doors of that hotel. That he wanted her in his bed.

There was something so compelling about Jessie. Compelling enough that the idea of missing out on it was stronger than the fear of what he'd be letting go.

"You're right, this wine is fantastic." Her words jarred him from his thoughts.

Gideon filled her wineglass and then poured himself two fingers of whiskey. He sipped his whiskey slowly, then sank onto the opposite sofa.

He crossed one ankle over his knee and assessed the woman seated across from him as she sipped her wine.

"A lot has happened tonight. I know you're disappointed, but maybe it wasn't as bad as you think. We should look at the live stream from the event."

"No. Please." Her bravado faded momentarily. "I shut my phone off for the rest of the night. I don't want to see it. Not yet. Just let me live in my little fantasy realm where I killed it on stage tonight and everything is right with the world."

"It isn't a fantasy, Jess. You *did* kill it on stage tonight. And I'll bet that ninety-nine percent of the people who saw your performance would agree."

"And that one percent?" Jessie raised a brow.

"They have terrible taste in music, so they don't count." He grinned when she laughed. He'd always loved the joyous sound of her laugh. "Seriously, if the vast majority of listeners think you were amazing, why do you care about what an infinitesimal fraction of people think?"

"It's the nature of the creative beast. I can't help it." Jessie shrugged. "Besides, I learn more from my critical reviews than I do from the glowing ones that tell me exactly what I want to hear." She paced the floor. "Which is why I need to work with producers like Chase and Dixon. They have this uncanny ability to take a track that might seem good on the surface and turn it into something spectacular."

"About that…" Gideon set his glass down. "I know you asked me not to interfere on this, but what if I could pull some strings and get you a meeting with one or both of them?"

Jessie folded her arms and plopped down in her seat. "I want a meeting with them, of course. But I'd like to do this on my own. The same way you built your business on your own. You didn't rely on anyone else."

"Not true." He leaned forward. "I owe my success to a lot of men and women who were willing to give me opportunities and teach me what they'd learned." Gideon shrugged. "I pay their generosity and kindness forward by doing the same."

Jessie had kicked off her heels and padded over to the sideboard where the bottle of wine was chilling. She refilled her glass of wine, then sat on the sofa with her feet folded beneath her. "I've read business articles about you. They always call you a self-made billionaire." Jessie didn't seem convinced.

"Because it's the more compelling story." Gideon groaned. He gave credit to the people who had helped him every single chance he got. But the importance of those relationships was inevitably minimized in magazines and interviews.

"My assistant Landon…the guy is a work in progress, for sure." Gideon chuckled, thinking of some of their conversations. "But he's good at what he does, and he has a hell of a lot of potential. If I can help him get closer to his goals, even if that means leaving my company and striking out on his own, I'm going to support him any way I can. So let me do the same for you."

Jessie drank a gulp of her wine, her eyes not meeting

his. "I don't like the idea of owing anyone anything. It gives people too much power over you."

"You think I'd want something in return?" He had to admit that one hurt. He thought she knew him better than that. Yes, it was fifteen years ago, but did she really think he'd changed that much? "Why would you ever think that?"

"It's happened before with someone I trusted."

Now he understood, and he wished he could give the fucker who'd made her feel that way a savage beatdown just to show him how it felt to be vulnerable.

"What happened?" Gideon sat on the edge of his seat, both of his feet firmly planted on the floor. "And whose ass do I need to beat?" There was a ticking in a vein in his forehead.

"Gideon, no." Jessie moved over to sit beside him. Her warmth enveloped him and her faint floral scent calmed the anger bubbling inside him over her revelation about her mentor. "I don't want to talk about that or the shitshow my performance turned into. Tonight, I want to talk about us."

She'd said it. Finally gotten it out into the open where they could discuss it like two rational adults. Though he found it difficult to have a reasonable discussion when she was sitting this close.

Jessie had already shed the sunglasses. Now she slipped off the hat and tossed it onto the sofa beside her, refluffing her headful of dark curls. Her short manicured nails were painted a deeper shade of pink and every other nail was affixed with a design.

"I'd like that." Gideon turned toward her and loosened his tie. "Spending these past few days with you has been special for me. I never stopped caring for you, Jess. The feelings I had for you then weren't romantic, but you were incredibly important to me. The loss of our friendship hurt as much as being dumped by Geneva."

Jessie frowned. Was it because he'd mentioned Geneva or because he'd admitted his feelings for her back then were platonic?

"One of my biggest regrets was how badly I'd bungled things between us. That my insensitivity that day hurt you." He traced the back of her hand with his thumb.

Jessie didn't respond to his confession, but her sensual lips spread in a slow smile. She leaned in, raised a hand to his cheek and kissed him again.

He wrapped his arms around her, his hand pressed to her back. Loving the feel of her in his arms and the taste of her warm mouth as he slid his tongue between her lips. He lost himself in her kiss. Lost all sense of time and place. Set aside his fears about what this meant for them.

He only knew he wanted more of this. More of her.

The longer he kissed her, the more sure he was that he would never get enough of her quiet murmurs. Or the way her soft, curvy body fit so neatly against the hard planes of his. That he would never tire of holding her in his arms.

Suddenly, Jessie pressed against his chest, creating space between them. She dragged her gaze to his, her chest heaving as she caught her breath. "There's one thing I need to know. It's about Geneva."

He already knew what she was going to ask, but she needed to say the words. "What do you want to know?"

She tucked strands of her hair behind one ear. "I need to know…if there was a chance for the two of you again, would you want it?"

"No." He kissed one corner of her mouth and then the other. "I loved your sister, but that was a long, long time ago. And we were never right for each other." He left a slow, lingering kiss on her mouth. Then pressed his lips to her ear. "It isn't Geneva I want, Jess. Or haven't you noticed?"

He lay her back on the sofa, his length pressed to her belly as he kissed her until they were both breathless.

He dropped kisses on her forehead and her eyelids. "Do you believe me?"

She nodded, her gaze meeting his. "I do," she whispered.

"Good." He kissed her again, savoring the taste of her sweet mouth and the feel of her body beneath his. "Because from the moment you strutted into that hotel lobby, I've only wanted you."

Twenty-Two

Teresa sat in the tan buttery leather seat on Brooks Abbingdon's private plane and fastened her seat belt. Then she double-checked to make sure her brother's seat belt was secure, since he was still fairly out of it.

One thing Teresa knew for sure, Joshua wasn't drunk. His clothing and skin were completely devoid of the scent of alcohol. Still, there was clearly something wrong with him.

Joshua had roused enough to walk onto the plane, but he was still babbling incoherently about rich liars and losers and the truth being exposed. When he wasn't ranting, he would doze off. So getting the truth from Joshua wasn't an option. In fact, as out of it as he seemed, she wondered if Josh would remember any of this, even once he became lucid.

He mumbled something that sounded vaguely like *sorry, love you, sis*. But then again, maybe that was just what Teresa wanted to hear. Something to make her feel the slightest bit better about the fact that her career was over. In fact, she was shocked that Brooks wanted anything to do with her once he learned that the party disrupter was her brother.

Joshua leaned his head on her shoulder, his dark brown hair tickling her nose. He muttered something again. This time she clearly heard *sorry* and *screwed up again.* Those words were followed by more incoherent babbling.

Joshua rubbed at his arm, complaining that it hurt like a bitch. *That* she heard quite clearly. He kept rubbing at his left arm, so she rolled up his sleeve and looked at it.

Teresa turned her head to one side and then the other, zeroing in on a small, nearly invisible mark on his forearm. She rummaged in her bag and took out her lighted pocket magnifier. Now she could see clearly what it was that Josh kept scratching at. It was a tiny, isolated puncture wound.

She breathed a sigh of relief that there was just the single mark. She checked his other arm and his ankle and saw no additional marks. If Joshua was an addict, he'd have several puncture wounds on his body, not just one. Which suggested that this was an isolated incident. But the more important question was, had her brother willingly injected himself with something?

"Your brother doesn't look very good." Brooks switched to the seat across from her once they were able to freely move about the plane.

"He's been conscious more often, and I'm beginning to understand more of what he's saying." Teresa swept the hair from her brother's sweaty forehead.

"Should I request that the driver take him to a hospital once we land?" Brooks studied Josh with concern.

She could only imagine how inconvenient it would be to have someone die on one's private plane. Teresa banished the snarky comment from her head. After all, Brooks had offered to help when she was persona non grata to everyone but Liam.

"No, but thank you for the offer just the same." Teresa smiled warmly at Brooks.

"You're sure?" He didn't seem convinced that it was a good idea.

In any other circumstance, Teresa would've insisted that they rush Joshua to the hospital. There they could identify the substance he'd been given and flush it from his system.

But that could mean trouble for Joshua. She'd paid a hefty price to ensure that his earlier offenses hadn't ended up on his record. If she took him to the hospital, the staff would need to report the incident. Was this all Josh's doing or was someone willing to put Josh's life in danger to ruin hers?

Nicolette's warning to Liam that they should be careful whom they trusted suddenly came to mind.

"I'm sure. Thank you, Brooks."

Teresa heaved a small sigh of relief when Brooks nodded and walked back to his seat. She glanced down at her still-shaking hands as she deliberated her next move.

Liam paced the floor of his cottage, still trying to figure out how everything had gone off the rails so quickly. The weekend started with so much promise and ended in a disaster, for which it would most likely be remembered. Particularly since the entire circus had been captured live on streaming video.

He was furious with Joshua for ruining his best friend's event and decimating what remained of the reputation of and goodwill toward Teresa and Limitless Events. He honestly couldn't imagine that her business could recover from what had just happened, especially in light of the fact that the person who'd crashed the party had been her brother.

Add to that his rant about rich people being liars and

losers…well, the wealthy set could overlook a lot of things. Calling them out like that wasn't one of them.

Liam's phone rang. He dug it out of his inside jacket pocket, hoping it was Teresa saying she'd changed her mind and would accept his offered plane ride tomorrow.

Shit.

He heaved a long sigh and answered the telephone. "Hello, Mother. What can I do for you?"

"You can stop making a fool of yourself by your insistence on associating with that Teresa person," Catherine Christopher said without hesitation. "You know what she's done, who she was to your father, and how she destroyed our family. Emilia Cartwright one of my oldest and closest friends, sent me a video of you dancing with that woman as if neither of you had a care in the world. And, just as I predicted, the evening turned into a disaster. That woman destroys everything in her path. And that poor singer, assaulted! Just horrible!"

"You watched the live stream?" That didn't sound like something that would interest his mother at all. If she wasn't in the room holding court as the center of attention, she simply wasn't interested.

"Only because I received dozens of calls from people who saw you canoodling with that witch earlier and I wanted to see what else was going on."

"We were dancing together on a crowded dance floor. It's not as if I had her up against the wall in the back of the room."

"Don't be vulgar, Liam." His mother's voice was strained. "I did everything I possibly could to warn your friend Matt Richmond not to associate his brand with that woman, but he just wouldn't listen. Now that millions of people have seen the train wreck his party turned into, he's the laughingstock of the entire internet. And who would want to attend another of his parties? A life-threatening disaster is practically sure to ensue."

"You're being melodramatic, Mother. You weren't there, and it wasn't seen by millions. The situation wasn't that serious. Matt's security team just wanted to be extra cautious after the man was able to get onto the stage. It was an overreaction to their initial screwup."

"Where is that woman now?"

Liam hesitated before responding. "Gone. Matt asked her to leave."

"Good riddance. All of us will be better off with Teresa St. Claire out of the picture."

Liam ended the call with his mother and gulped his Manhattan. Maybe his mother's life would be better without Teresa St. Claire in the mix. But he'd felt a gnawing in his chest from the moment she'd walked out the door.

Twenty-Three

Jessie was in heaven. Gideon's kiss, his touch, had been every bit as wonderful as her mind had imagined. But as the intensity of their kiss escalated, she wanted more.

Gideon had rolled them over so Jessie lay on top of him. She shifted so that she straddled him on the sofa. Both of them murmured at the sensation when she placed her hands on his chest and rocked the apex of her thighs against his steely length. He cupped her bottom, bringing her closer as she ground her hips against him, the sensation between them building.

He still seemed tentative. Or maybe he wanted to let her set the pace. But she knew what she wanted.

She wanted his large, strong hands to caress her bare skin. To glide her hands over his. And she wanted him inside her.

Jessie grasped the hem of her shirt and lifted it over her head, tossing it aside. Gideon quickly removed her sheer black bra and dropped it to the floor, too.

He pulled her toward him and laved one of her tight,

beaded nipples. Jessie arched into him with an involuntary whimper as he licked and sucked the sensitive tip.

Gideon gently scraped his teeth over the tight bud and she cursed under her breath at the sensation his actions elicited in the warm space between her thighs. He shifted his focus to her other breast, lavishing it with the same attention.

"God, I want you, Jess," he whispered against her skin.

His beard scraped her flesh, adding to the mélange of sensations.

Gideon's gaze met hers as he unbuttoned her jeans, then slowly unzipped them.

Jessie sank her teeth into her lower lip and lifted her hips, eager to help him slide the garment off one leg and then the other. He stood suddenly, taking her by surprise as he lifted her. She wrapped her long legs around him and held on to his neck as he carried her to the bed and laid her beneath the covers.

She had wanted this for as long as she could remember. But now that she was here in Gideon's bed, her hands trembled and butterflies flitted in her belly.

Her anticipation grew as Gideon slowly removed his tie and then his jacket. As if he was putting on a show just for her. He took off his shirt to reveal his strong, muscular chest and chiseled abs. Then he slowly unzipped his tuxedo pants and allowed the fabric to pool around his ankles.

Dayum.

Jessie swallowed hard, her eyes tracing the pronounced outline of his thick erection beneath his charcoal-gray boxers. She couldn't tear her gaze away from the darkened circle over the tip.

She licked her lower lip, the space between her thighs throbbing as she was struck by the sudden desire to taste him there.

Gideon reached into the bedside drawer and removed one of the foil packets stocked by the hotel. He slipped out of his boxers and sheathed himself, crawling into bed with her.

She'd never seen anything sexier than this man, completely naked, crawling toward her. Like a panther in pursuit of his next conquest.

He dragged her sheer panties down her legs and settled between her thighs as he kissed her again, his tongue searching hers.

Jessie wrapped her legs around his waist and her arms around his back as he kissed her. His hips rocked against hers.

His kiss was hungry and demanding. Making her more desperate for him. The space between her thighs pulsed and her nipples prickled as they moved against the hair on his broad chest.

Gideon broke their kiss, leaving her breathless and wanting. He trailed kisses down her neck and shoulder as he shifted off of her. She immediately missed the weight and warmth of his strong, hard body.

He moved beside her and thrust his hand between her thighs, gliding his fingers through her wetness, over her sensitive nub. She whimpered, overwhelmed by the sensation as she writhed against his hand. He inserted two large fingers, then three. Sliding them in and out of her as his thumb teased her hardened clit.

Gideon brought her close to the edge, her legs shaking. Then he'd back off just enough to keep her from going over.

"Gideon, please." It wasn't like her to whimper or beg. But she was so close, her body trembling with need. "I want you."

"And I have never wanted anyone as much as I want you, Jess." He pulled his fingers from inside her, moving them over the needy bundle of nerves and all of the slick, sensitive flesh surrounding it.

The muscles of her belly tensed and she cried out his name, the dam inside her bursting. Overflowing with intense pleasure.

He kissed her neck and shoulders as her body shuddered. Finally, he pressed the head of his erection to her entrance, slowly pushing his width inside her.

Jessie dug her short fingernails into his back, her body tense as Gideon slowly entered her.

"Relax, Jess," he whispered. "Breathe. I would never hurt you."

Jessie hadn't realized that she was holding her breath and her muscles were clenched in anticipation. She breathed in and out slowly, her eyes pressed shut.

Gideon rewarded her with a slow, sweet, tender kiss.

"Open your eyes, Jess." His voice was low and deep. "I want to see those beautiful brown eyes while I'm inside you. And I want you to see exactly what you do to me. How badly I want you."

He moved inside her slowly, allowing her body to adjust to the sensation of being completely filled by him.

They moved together, their skin slick with sweat. Her belly tensed as her heels dug into the mattress. Another orgasm rocked her to her core. She called his name, her body quivering.

Gideon tensed, her name on his lips as he tumbled over the edge into pleasure. The pulsing of his cock pulled her in deeper, her walls contracting around him.

Jessie released a contented sigh, her head lolling back on the pillow. She smiled up at Gideon. His forehead was beaded with sweat and his chest still heaved. He traced her cheekbone with his thumb.

"That was amazing." He kissed her. "Is it bad that I already want you again?"

"No. Because I plan on taking every meal right here in this bed until Monday morning when I have to go back to…" Her words trailed as the reality of the situation dimmed the buzz she was feeling.

"Let's not think about Monday morning right now." He caressed her cheek.

"Good plan."

Gideon dropped a tender kiss on her lips, then lay on his back and gathered her in his arms, pulling the covers around them.

Jessie pressed her cheek to his chest, their intense encounter replaying in her head. She tried to do as Gideon asked and not think about Monday. But she couldn't escape the knowledge that in thirty-six hours they would go their separate ways.

Gideon cradled Jessie in his arms as she slept soundly with her hand and cheek pressed to his chest. Her quiet exhalations skittered across his skin.

He couldn't remember the last time he'd felt so content. Or the last time he'd been with someone who made him feel the things that Jessie did. He glided a hand up and down the smooth skin of her bare arm as she slept.

It was well after one in the morning, but it had been several hours since he'd last checked his email. Gideon reached for his phone on the nightstand and turned it back on.

He checked his email, directing the light from the phone away from Jessie so he wouldn't disturb her sleep. He replied to a few urgent messages, then noticed that he had several alerts for Jessie's name.

She hadn't wanted to see the video, and he got that. But

at least one of them should see it. That way he could prepare her if it was as bad as she believed.

When he followed the link to view the video, there were already thousands of remarks. He sucked in a deep breath and started to read through them. He was pleasantly surprised.

"Jessie." He couldn't help waking her. She'd been so disappointed about how the performance ended. She needed to see this. "Sweetheart, you've got to see what people are saying about your performance last night."

She grumbled and buried her face in his chest before finally rolling over on her back and propping herself up on her elbows.

"All right, all right," she mumbled. "Let's get this over with."

He played the video and scrolled through some of the comments. The more she read them, the more excited she got.

"Oh my God. Did you see this? Dixon Benedict left an amazing comment. He said I'm one of the most talented singer/songwriters he's ever seen. He even says he'd love to work with me someday." Jessie sat up in bed, her back pressed against the headboard as she scrolled through the comments, most of which were rave reviews of her performance.

"This is incredible. Thank you, Gideon." She handed him back his phone and kissed him. "And I really do appreciate your offer to broker a meeting between me and Chase or Dixon. But I'd like to give it one more try on my own first. If I need your help, I'll ask. I promise."

"Whatever you want, beautiful." He cradled her cheek. "I told you, you're a star, Jessie Humphrey. And you're going to do amazing things." He kissed her.

She gave him a sly smile as she reached into the drawer

of the bedside table and climbed atop him. "There are a few amazing things I'd like to do right now."

"Oh yeah?" He rolled them over so that he hovered over her. "I'm all for that." He leaned down and kissed her. Then he made love to her again.

Jessie returned to her room on Sunday afternoon to gather some of her toiletries and fresh clothing. Gideon sat on the sofa watching the stock market news as he made calls to his assistant Landon.

There was a knock at her hotel room door.

"Gideon, would you get that, please?" Jessie called from the bathroom as she packed up her makeup and facial cleanser.

"Sure thing," he replied.

She'd expected him to call to her that it was the hotel staff or maybe Teresa or Matt looking for her. But there was silence in the other room.

"Gideon, who is it?" Jessie walked out into the main living space of the suite. She was stunned to see a face that resembled her own.

"Geneva, what are you doing here?" Jessie stammered. "I thought you were still in Amsterdam." Her voice faded and she wrapped her arms around herself.

"I was, but I thought I'd surprise my little sis. You said I should come to visit, so I thought I'd pop into Napa first and catch your performances. But my flights were delayed and I got in after your set ended last night." Geneva took a few steps closer to her sister. "But I saw the videos. Jessie, you were incredible. How is it that I didn't realize just how talented my sister is?"

Geneva opened her arms and Jessie stepped into them, hugging her sister tightly. Neither her parents nor Geneva had supported her decision to go into music. So it felt good to hear her sister's validation. It wasn't something she needed, but she hadn't realized until now how much she'd wanted it.

Her sister cupped her cheek and smiled, then turned to Gideon. She gave him what Jessie knew to be a forced smile.

"Gideon, it's good to see you." Geneva nodded toward him, awkwardness lingering between them.

"You, too, Geneva." He shoved his hands in his pockets, not moving toward her.

"So…you two, huh?" Geneva glanced from Jessie to Gideon, then back when neither of them responded. "Since when?"

"Since this weekend." Gideon pulled one hand out of his pocket and threaded his fingers through Jessie's. He squeezed her hand. "We hadn't seen each other in a really long time. We got a chance to get reacquainted during the retreat."

Jessie breathed a sigh of relief. She hadn't told Geneva or anyone else about the day she'd gone to Gideon's apartment. Maybe she'd tell her sister someday. But there was already enough tension between them. She wouldn't add to it.

Gideon wrapped an arm around Jessie's waist, as if he knew she needed his reassurance that he had no regrets about choosing her.

"I know you missed Jessie's show, Geneva, but there's lots to do here in Napa. Why don't I take you ladies to lunch later?"

"Great idea, Gideon." Jessie smiled at him gratefully. She turned to her sister. "What do you say, Gen? The food here is amazing and so is the wine."

"I'd like that." Geneva put on her biggest smile as she wiped dampness from beneath her eyes. "Can I meet you at the restaurant in say…an hour?"

"Geneva, I'm sorry if me being with Gideon feels uncomfortable right now. You're my sister and I love you. I'd never intentionally hurt you." Jessie took both of Geneva's hands in hers. "But... I love him. I think I always have." She glanced over her shoulder at Gideon. He grinned and mouthed the words, *I love you, too.* Jessie turned back to her sister. "And I did see him first."

"Yes, you did, Squirt." Geneva called Jessie by her childhood nickname through a teary-eyed laugh. "I guess technically I stole him first."

"You totally did." Jessie laughed, her eyes damp, too.

"Oh, Jessie." Geneva cradled her cheek. Her sister's smile seemed genuine, despite the tears that spilled down her face. "I'm so happy for you. For both of you." She turned to Gideon. "I've only ever wanted the best for both of you. I'm glad that the two sweetest people I've ever known eventually found happiness together. Things are just as they should be."

Geneva hugged Jessie again. Then she hugged Gideon. "You've always been a great guy, Gideon. So whatever happens between you two, I know you'll be good to my little sister." She turned to leave. "I'll see you two downstairs in an hour."

Jessie sighed with relief when the door closed behind Geneva. She turned to Gideon. "I'm sorry to have said that here, like this. I know it's only been a weekend and I wouldn't possibly expect you to—"

"Jess, breathe." Gideon pulled her to him. "Spending time with you this weekend reminded me what a rare gift it is to have someone in my life who believed in me from the beginning, when I had nothing. You were always in my corner, Jess. I want that again, and I want to do the same for you."

He pressed a soft kiss to her lips and stroked her cheek. "And when I said I love you, too, I meant it. I wanted to say it earlier, but I was afraid I'd scare you off."

"Your heart is racing." Jessie could feel Gideon's heart thumping against her palm, pressed to his chest. "Are you sure you're not the one who's terrified by this?"

"I haven't opened myself up to anyone like this in a really long time. So yeah…it feels a little scary. But I have never been so sure about what I want. And what I want is you."

"This weekend has been so amazing. What happens when we try to translate it into an actual relationship?" Jessie frowned, her eyes searching his. "I'm in New York and you're in Seattle. You'll be traveling to the Middle East and, eventually, I'll be out on tour."

"I know it seems insurmountable, but we don't get many do-overs in life. So I don't intend to take this second chance for granted."

"You know how long I've wanted this, Gideon. But I've worked really hard for my career, too. I don't want to give that up, either."

"I'd never ask you to." He kissed her forehead. "Look, no one said this would be easy, but for you, I'm willing to make sacrifices. I'd always planned to open an office in New York. Looks like I'll be opening it sooner than I thought." He kissed her again as he hauled her against him. "And I already own a penthouse in Manhattan with the perfect space to install a recording studio."

"You'd move to New York for me?" Jess pulled back to gaze up at him. "Are you serious?"

"I really do love you, Jessie Humphrey." He smiled. "And I look forward to making a life together. I don't know what the future holds, but I promise you, as long as you're all in, I am, too."

Jessie's eyes stung with tears and her heart felt full. She honestly couldn't ever remember being happier than she was right now. Lifting onto her toes, she kissed the man she'd loved for as long as she could remember.

Epilogue

An insidious grin spanned Catherine Christopher's face as she counted out a stack of crisp one-hundred-dollar bills. Liam's mother handed the stack to the man standing beside her desk.

"That went even better than expected." The woman snickered. "Everyone believes that Joshua St. Claire was out of his mind drunk or worse, high on something vile. What did you give him, anyway?"

The man opened his mouth to speak, but Catherine held up a hand and turned her head.

"On second thought, it's better if I don't know. The only thing that matters is that the little bitch got exactly what she deserves," Catherine announced gleefully.

"St. Claire probably won't even remember that he was drugged." The man counted the bills for himself before shoving them into his pocket.

"Perfect." Catherine smiled as she looked out the window and surveyed her vast estate. "His sister won't see what's coming, either. Just wait until Teresa St. Claire finds out what I have planned for her next."

* * * * *

ONE NIGHT, WHITE LIES

JESSICA LEMMON

For Aunt Beth.

Your passion for creating a life you love
continues to inspire me to do the same.

One

London-born Reid Singleton didn't know a damn thing about women's shoes. So when he became transfixed by a pair on the dance floor, fashion wasn't his dominating thought.

They were pink, but somehow also metallic, with long Grecian-style straps crisscrossing delicate, gorgeous ankles. He curled his scotch to his chest and backed into the shadows, content to watch the woman who owned those ankles for a bit.

Reid might not know women's brands or styles, but he knew women. He'd seen quite a lot of women in high heels and short skirts, but he couldn't recall one who'd snagged his attention this thoroughly.

From those pinkish metallic spikes, the picture only improved. He followed the straps to perfectly rounded calves and the outline of tantalizing thighs lost in a skirt that moved when she did. The cream-colored skirt led to a sparkling gold top. Her shoulders were slight, the swells of her breasts snagging his attention for a beat, and her hair fell in curls over those small shoulders. Dark hair with a touch of mahogany, or maybe rich cherry. Not quite red, but with a notable amount of warmth, the way a tree ended its journey from burnished gold to deep russet in the fall.

He sipped from his glass, again taking in the skirt, both flirty and fun in equal measures. A guy could get lost in there. Get lost in *her*.

An inviting thought, indeed.

When the opportunity to attend a technology trade show in San Diego, California, arose, Reid leaped at the chance. He'd been on high alert for the past two years, ever since his best friend, Flynn, survived a divorce, his dad's death and elevation to president of his company all within a relatively short period of time. Reid worked at said company, liked his job, respected the hell out of Flynn and wasn't willing to step away until the situation was sorted.

This trip to California was looked upon as a break by Reid and a necessity by Flynn. They'd implemented a lot of changes in the past twelve months, and Reid was intent on making the tech side of the company shine. He was the self-appointed King of Information. Data made sense to him.

So did women.

The brunette spun around, her skirt swirling, her smile a seemingly permanent feature. She was lively and vivid, and even in her muted gold-and-cream ensemble, somehow the brightest color in the room. A man approached her, and Reid promptly lost his smile, a strange feeling of propriety rolling over him and causing him to bristle.

The suited man was average height with a receding hairline. He was on the skinny side, but the vision in gold simply smiled up at him, dazzling the man like he'd cast a spell. When she shook her head in dismissal and the man ducked his head and moved on, relief swamped Reid, but he still didn't approach her.

Careful was the only way to proceed, or so instinct told him. She was open but somehow skittish, in an outfit he couldn't take his eyes from. And he wasn't the only one looking. Upon a second glance around, he saw that there were, in fact, many men looking at her.

Most were in clusters with one another, clinging to their own. The company Reid worked for had sent him alone, atypical since he worked closely with his best friends from college, but he didn't mind flying solo. He was a *Single*-ton, after all.

At Monarch Consulting, they shared the goal of helping other businesses grow and perform better. Flynn Parker—the aforementioned inheritor of the firm—was in charge and, while a bit straight-edged, definitely the best man for the job. Gage Fleming was in charge of sales, a good fit since he leaked charm like a noxious gas. Reid fancied himself a blend of both men, which was why they got on so well. The fourth musketeer, Sabrina Douglas, had been the bestie and plucky sidekick for years but recently became Flynn's wife-to-be. A kick in the nuts since Flynn was the one who initiated a pact with Gage and Reid never to wed in the first place.

But Reid couldn't deny that Sabrina and Flynn were meant to be together. It was obvious that they were in love, even to a cynic like Reid. Gage had agreed and they'd released Flynn from the pact, leaving Reid and Gage to hold strong.

Until Gage met Andrea Payne, a consultant superhero with strawberry-blond locks and a cunning smile. They were quite the dynamo couple, Andy and Gage. Their wedding was scheduled for next June. Flynn and Sabrina hadn't set an official date, but Reid guessed that announce-ment was forthcoming.

Weddings, weddings everywhere.

No matter. The breaking of the pact by both Flynn and Gage wasn't something Reid took personally. He'd de-cided a long time ago never to be married for a mountain of reasons he wasn't going to turn over in his head now. Gage's and Flynn's saying "I do" weren't going to change his mind.

Another swish of the brunette's skirt paired with her stepping from the dance floor. She aimed those tall shoes right for him. Reid reached up to straighten his tie, for-getting he'd tossed it on the bed in his hotel room along with his jacket. He settled for tugging his collar instead.

In his beige slacks, pale blue shirt, brown belt and brown leather shoes, he resembled every other man in the room save for a few slight differences.

Reid was thirty-one, not in his forties or fifties. He had a head full of wavy dark hair, no signs of male pattern bald-ness whatsoever. He also had a face that was perplexingly handsome, or so he'd been told. It was a face that aided him in bedding the many women who'd graced his sheets over the years, and he'd made it his mission to show them not just a good time but the *best* time while they were there.

Sabrina had once joked about Reid sleeping his way through their college campus. He'd responded that he'd been performing a service for women who otherwise wouldn't have known good sex if it showed up at their dorm room door wearing pasties on its nipples.

A joke, sure, but he hadn't been *completely* joking. He prided himself on his prowess as much as his service. He might be Clark Kent by day, glasses on when screen fa-tigue became too much, but at night he morphed into Su-perman in the bedroom.

Man of Steel, he thought with a smirk.

For those reasons he hadn't been in a rush to approach the goddess in the Grecian-style high heels like some of the other men in the room. Reid had already decided to carefully choose his moment, but as she made eye contact, he realized he wasn't going to have to approach her.

She was coming to him.

Two

Until this exact moment in time, Drew Fleming had never successfully captured Reid Singleton's undivided attention. She'd recognized him the instant their eyes locked across the room. He looked the same as when her brother, Gage, had introduced him years ago. To summarize: disgustingly, distractingly *hot*.

Reid, while *still* disgustingly, distractingly hot, was also somehow *more*. More mature. Slightly weathered. Handsome. Stately. Broader, too, his shoulders taking up more space in that button-up shirt than they had a right to.

Her heart pattered insistently against her rib cage as she walked toward him, and she forced herself to take deep breaths. She wasn't going to dissolve into Reid's biggest fan at a conference mixer, nor was she going to have a panic attack and run off in another direction. Drew was proud of who she was, of how far she'd come. She was no longer Gage's backward, chubby younger sister. She couldn't remember the last time she'd smiled shyly as she hid behind her hair.

She put a hop in her next step as she drew her chin up and shook her hair. Reid's tempting mouth slid into an expression that screamed *interested*. And who could blame him? She was *rocking* this skirt.

Reid and Drew didn't have much of a past to speak of, considering he'd only known her when she was fifty pounds heavier. She'd been the quiet girl sneaking frosting off the edge of her birthday cake because she couldn't wait for everyone to sing "Happy Birthday" before she tasted it.

Back then she'd had either white-blond hair with pink streaks, or jet black—that phase had lasted what felt like forever—before accepting her weight and her mouse-brown natural hair color as an adult. But today Reid was seeing her as her best self. Her rich, dark hair long and flowing over her shoulders. Her smile bright, her lipstick fresh, her new killer heels sexily laced up her ankles. If there was ever a perfect time to run into Reid Singleton, it was right now.

She'd have to call her roommate, Christina, the moment this mixer was over and thank her for coming down with the plague.

See, Drew might be herself, but she also *wasn't* herself. She was playing the role of her roommate, who'd had the unfortunate luck to contract the flu before the tech event for her company. Christina had been working at the Brentwood Corporation for just under a year and was worried if she missed the first conference they'd assigned her to, they'd never ask her to do another.

Drew was desperately in need of a break after a messy split with her ex a year ago. She felt was like she was emerging from the shadows after a long, deep slumber, so she volunteered to come here in Christina's stead.

Admittedly, manning—or *womanning*—the booth at the conference wasn't as fun as an *actual* vacation, but Drew made the best of it. She'd had a lot of visitors today and smiled and welcomed them even if she didn't understand what the heck the video she played on repeat was trying to convey. But what she was skilled at was small talk, and so whenever someone popped in, she'd winged it.

Tonight's mixer was a great excuse to wear the new shoes, admittedly a splurge, but she'd learned to spoil herself—to splurge on things *other* than food. Drew *splurged* on joy. *Splurged* on clothes. And tonight she might *splurge* on flirting with Reid Singleton. The way he was watching her hinted that he would enjoy that.

She ventured over to the quiet, darker part of the room only he was occupying. Reid set aside his glass, an inch of brown liquid in the bottom, and tilted his head as she approached.

She was tempted to duck her head to hide from the intense eye contact, but she forced herself to hold his cerulean gaze. "Hi."

"Hello." His voice was as rich as dark chocolate and every bit as sinful as those stolen swipes of frosting from her birthday cake. In spite of living in America for over a decade, his accent hadn't gone anywhere. He perused her from head to toe before those traveling eyes locked on her chest. "Christina. That's a pretty name."

Oh. Damn. Her badge! She'd clipped it on her top to make sure she would be admitted into the party but failed to tuck it away when she arrived.

Wait…

Reid knew she wasn't Christina, right? He had to be kidding. And so she laughed.

"Christina. Right."

"The tag's a bit of a formality but I'm glad for it. Saved me asking your name. I've been watching you dance."

Drew felt her smile slip. *Damn*. He didn't recognize her. A frisson of hurt rippled through her, and her smile was a little harder to hold. Was she so forgettable?

"You noticed me," he said.

"What?" She blinked as she reframed the situation in her head. She hadn't seen him in forever and she looked nothing like her former self. Still, she was halfway to offended that her brother's friend didn't know who she was... but she was also intrigued. What was the intrigue about?

Second chances, part of her whispered.

Reid knew Drew as Gage's little sis who was a fashion disaster, rarely spoke and was curled on the couch with a book whenever he had seen her. And though the summer she'd been rocking a black bikini at their family's backyard pool had been more about rebellion than catching Reid's attention, she remembered him noticing. In passing. He certainly hadn't looked at her the way he was looking at her now.

Like he *wanted* her.

What was that saying? That there wasn't a second chance to make a first impression. She'd bet there wasn't a single soul alive who didn't want to press a do-over button on something stupid they'd said or done in the past, to leave a totally different first impression. Evidently, she had the rare opportunity to do just that.

Reid and Drew both lived in Seattle—as did her brother—but she'd done her level best to keep from bumping into Reid on accident. Sure she'd undergone a transformation, but she wasn't willing to risk being overlooked again. He'd always seen Drew through the lens of "Gage's sister," and she doubted dropping weight and changing her

hair color would change that. Not that she had to try hard
to avoid him. Her social media footprint was almost invisible. She'd endured enough bullying in high school to
know better than put up a photo and expect likes and wait
for compliments. Nooooo thanks.

If she was running into him here, of all places, the universe must be nudging her to take action where he was
concerned. It was a sign.

"Can I buy you a drink?" he asked.

A laugh bubbled from her throat. A second chance to
make a first impression on Reid. To find out how long it
took him to realize that he was flirting and chatting with
none other than *Drew Fleming*, Gage's younger sister, and
not the mysterious "Christina" from the conference.

This should be fun. And no less than he deserved for
not recognizing her on sight.

"Only if it's golden yellow and bubbly."

He eyed her gold shirt. "Fitting."

He offered his arm and she curled her fingers around
his biceps. Whatever cool she had slipped from her like
rainwater off a duck's back. She'd easily navigated the
room in her high-heeled shoes all evening, but now worried
she might stumble and fall. She swiped her teeth with her
tongue in case her lipstick had transferred. She suddenly
worried there was something in her nose or—

"Champagne and scotch rocks, please," Reid ordered
from the bartender. Her palm was sweaty. So were her
teeth, for that matter.

Do not freak out. Do not freak out!

She'd play a role. Like an actor. Deep inside she was
the same Drew, but her outer appearance had changed
enough that some days she felt like someone else. She was
definitely a stronger version of herself. A *happier* version

of herself. She'd sprouted and then bloomed, and now a tender new bud was around the corner. She could feel it.

Screw Chef Devin Briggs for never seeing the rose he'd had.

She shook her head. She wasn't going to let thoughts of her ex-boyfriend ruin a one-on-one with Reid.

"Golden and bubbly." Reid handed her the champagne flute. "Should we sit or linger?" He leaned in when he asked, and she was so focused on the shape of his upper lip, the tempting fullness of his lower lip, that she didn't answer.

"Huh?" *Smooth, Drew.*

He gestured to a cluster of boxy-looking chairs and a sofa in the corner. Currently unoccupied.

"Sit. Let's sit." Before she had a case of the vapors and fell flat on her face.

He took her free hand this time, his blunt fingers and wide palm dwarfing her smaller ones. She walked toward the sofa with one thought dominating all others. *I'm holding Reid's hand.* I'm holding Reid's hand!

She felt like a teenager again, smitten by this gorgeous god of a man who seemed too perfect to be real. Except she was closer to his equal now, wasn't she? The playing field hadn't been leveled, but close. She was a professional with a great job and a great life, and her shoes were adding four inches of much-needed height. She was confident and strong, and she wouldn't trade this second chance for anything. His being attracted to her was doing wonders for her ego.

Shallow, but no less true.

Dipping his chin, he gestured for her to sit. She did, crossing one leg over the other and noticing when Reid noticed. She hid her smile at the rim of the champagne flute.

As bubbles tickled her throat and popped on her tongue, he settled in next to her.

"Where do you hail from, Christina—" another glance at her name tag "—Kolch?"

"And you pronounced it right. Impressive." Christina was always complaining that she'd heard everything from "Cock" to "Couch" whenever someone said her last name.

"Like the soda but with an *L*, I figured."

"You figured right." A weighty pause hovered in the air and she realized her faux pas. She recovered with a stilted, "What's your name?" and felt silly for asking.

"Singleton. Reid Singleton."

"Did you intentionally introduce yourself like James Bond, or did I hear it that way because of your accent?" His smile erased her mind like a powerful magnet, but thankfully she recovered quickly. "I assume you didn't grow up in California?"

"I'm from London, but I live in Seattle and have for years. Never developed a knack for you Americans' hard *R*s."

He overpronounced the *R* in *hard* and *Rs*, which made him sound a little like a pirate. Drew laughed again.

"Do you always giggle this much or only when you drink champagne?"

"Only when I drink champagne with handsome strangers," she said, enjoying the game and the new rules for it. When Reid figured out who she was in the next two minutes, she would shove his arm in an ole-buddy-ole-pal way and chastise him for his weak powers of observation.

But she was in no hurry. She liked him this way—trying to win her attention, sitting taller when she'd paid him a compliment he had to know was true. It wasn't like Reid didn't own a mirror. He was obviously good-looking to the nth degree.

It was unfair to every other man on the planet.

"Well played." His voice was a low murmur as he leaned in, his eyes touching her lips. He then sat back, taking her breath with him, and sipped his scotch while she drained half her champagne.

She suddenly didn't want this to end. She didn't want him to recognize her. She wanted to be seen as charming and playful and beautiful. She wanted to relax and have fun and flirt.

Her gaze locked on his full lower lip below his contoured top lip. She wanted to kiss him. Before it was too late. Before she lost her nerve, and her only chance with it. As soon as he figured out that she was Drew Fleming, the moment would be lost.

A wave of panic sailed through her chest. She'd regret not kissing him for the rest of her life if she didn't do it now. She set aside her champagne glass and faced him.

"Tell me more about—" he started, but she cut him off. In the most delicious way possible.

She grabbed his dashing, perfect face, tugged his mouth to hers and kissed him hard.

Three

Reid's spicy cologne tickled her nose as she tasted his amazing mouth. She'd sort of slammed her lips into his to start—blame years of pent-up lust—but now she eased into a more tender kiss, sliding her lips over his in gentle exploration.

She didn't know if he felt the same electric sizzle that flamed to life inside her the moment their mouths met, but she accepted that this couldn't go on forever. When they pulled apart, she'd come clean. She'd tell him her name—her real one—and then she would do the awkward dance of apologizing for the subterfuge.

But when she would've ended the kiss, Reid's fingers fed into her hair, holding her close. He opened his mouth wide and stroked his tongue against hers.

That ignited flame inside her burst into a five-alarm fire. He kissed like no man she'd ever known. The slide of his tongue was ten times more intoxicating than the champagne she'd been drinking—*in and out, in and out*. A needy sound resonated from her throat.

Reid Singleton was even more delicious than she'd imagined. And, oh, had she imagined. In the darkest corner of her bedroom with a flashlight and her journal. A shoebox in her closet held some truly horrible poetry. She'd imagined him saying her name in his proper accent—not in polite greeting, but with passion.

She might never know what it was like to hear him say her name in that way, but at least she knew how he tasted. Like smoky scotch and sexy male. Every part of her from her peaking nipples to her overheating thighs wanted to climb onto his lap and satisfy the insistent throbbing between her legs.

His kiss was both thorough but careful, his skill and his tongue almost too much to bear. Here was a man who knew how to please a woman, and Drew was a woman who needed pleasing. *Badly*. Not just sex for sex's sake, but sex with Reid. Sex with the man who'd noticed her from across the room, who had always been polite and friendly to her and her family. The man who, if she told him who she was, would end this fantasy in an instant because he would never take advantage of his best friend's little sister.

She wanted to hover in the in-between forever. Where they knew each other physically, where the past had no weight on the present.

She palmed his chest, and even over a shirt, he felt better than he had in her fantasies. Hard and firm, and real. So real. Greedily, she ran her fingers to the open placket of his shirt and touched the bare skin of his neck. That's when he broke their connection.

Blinking like he was having an epiphany, he took her hand from his chest and held it, her fingers gripped lightly in his. She watched in horror as he studied her, his eyebrows drawn. She waited for recognition to hit, her own fear and worry a toxic mix. He'd recognize her, reject her—and possibly apologize for kissing her back, which would be worse than the other two combined.

Turned out he did that first.

"Apologies for that," he said, his accent thick, his voice tight with what she hoped was lust and not disappointment.

"Don't be sorry. I'm the one who kissed you." She licked her lips, needing another drink of her champagne like her next breath. She reached for the flute, but he beat her to it, handing over her glass. "I've wanted to do that for a long time."

A deep chuckle brought her eyes to his, and she held his gaze and silently asked the question she wouldn't dare ask aloud. *Did you figure out who I am yet?*

"All seven minutes you've known me, Christina?" His lips twisted temptingly. If that didn't answer her question soundly, nothing would. He still had no idea who she was.

She polished off the remainder of her bubbly. Disappointment had no place in the moments following kissing him, but it was there anyway, making her chest tight and causing her to feel something else. Sad, if she wasn't mistaken.

Beggars can't be choosers, Drew. You wanted to kiss him, and this was your only opportunity. Did you expect more?

More.

She blinked, the rogue thought so far from her good-girl tendencies she instinctively wanted to shut it out. Reid's throat moved as he swallowed a sip of scotch. His Adam's apple bobbed, and she chased the line of his neck to the scant bit of chest hair visible where his shirt gaped open—just below where she'd touched him seconds ago.

Lie or confess?

"I'm an impatient woman. That's why I kissed you."
Lie, it was.

She wanted more. She wanted to run her tongue along his neck and kiss his bare chest. She wanted to kiss the firm, flat plane of his belly and trace that trail of hair down to the promised land. She wanted his mouth on hers, and lower. On her breasts and body, between her legs where she knew he'd be incredibly attentive and pleasing.

Although, if she walked out of this party without him— without telling him who she was—she'd be off the hook completely. She didn't hang around online and chat with old friends or new. She wouldn't cross Reid's path again unless Gage invited them to the same party—oh, shit.

Her brother's wedding!

Reid would *see Drew* at the wedding because he'd be there, obviously. Hell, he'd probably be the best man. He'd recognize her then, now wouldn't he?

That narrowed her options to an unfortunate one: confessing her real identity.

Reid tucked her hair behind her ear, then rested his arm over the back of the sofa. Leaning close, he watched her carefully. "I like impatience in a woman. And not to sound like a complete nutter, but I feel as if that kiss was inevitable. That even if you'd have waited seven more minutes, and seven more after that, it would've happened eventually."

Or maybe if I'd waited nine years. Ha ha ha…sigh.

He traced his finger along her jaw, his eyes following the path. Her heart rate was erratic. Could he see her pulse point thundering at the side of her neck? Then another, more devious, thought occurred. If she didn't tell him the truth just yet, how far could she take this night of fantasy? He'd forgive her. He'd have to. Gage and Reid weren't going to stop being friends because Drew told a white lie. Although one had to wonder if her own identity would be considered a "white" lie. Maybe off-white. Light gray...

"Like fate?" she whispered as he traced the scoop neckline of her shirt. This felt like fate to her.

"Bold word, but why not?" He continued touching her exposed skin, barely any pressure, the tickling sensation bringing forth goose bumps. "I also imagine that the evening will end with more than kissing if you'll allow it."

The skipped beat of her heart caused her breath to catch. "M-more?"

He trailed his hand to her palm and wove their fingers together. "A night together would amp up this conference to best-ever territory. I know you don't know me, Christina, but while I'm a man who enjoys a woman in my bed, I rarely mix work and play."

He lifted their entwined hands and kissed the top of hers, his stunning blue irises burning into her. She'd known Reid well enough to know that he didn't hold back in the physical affection department, but she'd never label him a player. That was too crass a word for him. He was simply a physical guy, acting on his instincts and his, she assumed, amazing skill. She couldn't imagine a single woman leaving his company being disappointed in his performance. Though many of them probably felt like she did: full of longing and worrying he wouldn't return her affections.

If ever there was a "seize the day" moment, this was it.

"What do you say? My room or yours? I'll let you choose, but mine is a suite with a kitchen, a balcony and a soaking tub."

"No piano?" She wanted to shout "yes!" but her nerves—or maybe her habit of always doing the right thing—had her stalling.

"No piano." His glorious chuckle might be the death of

her. She wasn't a swooner, but she was close. "Room service and I are acquainted. I arrived two days before the conference started, and there wasn't an after-party with a beautiful woman in gold waiting to share my steak and movie."

"What movie?"

He grinned, maybe knowing she was stalling and not caring. *"Jaws."*

"Jaws!" His answer startled a laugh out of her. "How did you sleep?"

He let go of her hand, charm dialed to eleven as he swept his hand to her nape. He said one word—"fitfully"—before covering her lips with his and drinking her in for a kiss that lasted long enough to turn her brain to mush.

"Christina." His warm breath coasted over her lips.

Drew's eyes were closed, the pretending still in play. She could carry on this farce, let him seduce her for real and agree not to regret the sex. It wasn't as if she would've had a prayer of seducing Reid as herself, but as "Christina" she had a chance.

"Let me make your dreams come true," he said. "Come to my room."

It was everything she wanted to hear, but guilt niggled at her.

"Isn't that a secondary location?" she breathed. "I learned never to be moved to a secondary location."

Another light press of his lips, and she opened her eyes. It was like seeing him for the first time, that angled jaw, those entrancing eyes, the full mouth slightly pink from her recent attention. How could she say no?

She couldn't.

"That was a joke." She gripped his shirt and kissed him. He let her, which was thrilling. "I'd like to see your room, Reid. I'd like to see much more than your room."

Her heart was tapping out a salsa, her palms sweaty, her stomach a Tilt-A-Whirl of excitement. This was happening—really happening—and since Drew was a woman accustomed to setting goals and achieving them, she decided to stop justifying and embrace the moment. *This* moment.

"That might be the yes of my life, Christina."

She didn't know if he said that to all the girls, but she wanted to believe that it was just for her. They stood, leaving their glasses on the low table by the sofa, and then he led her away from the thumping bass of the speakers and out of the room.

Four

Drew entered the elevator and Reid stepped in behind her. The doors swished shut as he punched the button for the twenty-first floor.

She was in an elevator, alone with Reid Singleton, heading skyward to his hotel room, where they would have sex. Drew smothered a smile as she examined her strappy shoes, a flush of heat creeping along her neck as she imagined him removing those shoes and kissing his way up her calves…

She was as confident in his ability as she was in herself, although admittedly her confidence was fairly recent. Three years ago, at age twenty-four, she decided she'd no longer hide behind the excess weight or comfort herself by eating. She hired a personal trainer and cut out processed and fried foods and quickly dropped the unwanted pounds.

Drew loved food. Of that she'd had no doubt. But she didn't feel an ounce of shame admitting she loved food now that she had a healthy relationship with it. No longer did she soothe her negative emotions by eating; now she exercised or worked. She'd changed her mind-set—decided she was worthy of the good things life had to offer—and that had made all the difference.

A little over a year ago she'd achieved another goal. She'd been featured in *Restauranteurs,* an industry magazine, as one of the "Top 30 under 30" professionals. She'd been the only restaurant public relations manager in the magazine.

Her employer, Fig & Truffle, owned several restaurants, cafés and bars in and around Seattle. It'd been Drew's job these four years to oversee the soft openings. Seattle's foodie scene was massive. And after the feature in the magazine, Fig & Truffle boosted her pay and made Drew *the* PR go-to.

She handled press, booked reviewers, interviewed top chefs from around the world...which was how she'd met her previous boyfriend. Chef Devin Briggs was the cherry on top of her "I've arrived" sundae, but they didn't last. How could they when he was a selfish ass in love with only himself?

Jerk.

"Second thoughts?" Reid's smooth voice interrupted as the elevator bumped to a soft stop. He was watching her with curiosity and *not* in recognition, thank goodness.

"Not at all." She stepped out when the doors parted, pausing in the long corridor for him to lead the way. He palmed her lower back as they walked side by side, and again she became intently aware of him—of the breadth of his shoulders and warm weight of his hand on her body. Of his comforting presence.

There was an innate kindness to Reid one might overlook upon first meeting him. Probably because he was insanely gorgeous. That sharp jaw, full mouth and the hint

of a dent at the center of his chin were so all-consuming
it took a few minutes to realize he was human and not
a futuristic sex toy designed solely for a woman's pleasure. Looking at him was a decadent treat—forget kissing him. Only she'd never, ever forget. Not even when she
was ninety and gumming her food.

At the end of the corridor, Reid guided her to the right
to a double-doored suite. He scanned his key, and gestured
for her to go in ahead of him.

The suite was about one hundred times nicer than her
room. She'd bunked at a hotel across the street from the
convention center. Her room had a rattling air-condition-
ing unit, pilled, nubby carpet and wall hangings the color
of pea soup. She'd have to tell Christina the next time her
company offered to send her out of town to upgrade the
room if possible.

Conversely, Reid's room was modern and posh. No
piano, but the palette was a tasteful dove gray and pale
ocean blue and minimally decorated with stylish furniture.
The door opened to a wide sitting room with a couch and
colorful throw pillows. A flat-screen television hung on
the wall. A kitchenette and bar were on the opposite side,
and the bedroom was visible through an open door across
the room. Her eyes snagged on that room for a beat, imagining being laid on that stone-colored bedspread under
Reid's blue-eyed attention...

Her recently earned confidence took a sudden dip.

"Nice. This is nice," she told him, her smile feeling
brittle and forced.

"My company spoils me." He walked to a desk in the
far corner, lifted the phone's receiver and murmured into
it while she meandered around the suite. The bathroom
was the size of her entire hotel room, the soaking tub wide
enough for three people to sit comfortably.

"Champagne and strawberries are on their way up."
She turned to see Reid stuff his hands in his pockets, his
expression handsome and affable. "You didn't think I'd
bring you up here and strip you bare right away, did you?
Where's the fun in that?"

He untucked his hands and came to her, cradling her
jaw. "If you change your mind at any time, Christina, say
the word. I'm not owed anything."

"That won't happen," she whispered. "I need this more
than you know."

A flicker of concern sparked in his eyes before a flame
of desire crowded it out. She rested both hands on his
chest, and he took the invitation to kiss her deeply. The
only sounds were the soft suctioning of their mouths and
the gentle scrape of the material of her shirt as he moved
his palms over her arms.

Drew hadn't been with anyone since Chef Devin Briggs
left her to start a family with another woman. Drew hadn't
been ready for a family. She'd been building her career and
enjoying her freedom. Devin, eleven years older than her,
had already established his career and was ready to settle down. It'd been a frequent topic of argument between
them, and had eventually led to their demise.

She'd been single since he left, working hard and skip-
ping sleep in pursuit of becoming the very best at what she
did. As a result, she hadn't had time to feel truly lonely.
Christina had been there to distract her, chattering away
about work or her own guy problems.

Drew had spent any free time she'd had researching and
reading about food service and public relations, or staying up until the wee hours to call chefs in other countries
who might be interested in lending their expertise to one
of Fig & Truffle's franchises.

In short, she hadn't had the time or inclination to indulge her fantasies.

Until tonight.

Her fingers twitched with the urge to undo each button on Reid's shirt and kiss a trail over his hard chest to the muscular bumps of his abdomen. At the same time, she worried that somehow he would see her—the former *her*. That the pounds she'd lost would reappear in his mind and he'd recoil, leaving her feeling unworthy all over again.

Ridiculous, she scolded silently.

He nipped her bottom lip before peppering kisses on the side of her neck. Her worries dissipated with each press of his lips. Overcome by longing and the sensations in her sex-starved body, Drew gave in to the experience that was Reid.

He must've sensed that she was through talking or stalling, because next he bent and lifted her, propping her back against the wall. He continued kissing her neck and collarbone as she wrapped her legs around his waist. He anchored her there with his hips between her open thighs and—*oh!*

Her center lined up perfectly with the hard ridge of his erection, which made its presence known as it pressed against her most sensitive spot.

"Ready, both of us, then." He ground against her, sending her into a mental free fall.

She'd never imagined sex with him would be a reality. When she'd last seen him, she'd been eighteen and awkward and shy and quiet, and at that birthday party where she'd decided to wear the damn bikini, she hadn't missed Reid flirting shamelessly with the female bartender. While he'd ordered a beer, Drew had sipped on mocktails without a drop of alcohol. It'd been a good reminder of the gaps between them—not only the handful of years separating their ages but also of his class and stature. Of his sheer beauty and her averageness. Like a great sequoia next to a plain maple tree, anyone could see how different they were.

Tonight, she'd prove to herself she was worthy of the great Reid Singleton.

"I've been ready longer than you know," she said. His hair was thick and soft against her fingers. He smiled, his lips damp from kissing her. Once again she worried he was looking at her. *Really looking.*

She worried he might see that beyond her dark hair and curvy yet slimmer physique was the once-shy younger sister of Gage. She didn't want to become suddenly undesirable or untouchable.

So not an option.

Distracting him as best she knew how, Drew stroked Reid's crotch, pleased when the material of his pants tented invitingly. He groaned, his tongue plunging into her mouth as he took his sweet time.

She was ready—absolutely aching to have him inside her. He loosened his hold on her, and she untangled her legs from his waist to stand on her feet. She unbuckled his belt and worked his fly open as he tore his mouth from hers to suck in a breath. He freed her from her shirt and once her lacy pale pink bra was revealed, he froze, his attention on her breasts. They were generous and always had been, but appeared even bigger in the silky demicup bra she'd purchased to match her shoes. Her D cups were swollen and pressed together, her deep cleavage an invitation.

It was an invitation he eagerly accepted, cupping her breasts and lowering his face to kiss the tops of each one.

She'd worked hard on her body—keeping her waist trim and legs toned took a lot of work and effort. And since she'd worked hard, she was going to enjoy her reward. *Him.*

She unbuttoned his shirt as he slipped the bra straps off

her shoulders, kissing her here and there as he did. She ran her hands over the expanse of his golden skin, and he tugged one bra cup down and sucked on her nipple. Her back arched, sending her breast deeper into his mouth, the resulting dampness in her panties a welcome warmth.

His mouth is the eighth wonder of the world, she thought, dazed by his skill.

He moved to her other nipple but before he could blow her mind, a sharp knock at the door preceded a call of "Room service!"

He lifted his face to hers, his eyes glazed with arousal. She fisted his hair in protest, and he winced in pain.

"Sorry," she muttered, letting him go.

"No, I'm sorry." He sent a baleful look in the direction of the door. She didn't want him to stop or even pause. She didn't want to give him a single moment to reconsider or change his mind. She couldn't bear the rejection.

He lifted her hand and kissed her palm before bending to retrieve her shirt and pressing it over her exposed breasts.

"Bedroom." His voice was rusty and sexy as hell. "I'll take care of this."

He crossed the room, his shirt and pants open, his hair a disaster.

Her grin was downright arrogant.

She'd weakened Reid Singleton's knees. What a powerful feeling that was. And he didn't seem anywhere near done with her yet.

At the door Reid buttoned his pants and ran his hands through his hair, sending her a wink as she backed into the shadows of the bedroom.

Five

Reid didn't bother closing his shirt or tidying himself much before letting the hotel employee in. He'd ordered champagne and strawberries, after all, which should've made it obvious that he was having a romantic interlude. He did tuck his hips behind the door when he opened it. What he was hiding from view would be too much information for whoever would wheel in the dessert cart.

A shaggy-haired guy who couldn't be more than twenty-one shuffled in looking bored and tired. Reid retrieved the first bill he saw from his wallet and stuffed it in the guy's palm.

Bloody hell. Reid had given him a fifty in his haste.

The kid held up the bill and blinked at it. "Wow. Thanks, man."

"No problem." Any amount of money was worth returning to his date as quickly as possible.

Door shut, Reid flipped the safety lock as Christina

appeared from the dark bedroom. Her skirt was in place, those incredible shoes crisscrossing up her ankles. Her shirt was still missing—a good sign—and she was wearing a pale pink bra that barely encased her gorgeous breasts.

Those breasts might be the death of him, but what a way to go.

She repositioned the cups almost self-consciously as she walked toward him. He knew her breasts were both beautiful and delicious. He'd have to take more time admiring and tasting them. He also wanted to taste those thighs and higher. He'd had her legs around his hips, her molten center warming his straining erection. He needed her, and he needed her *now*.

"The cart's arrived." Not what he wanted to say, but he thinking was a challenge with all the blood flowing to his nethers.

"I see that." Her smile was so sweet that he couldn't shake the idea that he was taking advantage of her somehow. The way she'd said earlier that she'd been ready longer than he knew hinted that it'd been a while since she'd had a man in her bed. Likely longer since she'd had a man *who knew what he was doing* in her bed.

Through the women he'd known, he'd learned that men didn't make it their priority to pleasure a woman. Which was criminal. When gifted with a beauty like the one standing before him, how could Reid not take his time exploring every inch of that body to learn what turned her on? What made her moan or giggle? What made her gasp in surprise or go to the brink of where only he'd be able to take her…

Best not to rush if that was his goal.

He grabbed the champagne bottle by the neck and took it from the ice bucket. His date's smile slipped as her eyes went to his hands working the cork. Worry puckered her brow.

"Did you…change your mind?" she asked, and bless her breasts, she actually sounded serious.

A rough chuckle escaped him as he popped the cork from the bottle. "Definitely not. I'm attempting to be a gentleman."

"What if I don't want you to be a gentleman? What if I prefer hurried over slow?" She glided across the room like a petite runway model, skimming the couch with her fingertips, her shoulders back, those inviting breasts jiggling as she walked.

"Why? Have you somewhere else to be?" He filled the two flutes and nestled the champagne into the ice before lifting a silver dome to reveal rows of ripe red strawberries and a bowl of melted dark chocolate.

Her pink tongue touched the corner of her lips.

"A gentleman wouldn't rush to undress you right away. A gentleman—" he dunked one berry into the chocolate "—would sample the chocolate off your nipples while feeding you a strawberry."

She sucked in an anticipatory breath. He had her full attention.

"A gentleman—" he carried one of the flutes over to her "—would sip this from your belly button before kissing you where it matters most. Ever had an *effervescent* orgasm, Christina?"

The heat in her eyes banked. "I prefer *love*."

A request he'd heard before. Some American women liked that term, he assumed because of his accent. He wasn't below fulfilling their fantasies.

He approached with the strawberry, chocolate delicately balanced on the tip. He lowered it to her mouth while saying, "Ever had an effervescent orgasm, *love*?"

She took a bite of the chocolate-covered berry, her eyelids, coated in a shimmery gold shadow, sinking shut. She moaned, a soft "mmm" that turned him on far more than it ought to. With this woman it seemed the anticipation of what came next was as exciting as the act.

Fantastic.

He polished off the rest of the berry, tossed the stem aside and kissed her. She tasted of chocolate and sweet red fruit. When she looked up at him, her cheeks were flushed, her eyes begging for what he'd promised.

"You've been with the wrong men, *love.*"

"Tell me about it."

He offered her the champagne, and she took a sip, licking her full, inviting lips, and his erection grew harder.

"We only have tonight, but that doesn't mean we have to rush," he told her. "In fact, since we have so little time together it makes sense to savor it."

He thought of this as "the talk." He didn't want to spoil the evening with overexplaining, but he wouldn't go forward before setting the expectation. Where Reid was concerned, there was no possibility for a relationship. He had no desire to go down that road.

"Believe me, Reid," she said on a throaty laugh. "I didn't expect things to get this far." She touched the dip in his chin and wiggled her finger. "Tonight will have to be enough for both of us."

A ribbon of unease curled in his chest. Already he wanted more than tonight, and he hadn't even had her yet.

"Unless we change our minds," he heard himself say.

"Why would we do that?" She narrowed one eye, her mouth a tempting purse.

"Are you staying for the entire conference?"

"I am."

"What if you find yourself bored while you're here and

crave my company?" He threw in a shrug like he wasn't anticipating her answer.

"Hmm. We'll see." With that noncommittal response, she put her palm on his chest and shoved him toward the couch. He was content to let her do as she pleased.

A side table lamp and the bathroom light glowed, but other than that the suite was dark. Even in shadow, Christina was inviting.

Despite the added height of her shoes, she had to stretch to kiss him. He held the flute out of reach and wrapped his arm around her waist, pulling her soft, supple curves against him and erasing every bit of his memory. He'd promised to do…something. With the berries, or was it the champagne…? She'd entranced him.

"We aren't rushing." That much he'd remembered.

"No. We're not." She stole the flute, drained the remainder of the champagne and set it aside. Then she pushed him onto the couch. "But we're not delaying, either."

She clicked off the lamp and straddled him, her breasts between them. He cupped his hands over her bra, rubbing his thumbs over her nipples until the hard nubs beaded beneath the fabric.

She gasped one word. *"Yes."*

"Does it hurt good, love?"

"*So* good," she agreed.

He unclasped the bra, freeing those bountiful orbs to the trusted homes of his palms. He took one nipple on his tongue and sucked hard, and she cried out—a sharp, high shout of pleasure.

When she wiggled her ass on his lap, his hips arched to find her—his cock eager to reach her warm, wet heat, his promises not to rush be damned.

Six

With his mouth on hers, it was easy for Drew to forget everything. Her past—*their* past—her insecurities, her stupid ex-boyfriend, her worries that Reid might recognize her…

Those yellow jacket-sized concerns had swarmed her mind earlier, but now they shrank to tiny fruit flies before vanishing in a puff of smoke.

Whenever he touched her, she was lost. Lost when he smoothed his hands up her legs, lost when he palmed her ass beneath her skirt and completely lost when his mouth teased her nipples once more.

"Yes, Reid." Damp heat pooled at the apex of her thighs as she moaned his name a second time. It was a plea. A plea for him to take her to physical release, to deliver her from the woman she'd been for the past year-plus. The overworked, sleep-deprived, slay-all-day boss she'd turned into… That woman was nowhere around when Reid Singleton kissed her. She was simply a woman—and for the moment, *his* woman.

He let loose her breast and propped his head on a bright yellow pillow. His elbows were locked, his hands wrapped around the spiked heels of her shoes. "You're beautiful."

The words struck like flint to stone. Words she'd always wanted to hear. She'd heard *cute* a lot growing up. She'd heard *pretty* once or twice. Hearing the word *beautiful* from him touched her in a deep, hidden place. He tugged her shoes gently by the heels and smiled. "Keep these on. These are what I first noticed about you. I'm afraid a fantasy brewed as a result."

Reid had a fantasy involving her and her shoes? How awesome was *that*?

"You wouldn't deny a desperate man his fantasy, would you, love?" He gave her his best puppy eyes.

She shook her head. She doubted he spent many, if any, nights lonely. He said all the right things. Looked the right way. Life's greatest pleasures must show up gift-wrapped on his doorstep.

Tonight, for example, she'd served herself up on a platter. And yet still he'd worked to seduce her. Not that there was any need. She'd been seduced by him years ago—the moment Gage stepped into their house for dinner and Reid walked in behind him. At the time she hadn't fully comprehended what that pinch in her gut was telling her. She'd stared, and when he'd waved hello in introduction, she'd hidden behind her hair and then run to her room. She hadn't had a single conversation alone with him, choosing to talk to her friends or her brother on the rare occasions she had seen Reid. Even on her eighteenth birthday, she'd climbed out of the swimming pool the moment he'd dived in. He was so out of her league, so unattainable, she hadn't even had the confidence to *converse* with him.

She noticed he'd been careful to mention that he didn't expect anything from her beyond what they shared physically. Probably he was used to delivering the bad news—that while he was glad to spend the night with a woman, he couldn't offer more.

But Drew had entered this situation knowing her time with Reid had an expiration date. Her eyes were wide open, her heart under firm direction to stay out of it. She was spending these precious moments with him to *carpe diem*, not because she expected forever. Besides, once he figured out who she was, this would be over faster than she could say the words "expiration date."

Lowering her lips to his for another kiss, she promised herself that after she made love with him tonight she'd tell him who she was in the morning. It wasn't right to continue to lie to him. Though she could forgive herself this indulgence, she thought as she opened the button and zipper of his pants. Telling him now would mean ruining everyone's fun. They might as well enjoy themselves.

"Your wish is my command." She offered her best saucy wink, raked her fingers over his bare chest and then scooted lower on his legs to pull down his boxer briefs. His erection sprang from the barrier, thick and inviting. "Oh God."

She hadn't meant to say that out loud, but it couldn't be helped. She'd never seen one quite this...*substantial*. Devin's was slightly above average—or what she'd come to think of as average. Reid's penis made others pale in comparison.

"Something the matter?" her cheeky Brit asked, his grin confident and sure.

"It's... You're beautiful. Everywhere I look. Every part I uncover." That was as honest as she'd ever been, but she wasn't going to do tonight halfway. She'd wanted Reid for so long there was only one way to be with him. *Completely*.

Before she'd gotten her fill of his nakedness, he sat up

and pulled her to him. His arms banded at her back, pressing her breasts flat to his chest as he kissed the underside of her chin.

"No, *beautiful* is my word for you. *Beautiful* describes these breasts I can't get enough of." He rubbed his chest against hers. "*Beautiful* describes the way you fit up against me, and the perfectly mind-numbing way I'll notch into you as soon as I'm done tasting you."

"T-tasting me?" She blinked at him, speechless and excited for that possibility.

"Mmm-hmm." He dragged his tongue in a slow line from her jaw to her throat before kissing her pulse point. "I'm going to bring you to orgasm with my mouth, and then I'm going to enter you and bring you that way, too. We'll throw in a few more during and after if you like. But I'm starting with my mouth here." He cupped her center, the pressure from his fingers teasing her clitoris. "Depending on how well you react depends on how long I stay down there. But be forewarned, I am very good."

A giggle bubbled out of her, a result of nerves and shock, or maybe the cocky, confident way he spoke. "Are you now?"

"Try me. We'll find out together."

Without waiting for her to answer, he stood and lifted her, his hands molding her butt. She held on as he walked her to the bedroom. Being carried to a bedroom by Reid Singleton ticked another box on her sexy bucket list.

Not that he could ever be reduced to an item on a list, but…well…he sort of *could*. He was an experience. One she was going to enjoy.

He plopped her onto the bedspread and shucked his pants, socks and shoes. The curtains were open, the star-pocked sky throwing meager light into the room. Just enough to highlight the dips and bumps of his chest and abs. She stood by her "beautiful" declaration. He was a sight to behold.

Especially when he lowered to his knees, his forearms resting on the bed near her feet. He lifted and inspected one high heel, the fire in his eyes evident even in the darkened room. He parted her legs gently and, gripping each ankle, dragged her down the bedspread toward him. Her skirt rucked up around her thighs, the pooling material bunching at her back.

Reid's hands disappeared beneath her skirt, smoothing the skin of her thighs and then, finding her satiny matching panties, dragged them off.

"Much as I want to see these on…" He didn't finish his thought, tossing the garment over his shoulders and returning his hands to her thighs. Broad, warm hands. His fingers gripped her flesh, and admittedly there was more there than she preferred. Drew might have drastically changed her body, but she was far from perfect.

But this is my perfect, she reminded herself.

He was.

"It's too dark in here. I have to see you. I'm sorry." He moved to stand and Drew slapped her hands over his and pushed them high on her thighs again.

"No! I need you now. Besides, it's sexier in the dark." And she was so, so close to having him.

She needed to share this with him, and it didn't matter what he thought her name was—she was giving Reid the real Drew. He was experiencing her physically and emotionally. She'd never fake that.

"Please," she whispered.

"I can't resist that plea, love." He eased to his knees and with another rough tug, pulled her to the edge of the bed. Tossing her legs over his shoulders, he lowered his face to her center and dragged his tongue slowly over her.

With a gasp, she dropped her head to the bed, her fists bunching the bedspread helplessly as he repeated the motion. His tongue delved and teased, fast then slow. He'd barely touched her and already she was dissolving.

"Please." She gave herself over to the sensations of his flicking tongue and attentive hands. Those hands climbed her body as he continued devouring her, and when he gave her nipples a light pinch, she came on contact.

Writhing, twisting, she belatedly realized she still wore her pointed-heeled shoes. It took some restraint not to accidentally skewer him.

Before she caught her breath, he declared, "One," and then lowered his face again, doing his best to turn her into mush. She entered the veil willingly, giving herself over to him and coming again in record time. He didn't count aloud this time, didn't give her a chance to recover before he renewed his efforts and took her over the brink for number three.

Three orgasms.

Never in her life had she tumbled over back-to-back-to-*back*. His hands were resting on her breasts, and she pushed up on her elbows. The pleased smile on his face framed by her parted thighs wasn't a picture she'd soon forget.

"Don't brag," she huffed. "It's ungentlemanly."

They both laughed at that one.

He kissed the insides of each of her legs and then vanished from sight before returning again with a foil packet in his hand. He climbed over her body, every inch of him bare and beautiful. "I'd say you're more than ready for this part, love. Correct me if I'm wrong."

She did love when he called her "love." She'd originally made the request to keep him from calling her "Christina," but "love" was working for Drew just fine, thank you very much.

"You're not wrong." She tugged him to her and kissed him thoroughly, stroking his hard-as-steel member once, twice before moving her hand so he could roll the condom on.

"Skirt off," he commanded.

She lifted her hips and allowed him to slide the layers of material from her legs. "Shoes, too?"

"Never."

She smiled what was probably a big dopey smile, and he returned it with one of his own. Then he cocked his head to one side, his lips pursing like he might say something. Perhaps something like, "Drew Fleming, is that you?"

Fear rattled through her like a roller coaster on an unstable track.

You're so close. Don't give up now.

"I need you." She wrapped her ankles around his ass, crossed them and tugged. The moment his cock brushed against her, the blip of concern erased from his face like it'd never been there. He shifted, nestling closer as he kissed her thoroughly. In between the heady slide of his tongue on hers, he shifted his hips and slid home.

She pulled her lips from his to yell, "Yes!" but her voice was no more than a strangled breath. A breath she lost when he slid out and then in again.

He fit, filling her, surrounding her. His scent, the rough, satisfied sounds coming from his throat—the entire experience of Reid—was better than she'd imagined. A growl rumbled in his chest as she smoothed her hands over his firm pectorals.

She'd never done this before—gone home with someone for one night. She never would've shared anything this intimate with someone she didn't know. She didn't know Reid that well, and yet there was something undeniably familiar about him.

"Ready for another?" he murmured against her lips. Their sweat-slicked bodies were smooth and damp against each other.

"Yes."

"Yes, what?" His smirk was too much.

"Yes...sir?"

"I was going for 'please,' but 'sir' will do." He tucked his arm beneath her knee and propped her calf on his shoulder. He drove deep, and that was the angle that sent her tumbling over for a fourth time. Before she could revel in the miracle of *Big O Number 4*, Reid gave in to his own hard-earned release. A guttural growl preceded a triumphant shout of completion.

She held on to him as the last of his orgasm shook his wide shoulders. He dropped his forehead to hers, panting out his release. When he let go of her leg, it drooped to the bed with the rest of her useless limbs. He gave her his weight, pressing her deeper into the bed, and resting his stubbled cheek on her shoulder. Satisfied and more than little sleepy, she tangled her fingers in his wavy hair.

She'd tell him the truth in the morning. After they both came down from cloud nine, or heaven, or wherever that last orgasm had taken her.

For now, she allowed her eyes to grow heavy. The radio-active hum in her body faded into a low buzz, and sleep's tendrils wrapped around her like a warm blanket. She became aware of Reid kissing her breast, her collarbone, her cheek. Of the bed shifting as he stood and shuffled into the bathroom.

The final words she recalled hearing were "Rest up, beautiful girl."

Seven

Reid listened to Christina's deep breaths in the dark, watched the rise and fall of the sheet he'd tucked her under, and smiled to himself. He'd been trying to fall asleep for a while. Four a.m. was an unholy hour to wake anyone. But as he brushed his fingers along her arm, the memory of touching her came crashing back, and parts of him refused to lie dormant.

They'd only just met and oddly enough, she felt familiar. It'd been a while since he'd connected—truly connected— with another person in bed. Sex was about satisfying a physical need, and yes, connection had happened before… on a purely physical level. With Christina, there was more than his body responding to her body. It was as if…his very *soul* responded to hers.

That was…that was…

Well, it was *insane* was what it was.

He blamed the hour, or maybe it was the lack of sleep. He couldn't possibly have a "soul" connection with someone he'd just met. It could've been due to the amazing sexual experience that had eclipsed any other from his past. He couldn't remember wanting anyone as badly as he'd wanted the woman lying next to him.

Not that it would change anything. Flynn's and Gage's recent betrothals weren't contagious. Reid had long beat the "I'm never marrying" drum, and now those drumbeats were more distant than ever. As much as turning over his heart as well as his bollocks scared him, thoughts of having a family sometimes intruded. Though that was definitely not in his best interest. Reid had lost his other half long ago, but still felt that loss as if it'd happened yesterday.

Physical connection was something Reid sought out and needed desperately, and tonight, when a beautiful stranger approached him, he hadn't had to think twice about throwing himself into an encounter with her. It was as simple as that. There was no sense in letting his past intrude in the present or in making this "connection" bigger than what it was:

Pure undiluted sexual attraction.

Christina hummed in her sleep and shifted, kicking the sheet off her body and baring her smooth back to him. She stuffed her hand beneath her pillow and revealed the side of her right breast and a splotch of color just behind it.

Familiarity prickled him. He had the strangest sense of having seen it before...

Then he realized he had.

Reid's brain skipped like a vinyl record. His eyes strained in the meager moonlight before he reached up to touch that spot, a distant memory warring with the present.

He traced the shape of the birthmark: the shape of the continent of Australia, and if he turned on the bedside lamp, he'd bet he'd see that it was grape jelly in color.

His body went cold as a flash of memory slapped itself onto the screen of his mind. Reid had gone at Gage's parents' house for a birthday party for his younger sister, Drew. She was turning eighteen, and Reid had brought a gift, though he had no memory of what it was now—and while he was flirting with the female bartender, Drew dropped her towel to reveal a black bikini. She'd scooped up her long blond—at the time—hair and tied it at the back of her head, clearly having embraced her curves enough to show them off at the privacy of her parents' pool. She'd lost the baby face—the rounder cheeks that she'd had when he'd met her. Reid had noticed the birthmark peeking over the string securing the barely-there top before she'd leaped into the water and avoided him the rest of the party.

He'd avoided her, as well.

There was no room for attraction to Drew. She was too young. Reid wasn't the boyfriend type. Plus, Gage's younger sister deserved only the best life had to offer—forever and a big diamond ring had always been in her future. They had never been in his.

Only now there was an attraction between them, wasn't there? It may or may not have been there at that birthday party years ago, but it sure as hell had burned between them tonight.

He snatched his hand away and scrambled out of bed, the mattress shaking as he did. Drew hummed once more but otherwise didn't move a muscle.

Hands fisted at his sides, he closed his eyes and prayed that when he opened them there'd be something in place of that splotch by her breast. An actual blob of grape jelly, or an illusion thanks to the shadows in the room.

No such luck. It was there in living color.

Drew Fleming was in his bed.

He swiped his forehead, irritated and angry in equal measures. She'd slimmed down since her eighteenth birthday. Her waist was nipped, though her breasts were large and ripe and her hips substantial. He should know—he'd touched, licked or kissed every luscious part of her tonight.

She was fit and strong, her hair no longer the blond with pink streaks he remembered but bold, sophisticated brown. And Drew herself was different. Even in that bikini that summer, she'd walked with her shoulders curled, her hair hiding her face.

It was the last time he'd seen her, so she hadn't been on his mind. Why would she? Other than the occasional mention Gage made of her, he'd had no interaction with her. He'd had no way of knowing the woman he'd taken to bed was Drew, especially when she'd introduced herself as *Christina*.

Reid's left eye twitched as he became aware of how naked he was—of how naked she was. He'd had sex— great sex—with a woman he couldn't easily disentangle himself from. It broke every rule he'd had for as long as he could remember.

Not to mention Gage would draw and quarter him if he ever found out Reid bedded his little sister with zero intention of a relationship.

Reid couldn't return to his life and she to hers like this had never happened. He'd shagged his best friend's sister while at a conference in California. He couldn't justify or rationalize that he was a male with needs and had thought she was a beautiful stranger with those same needs. Not now that he knew the woman in his bed was fucking *Drew Fleming*.

"Christ."

While Drew had undergone a radical physical transformation, Reid *hadn't*. He looked virtually the same. Sure, he'd gained muscle and mass, dressed more professionally. His hair was shorter than he'd worn it then. But aside from the lines around his eyes that hadn't been there in his twenties, he looked like himself. His hair hadn't fallen out, his belly hadn't grown fat and his accent hadn't changed, which meant Drew had known *exactly* who he was when she'd flounced over to him at that mixer.

He'd been so besotted by the beauty of the woman in gold, at the idea of charming her and getting her into his arms, that he'd overlooked that he *bloody knew her.*

She'd taken advantage of his single-mindedness, blinding him to her true identity. She'd allowed him to seduce her, to kiss her, to *go down on her,* all while knowing he had no idea who she was.

That not only made him feel completely daft, it pissed him off.

Was it an act of revenge? A plot against him? Had he done or said something to her in the past he didn't recall?

He pulled on his boxer briefs and rounded to her side of the bed, flicking on the bedside lamp. In the warm ambient light, Drew squeezed her eyes tighter in protest at the rude awakening.

She hadn't seen anything yet.

She reached for the sheet to cover her face, but Reid yanked it away, instantly regretting it. Her naked body was a beautiful sight and his cock, which didn't mind being misled, twitched in definitive interest.

Dammit. He concealed her beneath the sheet and snapped his fingers in front of her face.

Her eyes burst open, glazed and hazy with sleep before those sensual, full lips pulled into a crooked smile. She was gorgeous, but she was also a siren of the worst kind. She'd led him into the rocks. Tricked him. *Seduced* him.

She was gorgeous, all right.

A gorgeous *liar.*

Eight

Her night with Reid rolled over her like the tide sweeping the shore. It crashed into her with the ferocity of four—*count 'em, four!*—orgasms, and swept away memories of every lonely night spent bingeing sad movies and eating popcorn and feeling sorry for herself over stupid Chef Whatshisname. All that was left was Reid. Beautiful, charming, sexy Reid, who'd made love to her thoroughly... and was now waking her up abruptly.

She couldn't dredge up enough anger to take him to task for it, even though the bright bedside lamp was overkill.

"What time is it?" her morning voice croaked. She re-opened one eye to focus on him, expecting to find his charming smirk or affable half smile. Instead, he was glowering at her from his full height.

"A bit after four."

Mmm. She could listen to him talk all day in that yummy British lilt.

"Drew."

"Why on earth are you waking me up at four? We don't have to report to the display floor until—"

Drew.

He'd called her Drew.

Shit on a shingle. He *knew*. Wide-awake now, she sat up, her earlier explanations and justifications sounding lame even to her sleep-clogged brain.

She was so stupid for believing that she could not only pull the wool over his eyes but knit him a complete sweater out of it. Dumb. Dumb, dumb, *dumb*.

"Listen, I can explain." She sat up and pushed her hair off her forehead, the sheet falling to her lap. He jerked the blanket up to cover her. Oh, right, she was naked. She clutched the blankets to her chest, guilt weighing her down.

"You said your name was Christina," he bit out through clenched teeth.

"Actually… I didn't say that. I wore Christina's name tag and you assumed—"

"You let me assume!" His voice was a thunderclap of anger, his hands righteously propped on his hips. "You never thought to mention you were my best friend's younger sister all grown up?"

"Don't lecture me, Singleton!" she snapped, the warm and cozy bliss from great sex and deep sleep now fully shaken off. "Was I so easily overlooked you had no idea who I was? Even as we had sex and talked and looked into each other's eyes?"

"You wanted to be called *love*." His tone was so lethal she winced.

"I know. I didn't want you shouting out Christina be- cause it'd make me feel weird since she's my roommate."

A muscle in his jaw ticked, and she wished it would've

made him the slightest bit less attractive so that she could stay angry with him. Sadly, it only made him look hotter.

He turned and walked out and her guilt tripled, even as she admired his sexy backside shifting this way and that in his black boxer briefs.

"Crap." She reached to the floor and found her panties and slipped them on. And since her gold shirt was about the least comfortable item of clothing on the planet, she rummaged through a drawer and grabbed one of Reid's white T-shirts. She pulled it over her head, unable to keep from lifting the soft cotton to her nose for a laundry-commercial worthy sniff. Then she ventured out to find him.

He stood at the window, stone silent, his back to the room.

"How'd you figure out who I was?" she asked, her voice small.

Reid didn't turn around. One deep breath lifted his wide shoulders, then one more before he finally answered her.

"Australia," he said. Strangely.

"Australia?"

"Your birthmark." He peeked over his shoulder at her, one eyebrow winging skyward. "Behind your breast."

Right. Her birthmark. "Oh. That."

"Yeah, *that*. Australia and grape jelly in color."

"I always thought of it as raspberry."

Shirtless, thick forearms arms crossed over his chest, Reid was imposing and inviting all at once. The bump in his boxers was at half-mast, large enough that her gaze snagged on it for a beat longer than appropriate.

"Drew."

"Sorry." She rerouted her eyes to find his expression less ragey than before. Then she thought about what she was saying and how she was acting. Shame-filled, apologetic, guilty. That was the old Drew.

Old Drew had since transformed her life, her body, her *very being* to become who she was today. She wasn't going to let Reid take that away from her. Not after they'd shared the most intimate act between them.

"No. You know what? I'm not sorry. You had no complaints about my name, or my breasts or the incredible sex we had a few hours ago. I'm not going to apologize for rocking your world."

His expression showed a dash of chagrin. *Good.*

"The truth is if you had known it was me, you never would've taken me to bed!"

"You're damn right."

Ouch. She'd expected that, but still didn't like hearing it.

"What did I do?"

She blinked, confused. "Huh?"

He took a step toward her, and then another until they were toe-to-toe and she had to incline her chin to look up at him. He asked that strange question again, enunciating each word. "What did I do?"

"I don't follow."

"To you? What did I do to you that you wanted to exact revenge on me? How did you know I was going to be here? Do you spy on Monarch Consulting? Did you ask Gage my whereabouts? This isn't going to end well when he finds out, Drew, you have to know that."

She let out an exhalation of disbelief and a laugh of pure derision followed. "Oh…my gosh. You think this was about you." His turn to look confused. "You self-centered—" She poked him in the chest to make her *literal* point.

"Hey."

"—egomaniacal—" *Poke.*

"Hey!"

"—selfish bastard!" A third poke in the center of his breastbone had him swatting her away, only he held on to her hand, refusing to let go. "You think I did this *to you*? You think I held some revenge fantasy in my head so that I could take advantage of you nine years later? Maybe you think I lost weight for you. Dyed my hair for you. Arranged for my roommate to have to flu so I could pretend to be her, *just to get to you*!"

She succeeded in freeing herself from his hold. She sniffled, angry that she'd let her emotions overcome her. Angrier that tears were building behind her eyes. Well, those tears would have to wait, because she wasn't done being pissed off at Reid "I'm Every Woman's Reason for Getting Up in the Morning" Singleton.

"You weren't a target, Reid. I did this for me. I used to have a crush on you so big it nearly took my knees out from under me. And the handful of times I saw you after, that bolt of attraction returned. But I was too young, or too overweight—"

"Drew—"

"Shut up, I'm not done." Unwaveringly, she held his gaze, daring him to interrupt. He pressed his lips into a firm line and let her finish. "I was too young, or too overweight, or too short to grab your attention back then. But not tonight." Her smile returned when she remembered him noticing her. "Tonight you were watching me. You said you noticed my shoes first. You bought me a drink and you flirted with me. And then you brought me here and—"

"I *know* what happened." He held up a palm to stay her words.

"Was it that bad for you? Because for me, it was…" Vulnerability was not her strong suit, but here she went. "It was really great."

He surprised her by tucking his hand under her jaw and pegging her with a glare that rivaled the one he wore when he woke her up.

"How could you ask me that? You know how it was for me. You were there." His voice gentled.

"I knew you'd say no. That's why I didn't tell you my name. I had one chance for you to see me as someone other than Gage's little sister, and I took it." She shrugged. "I was going to tell you the truth in the morning. I thought I'd wake up before you did. I didn't know you'd knock me out with a four-pack of orgasms."

His rough laugh startled her as much as his fingers playing in her hair.

"I guess I didn't do as good a job of knocking you out since you were awake first," she said.

He dipped his chin, leveling her with an authoritative look. "I woke up ready to do it again. I was debating whether or not four a.m. was too early to wake you for another round."

Her "oh" was a startled puff of air. Round two sounded… wonderful. "Okay. I accept."

His headshake was subtle, but no less disappointing. But she could work with subtle.

"The conference lasts another four days. If we—"

"*No.* Are you aware that I see your brother each and every day at work? If he found out—"

"You think I'm anxious to tell Gage about who I'm sleeping with? I don't need his permission and neither do you. Unless you took some oath I'm not aware of not to date me I don't see the problem."

There it was. That smirk she found stupidly attractive. And since he'd given her an inch, she continued her side of the argument.

"I know you're not looking for anything permanent—trust me, after my last boyfriend, neither am I." She rested a hand on Reid's naked chest.

"Drew." He put his hand over hers. "We can't."

"Why not? Do you regret it?" A second passed. Two. Three. *Four.* "Tell me why we can't take off the clothes we're wearing right now and have sex like we did earlier. Tell me why we can't, and I promise I'll get dressed, leave and I won't bother you for the rest of the conference. Or ever again."

Part of her screamed in protest, but she wouldn't accept pity sex, especially from Reid. If he regretted sleeping with her that much, they'd be better off chalking last night up as a onetime thing. She'd have the memory of the best sex ever, and that would be enough.

That would *have to* be enough.

Nine

How could he look into Drew's warm coffee-brown eyes and lie? He couldn't. Even though he should. He should tell her that having sex with her was a mistake not to be repeated, and that while she didn't have to avoid him entirely, any physical endeavors between them were well and truly off.

He should tell her the reason *why* was because he wasn't a good guy for her to waste her time with. He should tell her that Gage was too good a friend to lie to, even by omission.

He *should*.

She was delicate swimming in his white T-shirt that covered her panties and hung low on her arms. Her eyes turned up to him in open vulnerability, and *dammit*, he couldn't lie to her. She siphoned the truth out of him like a needle in a vein.

"I don't have a good reason why," he admitted. "And no, I don't regret it. I was surprised when I saw that birthmark. I didn't recognize you last night, which made me feel daft. I should throw you out on principle alone," he added sternly.

She tucked her chin and batted her lashes, peering up at him with wide, doe-like eyes. That made her look like a naughty schoolgirl he'd like to take over his knee. It'd be no less than she deserved.

"But if I threw you out," he told her, gripping her nape, "I'd never again have the chance to do this—" He kissed her, sliding his tongue along hers and tasting that familiar-but-not flavor he'd become acquainted with. "And I want to do that again, Drew." He studied her carefully. "Or do you prefer to be called 'love'?"

"I prefer Drew." Her cheeks grew pink, lust darkening her widening pupils.

He lifted the hem of the T-shirt she wore and tossed it aside, taking a moment to admire those lush breasts begging for his tongue. He gave in to their plea, kissing the rosy buds as she moaned in his ear and tickled his scalp.

Hand between her legs, he pressed his fingers against her silky panties to find her damp and ready for him. "That didn't take long."

A sharp yank drew his head back, and he was facing Drew Fleming's wrath, her eyes twin pools of dark chocolate, her pursed, full lips determined. "You still have to work for it."

"Do I?" He loved teasing her. He'd enjoyed it last night, and he found himself looking even more forward to it in spite of knowing her true identity. She wasn't a one-night stand; she was someone he knew. Someone he shouldn't be with. *Forbidden*.

As much as he desired connection and release for himself, he craved her release even more. Craved those heady sounds of satisfaction as he gave her exactly what she wanted. Craved hearing his name roll off her lips, and saying her name as he lost himself inside her.

Her *real* name.

Propelling her backward, he walked her to the nearest wall and pressed her against it.

"Oh, back where we started," she said playfully.

"Yes, except this time we're doing everything against this wall. Later, if you like, we can have another round on that chair." He tipped his head to gesture to the chair sitting adjacent to the sofa. "And then over there on that kitchenette counter, or maybe the bathroom counter."

A flare of excitement widened her eyes.

"Bathroom counter, then?"

"What?" She blinked like she hadn't expected him to say that.

"You seemed excited by the prospect of the bathroom counter." He quickly carried her to the bathroom, plopping her onto the smooth marble surface. Only one sink, so the length of the counter was wide open for other endeavors. "I'm here to serve."

He smoothed his fingers from her neck to the valley between her breasts, purposely avoiding touching her exposed nipples. "Why did you like the idea of the bathroom, Drew?"

He suspected why, but he wanted to hear her say it. By everything she'd told him he could guess that she'd had a few fantasies that hadn't been sufficiently exceeded. He meant to change that.

"Um." Those cheeks went pink again before a nervous laugh parted her beautiful mouth. Just when he thought he'd have to tickle the answer out of her, she said, "Because of the mirror."

"You'd like to look in the mirror during?"

"Don't sound so shocked. Look at you. Like I wouldn't want to watch while we're…you know."

Could she be more darling? With all that dark hair coasting over her shoulders and her eye makeup slightly smudged, she was girl-next-door sexy with a million curves he wanted to road test at every possible speed. Breakneck, stop-and-go, snail's-pace slow…

"That's where you've got it wrong. You're the one to look at in that scenario." He slipped off her panties and discarded his boxers, helping her off the counter. He turned her to face the mirror. The lighting was bright and revealing, and the more he saw, the more he wanted. "Is it any wonder I was too gobsmacked to recognize who you were? Look at you."

He smoothed her narrow shoulders with his palms, slid over her biceps and took her hands in his. He held her arms to her side, and watched as her breasts lifted, the perfect quarter-sized nipples puckering in the cool air streaming in from the AC vent. From there he traced his hands along her ribs until she giggled and clasped his hands in hers.

"I wondered if I'd have to tickle that answer out of you earlier, and here you are, *ticklish*."

"Don't use that against me, okay?"

"Never," he lied, kissing her cheek as he clasped both her wrists behind her. "Now, where were we?"

He smoothed his hands over her belly, and she winced. "Not there."

"Why not? I like this part." Her belly wasn't completely flat, which he adored. Her curves were what he'd found most attractive. "I like how you feel against me."

He cupped her between her legs, gentling her open and swiping a finger along her seam. Kissing her ear, he watched her in the mirror. Her eyes were closed, her breasts heaving with her breaths, her mouth open in a pre-orgasmic O.

Bloody gorgeous—he was a lucky bastard.

He continued stroking and talking while she dissolved against him.

"I like all your soft bits against me. The soft and the hard make for great contrasts." He let go of her wrists and bumped her full bottom with his erection. She moaned her approval.

With one hand he increased the slick friction between her legs while toying with her nipple with the other. Then he offered a quick bite to her earlobe and breathed into her ear, "Drew. Open your eyes."

She obeyed Reid's command, and her gaze clashed with his in the mirror. She was surrounded by his tanned, broad form and thick shoulders. His fingers, dark against her pale skin, moved between her legs, and with each upward stroke she had to resist standing on her toes. She didn't know if she wanted more pressure or less. If she should ease away from the sensation or lean into it. He was too fantastic—too beautiful. Too…everything.

"My God, look at you."

He kept saying that, and as much as she wanted to stare at his perfect beauty, she obeyed his command and looked at herself. At her flushed face and neck, at the rosy nipples, one of which was being plucked lazily by the man behind her. At her hips and belly she'd never quite been able to rid herself of, damn her love of bread.

"You're perfect," he whispered.

"I've already agreed to sleep with you. You don't have to seduce me." She released a nervous laugh.

Reid straightened behind her, taking his tantalizing

touch with him when he went. His face was an unreadable mask.

"What happened?"

"You think I'm lying?"

"Not exactly. I think you're being nice, and I was letting you know you don't have to be." She gave him a brittle smile. He took one final look at her and left the room. Left!

Before she could follow him out, he returned, condom in hand. He tore the packet open with his teeth, sheathed himself and returned his gaze to the mirror. She was forced to regard their reflections to meet eyes with him.

"I—"

"Do you want to have sex with me, Drew?"

"Of course."

"Do you want to have sex with me in front of this mirror… *Drew*?"

"Yes."

"While we have sex in front of this mirror, I will tell you how beautiful every part of you is while we do it, is that understood?"

His commanding tone excited her as much as the promise. She'd never been great at admitting she was beautiful or desirable. She'd never been that great at sex with the lights on. But she wanted to be different and she wanted Reid, and what he was offering was bold and inviting. It was exactly what she craved. Her entire body vibrated with *yes* at his offer.

"Understood."

"You have the most beautiful ass." He grabbed a handful of her butt, and she stood to her toes. At the same time, he bent his knees, lining himself up with her slick center. "Say yes, Drew."

She gave him a sweet smile in the mirror. "Yes, Drew."

"Cheeky." He notched into her, and she gasped in anticipation. She didn't have to wait long to feel the rest of him. He slid in deep, each rocking motion slow and intentional, and the entire time he praised a different part of her body that he liked.

He held her chin and kept his gaze on hers, his voice turning her on and filling a deep cavern she hadn't known existed until just now.

This time with Reid was bold. It was different. It was *amazing*. And when he came, it was her name—*her real name*—that fell from his lips on a harsh growl.

Ten

"The Bachelor *What*?" Drew rolled and faced him in bed, the sheet slipping down revealing those luscious breasts, and everything Reid had been saying flew right from his head.

One finger on his jaw, she turned his head to hers meaningfully. "You really are a boob guy."

"I happen to like breasts, yes, and yours happen to be a very fine pair." Unable to help himself, he cradled one and tested its weight, brushing his thumb over the nipple for the sheer joy of watching it pebble in reaction. "They're magical."

"Uh-huh. Anyway. The bachelor thing…"

"Pact. The Bachelor Pact. Gage, Flynn and I agreed never to marry, swore on our—" He thought of what they'd sworn on and decided against sharing. Swearing on their dicks sounded immature at best and sadistic at worst. "We swore an oath not to abandon the others. And then they all abandoned me and left me the only man standing. Wankers."

"I love that word." She grinned. "I can't believe Gage is engaged…again. I didn't know about the pact, but it doesn't surprise me that he entered into such an agreement. I never thought he'd marry after the way his ex left him."

"We all have our sad stories."

She hummed in her throat, her eyes darting away. She'd hinted at her own sad story earlier but now didn't feel like the time to bring it up. His eyes slid to the alarm clock on the nightstand. The symposium opened at 9:30 a.m., and it was half past six now. Closer and closer to the time for them to pack up and hustle to work for the day.

"When do you need to go back to your floor?"

"My *floor*? I only wish I were staying at this glam hotel. I'm in the terra-cotta-colored flophouse across the street. It has three floors and the elevator is busted. My roommate evidently has a cheap boss. Unlike you."

He didn't like hearing that she had to schlep across the street and then back again. "I'll walk you over."

"Don't be ridiculous." With the tip of her finger, she *booped* his nose like she might a kitten's. "But that's sweet, thanks."

He snatched up her hand. "I wasn't being sweet. I was being protective, and it wasn't a question. *I'll walk you over.*"

He could've done without the eye roll.

"Fine."

He took advantage of her nearness to press a kiss to her lips. She lingered and he let her, and when they pulled apart he grunted in protest.

"I don't have that much time, Romeo. I can pull myself together fast, but not fast enough for another hour-long *sex*travaganza."

He enjoyed listening to her talk. The words she used, the unabashed way she complimented him.

"*Fine*. We'll talk instead. Tell me about your job. Your real job when you're not moonlighting as your roommate." He raised an eyebrow, and she beamed at him. Gorgeous girl.

"I'm the go-to public relations guru for Fig & Truffle restaurants. They have several local Seattle chains, and I'm in charge of running their soft openings, interviewing chefs to design their menus and a bunch of other stuff you'd find boring."

He didn't find her boring. He found her fascinating. "What's involved in a soft opening?"

"Well, it's when the restaurant is staffed, the menus finalized, the kitchen staff hired. Everyone is green and not quite ready for prime time. They hold a soft opening for friends and family so that the staff can practice, and then sometimes they'll do one for industry, like food critics. After that, the restaurant will open to the public, hopefully with a long line wrapped around the block."

"And you bustle around making sure everything is in place?"

"Pretty much. But it always is. I'm incredibly organized and meticulous."

He could envision her now, dressed in a sleek black dress, that dark hair pinned up in a fancy twist, her high-heeled shoes in place, her jewelry and makeup just so. In charge and confident in her abilities. A confidence that was newly won. From what he remembered of Drew when she was younger, she'd mostly hid her face from him.

"You're thinking something you're afraid will be rude to say." She squinted at him. "I can tell."

"I'm not."

"You are. Go on. Ask."

"It's not a question, more an observation. You've changed is all."

"Yes. I lost a lot of weight."

"That's not what I was thinking about."

Genuine surprise colored her features. "Really?"

"Really. I was remembering how shy you used to be, and now you're this bold, beautiful, confident creature who clearly gets what she wants when she wants it." He gestured to himself. "Look at me. I said we were done, and you've convinced me otherwise."

"It didn't take much convincing."

He kissed the smile off her lips and stole a glance at the clock. "I think we can fit in one more round and still have you ready in time. Especially with a capable escort chaperoning you to your hotel and back again."

Her eyes sparkled, a thousand yeses twinkling in their depths.

He parted her legs and climbed over her, staring down at Drew Fleming. How had he never looked this closely at her? Granted, he'd only seen her a handful of times, but how had he overlooked her slightly crooked smile, her infectious laugh, the alluring way she said his name...

"I should've known it was you," he told her.

"It's okay. I'm different."

"Yes, but I don't recall how you were before, short of a few sparse details. I should've paid more attention."

She twined her fingers into his hair. "Hmm. How could you possibly make it up to me?"

"I don't know that I can." He kissed one breast and then the other. "But I'm damn sure going to try."

Drew had spent so long in bed with Reid this morning, they'd been late to the symposium. He'd dropped her off at her booth, handing over the leather bag that he'd insisted on carrying for her. Then he'd kissed her sweetly before jogging to his own booth.

She'd set up with a smile on her face and her head in the clouds. She still couldn't believe that she'd spent the night with Reid Singleton, or that she was going to spend another night with him. He'd told her in her room—after agreeing that it was as subpar as she'd described—that he'd like to see her again tonight. She should've played coy or hard to get, but she'd blurted "Absolutely!" before she'd thought better of it.

The hours passed slowly, the crowds slower than yesterday. That gave her time to daydream, and she had plenty of fantasy fodder after what she'd spent the night and this morning doing with Reid. About fifteen minutes before she could close her booth, Drew began putting small things away to save herself time, like business cards and plush squishy balls with Christina's company's name on them. Her phone vibrated on the counter as she bent to toss the squishies into a cabinet.

"Hello, Christina," she said with a smile as she put the phone to her ear.

"Hello, Christina Two," her roommate said.

"You sound better. Out of the woods?"

"Eh. I managed to shower and heat a can of soup, but my energy level isn't great. Couch and TV are the only activities on my agenda."

"If that what it takes to get better, do it!"

"Are you ready to choke me yet for sending you to the symposium in my stead?" Christina let out a rattling cough, and Drew bristled in sympathy.

"Of course not. Plus you didn't *send* me, I practically begged to come." She debated for a full half a second before deciding to broach the topic of Reid. Christina didn't know him, and Drew needed someone to talk to. "I ran into someone I knew from a long time ago, so it hasn't been that bad."

Ha! Understatement of the millennium. Not only was her evening "not bad" it was so good it needed its own category.

"Anyone I know?"

"No. Friend of my brother's. His name's Reid."

"Whoa." Christina's cough sounded distant, like she'd held the phone away from her face. "Sorry about that," she groaned, and then sniffed. "As I was saying before my case of tuberculosis rudely interrupted: *whoa.*"

She loved her friend's sense of humor. "'Whoa' what?"

"Your voice went all breathy when you said 'Reid,' only I can't do it because I sound like Stevie Nicks right now. Let's hear it. What happened?"

"Well, he...he thought I was you."

Silence.

"I don't mean that he thought I was *you* you. He didn't recognize me at the mixer and kept calling me 'Christina.'" She recapped Reid's flirting with her and how she hadn't corrected him when he assumed she was someone else. "And then I sort of...kissed him and agreed to go to his room. Which is a hell of a lot nicer than yours, by the way. You tell your boss the next time—"

"Drew Marie Fleming!" Christina exclaimed, probably using the last of her energy reserves. "You saucy tart!"

Drew shushed her friend and drew a curious glance from her booth neighbor across the aisle.

"Did he figure out your true identity?"

"Yes. He did. Sadly, before I told him. I was asleep... after, and he recognized my birthmark."

"Ah, rookie move, Fleming. You should've hidden that with makeup before taking him up to his room to blow his mind. Oh my God! I'm still in shock. Tell me everything. How was he? Are you seeing him again? How mad was he, or is he still mad?"

"I'd love to linger, but I'm about to close the booth for the day and I promised I'd meet him for dinner."

"That answers that. Oh, honey. You owe me so many details. And I owe you for going for me. Name it. Want me to cover your half of the rent this month?"

"You don't owe me. As good as last night was, and as promising as tonight is, I'm the one who owes you."

"That makes me happy." Christina's smile could be felt through the phone. "You deserve good things, Drew."

Drew teared up a little at that. She did deserve good things. And Reid was a very, very good thing. "Talk later, babe. Get well."

"Bye, hon."

She pocketed her cell phone and made quick work of clearing out the booth. After an arduously long day of boring tech talk, Drew was ready for a cocktail. She locked the expensive projector and other technological wonders for her display into the cabinet. Then she headed into the melee of hardworking men and women who had staffed their company's booths, and who all looked equally ready for a cocktail.

She found a sign in the aisle with a map of company names and booth numbers. Monarch Consulting, both three-zero-three, was one aisle over from where she stood now. She wandered past booths that were either empty or quickly emptying, and spotted Reid bent over a counter chatting with a prospective client...

At least she hoped the lithe, leggy redhead talking to him was a prospective client.

Eleven

Drew ducked behind a plant to watch Reid laugh and charm the redheaded woman. Even from the back she seemed pretty, in a well-fitting pair of pants and a shirt. And she was tall, which was something Drew would never be no matter how much she worked out.

She self-consciously smoothed a hand over her floral skirt. She'd paired the slim skirt with a bright pink top and gold jewelry, her heels gold and glittery. Reid had commented on how she liked to sparkle when she'd slipped them on. He'd been sitting on her ugly olive-green-and-pink bedspread in her room and she'd remarked how he looked good in everything—even the hotel's putrid decor.

And now that dazzling smile and his full attention were turned on another woman.

Memories of being with Chef Devin Briggs crashed onto her like a stack of toppling boxes. When he'd pitched the idea of them traveling the world together, she'd been intrigued, but also wary. She loved her job and living close to her family and wasn't ready to give either one up. Heck, she had her job to thank for meeting Devin—who'd she'd called to design the menu for Parity, a swanky café downtown.

She'd told him she wasn't ready. He told her he should've known better than to date someone "so immature" who didn't take life "seriously."

They broke up that night, and his infamous chef's temper she'd seen many times in the test kitchen made its final appearance. Only two weeks passed before he found Drew's replacement. Last she'd heard Devin and his new wife were opening a restaurant in France.

Even though Drew knew Devin was a selfish ass and turning him down had been the right call, getting dumped stung. When she'd heard he was "in love" via mutual friends at work, she'd felt replaceable and worthless.

As she watched Reid flirt with a woman the way he'd flirted with Drew last night, jealousy blazed brighter than ever. She stepped out from behind the decorative plant, determined to tell him exactly where he could shove that thousand-watt smile.

Screw this. Screw *him*.

Reid spotted her and straightened from his lean, his smile fading. The slender woman—in a pressed pair of black slacks and a blue silk shirt—turned, her smile catching, as well.

Drew stopped dead in her tracks, blinking in shock at the redhead. "Andy?"

"Drew!" Andrea Payne jogged over and scooped Drew into a hug. Andy was Gage's fiancée, Drew's future sister-in-law. She could kick herself for not recognizing the other woman's unique shade of strawberry blond.

"I'm so relieved that it's you. I thought…" Drew flashed a glance at a bemused Reid before pasting a smile on her face for Andy. "Never mind what I thought. What are you doing here?"

"I was hired to help a company across the street, and I saw the symposium signs. I thought I'd come say hi to Reid. Gage didn't mention you were going to be here." She frowned in confusion. "If I'd known I would've taken you to lunch."

"Thanks a lot." Reid folded his arms over his chest. "You barely fit me in five seconds before closing time, but Drew you'd treat to lunch."

"I like her more than I like you." Andy smiled sweetly at Reid, then turned to Drew. "So? What gives?"

"My roommate has the flu, and I offered to stand in for her." Drew pointed at her name badge that read "Christina" before removing it and tucking it into her purse.

"Did you know she was here?" Andy asked Reid.

"I saw her at a mixer last night. We, um…chatted."

"Reid and I haven't seen each other for years. He didn't recognize me." Drew liked having sharing a secret with Reid, but Andy's being here made playing with fire feel more like playing with a live grenade.

So much for her brother not finding out Drew was in California at the same time as Reid.

"I wish I could take you both to dinner, but I have to get back to my client. What a fun coincidence." Andy cocked her head at Drew. "Where's your booth?"

"One aisle and three booths over." Drew pointed to the general direction of where she'd spent the day.

"What are you doing in this aisle? Did you two have plans or something?"

"Yes," Reid said. "I offered to buy Drew dinner in retribution for not recognizing her, so that's where we're headed."

"That was…thoughtful." Andy's blue eyes broadcast her

suspicion, but then she blinked and it vanished like it'd never been there. "Well, I should go. Drew, great seeing you."

"You, too."

Andy whisked away, and Reid slipped his laptop into his bag, whistling as he locked up his booth with quick efficiency.

"Do you think she figured us out?" Drew murmured, eyes glued to the aisle where Andy had vanished.

"Do I think she saw us here, outside the Monarch booth, and assumed we spent the night in various stages of nakedness interspersed with champagne and bathroom counter sex? No. I do not think she figured us out."

Drew opened her mouth to tell him his smart-ass comments weren't appreciated, but he grabbed her and kissed her soundly before she could. She fisted his button-down shirt to shove him away but then ended up pulling him in as she enjoyed the firm feel of his lips on hers.

Mmm. He was addicting.

He ended the kiss and dropped another brief peck on the center of her mouth. "Now, if I'd done *that*, I do think she'd have suspected something. Also, what'd you mean when you told her you were relieved it was her? Who did you think I was talking with?"

"No one."

"Drew."

"I like when you say my name in ecstasy, but not in that scolding tone."

He reminded silent. *Waiting.*

Dammit.

"My ex didn't waste any time hooking up with someone else after our breakup, okay?" She lifted her arms and dropped them at her sides again.

"No. It's not okay."

"You're right. It's not. After that, I spent a lot of time

believing I'm replaceable. I guess seeing you turn your flirt-o-meter up to eleven made me a little…concerned."

His eyebrows rose. "You mean jealous."

"*Concerned*. For myself."

"Mmm-hmm."

"Take that smirk off your face, Singleton, or I'll remove it for you."

"Promises, promises." He nuzzled her nose with his, the scent of his cologne tickling her senses and doing a good job of making her forget why she was upset.

"Did you decide on what to have for dinner?" He released her, and she missed being in his arms instantly.

That wasn't good.

She'd have to figure out how to have a casual affair since she'd never had one before. The trick would be walking away without developing feelings for Reid. And now, thanks to Andy's surprise visit, she'd also have to practice not looking as guilty when her brother inevitably brought up her running into Reid.

"Italian? Indian? Burgers and fries?" The man occupying her thoughts ducked into view, and she realized she'd spaced out for a second.

"Wherever is fine."

He shook his head. "You're a foodie. 'Wherever' is not fine."

Okay, he had a point. She wasn't sure it was a good idea to go to dinner with him, especially since she knew she'd end up in his bed afterward. But he was so…*yummy*. Plus she liked that he was standing there waiting for her answer, like what she said would alter the course of his evening. That kind of power was heady.

"Masala is good, and it's four blocks from here. We can walk. I need to drop off my stuff at my room first. Meet you there?"

"Meet me there? Good God, woman, who besides that asshole chef have you been dating? I'll take your things up to my room. We can walk together." He gestured for her leather bag. "I was thinking about how inconveniently located your room is from here. Why not stay with me for the remainder of the conference?"

"Wh-what?"

"You heard me. I have plans for us. You're not going to be in your room anyway. Just check out on Sunday and Christina's boss will be none the wiser. We've agreed to spend these days together, so might as well spend them *together*."

Everything sounded so good when he said it. Even— *gulp*—what translated loosely into moving in together. A little prickle of concern tickled the back of her mind, but she shoved it away. Staying in the same hotel room with Reid wasn't the same as embarking on a yearlong relationship destined to end in disaster. When Sunday came, they'd return to their separate lives in the same big city and everything would go back to the way it was before they slept together. She'd see to it.

Just because she'd had a Devin Briggs flashback a few minutes ago was no reason not to have fun with Reid. Besides, they were nothing alike. Reid didn't have OCD, wasn't temper-prone and didn't order her around. She didn't count his insisting on walking her to her hotel, or the sexy, commanding tone he'd used when they were having sex in front of the mirror. That was more about him taking care of her needs than throwing his weight around.

"Masala it is," Reid said. "I'll run your bag upstairs."

"I'll come with you."

"Oh, you will, will you?"

"I'd like to move my legs. Other than fetching a sandwich from the food cart, I haven't had a chance to raise my heart rate."

"Love, I can think of many more fun ways to raise your heart rate." He sent her a foxy wink, shouldering her bag as they walked to the elevators.

He wasn't wrong. That wink alone had elevated her heart rate better than power walking or taking the stairs.

"But you can't seduce me yet," he told her as they stepped into the elevator. "I deserve a nice night out, I've been stuck in my room since I arrived. I won't let you keep me there like some kind of sex slave."

"Me?" she asked as the doors swished shut. "You were the one who was all 'my room or yours.'"

"First, I do not sound like that."

He didn't. Her British accent was rubbish.

"Second, I want to talk. We've a lot of history to catch up, you and me." He winked again. So sexy.

"What if Andy sees us?" she asked, her concern returning.

"It's a big city. Plus I wasn't planning on shagging on the table when we went out."

She snorted.

"Do you always snort when you laugh?" He smiled at her, and she realized that she really liked when he smiled at her. There was something possessive behind it, and yet that possession didn't make her feel smothered.

"That was embarrassing, and you pointed it out."

"It was embarrassing? I thought it was cute."

"*Cute*. I hate that word."

The doors opened, and he held them for her to step out. "Why?"

"It's nothing." In the corridor, she turned the direction of his suite.

"Might as well tell me. I'll find out for sure now that I know you're ticklish." He swiped his key card and opened his hotel room door to reveal a room tidier than they'd left it. The maid must've been in. Reid dumped his bag and hers onto the couch.

"Why do you hate the word *cute*?"

She shrugged one shoulder. She didn't exactly relish revealing her vulnerabilities. But again, something told her she was safe in sharing them with Reid.

"I…don't ever remember being told I was beautiful until you said it last night."

"I see." His mouth pulled into a deep frown. "So you've not only dated assholes, but blind ones."

"Kind of. Yes."

"Well, let me be the first to dispel this ridiculous notion." He tucked her hair behind her ear—a sweet gesture she was finding to be uniquely his. "Cute and beautiful are not mutually exclusive. You're honestly one of the most beautiful women I've had the pleasure of knowing, and I don't only mean because you have breasts that make me want to weep with joy."

"Boob guy," she accused.

"Guilty." His serious expression didn't waver. "But you're also damn cute. And if you believed that 'cute' was an insult when I said it before, I apologize and ask that you don't hold that against me now." He pulled her into the circle of his arms. "Your boobs, however, I encourage you to hold against me as often as possible."

She couldn't resist kissing him for that, and when he kissed her back and she melted into him, she knew she was going to break her promise of going out.

They were definitely ordering room service tonight.

Twelve

"How about this one?" Christina held up a frilly-necked shirt.

"Hmm. Not doing it for me." Drew continued sliding the hangers on the rack in search of…she didn't know what.

She'd returned home to Seattle from California on Sunday and now was shopping for her next soft opening. It was happening next week for a sushi restaurant named Soo-She.

She wanted to be prepared with the right outfit for the swanky and minimalist restaurant. The food ranged from traditional raw fish sashimi to inventive new options made with grilled chicken, pork and even steak. There was a lot of buzz surrounding the restaurant because of its unique style—including several VIP floating islands and an open kitchen format that encouraged interaction with the chefs.

Drew was searching for a shirt that complemented the restaurant: noticeable and minimalist. One that made her stand out in case the staff needed to flag her down, but also professional. A shimmery silver blouse caught her eye on the wall, and she was pulled toward it as if by a tractor beam.

"That's the one," she said. "I can pair it with my knee-length slim black skirt and my Choos."

"It suits you. Sparkly and fun." Christina plucked the hanger from its station and flipped over the price tag. "Also, fussily expensive."

"It doesn't matter how expensive it is. I'm buying it." Drew draped the shirt over her arm. "Along with jewelry. I'm thinking a row of silver bangles."

"I'm so jealous of your style. I wish I had somewhere fancy to go." Christina pushed out her bottom lip. Drew had always thought of Chris as pretty, from the moment they'd met last year at the soft opening for the Fig & Truffle on Smithfield. Christina was a waitress at the time, and Drew had been drawn to her take-no-crap attitude. Her friend's style had changed since then. Christina had lost the ponytail, her light brown hair now short and sassy. She favored slacks and striped blouses, and never was without her favorite accessory: a red belt.

"You *do* have somewhere fancy to go. You're coming to the opening of Soo-She, right?"

"Alone?"

"I'll be there!"

"You'll be too busy to babysit me. Is anyone else I know going to this friends-and-family soirée that I can sit with?" They stopped at a clearance jewelry section and began rummaging. "What about Reid?"

"What *about* Reid?" Drew held a pair of hoop earrings to her ear and examined them in the mirror before deciding they were too large for her face.

"You spent several sweaty nights in the man's arms and now you're never going to see him again?"

Drew gave her reflection a wan smile. The latter part of the week had been like a magical fairy tale. She'd let Reid talk her into moving her luggage to his hotel room, and they'd gone to bed together every night and woken up side by side every morning. That second night they didn't make it out to Masala, choosing room service dinner instead, but on night three they did. They ate some of the best Indian food in the city and laughed over shared stories about Gage and Reid's college years.

She'd had sex with Reid every single night. And each time it was mind-blowing and all-consuming. Each time she mused how easy it would be to fall for him. Then she shut down that possibility before she did something she regretted.

Falling for Reid Singleton wasn't an option.

"It doesn't serve me to continue seeing him," she told Christina matter-of-factly. "He isn't looking for a girlfriend, and I don't have time for a boyfriend."

A white lie. She had time, but there was no sense in entertaining a Reid-boyfriend fantasy if it wasn't going to come to fruition.

Christina pointed at Drew with a studded leather bracelet. "If neither of you wants a future, then it doesn't sound like there is any risk to you sleeping together. All I'm saying is that if I could get laid on the regular without strings, I'd do it."

An older woman with tight gray curls grunted disapprovingly as she wheeled by with her walker.

"Oh, like she never used up a man and spit him out," Christina whispered to Drew. "Look at those legs. I bet she was a pistol."

Laughter shook Drew's shoulders as she held up a necklace to her throat. "This would be cute with your navy-blue-and-white-striped shirt. Look, the pendant is a little anchor."

"And half off. Sold!" Christina snagged the necklace and then tilted her head, a look of patience or pity—or maybe both—on her face. "At least ask him to the soft opening. What could it hurt? Invite him and your brother and his fiancée. Make it a group thing. I can sit with them and then I won't have to go by myself."

"Why don't you ask Jerry from work?"

"No." Christina shook her head fervently. "I'm not dating right now. But I'll be happy to grill Reid for you. Is there any intel you'd like to glean? I'll go undercover."

"I'm not sure he'll agree to come!" Drew protested, but she did so through a smile. She did want to see him again.

"Aha! So you *are* asking him."

"Only because we have seats to fill." Drew slipped a fat, jewel-studded bracelet onto her wrist and forgave herself yet another white lie.

Reid carefully removed the wee cup from the espresso maker, and the surface wobbled dangerously. He sipped the hot liquid from the edge, savoring the coffee he needed more than his next breath. He'd come home from California nearly sexed out and didn't know what to think about that. Not only had he had more sex over the weekend than he'd ever had with one woman in a condensed period of time, but he'd had it with *Drew*.

He'd returned home Sunday night and sent an email to Flynn and Gage letting them know he wouldn't be at the office on Monday. He'd worked from home instead, catching up on email he'd been ignoring. He'd told his friends-slash-coworkers that he was behind because of the mixers and client dinners at the symposium.

The real reason was that he'd spent every spare second over the last weekend-plus in bed with Gage's younger sister.

During the last night they were together Drew had once again sworn Reid to secrecy. She'd brought up the lucid argument that what was done was done and Gage would only worry about her, or worse, lecture her.

"There's a double standard where men are concerned in this sort of arrangement," she'd told him.

He thought it was complete bullshit—to use an American term—and Drew should be able to have sex with whomever she pleased for whatever reason and without judgment. At the same time, Reid also saw the situation through Gage's point of view.

Reid wasn't a cad, but he had taken a vow to stay unwed for the rest of his days. Friends for over a decade, Gage knew Reid better than most. Gage knew Reid's view on serious relationships—*pass*—and Reid's dating habits—frequent and fleeting. Now that Gage had been bitten—nay, *infested*—by the love bug, he might also believe that Drew deserved better than a man who would use her for a few nights of pleasure. Drew meant more to Reid than that, but he didn't care to have that discussion with Gage, either.

Now it was Tuesday, and the email was caught up and Reid couldn't avoid his best friend any longer.

"Morning, Singleton." Gage announced.

Startled, Reid nearly spilled his coffee after all.

"How was vacation?"

"Hardly a vacation." But Reid couldn't deny it'd been every bit as fun as a vacation. Turned out it was impossible to be stressed when he spent every evening bare-ass naked, Drew at his side.

"Andy said Drew was there."

"Was she?"

Gage's face twisted into an expression of disbelief. "Yeah."

So probably Reid shouldn't exaggerate.

"Kidding. Yes, she was there. I didn't recognize her, to be honest. She looked like a different person."

"I talked to her on Monday and she said you thought her name was Christina and that you tried flirting with her." Gage slapped Reid's shoulder, and Reid nearly choked on his coffee. She'd talked to Gage? And she didn't clue Reid in as to what she said?

"She blew me off," Reid said, careful not to put too much of a gap between the words *blew me* and *off*. She'd paid particular attention to that favorite part of his anatomy Saturday night, and he'd not soon forget it.

"She said you took her to dinner, though, which was nice of you. Thanks for that."

"Not like she's a charity case, mate."

"I'm sure you would've rather been out buying drinks for beautiful women than stuck entertaining my little sister."

Incensed, Reid blurted, "Drew *is* beautiful," even as he reasoned that Gage was her brother and didn't look at her the same way.

"Yes," Gage admitted. "She is. I meant I'm sure you would've rather been servicing the greater part of San Diego than hanging out with Drew."

"You say that like she's uninteresting. I found her lovely." *And receptive, responsive, easy to ravish...*

"You're right, I'm a jerk. I sometimes forget she's a grown woman, you know? I look at her and see a teenager. I overlook the fancy clothes and the new hair color and that air of..." Gage gestured for help. "What word am I looking for?"

"Sophistication."

Gage snapped his fingers. "That's the word. Who'd have ever thought my sister, who spent her time coloring her hair weird colors and doodling in her journals, would be sophisticated?" He laughed, bemused by his own observation. "Did she call you yet?"

"What? No. Why? I mean, why would she call me?" *Smooth.*

"Yeah, I guess that would be weird. I gave her your number. She invited Andy and me to a soft opening at some sushi joint on Friday night. Asked if you wanted to come, too."

Oh, really? Reid couldn't stop his smile. Seemed Drew hadn't had her fill of him after all.

"She said her friend Christina would be there. *Alone.*" Gage waggled his eyebrows meaningfully. Under normal circumstances, Reid's ears would've pricked upon hearing of a woman he didn't know.

Gage watched him expectedly.

Right. Reid should probably feign interest. "What does she look like?"

While Gage described Drew's roommate, Reid swapped his espresso for his cell phone. Thought she'd set him up on a date, did she? Not as long as he had something to say about it. "You'd better give me Drew's phone number. So that I know not to screen her call."

Gage rattled off the number without suspicion. And why should he suspect anything? Reid was a family friend, and news of him running into Drew would be as unremarkable as if he'd run into any other platonic friend anywhere in the country.

Except that Drew had transformed into a goddess who'd wooed the knickers off him.

Except for that part.

Thirteen

Drew sprinkled smoked, flaked sea salt on top of a perfectly grill-marked portion of halibut and assessed her handiwork. She screwed her lips to one side as she examined the green and red sauces. *Too much green*, she decided. She should've left more of the square white plate visible. She balanced a bouquet of microgreens on top of the fish and admired her creation anyway.

There was no Chef Devin Briggs in her kitchen to critique her work, but credit where it was due, he'd given her an eye for plating that would serve her well in her career for years to come.

Fork, knife and napkin in hand, she sat at the kitchen table to enjoy her dinner. Christina was out with her girl-friends tonight, and had been polite enough to invite Drew along, but Drew had passed. She needed a night in to recharge after the social melee of the past weekend.

Her cell phone chimed as she forked the first bite into

her mouth. She ignored the text message notification and savored the flavors of her meal. The subtle lemony sauce, the black peppercorns… The chime sounded again, and with a sigh, she dropped her fork.

The first text read: You talked to your brother about us. Followed by: This is Reid btw.

Smiling, she keyed back, Reid who?

Dinner forgotten, she watched the screen for a reply. Two words popped up—Not funny—before the phone rang in her hand. She didn't hesitate for a second.

"Hi," she breathed.

"I'm in the car. Can't text and drive, you know," came Reid's smooth British lilt. Her chest flooded with longing. She'd missed him so much. "You were supposed to call me, Gage said."

"Yes. I was." She ate a bite of fish to stall.

"And invite me on a date with your roommate," he said flatly.

"No, no. Not really." Drew didn't want to think about Reid dating anyone, let alone Christina. The very idea of him kissing another woman made her lose her appetite. "I didn't want him to be suspicious."

"I see. I thought you were sick of me and pawning me off to someone else. I'm not merely a toy to be passed around."

He was joking. She could read him so well now, after just four days together.

"What are you doing after the soft opening?" Reid asked.

"Not much. I typically stick around until the kitchen closes, and then I go home and go to bed. Exciting, I know."

"Are you required to 'stick around until the kitchen closes'?" His voice dipped seductively, and she found herself twirling her hair around one finger as she responded.

"No. My work is done when the guests leave."

"In that case, you can stay the night at my place."

Her heart skipped a beat. Excitement swam through her bloodstream.

"But we were done…after the weekend."

"I've changed my mind."

She bit her lip, a million reasons why she shouldn't be with Reid flickering on the screen inside her head. He was her brother's best friend, and keeping a secret this huge from Gage had already proven challenging. She had no interest in a relationship and neither did Reid, so why continue one? Plus, her brother's wedding next June would be even more awkward if Drew couldn't ignore the crazy, insane chemistry between her and Reid. The smartest tack was to end things now and avoid any sort of romantic entanglement.

But no matter how hard she tried to focus on the future and warn herself of the consequences, the pull to him was too great.

There was only one reason to continue this affair with Reid: because she wanted to.

"Okay," she said. Apparently, that was enough of a reason for her.

"Great. I'll see you on Friday. In the meantime, I have your number and you have mine. So if you're lonesome for me…"

"Reach out?"

"With both hands," he murmured, his accent thick. "Oh, and Drew?"

"Yes?"

"While I'll enjoy unwrapping you no matter what you wear, I really like black lace. Choose your undergarments thoughtfully."

"Yes, sir," she purred.

"Good night, beautiful," he said, and then he was gone.

She ate the rest of her dinner quickly, then grabbed her laptop and glass of wine and curled up on the couch. High-end, sexy lingerie was a click away, and she intended to find the perfect black lace set that would drop Reid's chiseled jaw straight to the floor.

Black lace was itchy.

Or at least the garments she'd purchased were. That's what she got for shopping online for a brand she'd never heard of. Apparently, high price didn't necessarily signify high quality. At the last moment, she'd decided on a slim black dress instead of the shirt she bought for this occasion.

The dress boasted spaghetti straps, perfect since she loved showing off her shoulders and arms. She worked hard keeping them fit. The skirt stopped just above her knee, and her heels were platforms—sturdy so that she wouldn't slip on the kitchen's slick floors—though she would spend most of her time in the dining room, overseeing tables and communicating to the bartenders, busboys and waitstaff.

She loved the restaurant business. There was an anticipatory hum of excitement in the air as everyone from the dishwasher to the hostess focused on the night going smoothly. They were one cohesive unit, working together for a common goal.

It was exhilarating.

The doors opened to a line out front, and one of the hostesses took the invitations required to enter the restaurant as three other hostesses quickly filled the empty tables. Servers bustled over to take drink orders, and bartenders mixed concoctions in metal shakers with as much flair as they could muster.

"Drew," came a sharp whisper over her shoulder. Chris-

tina had shown up early, and Drew seated her at one of the VIP islands that sat four on each side of the chef's station. It was intimate, and in Drew's opinion the best seat in the house. "Are they here yet?"

"I don't think so, but—" Then she saw him. Reid held the door open for Andy and Gage and then stepped in behind them. He was wearing dark slacks that made him seem even taller, a lavender button-down shirt and an eggplant-colored tie. His wavy hair was styled neatly against his head, and you could slice vegetables on that knife-sharp jaw. Her stomach fluttered, and only then did she realize what a bad idea it was to have invited him here. She'd never be able to hide her attraction to him. She was glowing like a neon sign.

"I see Gage!" Christina said excitedly, then, "Oh…my gosh. Drew. *Drew!* Is that him? The guy—the model-looking guy? Is that Reid?"

"That's him." Every wide, tall, capable inch of him was glorious to behold.

Gage pointed in Drew's direction and walked over, and as much as she tried to keep her eyes on Andy's friendly smile, her gaze strayed to Reid. Reid winked at her, his hands in his pockets like he hadn't a care in the world.

She couldn't believe in a few short hours she'd be going home with him. It was heady. It was amazing. It was—

"Hey, sis." Gage pulled her into a hug before turning her over to Andy for another hug. She turned to greet Reid next, but then didn't know what to do. Offering her hand for him to shake seemed formal. He erased the need for her to overthink it as he embraced her gently.

"Drew. Good to see you again," he murmured before placing a kiss on her temple. "You're looking well."

Was it hot in here or was it her? One more look at Reid, and she disagreed with herself. It was him. Most definitely.

"This, uh, this is my roommate, Christina," Drew introduced, and everyone said a quick hello.

"Ah, the *real* Christina. Finally, we meet. Did you know Drew impersonated you to an entire symposium filled with potential clients?" He kissed Christina's hand and she giggled, dissolving like any woman would with Reid's attention squarely on her.

"I begged her to go in my place. I was dying of the plague, but I've made a miraculous recovery."

"I can see that." He held Christina's hand for another beat before letting it go and taking the chair right next to her. Drew frowned, not liking that at all.

"Go do your thing," Gage told her, and then said to the table, "Take a good look at her while you can. When Drew's at these things she's running ninety miles a minute and barely stops to be cordial to the people she knows.

"It's true," Christina agreed. "She has focus like I've never seen. It's like she's powered by the energy surrounding her. I've never seen someone so turned on by food."

Christina didn't mean it in any other way than it sounded, but with Reid smiling at her, all Drew could think about was that once, in her not-so-distant history, she'd been turned on by food exclusively, and in an unhealthy way. What didn't help was that her roommate had never had such a problem.

Christina was narrow and tall, her limbs delicate and graceful. She *barely* worked out and had been blessed with a metabolism that would make any woman jealous. She was also taller than Drew by about four inches, and even in a plain ensemble of slacks, a striped shirt and a red belt, the other woman seemed to *fit* with Reid better than Drew.

At times like these Drew felt as if she were playing dress-up. Like she was faking her success in her new clothes and new hair and new body, and soon the spell would be broken. The clock would strike midnight and she'd transform into the shy, unconfident girl with a bigger waistline. The second that thought walked to the front of her mind, her hard-won confidence flagged.

"I love sushi," Christina told Reid, her smile beaming. "Don't you?"

"I love to eat just about anything," he said with a healthy dose of his typical charm. Christina giggled.

Drew ignored the blaze of jealousy in her chest. She trusted Christina, and being charmed by Reid was inevitable. He was a potent mix of masculine attributes. The man could woo a nun out of her habit.

Drew excused herself and left her friends and her brother to their evening. She had a job to do. Before she disappeared into the kitchen, she stole one final glance over her shoulder.

Reid's eyes were glued to Christina.

Fourteen

Christina, on Reid's left, leaned to make eye contact with Andy on Reid's right. "Tell me more about your wedding next year. Drew said it was going to be in Ohio?"

"Crown, Ohio. At a vineyard. With a lake." Andy's smile brightened her entire face. She chattered about the venue excitedly, how it'd be a weekend-long affair and how each of her sisters had been married at the same lake. "It's a family tradition. It's also where Gage and I fell in love. You probably already heard about that."

"Drew mentioned that you two pretended to be together, even though you barely knew each other." Christina's eyes snapped to Gage.

"The connection was instant," Gage said with a man-in-love's smile on his face. "There was no denying it."

Reid swallowed thickly as he recalled the first time he'd seen the "new" Drew on that dance floor. Recalled the way she'd moved in that skirt, and those shoes he couldn't tear his eyes from. The way she'd approached with a bubbly confidence that had drawn him to her.

Like a moth to a flame, Janet Jackson sang in his head.

Even if Reid could've written off the encounter as sheer physical attraction, that excuse fell flat after he'd figured out who Drew really was. Hell, moments before he'd recognized the birthmark he was musing over the connection he'd had with the beautiful brunette.

"…and your plus-one, of course," Andy told Christina, sending a lingering, meaningful glance at Reid. "Whoever that might be."

He'd zoned out and missed a hell of a conversation. He blinked over at Christina, who looked visibly uncomfortable. "Oh, well. You know. I don't…um…thank you for the invite."

"We liked the idea of having a joint bachelorette/bachelor party at the lake," Andy explained. "Reid'll be there."

Ah, hell. They were trying to set Reid up with Christina. Yes, he'd been flirting a little to reroute the attention from the way he was reacting to Drew. Apparently, it'd worked a little too well.

But a wedding *one year* in the future? *Andy, darling.* Evidently Gage wasn't the only one infested by the love bug. In the interest of not making things awkward, Reid played along with her Cupid-like intentions.

"I wouldn't miss your commingling cock-and-hen party. I enjoy a good F-you to tradition." Reid raised his glass of sake and said a cheers to everyone at the table.

The chef at the center of their cozy table served their sushi rolls and bento boxes. Gage struck up a conversation about the skill it took to create their food, and Andy leaned on her elbow and smiled, listening as the chef talked at length about his training. Reid used that opportunity to turn his back to friends.

"Sorry about that," he whispered to Christina. "It seems they believe we belong together."

"Yeah, well, if you weren't laying it on so thick, we might not be in this mess. You'd better not talk to every girl like you're talking to me. Drew is a good person."

Reid couldn't help smiling. He liked that Christina was standing up for Drew. "You're a good friend. I didn't mean to oversell it."

"You can't help it, I guess." Christina picked up her chopsticks and lifted a crab roll. Around a mouthful she added, "Look at you."

"Can't a man be polite without being thought of as a player?"

Vehemently, she shook her head, gesturing to him with her chopsticks as she chewed. "You're great-looking. Not good-looking. *Great*. I imagine attention from the opposite sex isn't hard for you to obtain."

"You make it sound criminal." Her comment peeved him, probably because it'd sounded more like an accusation. He grumpily ate a piece of sushi.

"It's not criminal." Christina returned to her meal. "But it certainly doesn't make me feel special. Is...*you-know-who* special?"

"Of course she's special." Reid had known Drew for years—true, he hadn't seen her in several of those years, but she was related to one of his closest friends. She automatically meant more to him than a stranger. Was Christina implying he'd taken advantage of Drew? Simply used her up and spat her out?

"She's a good person," Christina reminded him again—as if he needed reminding.

"I know that." The muscles in his neck went taut. He'd graduated from peeved to pissed off.

"She deserves more than a playboy is all I'm saying."

The thread of his patience snapped. "Why don't we enjoy our dinners and attempt to survive tonight as amenably as possible?"

"Reid." That scolding whisper came from the woman at his right elbow. He turned to meet eyes with Andy, whose auburn eyebrows climbed her forehead.

"He's fine, Andy." Christina smiled. "It's my fault for bringing up football."

"Reid hates American football," Gage paused eating his own dinner to say.

"I—I know. That was the disagreement." Christina leaned out of view of Andy and Gage to mouth "sorry" to Reid.

Reid leaned over his food to shield them from Andy's and Gage's prying eyes. "We need to be more convincing than this. For Drew's sake."

He'd already vowed not to speak to Gage about what'd happened in California and, given Christina's presence, it wasn't hard to guess that Drew wanted to keep up the ruse.

He guessed there was a certain logic to keeping mum. This thing between him and Drew would be short-lived. She didn't want a boyfriend any more than he wanted to be one, or so she'd confessed that last morning they'd spent together. It'd been an unwelcome goodbye. When she'd offered a kiss on his cheek and whispered, "Don't worry, Reid, I won't make this weird," he'd felt an odd pang of regret that their time together was well and truly over.

Only now it wasn't. As long as no one was the wiser that Drew and Reid were together, all would end well.

Christina threw her head back and laughed, making it a point to touch his arm. "Oh, stop!" She laughed again heartily and sent him a meaningful nod.

Right. They needed to be more convincing.

"Well, you asked," he played along, pasting on a wide

smile. At that same moment, he saw Drew pause in the mouth of the kitchen, a stricken expression on her face.

Bloody hell.

"Um, pardon me for a moment." He stood from his seat and angled for Drew, who tore off through the dining room. He caught her in the hallway leading to the restrooms.

Snagging her upper arm, he tugged her deeper into the corridor. Thankfully, they were on the opposite side of the restaurant from their friends, and out of sight.

"What are you doing?" Drew shook out of his grip.

"Coming to explain that I am not flirting with your roommate. Well, I am," he amended, "but not because I want to."

Drew folded her arms over her breasts—God, those breasts. He had to mentally will his attention back to the conversation he'd started. At least they were alone for the moment.

"You don't seem too broken up about having to flirt with her," Drew said. "Apparently, you've got her eating from your hand."

"She threatened me two seconds ago," he said in her roommate's defense—and a bit in his own. "If you want to blame anyone for this situation, blame yourself. You're the one who doesn't want to tell Gage the truth."

"You didn't seem to have a problem agreeing with me. What's the matter, Reid? Worried that my brother will lose his hero worship for you now that you've stooped to have sex with someone like me?"

What the—?

If Reid was upset before it paled to the rage roaring through his bloodstream now. How dare Drew talk about herself that way? And what the hell did she mean "someone like her"?

"Stoop?" He wheeled her backward and they bumped

into a door that read Employees Only. He tried the knob, hoping someone had been careless. As luck would have it, the door opened. He shoved them both inside the pitch-black closet and shut the door. He flipped on the light switch, illuminating the cramped space in a yellow glow. Stacks of paper towels, takeaway containers and other items towered on shelves lining the small closet.

"I do not stoop, Drew." He pressed her back against a blank wall. "*Ever.* Are we clear?"

Some of the anger bled from her expression, leaving behind beautiful, raw vulnerability. Whatever issues she had about her worth were her own. He'd do well remembering that. But he wasn't above teaching her a lesson.

"Unless by stoop you mean…" He dropped to his knees and pushed her skirt up her thighs.

"Reid! What are you doing? I'm at work."

"Proving you wrong," he answered as he slipped her panties off. "Or right, depending on your perspective."

He hiked the dress up over her hips and buried his face between her legs. She sagged against the wall, her fingers twining in his hair. Soon, her incoherent noises mingled with low moans of pleasure.

She tasted like heaven when she came—the same way she'd tasted last weekend. He'd missed being with her already. That wasn't normal for him.

He ignored the stray thought and placed another loving kiss on her most precious part before standing to his full height.

She blinked heavy eyes at him as he tugged her dress down, then she frowned as if belatedly realizing an important component of her wardrobe was missing.

"Panties." She held out a hand.

Pretending to be angry with me? I know better, love.

He thumbed the scrap of black lace and then shoved

the garment into his pocket. "I believe I'll keep these as a souvenir of our time together tonight. Whenever you catch me play-flirting with Christina I want you to remember my lips on, well, *your* lips, quite frankly."

Her mouth dropped open into a stunned smile. She liked him slightly crass and under her command. That much he knew.

"And then I want you to remember that I have your underpants in my pocket. That I came to find you, kiss you and drop to my knees at your feet." He pressed a firm kiss to her mouth. "That, *love*, is the only time I stoop."

On that brilliant parting line he left the closet, brushed the dust off the knees of his trousers and walked out to rejoin his pretend date for the evening. He stuffed his hands into his pocket and touched the lace panties he wished he'd gotten a better look at in the dim light of the supply closet.

No matter. That was only a preview of what was to come this evening. Specifically, *Drew*. As many times as she'd allow him to take her to the edge and over.

Fifteen

Reid was spent.

Through and through, just an absolute goner.

He'd told Gage and Andy he'd take a car home, wished Christina well, and then he'd waited at the bar with a scotch while Drew finished up. She had, in what had seemed like record time, and was gliding over to him in the black dress that rocketed a punch of anticipation straight to his gut. He'd put his arm around her and kissed her temple the moment she was close enough for him to do so, and then he'd put his lips to her ear and whispered, "Missing something?"

Knowing he was referring to her panties, she'd laughed and her cheeks had turned pink, and that'd simply made his night.

Or so he'd thought. What had *actually* made his night was bringing her to his apartment, sweeping aside her dress and shoes, and taking her to orgasm half a dozen times.

"Doesn't seem fair that you can have six of them while I only get the one," he teased. He was still lying flat on his back in bed. She was out of sight, somewhere in his walk-in closet, where she'd disappeared a few minutes ago.

"Six what?" she called from the recesses.

"Orgasms."

She stepped from his closet wearing one of his navy blue button-down shirts. The tails came to her thighs, and she was fiddling with one of his striped ties, attempting to knot it at her neck.

"I think it's fair." She paused in her task to grin, all pearly whites and mischief.

He sat up and scooted to the edge of the bed, gesturing for her to come to him. When she was standing between his legs, he finished knotting the tie for her.

"Have an important business meeting to attend?" he joked as he tightened the tie at the collar of the shirt. He liked her this close, her breath dusting his cheek. There was something about Drew that towed him in. Her inherent sweetness, perhaps...

Or her lack of experience.

If he thought too much about that, he'd feel a heap of guilt, so he shoved it aside.

"I like your clothes." She stepped away and held out her arms to show off her outfit. Navy blue shirt, tie and the shiny black heels she'd worn tonight.

"I like you in my clothes." He'd been allowed to spend another evening pleasuring this amazing woman. He was a lucky bastard.

She stepped toward him in the exaggerated walk of a model on a runway, before losing her nerve and laughing.

"If you had any idea how sexy you looked doing that, you wouldn't laugh."

She shoved the shirtsleeves, which had swallowed her hands, to her elbows.

"You're good for my ego." She patted his cheek, and he caught her hand, the words *You're good for me* on the tip of his tongue.

He didn't say them, figuring she'd take them the only way she knew how—to mean more than they actually did. Though he wouldn't be lying. Drew *was* good for him. It was he who wasn't good for her. She was sweet and open, learning about all life had to offer her, and from what he'd seen tonight, life would continue delivering more to her capable hands.

In the restaurant, she'd been poised and confident, impossible for him not to admire. Even while pretending with Christina, he hadn't been able to keep from stealing glances at Drew. But he'd seen the girl she used to be beneath that womanly exterior. That bashful, sweet girl who had much more potential than she gave herself credit for.

Reid, on the other hand, was jaded, broken. Not a good prospect for a commitment. As long as she wasn't with him long-term, she had a chance at having a full and complete relationship with someone else. He'd not rob her of the chance to be more, have more and do more.

Arguably he was taking advantage of her weakness for him to fill a void that had been cavernous since he was a child. It was unfair, but he also believed in Drew's strength. She'd recover from him in no time at all. He'd see to it.

"Do you miss London?" she asked out of the blue. "Your family? I'd miss my family if they weren't a car's ride away."

"Sometimes," he answered honestly. Family wasn't a topic he liked to discuss with anyone—not even his closest comrades, Gage, Flynn and Sabrina. And he most certainly hadn't traipsed down Family Lane with any woman in his life. Oddly enough, Drew felt like a safe zone for Reid. Again he thought about how they'd "connected," and as perplexing as it was for him to admit he felt that way about her, he couldn't deny it.

"That was the heaviest 'sometimes' I ever heard." She stroked his hair. This time of year was always hard for him. His birthday was around the corner, and there was no way to avoid what came with it. The past. The memories. The sorrow.

"You know, in spite of your rakish reputation, Gage never warned me about you. And I'll bet he never threatened you to stay away from me, either."

Reid blinked away the thoughts of his family's tragedy to focus on Drew. There, in his shirt and tie, looking for all the world like a woman who belonged in his bedroom. Typically, a woman in his bedroom was doing one of two things: asking for more or putting on her clothes to leave. And that was because *typically* he wouldn't have lingered in the bedroom. He'd have kissed her lightly and made the excuse that he couldn't sleep. Then he'd hide behind his laptop at the dining room table until she fell asleep or decided to call it a night.

He hadn't thought too hard about that before now. He'd seen it as polite; a good way to avoid awkward conversations about family, friends, past or future. But with Drew, he'd lingered. Hell, he hadn't even gotten dressed.

"You're correct," he told her. "Gage never warned me off."

"Know why?" She loosened the tie. "I was never on your radar. And he never told me to stay away from you because he knew I didn't stand a chance of winning you. You've always been out of my league."

He caught the length of silk around her neck and pulled

her to him, then threw the tie aside and unbuttoned the top two buttons of the shirt she wore.

"To be fair, I never had the chance to see you outside of a family gathering." He kissed the space between her collarbones. "One normally doesn't prowl family events in search of a date, you know."

"*Ew.* I'm not family."

"You were eighteen, Drew. You'd just graduated from high school, were ensconced with friends your age and had no interest in me whatsoever."

She clucked her tongue, which told him he was dead wrong about that.

"And I was an idiot twentysomething who wouldn't have dreamed of hitting on you lest Gage have my ass. I couldn't have acted on my attraction if I'd stopped for a second to allow it to form." He cocked an eyebrow. "How was I to know you'd morph into a foxy siren who knows exactly how to turn me on?"

"Or that I'd avoid any gathering where you'd possibly be present?"

"No." He frowned, not liking the sound of that.

"Gage and I don't have a lot of friends in common, so it didn't come up often. But, yeah, I was sure to tell him to arrive at soft openings with a date and not a friend, just in case."

"Just in case what?"

"Just in case." She shrugged one shoulder and didn't give him any more than that.

"Just in case," he repeated as he unbuttoned another two buttons and parted the shirt. "I saw you and couldn't contain myself?" Her breasts, large and full, sat on display before him. He sucked one nipple and then the other as she raked her nails into his hair. After a minute of leisurely exploration he wasn't sure who was enjoying it more.

"Seriously. You are *so* good at that." She moaned, the earlier topic forgotten. Which he preferred. He didn't want to hear her reason for why she hadn't wanted to bump into him. Given her comment earlier about him "stooping" he could guess it wasn't a positive one.

He rested his face between her breasts and, his voice muffled, proclaimed, "Anytime." When he lifted his eyes to hers, she was smiling down at him.

Much better.

She pulled the shirt closed and crawled into bed. Content to stay a while longer with her, he moved to settle in at her side.

"Regardless of what we do or don't do together, you know you can talk to me, right?" she asked.

"About?" He half expected red emergency lights to flash or a siren's wail to pierce his eardrums at the inference of "talking." Definitely, he should climb from bed and beg off to work. *Talking* was never a good idea, but he didn't budge.

"Anything."

"I have nothing to talk about." He tucked her dark hair behind her ear, loving the silken feel of the strands. "I prefer you as a brunette."

"And in black lace," she added.

"Yes. But mostly *out of* black lace." He wrapped his arms around her and kissed her, and she shoved against his chest gently.

"I'm a great secret keeper. I never gossip. I don't share privileged information."

"Christina knows about us. Not so great, I fear."

"We weren't together when I told her. You were part of my past. Completely fair game. How can I be sure you won't spill the coffee beans to your bros? To *my bro*, in particular? You and Gage are like this." She crossed her index and middle fingers to illustrate. "He'll pry it out of you eventually."

"I'm a better secret keeper than you, guaranteed."

She harrumphed.

"I've kept a secret from Flynn, Sabrina and Gage since I met them. I've never once 'spilled the *coffee beans*.'" He grinned at the cute way she switched up the phrase. He'd learned over the course of spending several mornings with her that Drew liked coffee almost as much as he liked her breasts.

And that was saying something.

"I don't believe you." She jutted her chin stubbornly.

"Drew. I once swore an oath on my tallywacker that I wouldn't wed and never broke that pact even though *both* Flynn and Gage pussed out. Believe me. My word is oak."

"I'm already trusting you to take the you-and-me secret to your grave."

Unbeknownst to her, that phrase was apt when it came to the other secret he harbored. A shadow stretched over the room and consumed him with dark thoughts.

"You can tell me what happened, Reid." She played with the wavy hair atop his head. "Be brave and tell me about the girl back home who broke your heart."

He met her seeking gaze. A decade was too long to harbor a secret from friends. He'd sworn years ago that he'd tell them eventually, but the timing was always wrong. When was the best time to bring up tragedy? He still didn't know when he'd tell Gage, Flynn or Sabrina, but his gut told him now was the exact right time to talk about Wesley with Drew.

"You're completely wrong," Reid told her, his eyes losing focus as his gaze slid away. "It wasn't a girl back home who broke my heart. It was my twin brother."

Sixteen

"Twin brother?" Drew had no idea he had a twin brother. "Are you two estranged?"

"He died. We came to believe."

Her heart sank to her toes. She didn't understand what he'd meant by that, but he seemed ready to talk about it, so she was here for him. She rested a hand on his chest in silent support.

"He disappeared during our birthday party." Reid shoved a pillow under his neck. His gaze was on the ceiling, but she didn't move into his frame of vision. She sensed this wasn't a story he told often. He'd probably appreciate her presence more than her sympathy.

She waited for him to continue, idly stroking her fingers through his chest hair and watching her own hand rather than staring at him. Eventually, he must've felt comfortable, because he spoke again and didn't stop for a long while.

"It was a hot afternoon. I don't know how, at three years

old, I remember that. But I do. Mum and Dad planned a massive circus-themed birthday party. It was packed with face-painting clowns, jugglers, a petting zoo. Mum had insisted on a huge inflatable castle packed with plastic balls. When I could get her to talk about the day, she'd tell me how she'd fought for that inflatable with Dad for a week solid before he'd given in. He'd thought it a monstrosity."

Reid smiled at the memory, and even though it was sad at the edges, it transformed his handsome face. He looked at once older and younger.

"Within a half hour of the festivities and among legions of neighborhood friends, my twin brother, Wesley, went missing." Reid sucked in a breath, but it barely lifted her hand where it rested on his chest. As if the oxygen hadn't quite reached his lungs. "Dad dived into the in-ground pool to look for him there, just in case Wes had fallen in. I don't remember that part. But he told me that he'd had a vision of Wes at the bottom of that cement box, blue in the face. When he came up out of the water to an expectant crowd of onlookers, he shook his head and they dispersed.

"The search party blanketed the yard, the surrounding neighborhood and the patch of woods beyond the house. It wasn't a large area to canvass, but everyone came up empty-handed. Police took over the search at nightfall, blanketing an even bigger swath of land. They'd interviewed the clowns and the jugglers, the animal handlers. None of them had any idea where Wes was. No one saw him wander off."

Reid paused to swallow, his Adam's apple bobbing as if pushing past a lump of dread. Drew's stomach turned in anticipation of the story that wouldn't end well.

"Five years later—"

"Oh my God," she couldn't keep from whispering.

"—my folks decided to have a funeral. Trying to find

Wesley had become their life. They'd gone on television to share the story, had been interviewed by papers and had covered the surrounding towns and villages in posters with Wesley's photo on them. My mother was a functioning alcoholic by then, having turned to the bottle when the grief became too much. My father was simply exhausted. He'd told me he'd never felt so impotent in his life not being able to protect his family.

"I can relate to that. I couldn't protect Wes, either. I was too small, just as helpless, but I'm older and when I grew up I still felt... I don't know. *Responsible*. It's hard being the one left behind and feeling as if a part of yourself died, as well. I know everyone believes that my reasoning for the pact not to marry has everything to do with sowing my wild oats forever, but it's more about what I've to offer someone. To be honest—" he slid his eyes to her, his face a mask of sadness "—I don't have a lot left to offer."

"Oh, Reid." She hugged him close, holding him until his breathing returned to normal instead of shallow bursts. "I'm so sorry."

"Thank you. By the way, Mum's graduated from drinking daily to drinking occasionally."

"So she's well now?"

"Yes." He frowned like he didn't want to say more, but then he did. "Sometimes I wonder if life would've been better if my dad had found Wesley at the bottom of that pool. I'd give anything to have my brother back, but if it had to happen then—if I could choose the way he'd die— it'd be that. We have no idea what happened to him. His body never turned up. He was simply...gone."

Her heart snapped clean in two at the anguish in Reid's voice.

"And you've dealt with it by keeping quiet."

"Not too bright, eh?" He smiled over at her, but it was

forced. She touched his chin, resting her index finger in
the dent there.

"I won't tell Gage. I won't tell anyone. No matter what.
I swear."

"I trust you." He squeezed her against him and kissed
her forehead. She loved being this close to him, being held
by him. It made her feel safe. She liked being the person he
could rest his burdens on, too. "Though it's probably time
I told my friends about my brother. They think I don't like
aging and that's why I never allow them to make a fuss
over my birthday. Truth is, my family doesn't celebrate
it. We haven't since the day we lost Wesley. After the funeral, it felt like a betrayal to continue celebrating. Every
day I'm on this planet is a day he's not."

Oh, Reid. That guilt must've eaten a hole through his
gut like battery acid.

"You've never told anyone this," she said.

"No. What I just told you was more than I've admitted
to family, to friends."

"Girlfriends?"

"I don't have girlfriends. For reasons you've now
gleaned."

"I always wondered why you weren't a one-gal kind
of guy. Now I know." She could understand how he'd become gun-shy. His parents sounded like part of them had
died alongside Wesley that ill-fated day. Reid must've felt
overlooked, soaked in all those negative vibes as a child,
all while struggling to understand what had happened to
his brother.

"I still feel him." Reid's mouth tugged down at the corners. "That's the strange part. Like there's a chip embed-
ded here—" he pointed to the center of his chest "—and
I can still sense Wes somehow." A quick jump of his eyebrows dismissed the subject. "You must think me barmy."

"Barmy?" That was a new one.

"Crazy."

"Ah. No. It's not crazy. When my grandmother Adele died, I was fifteen years old. I had dream after dream about her. In those dreams, she always said the same thing. 'Look for me in the sky, Drew. I have my wings.'" She smiled at the thought. "Every time I see a bird, a butterfly or a bumblebee, I say to myself, 'Hello, Gran.'"

"Sweet *and* cute."

He shook his head. "Definitely you deserve better than me."

"Why don't we not talk about who deserves what when it comes to us?" She wanted to sooth and comfort him. Wanted to see his easy smile return even though she knew there was a shadow hiding behind it.

"What shall we discuss, then?" His smile wasn't quite easy but it was there. Evidently he was ready to cast off the bleak topic. She knew just how to do that.

"I should amend that we aren't talking about who deserves what unless we're talking about orgasms, which I can hereby state with clarity that I need a minimum of six each and every time you and I are naked together. Even though it's unfair for you and your pitiable one at a time." She poked her bottom lip out into an exaggerated pout, and Reid laughed. It was a small laugh, with barely any breath behind it, but she considered it a win.

"It's not my fault I'm much better at delivering than you are, love."

"Not funny!" She swatted him with the sleeve of the shirt she wore, belatedly realizing it was going to be unwearable if she continued wrinkling it. She sat up abruptly. "I should hang this up."

"Wrong. You're not leaving this bed." He was on top of her in a flash, pinning her down and tearing open the shirt. She let her eyes wander over her own nude body, at her large breasts with nipples pointing at Reid as if saying, "Here we are!" Her legs and thighs, while not perfectly slender, had plenty of muscle. She admired the way her smooth skin was juxtaposed against Reid's hard planes, thick thigh muscles and wiry hair on his legs. She marveled at the heavy penis brushing against her tender sex.

"Make love to me." She flexed her arms uselessly since he held her wrists. "I need it. And so do you."

His eyes held weighted darkness behind them. She couldn't erase it any more than she could fill the empty part of him, but she could help take his mind off his loss.

And maybe that's what they were to each other, a way to forget the past and heal parts of themselves that no one else could. Her by being the person he needed most right now, him by being the only man who could fulfill a decadelong fantasy for her.

"My pleasure." He kissed her, accepting her offers—spoken and unspoken—and taking them to the pinnacle of passion yet again.

Seventeen

Drew sipped her coffee and tried her damnedest to wake up. When she wasn't participating in an opening for a restaurant, she worked from home scheduling, interviewing and planning the next opening. Even on a Sunday like today, she'd normally be awake and handling her email. She hadn't so much as made it to the shower yet, and it was almost ten o'clock.

Reid had kept her up way too late doing amazing things to her body she wouldn't soon forget. She shivered, her tired smile resting on the edge of her coffee mug.

Friday night after the opening at Soo-She, he'd told her about Wesley. Last night she'd cooked for him at her place—chicken piccata—and he'd stayed the night. Christina had gone away for the weekend, leaving the house blessedly empty.

Drew had managed to get out of bed an hour ago, but hadn't wanted to wake him with running water and the sound of the blow-dryer.

She'd lingered in the doorway of her bedroom and admired the sculpted, firm globes of his solid buttocks, the muscles in his back and how good his dark wavy hair looked against the bright white of her bedsheets.

Reid Singleton in her bed, bare-ass naked, wasn't a sight to rush. So she'd stood there until she felt like a creeper and finally forced herself into the kitchen for coffee.

She'd been there since, but after cup number two failed to motivate her she wondered if she should give up and crawl into bed next to him.

"Morning," came a raspy male voice from the hallway. Reid was in the gray T-shirt and worn soft jeans he'd arrived wearing, but he hadn't bothered with socks and shoes. And his hair was finger-combed by the looks of it.

"No fair. No one should look as good as you do in the morning."

"Hah. Nice try. Where's mine?" He gestured to her coffee, and she pointed at the mug on the counter. "Thoughtful," he praised as he poured himself a cup. He took the chair next to her at the kitchen table. She had one leg curled under the other, her heel resting on the edge of the seat. He wrapped one big, warm hand around her toes.

"What's on your docket today?" Much as she'd love to lounge around in her apartment with Mr. Perfect Ass, she really should get to work.

"Sundays I head to the market to find something to eat for the week. I drop off my dry cleaning. The usual exciting weekend stuff. You?"

"Work."

"On a Sunday?"

"Yeah. I work from home a lot. It's a gig that can't only be handled nine to five, Monday through Friday."

"I suppose that's true. I've always been grateful for my

nights and weekends free. It's the appeal of Monarch and being your own boss."

"I thought Flynn was your boss."

"Well. We let him believe he is." Reid grinned.

He was too damned charming for his own good. And far more layered than she ever would've guessed. She'd only ever seen a fun-loving, hotter than Hades Brit who was utterly unattainable. Now that she'd been with him on multiple occasions, she saw how unfair she'd been to him. He was human, with feelings and hurts and a past that was darker than any of them knew. She'd never sensed anything ominous surrounding him, but she supposed she was too busy keeping her distance to have noticed.

"When is Christina returning?"

"Tonight."

"My place, then? You can bring your work if you need to. No sense in both of us running off in the morning." He sipped his coffee while he checked a weather app on his phone. "Eighty-four degrees today," he mumbled almost to himself. As if he felt the weight of her stare, he met her gaze. "What?"

"For a guy who doesn't want to be involved with a woman, you make a lot of plans with me."

"Am I to believe you're finished with me?" He raised one cocky British eyebrow. "I'm to believe you want nothing to do with me and your pending six orgasms tonight?"

"Are you so content to let me use you?" she teased with a giggle, but there was some truth to what she was asking. She didn't feel the least bit used by him. He'd made her feel like a princess, and had soothed her most tender spots since the night he'd found out her true identity.

"Yes." He narrowed his eyelids. "Perhaps we should outline a few ground rules to keep from getting in too deep."

"It's not a bad idea." She wasn't accustomed to open-ended anything. Her next six months were planned to the minute. Her dated planner was decorated in washi tape and appointment stickers. Her to-do list was bullet-pointed and detailed. "How about we set an end date?"

"Okay." He nodded as if this was par for course, an idea that made her slightly uncomfortable. Nevertheless, she pressed on.

"Probably before the holidays." She couldn't imagine sneaking around during Thanksgiving or Christmas. The guilt of lying to her brother and family would eat her alive. "Should we count Halloween as a holiday?"

"Are you invited to any costume parties?"

"I go to at least one every year."

"And we don't want to navigate couple *costumery*."

"I'll be busy that entire month anyway. I'm opening three different restaurants."

"Very well. That gives us August and September."

"When…um. When's your birthday?" She felt uncomfortable asking since she'd learned it was a sore topic, but she couldn't not ask. Reid didn't have a single good birthday memory and she wanted him to have one. One he could be happy with and not overwhelmed by.

"September fifth."

"I can't believe you told me that."

"Neither can I." His eyebrows jumped in a show of adorable self-deprecation before he stood from his chair. He finished his coffee and bent to place a kiss on her forehead. "I have to run. Tonight? My place?" At the sink he rinsed his mug. He looked in her kitchen.

My place in your life?

"Tonight. Your place," she confirmed.

"Uber will be here in a bit," Reid said of the car service coming to pick him up. He gathered his things from the bedroom, and she met him at the front door.

"Seeing me out?" he asked. "So sweet."

"And cute. I know. I know." She rolled her eyes, but she didn't take offense to him thinking of her as "cute." Not now that she knew "cute" and "sexy" weren't mutually exclusive.

"Damn cute," he agreed in a low, sexy murmur. Then he kissed her, holding on long enough to make her want to grab him by the shirt and drag him back to bed. He hummed softly as he ended their kiss and pulled open the door.

There, in the threshold, stood Gage, fist raised to knock.

"Reid?" Gage's eyebrows crashed over his nose, then he snapped his attention to Drew. "What the hell?"

"What are you doing here?" She tried to keep her voice steady, but it wobbled slightly.

Her brother lifted a foam cooler. "Dad came into town and left this. You know I eat fish as rarely as possible. I only did that Soo-She thing because they offer a chicken option."

Their father worked at a fish hatchery in Leavenworth, Washington. He often brought his work home with him and more often brought his work to Drew and Gage.

"Why is Reid here?" Gage asked, again skewering his best friend with a glare.

"Because, dummy," she stalled. She always went with confidence when she had no idea how to escape the predicament before her. "He was visiting Christina." She waved a hand at Reid, who gave her an incredulous look. "I don't understand his appeal, but whatever."

She crossed her arms over her chest and shrugged. If confidence didn't sell it, indifference would.

"I thought you and Christina didn't work out." Contrary to her accusation, Gage was no dummy. It was up to Reid to back her up. Drew almost doubted he would. It was one thing to keep a secret from her brother, but it was another to lie to his face. She sent telepathic messages to Reid asking him to support her white lie with one of his own.

"Well, it may not last, but it worked out for the night," Reid said, charm oozing from his every pore. "Don't wake her. She had a long, *long* night," he told Drew, going as far as to point toward Christina's empty bedroom.

"I won't." Even though they were pretending, she felt a spike of jealousy at the thought of Reid and Christina having a long night together. Which made no sense, so she flashed Reid a quick smile of thanks and then took the cooler from Gage. "Thanks for the fish."

"Where you headed?" Gage nodded at Reid.

"Home. My car will be here—" he consulted his cell phone's app "—in two minutes."

"Cancel it. I'll give you a ride home."

"You're sure?"

"Positive."

Reid pressed a button, declared that it was "done" and resumed his walk out the door. "Let's go, then. Drew, always a pleasure."

She bit her lip, hoping with all she had that Gage wouldn't grill Reid on the way home and that she wouldn't have to hear a lecture from her big bad brother about how Reid wasn't the man for her. Gage might think he knew his best friend, but after last night she knew him better.

She shut the door behind her brother and her temporary boyfriend and sagged against it for a full minute. She'd been taken advantage of by men in the past, and there was no doubt in her mind that Gage would see this as another mistake in the making. He would worry she'd fall in love with Reid the way she had with Devin, and before him, Ronnie, and before him…she didn't even want to think about how many romantic mistakes she'd made in the past.

And since Gage knew his friend was as unobtainable as plucking a star from the sky and putting it in her pocket, he'd have warnings for her—and probably a few for Reid about what they were doing together.

The trouble wasn't that Gage would be wrong to worry, the trouble was that he would be *right*. But she had a sixth sense about Reid. Even though she'd just agreed to an end date and even though Reid had professed himself unable to have a long-term relationship, she believed he could come to mean more to her than either of them had ever dreamed.

He'd already been a better boyfriend than Devin and Ronnie combined. And he hadn't even been trying.

Her eyes sank closed. She couldn't—wouldn't—allow herself to fall in love with Reid Singleton. No matter how amazing he was in bed or how sweet he could be in the morning. No matter that he'd shared his broken, sad past, trusting her with that information and no one else. She could keep this light and walk away unscathed. That would be best for both of them.

"Keep telling yourself that, Drew," she said on a sigh. Then she walked the kitchen to put her freshly delivered fish in the fridge.

Eighteen

"Thanks for the lift," Reid said, breaking the stifling silence. If it weren't for Drew's insistence that they keep the affair from her brother, he'd just as soon tell Gage what was going on. Reid was a grown man; he could handle whatever his best friend had to say. And Gage could use a reminder that his sister was a grown woman, whether he wanted to admit it or not.

"Christina is an odd choice for you." Gage kept his eyes on the road, his mouth firmly set.

"Is she?" Reid tried to sound bored, but some of his irritation bled through.

"Yeah. You usually gravitate toward bubbly and bouncy, and Christina is neither of those things."

"Opposites attract. I suppose your and Drew's matchmaking worked."

"Uh-huh." More silence infiltrated the car.

"What is it, Gage? Stop being so damned stubborn and say what you're thinking."

"Drew is…she's an adult and I know that. But she's also a lot like she was when we were growing up. There's a new, hard-won confidence to her, but there is also a naive side. She believes in dreams coming true and fairy tales, and it's gotten her into trouble in the past. With men."

Reid hated thinking of Drew with any of the *gits* she'd dated in the past, but he couldn't exactly show his anger lest he tip his hand.

"She seems to be holding her own fine now. How do you know she's not seeing someone?" Reid grumbled. "Does she tell you everything?"

"She tells everyone everything about the guys she dates. Although after the way Mom gave her hell about the chef who dumped her, she might be keeping quiet. You were at her place, did you notice her texting someone a lot? Any phone calls? She's been acting differently these past two weeks. She seems…happier."

"And you're unhappy about that?" Reid asked his friend, trying not to gloat over Drew's happiness. He liked knowing he'd brightened her world. She'd shined a spotlight on his, as well.

"I'm not unhappy she's happy, I'm wondering how long this one will last before it fizzles out and I have to go over there with Ben & Jerry's dairy-free ice cream, or gelato and help her through another devastating breakup. I can't bear to see her hurt again." Gage let out a sigh, and Reid felt his friend's concern for Drew in that gust of air. Gage loved his sister more than anyone. Reid knew what it was like to love a sibling that much. He could relate to feeling their pain like his own. Why should it be any different between Gage and Drew?

"Worrying comes from my mother's side, I guess. I should stop being such a pussy, yeah?" Gage tagged Reid's arm. "Anyway. You and Christina make a good couple. She's smart, and she's adorable. She's been fiercely loyal to Drew, which I appreciate. Did you know she moved in with Drew last year after the Devin Briggs debacle?"

"No, she, ah, didn't mention that." Reid frowned in thought. He didn't know much about Drew, actually. He didn't usually know a lot about the women he dated. Knowing a lot about them opened up the conversation to them knowing a lot about *him*, and he tried to avoid that sort of depth if possible.

Until Drew. She knew an awful lot about him. More than he'd meant for her to know. His time spent with her had dredged up his painful past and was making him face his biggest fears, but he could swear…it was ridiculous but it seemed as if…she was *healing* him.

"You okay? You look, to use your term, completely *knackered*." Gage grinned, proud of his Britishism for "tired."

"I am knackered," Reid admitted.

"Christina wild in the sack, is she?"

"Keeps me on my toes," Reid answered with a wily grin. This was territory he was comfortable with when it came to nattering away with his friends. Sex was fair game, and he often had tales of prowess to tell. Gage would expect no less.

"She's a firecracker. Multiple orgasms, right in a row." He snapped his fingers. "Bam, bam, bam."

"Nice." Gage nodded his approval, but Reid doubted he'd be nodding his approval if he knew they were talking about Drew.

Drew had been right in the assessment of her brother. Gage loved her, but was overly protective of her. He believed she was bouncing about falling in love with any git who came to call, but Reid knew differently. He and

Drew had made an agreement to end this affair—they'd even given it a time line.

Drew wasn't going to be sobbing into her ice cream when Reid walked away. He wouldn't allow it. Besides, she'd already seen some of the bones in his closet and he doubted she wanted to see the rest of the skeleton.

He'd take the gift of spending time with her and in turn make it the best of her life. And hopefully teach her a thing or two about how she should be treated by the next man who enters her life. He'd make sure she knew that no one less than Prince Charming was worthy of her, and he'd make sure she understood as much when they kissed goodbye for the final time.

It was all in a day's work, he lied to himself. *No less than what you'd do for any other woman in your bed*, he argued.

What bothered him all the way down to his bollocks was that whenever he thought of saying good-bye to Drew, a bit of loss snuggled in next to the bit that resided in his chest. Drew, the perfect yin and to the yang of Wesley. He'd miss her. But he would let her go when it was time.

"Anyway, sorry for pumping you for intel," Gage said. "I just want Drew to find someone who treats her with respect."

And treats her to multiple orgasms, Reid thought with a smile.

Drew carefully folded the final French crepe and stacked it on top of the others.

"I'm ridiculously excited to eat." Reid rubbed his hands together, all but drooling at the sight of the tower of fluffy, thin crepes.

"I love feeding people. Because of that ravenous look right there."

He snagged her waist and pulled her onto his lap. She nearly upended it onto her own lap before resting it safely on the table. "Careful!"

"Never," he proclaimed before sliding her hair aside and kissing her neck. He wrapped his hands around her front and cradled her breasts, fingering her nipples through her thin T-shirt. After they'd had sex on the sofa, he'd complained he was "famished," and she offered to cook for him. When she went to get dressed he argued that he didn't want her to put clothes on. She'd explained the dangers of cooking naked, and he'd allowed the clothes, but only if "you sleep next to me without them."

It wasn't a hard-fought argument. She'd agreed immediately.

"Now what?" he asked as she slid from his lap to sit in the chair at the table next to him.

"Now you fill them with berries." She demonstrated by lifting a delicate crepe onto her plate, filling it with a line of macerated strawberries and blueberries and rolling it up like a skinny burrito. "And then…" She reached for a can of spray whipped cream and wrinkled her nose. "This is sacrilege but since you have no cream to whip, we'll have to make do." She squirted a dollop of whipped cream onto her crepe and then held the can between them. "Do I want to know why you have this in your refrigerator?"

"Probably not."

"Ugh."

She reached for her fork, but Reid caught her hand. "I'm *joking*. I have it because I like it on my ice cream sundaes."

"Oh."

"Sounds like your filthy mind had a better idea."

She felt her cheeks warm, and she smiled at her plate. "Maybe."

"I promise to save some for later." He cocked an eyebrow and then filled his crepe, topping it with whipped cream and digging in. She stopped eating to watch him eat. Watching the way he closed his eyes, moaned in appreciation and sagged in his chair like he'd been overcome. "Why are you planning restaurant openings when you should clearly be head chef at one?" He forked another bite into his mouth and caught her staring. "Something wrong?"

"No. Not at all. It's just… I've never told anyone this but lately I've been writing recipes, designing menus. Instead of fussing over schedules like an underpaid party planner, I'd much rather be wooing people's taste buds with my creations."

"Well, you should," he said simply, and then pulled another crepe onto his plate to assemble. "These are incredible."

She watched his long, blunt fingers as they rolled the crepe. He had such a sure and strong way about him. Talk about confidence. She couldn't imagine there was ever a time he didn't have it. But that time had existed, hadn't it? Only in leaving London and finding friends in Seattle had he escaped the oppressive atmosphere of living with parents who mourned his twin brother.

"Why don't you do it?" he asked.

"Do what?"

"Open a restaurant."

She chuckled. "Most restaurants fail, Reid."

"Fig & Truffle restaurants seem to do okay."

"They're a huge corporate conglomerate. They have a safety net wider than the Pacific Coast."

"So open a restaurant with them. Like Soo-She or whatever. You can call it, I don't know, Drew's Diner."

"I don't want a diner. I want a fancy eatery where every morsel is more mouthwatering than any you've tasted before."

He held her gaze for a protracted moment before finally saying, "Sounds like you."

She blushed again. She'd never get over this gorgeous, godlike man flattering her.

"You know during the ride home, Gage mentioned that he thought you were seeing someone. He was worried it'd be another wanker like Devin Briggs. Or the guy before him."

"Ronnie."

"Whoever." Reid dismissed the topic with a wave of his fork before digging into his second crepe. "Your brother worries about you settling. You shouldn't do that."

Reid regarded her sincerely. Kind of like when he confessed about Wesley, there was no cover-up, no cocksure tilt to his mouth.

"I *don't* do that."

"Do you want a family, Drew?"

"What kind of question is that?" She busied herself taking another bite while she decided how to answer. "Not now. Right now I want a career I love. I want a relationship with someone who understands I have to work to make my dreams happen. I want—" She cut herself off when she knew the end of that sentence. *I want to be with someone who encourages me to pursue those dreams.* Reid had just plainly told her that she should be creating menus and cooking for a living and that she should go for it.

"Of course not right now, but eventually, I can see you with a family man. The trick is to find a man who fits that bill at the right time. Someone who loves and respects you and wants to put down roots."

She chewed a strawberry thoughtfully before asking, "Do you want a family?"

"Never." There wasn't a second's hesitation in his answer.

"How can you say never?"

"Easy. I watched mine turn to dust. It's not a pretty sight. The only family I need is the one I have in Gage and Flynn and Sabrina." He opened his mouth and shut it again, like he decided not to say more. She wondered if he was going to include her in that "family" label but had changed his mind. Because they were sleeping together? Or because soon they wouldn't be, and friends was too big an ask after all they'd done together?

"You're worthy of your dreams, Drew. Don't let anyone talk you out of them, whether it's a chef who wants to pigeonhole you, or a guy who's obviously not cut out to be who you'll need him to be in the future." Reid rested his hand on hers, his expression one bordering on regret. Like maybe the second guy he mentioned was himself.

"Thanks, Reid." She squeezed his hand and smiled.

"You're welcome."

They went back to eating their late-night snack, and she thought about how Reid was wrong about who he was, if that's who he'd been referring to. He was capable of being who she needed in the future.

He was who she needed right now.

Nineteen

Using the key entrusted to her from Fig & Truffle, Drew unlocked the Market location of the elegant restaurant. It was a standalone building just off the pier, facing the water with an amazing view of the sunset.

Inside, the restaurant was polished to perfection, deep red-brown woods and pale cream-in-coffee painted walls. The floors were charcoal gray, the chairs a tasteful blend of neutral colors. The soft opening for this location of Fig & Truffle was soon, so Drew considered herself lucky that her boss agreed to let her borrow it.

She held the door open for Christina, who followed with a cup of strong coffee they'd picked up on their walk to the pier. It was the ungodly hour of 7:00 a.m., hours before the management team came in here to train the myriad servers, cooks and other staff who would have this place humming like a well-oiled machine on opening day.

"It's beautiful." Christina ran her hand along one of

the smooth vinyl booths. "This is my surprise? I thought it was this." She held up her coffee cup.

"Well, the coffee was a bribe to coax you out here with me." Drew walked to a darkened corner of the restaurant and flipped on the lights. Soft orange-yellow bulbs spotlighted the tables. "I'm borrowing it." Christina had slid into one of the empty booths across from the bar, her eyes on the neat rows of liquor bottles lining the wall. Until Drew added, "For Reid's birthday."

"Excuse me?" Chris pegged her with a stern glare.

"I talked to my boss, and his boss and a few other bosses, and then I begged a little and they agreed to lend me the restaurant, a chef, a server and a bartender for Reid's birthday dinner. I'm thinking gold and black streamers here." Drew pointed to the bar. Then she gestured to the table where Christina sat. "Candlelight, black place mats and gold chargers, and Fig & Truffle's signature square white plates and bowls. Reid and I will have the entire place to ourselves."

"Drew, honey." Christina's face was a mask of concern.

Drew could guess what was coming. She'd already shared with her roommate that Reid didn't celebrate birthdays, which, to Drew, was a crime. Sure, he had a good reason for not celebrating, which she *hadn't* shared with her friend, but she couldn't bear the idea of another birthday passing him by without creating a new, happier memory.

"It's just the two of us," Drew reiterated in her own defense. "I'm not going to invite a hundred people or anything."

"Yes, but is this your place? I mean, even though you two are..." Chris waved a hand. "Whatever you are to each other."

"We're together...for now. That's what matters."

The month of August had flown by in a blur of happiness. She and Reid saw each other every night during the weekends and two to three nights during the week—whenever she didn't have to work in the evening. She'd mostly stayed at his place, toting her laptop with her. She'd spent her mornings off lounging on his fantastic L-shaped sofa and drinking espresso from the machine on his counter that was even more expensive than the one she'd splurged on for herself.

She cared about him. Deeply. And knowing that his birthday was a source of pain for him, she wanted to do something for him no one else had done. His family might not believe it was important to celebrate the day of his birth, but Drew did.

She knew from their many conversations that Reid wasn't ever in a relationship for long, yet he'd been with her almost two months. They'd agreed to end things this month, but she couldn't let him go without showing him how much better things could be. He'd suffered cut-to-the-bone pain when he'd lost his twin brother, but the future didn't have to be so bleak.

She wanted to help him. And while she knew throwing him an intimate birthday dinner wouldn't heal him completely, she thought it would be a good start.

"Isn't he going to be upset with you for doing this?" Christina's brow dented with concern.

"He doesn't know what it's like to be celebrated, Chris. Everyone deserves that. He spends so much of his time telling me I'm worthy and capable. It's past time someone did that for him."

Her friend smiled. "You're a great person, Drew."

"So are you. Because you're going to help me decide on a menu." Drew hustled to the hostess station and grabbed a leather-bound menu. Back at the booth where Christina sat sipping her coffee, Drew slid into the other side and pushed the menu across the table. "Steak, fish, or should I go out of the box and choose something like lamb or pasta? Chicken seems too pedestrian."

Reid's birthday was two days away and she was very aware that this little dinner celebration was close to their farewell. Neither of them had talked about it lately. She wondered if he'd changed his mind about "getting in deep" with her. She already knew she was in over her head.

"Why are you asking me instead of a chef?" The pained look in Christina's eyes suggested she already knew.

Drew sighed in defeat. "Because the chef can't advise me how to tell Reid I'm in love with him. And I was hoping you could."

Christina reached over the menu to grasp Drew's hand. "I thought you were breaking up soon."

"This month, though we didn't set a specific date."

"I guess… I don't know why you're doing this."

"Reid deserves an amazing birthday celebration. I can't say why, but I can tell you it hasn't been a happy occasion for him for most of his life. If I can give him the gift of a happy memory when he turns thirty-two, I know he'll appreciate it more than he'll ever be able to say."

"It's sweet, Drew. It's amazing." Christina shook her head sadly. "That's why I'm friends with you. Because you're sweet and amazing and you do these incredible acts of kindness for those you love."

"I'm sensing a 'but.'"

"But." Christina smiled softly. "If you're not sure that Reid loves you, too, you're taking a really big risk. You know things are ending soon, and since he's a man it's not hard to guess that he's taking whatever you're telling him at face value. He thinks you're all in for the good time you're having. *Without* strings."

"I am." Drew tugged her hand away. "I absolutely am.

But that's the point. I'm in love with him and I suspect that under the playboy facade—that's not even the right word for him—he cares for me a lot. Why would we call this quits if it's working so well?"

"This plan isn't only about his birthday, is it?"

Drew pressed her lips together, debating how to answer that question. If she said no it would be as honest as she'd been with herself while she was planning the entire thing.

"It's *mostly* about his birthday," Drew said. "It's also about showing him what could be possible if we leaned in *a smidge* more." She measured out half an inch between her index finger and thumb and held it in front of her face, watching Christina though the gap.

Drew couldn't help how she felt, and she couldn't deny she wanted more. She wanted more nights in Reid's bed. She wanted more snuggling on the couch. She wanted more Sunday mornings making him scrambled eggs and cups of espresso. She wanted to tell everyone that he was hers.

Including her parents, Gage and anyone residing on planet Earth. She was hopelessly in love with him and wanted everyone to know it.

"I'm tired of keeping us a secret. We're worthy of good things, and finding each other was the ultimate good thing."

"I know. It really has been," Christina surprised her by saying. "I'm all for banging the Drew-and-Reid-forever drum. What I don't want is for you to go in with expectations that aren't what Reid wants at all. I don't want to see you hurt when you're on the totally opposite shore from him. When he does exactly what he says he would do, and you blindside him."

"What's that supposed to mean?" Adrenaline poured through Drew's veins, taking her buoyant mood with it. She sensed her friend was about to share an unwelcome observation. When Christina said, "Hear me out," Drew knew she was right.

"Didn't Devin tell you several times while you dated that he wanted to travel and have a family? Hadn't he been exploring being a personal chef and working with a few wealthy families overseas the entire time you two dated?"

Drew frowned. "Yes, but—"

"You told me he was done being in Seattle. You told me all he talked about was not being stuck in a restaurant kitchen."

"If you're taking his side—"

"I'm not taking his side, Drew. I'm taking *yours*. He told you exactly what he wanted and you told me that you didn't want that. You wanted to be here in Seattle. You wanted to build your Fig & Truffle dream. You wanted to be career-minded and rock the foodie scene. Devin left you and it was a rotten thing to do. Just terrible, but he did exactly what he told you he wanted to do."

"We could've compromised."

"You were clear with him about what you wanted. He tried to change your mind. Did it work?"

"You're not helping!" Drew sprang out of her seat and paced the length of the bar. "I'm over Devin. I'm with Reid. This is about Reid!"

"It's about you, too, sweetie. You want him to go along with how great the two of you can be together, but he's already stated exactly what he wants. You can't dazzle him into changing his mind with the ultimate Pinterest birthday celebration. Tell him you love him *before* you try this tack."

"No. I have to *show* him. I have to show him that this is what we can be." Drew rested her hands on the table. "Chris, I told Reid I wanted a restaurant of my own and he told me to go for it. I made him crepes and he saw my potential. But I had to show him. He sees me in a way no one else does. He just doesn't know what he's capable of yet. I'm going to bring him here on his birthday and show him what our future could look like. Trust me."

Christina nodded, but she looked unconvinced. So much for backup. But no matter what her friend thought, Drew was as certain of her plan as she was of its outcome. Once she wooed Reid with a perfect evening, once she gave him the gift of a second chance at a real, meaningful relationship, she knew he'd see things her way. They had potential—a truckload of it—and she wasn't going to let him go when it was so obvious they belonged together.

"Steak or fish?" Drew nudged the menu.

God bless Christina, who perused the options before meeting Drew's seeking gaze. With a sigh, she said, "Tell me more about the ribeye with thyme butter."

Twenty

Lost in thought on the code he was writing for work, Reid didn't hear Gage come in. Reid jumped when a black box with a white ribbon landed on his desk in front of his keyboard. He surfaced from his concentration and allowed the two computer screens in front of him to recede into the background—after first hitting the save key. If he lost even a line of coding, he'd tear his hair out.

Gage stood at the other side of Reid's desk, arms folded over his chest. "That's for you."

"What for?" Reid took off his glasses and set them aside.

"Your birthday, dimwit."

Reid stared up at his best friend, half in shock, half in irritation. Gage knew as well as anyone that Reid didn't like celebrating his birthday. Gage and Flynn used to give him shit about it, but they'd eventually stopped.

"Since I'm not allowed to give you birthday gifts, consider this my official bribe."

"Bribe?" Reid popped the ribbon and opened the black box, revealing a watch inside crafted completely of wood. He'd never seen anything like it. "This is incredible. Why does it smell of whiskey?"

"It's made from bourbon barrels."

Points for being unique, Reid thought, impressed.

"What's the bribe for?" He took the watch from the box, admiring the style. The numbers 12, 3, 6 and 9 were burned into the wooden face. The weight was nice, the size perfect, and the metal clasp a brown-tinted stainless steel. He snapped it around his wrist.

"It's also water-resistant in case you jump into the lake at the wedding with it on. The bribe is that I'm making you my best man. I know you don't do the wedding thing. Hell, I don't do the wedding thing. But Andy and I are doing the wedding thing, Reid, and I need you at my side."

Reid never wore his emotions on his sleeve. He preferred acting aloof to vulnerable, ever the sincere smart-ass. In this case, however, he couldn't hide his happiness for his friend. Before he thought about his actions, he was out of his chair and wrapping Gage in a manly hug, and slapping his back for good measure.

"I'll do it," he vowed, and then because old habits died hard, added on, "but only in case you change your mind about being married and need a ride to the airport."

Gage clapped Reid's arm and laughed, taking the comment the way it was intended. "Yeah, yeah. Anyway. I'm giving Flynn a flask. He's my other best man."

"You can't have two best men." Reid feigned offense. Flynn and Gage were like his honorary brothers, and he didn't mind sharing the spotlight with Flynn a bit. "I'm clearly *the best* man because you came to me first."

"Luke's going to be in the wedding party, too. I'm running out of friends," Gage said of Sabrina's brother. "Andy has five sisters and they're all in it, and my side's a little light. How weird would it be to ask Sabrina and Drew to stand up on my side?"

"Drew?" Reid croaked. "Drew. Right. Of course. She's your sister, after all. You should absolutely include her."

Gage frowned. As well he should. Reid had gotten emotional, which he never did, and then overreacted about Drew, which he never would've done had it not been for the sneaking around with her on the regular.

"We'll figure it out. Maybe do something nontraditional like have everyone walk down the aisle in pairs. Like, you and Drew could walk together, Flynn and Sabrina, and then Luke can escort one of Andy's sisters... I don't know. We haven't figured it out yet."

Reid nodded, his mouth as dry as if he'd just eaten sand. Walk down the aisle with Drew? It shouldn't be awkward, but since he'd been sleeping with her for the better part of the past two months and knew the end was nigh, it might be weird to see her next June. What if she had a date? What if *he* did?

Gage was blissfully in the dark, having given up the notion that it was odd finding Reid in Drew's apartment. He'd asked about Christina a time or two when they'd been out for beers. Reid had played it off, saying they were doing "okay" and then adding that he wasn't "ready to let this one go yet" in case Gage popped in at either Drew's or Reid's house and caught them together. At least if the Christina lie was in circulation, he'd have a prayer of playing it off.

What was making him so damned uncomfortable with the situation wasn't keeping Gage in the dark, though that was inconvenient, but that Reid had started suspecting Drew was on the brink of wanting more. He'd had enough experience with women to know when it was time to pull up. Drew might not be in love with him yet, but she was close.

Every time thcy were together, there was a lot more than sex between them. They'd become friends—close friends—in a short time, and had shared secrets and stories with each other. Making love with her was healing a deep wound that'd occurred when Wesley vanished, and no other woman could claim the same.

Reid swiped his brow, sweat popping out on his forehead. He had to get out of here, just for a while.

"I, um, I forgot." He put his computer in sleep mode before grabbing his bag and stuffing his laptop into it. "I have to be across town for a thing."

"What thing?"

"Meeting with a guy—it's too boring to talk about. Probably why I forgot." Reid cleared his throat and checked the time. It was nearly two o'clock. "Yep, running late. Thank you for the watch. It's already come in handy. June. I'm excited."

With that off-kilter farewell, Reid and Gage stepped out of the office. As Reid locked up, Yasmine, their assistant, called Gage over. Reid used the distraction to bolt to the elevator, but not before Sabrina stopped him on the way.

"Hey. You okay?" She was wearing her black-framed glasses today and a royal blue dress that made her green eyes appear even brighter.

"Perfect. Late for a meeting."

"Oh, well, I'll let you go." She pointed at his wrist and smiled. "I see Gage asked you to help marry him." She winked, and Reid felt something loosen in his chest. No sense in being dramatic about it. What was with him today? He wasn't big on premonitions, but he felt as if someone'd walked over his grave.

"Yeah. He did ask." He gave her a smile.

"And you said yes." She beamed. "I'm glad."

"Me, too."

"You set a date yet?"

"Not yet, but we will." Her smile brightened. "Are you eagerly anticipating standing up at our wedding, too?"

"You know me. I never miss a good wedding."

"Uh-huh." She chuckled and turned for her office, calling over her shoulder, "Have a good one, Singleton."

He smiled to himself, shaking his head at his own bout of random anxiety—which he considered perfectly normal now that he thought about it. His birthday was tomorrow, after all. It'd been an off day for his family for as long as he could remember.

Drew had invited him to dinner on his birthday. Fig & Truffle at the Market was opening soon, and the staff was doing a practice run even before the soft opening. They needed extra mouths to feed, and she'd invited him since she knew he wouldn't be busy. He'd warned her not to sneak in a birthday celebration, and she'd sworn by drawing an X over her left breast that she'd do nothing of the sort. He trusted that to be true. *It'd better be true.*

Surely, she knew after he'd shared with her the tragic loss of Wesley that a surprise party wasn't a good idea.

Besides, he had further reasoned, she'd have to invite Gage, Sabrina and Flynn, which would mean telling them about the relationship. He doubted any of his marriage-bound friends would be happy to hear about them—especially when they found out Reid and Drew were temporary.

Tired from the afternoon slump, Reid drove to Brewdog's, deciding that a hot drink and some time alone with his laptop was in order. He needed to escape the office and have a bit of solitude. Solitude in public. Coffee, or maybe a cuppa, sounded incredible right about now.

He stepped inside, displeased to find a line. Figures. This week had been a kick in the bollocks all the way around.

Almost all the way around. Drew had been the highlight of his night on most nights. He hadn't seen her in a few days, which shouldn't have been a big deal but here he was, standing at Brewdog's wearing a watch made of bourbon barrel, feeling melancholy and displaced, and missing her. Missing her because she knew how to take his mind off his troubles. And it was about more than her shedding her clothes—though that certainly took his mind off *everything*. Drew knew when to needle him, when to push, when to sit back and wait for him to speak. She also cooked a mean omelet. He'd found risotto unimaginative and dull until the other night, when she fed him a bite she'd cooked on the range in his kitchen. Truffles truly changed everything.

She was becoming special to him in a way that he hadn't been able to fathom. How about that?

Lost in thought, he wasn't aware the line had moved until the guy behind him tapped his arm and murmured a polite, "Excuse me. The line's moving."

Reid shuffled forward and turned to apologize but stopped cold when he found himself looking into blue eyes that were eerily similar to his own. Actually, *everything* went cold. His face, his hands, his arms. The laptop bag he was holding felt as heavy as if he'd toted in a cinder block. The sounds around him receded, replaced by a high-pitched hum inside his head.

The man who'd tapped him cocked his head slightly but before he could get a word out, Reid felt tears prick the corners of his eyes.

"Wesley?" His voice was barely audible over the chatter of the café, a dry croak of sound he'd desperately tried to

make audible. Every part of his being, every cell within, told him that the man with eyes that matched his own was his deceased brother.

"Tate." The man shook his head and offered what might've been an uncomfortable smile. "Tate Duncan."

He offered a hand, and Reid stared at it for a beat longer than appropriate before taking it in his own. "Reid Singleton."

On contact, "Tate's" face went slack. They stood there, hands clasped, staring silently for an awkward beat before Reid let go.

"Next customer," the barista called out. "Sir?"

"Um, right." Reid faced the barista, determined to shake the eerie moment. "Americano. Two pumps vanilla." He gestured to Tate and said, "Put his on mine."

"You don't have to—" Tate started.

"I insist."

Tate let out a small laugh and then gave his order. "Black coffee."

It's a coincidence, Reid told himself as he paid. The shake in his arm receded, his limbs warming as the cold sensation went away. It didn't change the certainty in his gut, though.

Reid and Wesley weren't identical twins, but they'd had the same eyes. Their mother had dressed them in matching clothes at that age, and even now they didn't look that dissimilar, each in chinos and button-down shirts.

Reid watched Tate from his periphery as he walked to the other counter to await their beverages, and that gut certainty that this man was Wesley back from the dead returned with a sickening twist. And Reid had no idea how to broach that topic without sounding like a complete and utter loon.

"Thanks for the coffee, man." Tate's accent was American with a dose of cool, calm California. Not a note of English in it that Reid could detect.

"You're welcome." Reid swallowed thickly, trying to reason a way to keep Tate from leaving. To tell him that he was not Tate, but the twin brother who went missing on their third birthday.

Reid *knew* it.

"Do we...know each other?" Tate laughed awkwardly. "I usually remember everyone, and I can't get over the familiarity. But your name doesn't ring a single bell. Sorry if that's rude."

"No. You're right. We do know each other." Reid spotted the hairline scar beneath Tate's right eye and once again, reality tilted on its axis. Wesley had been bitten by the neighbor's nasty poodle a few weeks before their birthday. The scar had been an ugly one and had required stitches. It was now faint and white and exactly the spot Reid remembered from the many photos their parents kept around the house.

He couldn't let Tate leave this café without telling him the truth.

"You're not Tate," Reid blurted, knowing he sounded bonkers.

"An Americano and a coffee, black," called out one of the baristas.

Tate grabbed the drinks and handed over Reid's cup, offering yet another polite smile. "I am. Trust me."

"Trust *me*. You're not." Reid cuffed his brother's arm and moved him aside, feeling the resistance in his younger-than-him-by-two-minutes twin. He spoke quickly, afraid to pause for even a second and lose his nerve. "You're Wesley Singleton and you were born in London. Your birthday is tomorrow. Your mother's name is Jane and your father's name is George and I'm Reid—" he cleared his throat "—your twin brother."

Despite the stark shock on Tate's face, and the onlookers who paused to take in the dramatic scene, Reid pressed on. He had one shot to get through to his brother or he would never see him again. He knew it in his bones.

"Our third birthday party was a circus theme and there were clowns," Reid continued. "And jugglers an-and a big inflatable house filled with plastic balls. And a pool!" He knew how he must look: wild-eyed and crazed. He didn't care. He'd spent his entire childhood looking at children his age for any sign that they were Wesley. There'd been a feeling so strongly within him at the funeral that Wes hadn't died. That he was alive and well. Over the years he'd lost hope, but he wouldn't lose Wesley again.

"Listen, please. There was a pool, Wes." Reid tightened his grip on his brother's arm. "And your favorite toy was a Curious George soft toy and I threw it into the pool once and Mum dived in with all her clothes on to get it for you."

"Look, man…" Tate's expression turned thunderous as he shook out of Reid's grasp.

But Reid was nowhere near giving up.

"You went missing," he told Tate as calmly as he could manage. "We looked and looked. For years. Your funeral was five years after that, and we buried an empty casket. I have no idea how you're here and why you don't sound like you should, but you are and you don't. I know as I stand here that you're not Tate Duncan. You're my brother, Wesley Singleton."

Tate's face had gone stark white; his blue eyes were wide and frightened.

"I don't mean to scare you." With one shaking hand Reid pulled a business card out of his bag and thrust it into Tate's palm. "Try and remember and then call me if—"

"Look, buddy." Tate's voice shook with anger. "I appreciate the coffee but whatever scam you're running, I'm not interested."

"Wait, Wes—"

"It's *Tate*. Leave me alone." He looked at the business card gripped between his fingers and then tossed it, along with his untouched coffee, into the nearest trash can. "Don't follow me or I'm calling the police."

Twenty-One

Tate Duncan's hands were shaking so badly on the steering wheel of his Mercedes he considered pulling over at the nearest curb and waiting for the sensation to pass. Instead he kept his hands wrapped around the leather and took in what he could see, hear, touch and smell.

His name was Tate Duncan. His parents were William and Marion Duncan. His fiancée was Claire Waterson.

He'd been adopted—and yes, he'd had an accent when he was a toddler. But his birth mother had given him up for adoption after his father had died, and then she'd died shortly after that. He had his birth parents' death certificates, for Christ's sake.

"Scott and Natalie Winters." He spoke his birth parents' name aloud in the car, his voice sounding hollow and desperate. If what the stranger in the café had said to him was true, then that meant…what…his adoptive parents had lied to him his entire life? Or worse—had they arranged to have him kidnapped?

"It's ridiculous," he said aloud, but his body betrayed him and the shakes in his arm started anew.

He pulled into a hotel parking lot. He was in town on business today to finish up the plans for his new build on Spright Island, but now he'd rather take the ferry home and have the damn plans sent by courier.

Fear and confusion swam in his bloodstream. The run-in with Reid left behind enough doubt that Tate touched the screen on the dashboard of his Mercedes and called his parents in Santa Clarita.

"Hi, sweetheart," his mother's voice said over the speaker.

"Mom."

"What's wrong? You sound like something's wrong." Always the sensitive sort, Marion Duncan detected a problem immediately.

"I'm going to tell you a story, and I don't want you to interrupt until the end." He carefully recounted what had happened at the coffee shop, sharing every detail except for one. What he didn't tell his mother was that when that Reid guy shook his hand, Tate felt such a sense of peace it overwhelmed him. It was like seeing an old friend after years apart. And that, he realized, was exactly why he'd called his mom to tell her about what had happened. "Then I threw away the coffee and business card and walked out."

Tate raked his hands into his hair and waited for the silence to be interrupted by his mother's chiming laughter. He hoped with every fiber of his being that she'd tell him Reid sounded like he was in need of psychiatric attention. Then she'd reassure Tate that everything was fine and tell him not to worry, and they'd talk about something else.

Like his birthday plans for tomorrow night.

Your birthday is tomorrow.

How the hell had Reid known that? It had to be a scam. That was the only reasonable explanation.

"Mom." He said her name insistently, praying that the call had dropped or there was some other reason for her silence.

"Tate, honey," she managed, her tone so grave it sent chills skittering down his spine. "We need to talk."

Twenty-Two

Drew was so excited she could burst clean open and out would spray gold confetti. Her smile had been incurable most of the day as she picked up the final details for Reid's birthday dinner.

She'd decided to call the chef she'd hired for the night and ask his specialty. Turned out it was a gorgonzola New York strip steak atop pureed vegetables and garlic potato wedges. It sounded so incredible she ordered the same dish for herself.

Once the meal was decided, the only plans left to complete were decorations. Black and gold was the theme, and she'd spent the past hour hanging foil streamers and tying balloons to the barstools. The table was set in black and gold and white, and she planned on soft jazz as the background music.

Once the restaurant was set and the staff of three had arrived, she changed in the women's restroom. She'd cho-

sen a red dress for the evening, forgoing her habit of being
modest by wearing a plunging neckline. That, as much as
the rest of tonight, was part of her gift for Reid.

She was excited about giving him a new memory of his
birthday. One that would stand out in his mind and make
him smile. He'd know that she cared about him enough to
make the effort, and, she hoped, he'd also have a glimpse
of what their future together would look like.

The past, however, was a tricky beast. Even in her current state of well-being and confidence, she had moments
of fear and anxiety, and deep-seated feelings of not being
good enough or pretty enough or worthy enough.

Reid was a reminder that anything was possible. That
the dream she'd once harbored in the quiet of her heart
had come to fruition. They'd found each other at the perfect time, and she planned on showing him that tonight.

And then she was going to tell him she was in love
with him.

She checked her phone, but no word from Reid despite
her earlier texts. She called in case he was driving. No
answer. She settled on sending another text: Starting at 7
sharp. Does that work for you?

She watched the screen for a few moments but then
decided not to be weird about it, filling the time by turning the lights down low and locking the front door. That
way, Reid would have to let her know he was here, plus
she didn't want a person off the street disturbing her private party.

At five after seven she checked her phone again. Nothing.

She called. No answer.

He could've been held up in traffic. Maybe his phone
died. Reid had never played games with her before, and had
always done what he'd said. She knew he hadn't forgotten.

Unless…

She chewed her lip, remembering her early-morning text to him. She'd wished him a "happy birthday" followed by a "can't wait for tonight!" At the last second, she'd added a heart emoji to her text and sent it.

Surely that wouldn't have scared him off?

"He's on his way," she said aloud. She refused to let her confidence do a free fall. Tonight was too important to give into timidity.

At nine o'clock, Drew gave up the hope she'd held so dear. He wasn't coming.

She locked the door behind her borrowed staff, Beaux, Dana and Rocko, apologizing again for the hiccup in plans. Fear and worry mingling in a volatile mix, she lifted her cell phone and tried one last time to call Reid. After the fourth ring her heart sank, and this time she left a voice mail.

"Reid. It's nine o'clock. I'm at Fig & Truffle. You didn't call, you didn't text. You didn't show up. I don't know what to think. I'm scared to death you've been in an accident. I'm probably overreacting. Things happen. Delays occur. Hell, maybe you had a family emergency. Anyway, happy birthday."

She pressed End and stared at the screen of her phone, her stomach churning. She was worried, but she was also pissed. Was this his way of ending things? Was he going to ghost her until she went away? It seemed cruel, especially after how certain she'd been that they were growing to love each other, but…

Maybe Christina had been right.

Drew hadn't come clean about her feelings to Reid, and now he didn't show up to the evening she'd planned.

"Or…" she told herself. "He's reeling because it's his birthday."

Reid had not only shared the truth about his deceased brother, he'd told her plainly that birthdays weren't celebrated since Wesley's disappearance and subsequent funeral. Reid had warned her off from planning anything, and she'd told him not to worry, assuming he'd be grateful once he'd arrived. She'd convinced herself that she was doing this for him, *for them*, but was she? Or did she become so wrapped up in the planning that she never stopped to think about what he wanted?

Christina was absolutely right. Drew hadn't leveled with him about *anything*.

Reid must've caught wind of her plans, or maybe he'd sensed via her texts and the heart emoji that tonight wasn't a soft opening after all. If he'd suspected her of luring him here for a birthday celebration—one he hadn't asked for and didn't want—there's no way he'd show up.

She'd accept her share of the blame, but he should've communicated his feelings—no matter what they were. He could've at least given her the courtesy of a reply text.

"Bastard," she growled under her breath. Anger took the controls from worry as Drew drove to Reid's apartment. She vowed to keep a cool head and let him say his piece, but if she found out he'd blown her off on purpose, they were going to have a lot to talk about.

Short of death, there was *zero* excuse for him not contacting her to tell her he wouldn't be there tonight.

She banged on Reid's door after sweet-talking the front desk—Ralph knew her by now, so it hadn't been that hard—but there wasn't an answer. She knocked one last time before trying the knob, and the door opened.

Inside his apartment she heard the TV around the corner, and took a deep breath of relief when she saw him sitting on the couch. Now that she knew he was okay, she was going to kill him.

"It's Drew," she announced. The back of Reid's head was visible over the sofa and a war movie was on the screen—her least favorite.

"Reid?"

She rounded the couch to find him slumped, eyes closed, a half-empty bottle of Jack Daniel's in one hand. She reached for the bottle before he spilled liquor on the couch, and he jerked awake.

"What the hell!" he barked. His eyes were dark with fury, his mouth a hateful tilt.

"Are you… What happened to you tonight?"

He avoided looking her in the eye. "You're in my way," he growled. "What the bloody hell are you doing here, anyway?"

Okay, she had no idea what was with his Jekyll/Hyde behavior, but she wasn't going to stand here and take it. He'd never talked to her this way. She snatched away the remote and flicked off the TV.

"Hand it over!" He tried to stand but he stumbled, crashing onto the couch in an inelegant heap.

"Give me the bottle and I'll give you the remote."

"No deal." He took another swig, spilling whiskey over his chin before setting aside the bottle.

"I waited for you for over two hours," she told him. "And you were here the whole time…getting drunk?"

"It's *my* birthday."

"I thought you wanted to spend it with—" *someone you love* "—me."

A flash of guilt lit his expression and vanished just as fast. "Yeah, well."

"Why didn't you call me? Or answer my text?" Things

couldn't end this way. She wouldn't *let them* end this way. "At the very least, I'm owed the respect of a reply."

"With a heart emoji," he slurred, glowering up at her.

There it was. Her fear confirmed. She'd convinced herself on the way over here that she'd been overreacting. He had held that stupid red heart emoji against her.

"I—"

"Get out, Drew." Those words were spoken plainly, not an iota of a slur or hesitation, which made them all the harder to hear. He pointed to the door. "Before I call security."

"I am not going to let you kick me out of here without an explanation."

"Yes, you are." This time he did stand, bearing down on her with nostrils flared. "You'll do it because I asked. And because you deserve better than someone who can't be who you need. You deserve someone who texts hearts back to you… Someone who shows up. Someone without all this baggage." Pain crept into Reid's eyes. "You deserve someone—" he touched her cheek gently "—better than me."

His eyes fluttered, and he swayed, nearly toppling over. She grabbed his arms and—thank God for the trainers at the gym—was able to reroute him to the couch, where he fell with a *whump*. He lay on his left shoulder, awkwardly positioned, eyes shut. A soft snore came next.

There was something else going on with him—something bigger than heart emojis and birthday dinners. Maybe he'd gotten a call from his father that his mother wasn't okay, or maybe he'd called his mum for support and she hadn't offered any.

No matter what had happened, Drew couldn't leave him here alone. She'd never seen Reid behave this way. She couldn't be certain that he was in his right mind, or that he wouldn't attempt to drive somewhere. Someone had to stay with him and make sure he was okay, and that someone couldn't be her. Reid didn't want her here. He'd made that clear.

But she knew who could help. The same person she'd always turned to first whenever she'd been in trouble. After the second ring, her brother answered.

"Hey, sis."

"Gage," she spoke around a lump in her throat, frightened and worried now that the anger had passed. "I need you to come to Reid's."

Twenty-Three

Tate had drunk enough wine at his birthday celebration to tranquilize a grizzly bear, but apparently it hadn't been enough to keep him asleep through the night.

He bolted upright, his chest heaving. A sheen of cold sweat covered him, and his head throbbed like hell.

He was momentarily disoriented by the pale blue walls and the pink floral comforter, the whitewashed dresser that glowed in the moonlight streaming in through the window. Then he remembered he was at Claire's apartment. She'd driven him here after the restaurant where Tate had wine. Like, *all* the wine.

His fiancée was fast asleep, her perfect bone structure aglow and her neatly brushed blond hair fanning over the pillow.

He touched her gently, half expecting her to turn into smoke and vanish altogether. That's the way he'd felt ever since the phone call with his mother yesterday. As if his entire life had been a mirage. She'd said they needed to talk, and that hadn't been the half of it…

"We need to talk."

"Then talk."

"Not over the phone. Plus, your father will want to be there."

"Don't do this to me, dammit." He'd never spoken to his mother that way his whole life, but desperate times… "I'm sorry. I can't… You have to tell me something, Mom. I feel like I'm losing my mind."

She sighed, a ragged sound from the depths. Frankly, he was terrified what she'd say next.

"Everything your father and I have told you about your past, your parentage and your childhood is true."

Tate released the breath he was holding. The back of his head hit the headrest in relief. "Thank God."

But before he could completely relax, his mother added, "As far as we know."

When she'd started to cry, he'd known something was severely off. She refused to tell him any more over the phone. He'd boarded the ferry and returned to Spright Island. But even his sanctuary within the luxury wellness community he ran and operated wasn't enough to lift the weight of dread from his shoulders.

His parents had traveled to his house to talk to him in person this morning, and what they'd told him was at once better and worse than Tate had imagined.

He ran through the list of what he now knew for sure.

One, he was adopted at age three.

He pictured Reid in the café. *Our third birthday party was a circus theme…*

Two, he was born to British parents, which was why he used to have an accent.

You're Wesley Singleton and you were born in London.

And finally, the new information that had come to light: his parents had always been suspicious of the agency from where they'd adopted Tate.

"We fell in love with you on sight," his mother had said through heaving sobs as she stood in his living room.

His father hadn't been crying, but his throat had been choked with emotion when he admitted that he, too, had been suspicious. *"But we never doubted your parents were dead. We knew it was unscrupulous for the agency to ask for an extra fee, but we loved you so very much."*

They'd paid over $100,000 in "processing fees" to rush the adoption process. The agency had provided the death certificates of Tate's alleged birth parents, and that had been the end of their communication with the agency.

"We *still* love you so much," his mother had said.

Tate loved them, too, but hadn't been able to return the sentiment at that moment. Instead, he'd given them his spare key and invited them to stay at his home on Spright Island for a while.

He'd returned to Seattle to Claire, arriving about six hours earlier than he'd planned and with a packed bag. Then he'd pasted on a smile as fake as he suspected those death certificates were and told her he missed her.

They'd been dating a little over a year, and he'd proposed a month ago. They hadn't decided yet where to live, though it made more sense to him to stay in Spright Island since he owned a home there and Claire rented. They'd tabled the discussion for the time being. To think he'd believed her hesitation was the biggest cause for turmoil in his otherwise worry-free life.

Worry-free until now.

He'd spent the day and evening with Claire and two couples who had started out as friends of hers. Tate hadn't enjoyed the dinner or the company, or even the wine. He'd used the substance to numb himself.

He'd kept what his parents told him secret and vowed to keep it secret until the day he *actually* died. No good could come from rocking the boat. None at all.

Claire made a soft noise and touched his arm.

"Okay?" she murmured, her eyes closed.

"Yeah. Fine." He bent and kissed her smooth cheek and slid out of bed. "Just hungry," he lied.

In the kitchen he stood with a bottle of water and stared at the black sky, at the barely visible stars struggling to twinkle through the light pollution of the city.

Somewhere out there was a man named Reid Singleton who believed that Tate was his brother. Who believed that Tate was named *Wesley*.

"And that I was kidnapped by a circus clown," he said aloud with a hoarse chuckle. The laugh died on his lips as a vision flashed on the screen of his mind.

No, not a vision.

A memory.

A memory of a little boy with the same color eyes as him snatching a stuffed Curious George toy and throwing it into a swimming pool.

Then another vision attacked like virtual reality—he could practically feel the large, rough hands that caught him under the armpits. Smell gasoline on the fingers that had covered his mouth.

And as three-year-old Tate had been carried into the woods, he saw a blur of bright colors—a red-and-yellow inflatable where kids played in a sea of plastic blue and green balls—against a brown cottage in a lush yard.

Home.

The word hit him with such a certainty that his knees weakened. The pounding in his head dialed up to ten. He sank to his ass on Claire's mahogany wood flooring, no longer able to find the strength to stand.

It was real.

Everything Reid had said.

"My brother," he whispered to the dark room.

"Tate?" Claire, wrapping a short silk robe over her lithe frame, padded out into the kitchen. "Are you okay?".

"I'm not Tate." He smiled up at his fiancée but his mind was in a sad, distant place. "My name is Wesley," he told her in as good a British accent as he could muster.

Twenty-Four

When Drew heard the light rap at the front door, she was next to it, having waited for her brother to arrive in the foyer rather than watch over Reid. First off, he was fine—drunk, sure, but fine. At least physically. Second, she was still pretty angry with him, and standing over him fuming wasn't productive.

She pulled open Reid's front door and Gage scanned her red dress and heels darkly. "Where is he?"

"Passed out on the couch."

Gage stalked past her. In the living room, he took inventory of Reid's position before bending over and hauling his best friend into a sitting position.

Drew stood off to the side as Gage slapped Reid's face—not hard enough to rattle his teeth but hard enough that Reid's eyes rolled open.

Reid threw himself forward and squeezed Gage into a hug. "Wesley."

Gage peeled his friend off his shoulders. "Reid. Man. What is going on with you?"

"Gage?" Reid blinked a few times, his eyes damp with tears. "I thought you were my brother."

His brother? Ho boy. She'd been right. Something was going on with him that had nothing to do with her.

"It's our birthday."

"I know it's your birthday."

"*Our* birthday. I stood up Drew." Reid sent her a glare. "She won't leave."

Gage's jaw tightened, and he slid a withering glare Drew's way. Then he told his friend, "You are going to owe her a really big thank-you in the morning for putting up with your shit." He pulled Reid up by the shoulders, wrapped one arm around him and dragged him into the bedroom.

Drew lifted her purse from the barstool in the kitchen and tiptoed toward the front door.

"Sit your ass down." Gage bypassed her to go to the fridge and grab a bottle of water. "Give me thirty seconds."

She wanted to tell him she didn't owe him an explanation, but she did. They'd always been close. She confided in her brother about everything. Hell, he was the one she called when her heart was broken. Him, not a girlfriend. Gage always knew what to say to make it better, and she trusted him not to spill her secrets to anyone—especially Mom and Dad. And right now her heart was definitely broken.

She dropped her purse on the kitchen counter and sat on the barstool, her chin in her hands while she waited for Gage's return.

He arrived a minute later and pulled two bottles of beer from Reid's fridge. Uncapping them, he watched her with a look of disappointment—which was worse than if he'd been angry.

"Him, I'll take to task when he's good and hungover." Gage took a long guzzle of beer, and she did the same. "You, I'm dealing with now." He leaned on the counter. "What's going on, Drew?"

"Reid and I have been…seeing each other."

"You mean sleeping together."

She winced. "Yeah."

Gage shut his eyes slowly, took a deep breath, and after steeling himself, nodded. "Go on."

She told him about California and about Reid not recognizing her.

She told him about the crush she'd had when she was younger. She told him how Reid had come to mean more to her than she'd expected. How it was her idea that they not tell Gage. Then she told him that Reid never dated Christina. How Drew planned his birthday party because Reid told her a big secret about why his birthday was such an unhappy time of year.

"Why?"

She averted her eyes. "I can't tell you that."

"Yes, you can."

"I really can't." She picked the label on the beer bottle with her thumbnail. "It's something you're going to have to hear from Reid himself. I promised."

Her brother nodded, but still didn't seem happy about… well, any of it. "You're in love with him, aren't you?"

She nodded, and a tear spilled down her cheek.

Gage pulled her into a tight hug. "Why'd you do that?"

"I don't know," she sobbed. "I thought he'd want to make this last a little longer. I was going to tell him how I felt tonight."

"Shh-shh. Listen." He held her face in his hands and

gave her a soft smile. "Try not to worry, okay? I'm going to stay here. I'll talk to him. I'll find out why he was such a dick to you earlier. No matter what big secret he has, Drew, you know you deserve more than what he's offering."

"Funny. That's what he said to me." She offered a watery smile. "I thought I'd change his mind. That he'd see how great we are together. How good I am for him."

"This doesn't have anything to do with you. If anything, you're too good for him." Gage kissed her forehead. "You okay to drive home?"

"Completely sober," she said instead, because she wasn't okay. Not even a little. But she took her brother's advice and left. The only other option was to stay here, and she sure as hell wasn't doing that.

At home, Drew kicked off her shoes and crawled into bed, still wearing her red dress. She was exhausted from the taxing emotions of the day. The last thing she thought about before sleep took hold were Reid's words to Gage.

I thought you were my brother.

What was that about?

The second cup of coffee was helping. He hoped.

Reid hovered over his half-empty mug, cupping his aching head in both hands. It was like a nuclear bomb had gone off in his skull. Gage stood sentinel at the countertop, arms folded over his chest. He'd been like that all morning. He hadn't done a damn thing to help Reid get over his hangover, either. He'd started off by coming into Reid's room and clapping his hands together while yelling, "Time to get up!" over and over.

Reid had dragged his aching carcass into the shower and emerged feeling not much better. In his kitchen, Gage stood, mug of coffee in hand, and when Reid asked for one he poured the entire pot down the drain.

So much for best friends.

Reid had made another pot of coffee and poured himself a cup while Gage made himself a plate of scrambled eggs. He ate, and Reid refilled his coffee mug. And that's when Gage decided to speak.

"Talk, Singleton. Why are you messing with Drew?"

"I'm not messing with her."

"But you are fucking her."

"Do you want your ass kicked?" Reid barked, adrenaline pouring through his veins like hot lava.

"That's my line."

He'd never seen his friend this pissed off before. Gage had every right. Reid was in the wrong pursuing Drew and hadn't treated her well last night. He hadn't been able to reconcile having a birthday now that he knew his brother was alive and well and in the same damn city. After a night and day of emotional upheaval was it any wonder he'd turned to whiskey for a reprieve? His thoughts had been an unsortable mess since he'd found Wesley returned from the dead, and then lost him all over again.

Reid wouldn't have been good company at Drew's soft opening anyhow. Yes, he should've contacted her, but what the hell would he have said? *Sorry, too drunk to show up after finding my brother alive.* He had no idea how to tell her what he'd learned…how to tell anyone.

"My life took a complicated turn last night," Reid mumbled.

"What's so complicated?" Gage pressed. "You can't sort your heart from your dick? So you slept with my sister until she got in too deep and now you're punishing her for liking you too much?"

"No. That's not—this isn't about Drew." Reid palmed

his head. It ached 5 percent less than when he woke up this morning, which was a crowning achievement. His pending breakdown was far more than Drew had signed up for. If she thought he'd had baggage before, it was nothing compared to the entire airport's worth he had now.

"I'm trying to protect her," Reid told Gage, but the excuse sounded lame even to his own ears.

Gage narrowed his eyelids. "That's my job."

"I…" Reid swallowed thickly, worried that Gage would think him bonkers once he told him about Tate. Worried more that Gage would write him off completely when he found out that Drew wasn't the only secret Reid had kept from him over the years. But Reid owed him an explanation, not to save his own hide but because Gage was his oldest friend.

"I have a twin brother," he said. "And up until two days ago I thought he was dead." Reid told him about the birthday party that ended up being a search party and everything else leading up until now. How his parents had never handled the day well. How Reid hadn't celebrated a birthday since.

While he spoke, Gage's face grew pale.

"I was in Brewdog's for coffee and, Gage, I swear as I sit here he was right behind me in line."

"How?"

"I have no idea. I told him who he was. He didn't believe me. He introduced himself as Tate Duncan from California. But he had a scar I recognized. He has my eyes. It was my brother, Wesley. I'd know him anywhere." A fresh wave of pain zapped his chest. "He threw away my card. He didn't believe me," he repeated numbly.

"Reid… I… And now? Do you still believe that was Wesley?"

"With everything I am." Reid shoved his coffee away, his stomach on fire. "I might be more certain than before."

"And you didn't tell Drew about him?"

"I told her about his death, but I didn't tell her I saw him." Reid blinked in shock. "That he wasn't dead." He blinked up at Gage. "I was processing."

"You were processing," Gage bit out. "Not only have you been keeping the relationship between you and Drew from me, but you've been keeping this secret, as well? From me, from Flynn and Sabrina? We've been friends for years, Reid. You could've told us."

"I know." Reid hung his pounding head.

"Drew would've understood."

Reid was beginning the suspect Gage was right. But finding his brother was alive hadn't changed who Reid was—he hadn't suddenly become whole. In fact, he felt more broken than ever. "Drew and I were supposed to break up this month, anyway. Last night seemed apt."

"Did you really think she would let you go after she was with you for nearly *two months*?"

When Gage put it that way, it made Reid feel daft. Of course she wouldn't shrug their time off together. She was different, and with her, Reid had been different.

Gage shook his head pitiably. "Lucky for you I fell in love with someone who wasn't honest about her identity at first, either. I have a high tolerance for understanding."

"You thought she was a man," Reid teased. Andy's website hadn't featured her photo so they'd assumed by name and reputation alone that she was a male. What a bunch of sexist bastards they'd been. "Until we laid eyes on her, we all thought that."

Gage smiled, unable to keep a stone face when his fiancée was mentioned. He refilled his coffee mug, topping off Reid's as well—a good sign Reid was on his way to being forgiven. "How have you not tracked this Tate guy down yet?"

"I used to search online for him once I was old enough to know what I was doing. Just in case we'd been mistaken. I researched adoption agencies, missing children reports. I finally gave up. Accepted the inevitable. That casket was empty, but Wesley may as well have been inside it. He was a ghost."

"A ghost who has returned." Gage raised his eyebrows. "And now you know his name and where he's from."

"I do." Hope dawned, sharp and bold. He knew enough to track him down.

"We'll call every Duncan household in California," Gage said as he lifted his phone to his ear. "Every Tate Duncan in the Pacific Northwest."

"Who're you calling?"

"We need help." Then into the phone, Gage said, "Flynn. Can you and Sabrina come to Reid's? Yes. Now."

Twenty-Five

It was hard to mourn Reid when she wasn't sure they'd ever had anything to begin with. Drew wasn't even sure they were broken up.

Reid was gone. That much she knew.

Gage had called her late on Sunday to tell her…well, not much. She knew that Reid woke with a killer hangover, that Flynn and Sabrina and Gage had spent the day together. That they all knew Reid's secret about his twin brother going missing when Reid was three years old, and about the funeral when Reid was eight.

What she didn't know was what had driven Reid to drown his sorrows in whiskey and treat her like she'd never mattered. She'd told Gage as much and he'd given her the best big-brother speech ever.

"It's inexcusable the way he talked to you that night and I'm sorry," Gage had said. "I love you so much. I'm trying to be there for him, but trust me, I'm on your side.

If he doesn't make some sort of amends with you soon, I'm not sure we'll be friends much longer. I choose you, kiddo."

She'd burst into tears and cried on her phone's screen, telling Gage that she was at fault as well, and that he shouldn't leave his best friend for her. She should've told Reid how she felt about him a long time ago. She'd dreamed up the plan for a perfect evening when, really, wouldn't a simple heart-to-heart have been enough?

"He has a lot to make up for with all of us," Gage had said, sounding as hollow as she felt.

It seemed everyone was in a holding pattern while Reid was in London. She didn't know why he was there, but assumed he was trying to find some closure with his family. She didn't know why this birthday in particular had been a trigger for him, but there was more to the story that she didn't know about. Gage let on that he knew, but refused to tell her, even though she'd begged.

"I can't, Drew. The same way you knew I had to hear from Reid, you are going to have to hear this from Reid, too. He swore all of us to secrecy, saying he had to sort it out for himself. We owe him that."

"It's that big, huh?" she'd asked, acceptance an arrow through her heart.

"Yes. It is."

So that was that. Reid was in London and she was in Seattle and had no idea when he'd be back, why he'd gone there or if he'd ever speak to her again.

As much as it'd hurt to do it she'd deleted his phone number and text messages from her phone. She needed a clean break. Seeing that damn heart emoji in her text messages only reminded her of the worst night of her life. She needed to pull on her big-girl panties and remember who she'd become.

A woman who was building a career without the support or help of a man. Reid was no Devin Briggs, but somehow he'd managed to hurt her more than Devin, and in a much shorter span of time.

She hated Reid for that as much as she loved him in spite of it. It would be a long road, but she wasn't going to lie around in wait for him to come to some conclusion about them. Good God, it'd taken him a decade to tell his best friends about his loss. How long would he keep her in the dark about this new turn of events?

"Hey, Drew." She turned to find Beaux, the bartender, a bottle of white wine in hand. Fig & Truffle, the Market location, was opening tonight, and she was ready. They all were. "Do we have more chardonnay?"

"Let me check." She walked past him, but he caught her arm gently, his blond eyebrows lowering in concern.

"You're better off without him." Beaux nodded resolutely, and she forced a grin. He'd been there the night of the failed birthday dinner. It wasn't much of a leap to put Reid's absence together with her sadness and arrive at the logical conclusion she'd been dumped.

"You're absolutely right. I'll check on the chardonnay." Keys in hand, she walked to the wine cellar as the cliché Beaux offered echoed in her mind. She didn't believe she'd be better off without Reid, but she had to believe that to make it through tonight. And the next night. And the night after that.

However long it took for her heart to heal after being torn apart.

Reid had been in London for nearly two weeks. He'd gone to his parents' home to stay, and they'd been delighted to see him. It was rare he popped in for a surprise visit. Hell, he'd never popped in for a surprise visit.

As glad as they were to see him, however, he couldn't feel good about being here. He had news for them he knew wouldn't be welcome.

And he'd put it off for too long.

He'd played off the extended visit as "old home week," and he'd made good on that bargain as well, hunting down old friends and cousins he'd not seen in years. He'd spent a lot of time at the pub—every damned night. Last night he and his father had downed their fair share of scotch while sitting at the fire. Mum had long since gone to bed, and the scotch warm in his veins, Reid found it the perfect time to tell his father what had happened in Seattle.

George Singleton had taken the news well. Stoically, actually. The tremor in his hand had rattled his half-empty glass, but he'd listened intently as Reid caught him up.

Flynn was the one who'd called the correct Tate Duncan. He'd reached him via Spright Island's realty office. A woman named Shelley had answered the phone. Flynn had convinced her that he and Tate had met up in Seattle, but he'd lost Tate's number and was interested in bringing more business to their community. She'd mentioned that Tate had taken the week off. "I believe he's in Seattle now at his fiancée's house," Shelley had said. "Would you like me to leave him a message to call you?"

"It's urgent. So, yes." Flynn had relayed Reid's phone number. "If you could give him the name Reid Singleton and tell him it's an emergency. He'll understand."

Flynn had ended the call and nodded to the four of them seated at Reid's kitchen table, each in front of their own laptops. "I think that was him."

Sabrina had reached for Reid's hand, and he'd held on to her tightly, feeling as if his friends were the only thing keeping him bolted to the earth. Like without them he'd go hurtling into space until the oxygen was robbed of his body and he collapsed like a meaningless black hole.

Reid sat across from his mother at the breakfast table now, who was wholly ignoring her sausage and eggs. His father held her hand, his expression unreadable. She cried softly, and Reid wanted to stop talking. To stop breaking her heart into tiny pieces. Unfortunately, there was more to tell her.

No going back now.

"Wes—Tate Duncan called me, Mum. That afternoon. Within an hour of Flynn's phone call, he called me back." He drew in a deep breath as his mother's face filled with hope. "He's…not ready. To meet either of you."

She collapsed into his father's arms, her wailing sobs drawing wetness to Reid's own eyes. George shushed his wife and rubbed her shoulders, there for her when she needed him most.

Exactly the opposite of Reid's reaction to Drew, and he'd needed her even more than she'd needed him.

Reid hadn't been able to lean on her even when he'd received the knee-weakening call from his brother. The one where Wesley plainly stated that he'd remembered being snatched.

"Must've been a repressed memory or something." *Tate's voice was low, his tone flat. Reid remained silent.* *"I spoke with my parents. My adoptive parents. They told me something I've never known before. The agency that facilitated the adoption was…sketchy. They extorted money from them. A lot of it. My mom said she was too in love with me to see the truth for what it was. That the death certificates for my birth parents could've been faked."*

It was a lot to take in—then and now. It was so much that Reid didn't say any more to his mother about what

Tate had relayed to him about the adoption. But there was a sliver of hope he could give her, and thank God for that.

"I need to tell you some good news." Reid patted her arm and his mother—his beautiful mother with her stylish gray hair and trim figure, and green-blue eyes—pulled her face from George's neck to fasten Reid with a look that conveyed so much hope his heart broke for her.

"He's agreed to meet me for dinner when I go home. It's a start at building a relationship. He has a lot to sort out. And so do we." Reid wasn't sure how he'd handle a man he didn't know coming up to him in a coffee shop and saying he was his long-lost twin brother. He supposed he'd have become angry and stormed out, like Wesley had. How did anyone even begin to accept their entire life was a lie?

"I promise you both," Reid told his parents, "that I will do everything in my power to bring him to meet you."

"Or us to meet him." Jane wiped away her tears and offered a brittle smile. "We will fly to Washington, darling. We will."

"I know you will. And as soon as I navigate around this very sensitive subject of Wes—Tate accepting that we're his family, I will put you on a plane myself. But keep your hopes in check. Just in case."

She nodded excitedly, and he could see that her hopes were most certainly not in check.

"Can we call him?" she asked.

"I don't know. But you can call me." He held his mother's hand. "You can call me and I'll tell you everything about him and how our dinner went. And I will tell him that it's best for all of us if we reunite as soon as possible."

Jane's tender smile was like the sun bursting through dark clouds. "My baby boy."

Reid assumed she was referring to Wesley until she

moved from George's embrace and into Reid's. He held his mother as she cried against him and vowed that no matter what, he'd make that reunion happen. If it took him the rest of his mother's life to convince Wesley to reunite with his actual family, Reid wouldn't give up on his twin brother.

Not ever, ever again.

"There's more I have to tell you," he told his mother as she calmed. He smoothed his hand along her back. "I've met someone."

Jane pulled herself from his arms, her face a comical expression of shock. She didn't know details about his love life, but she knew he wasn't one to settle down. "Have you?"

"*The* one."

He was as sure of it as he was sure that Tate Duncan was Wesley Singleton. He was as sure of Drew being his destiny as he was the sun would rise in the east. He was sure, for the first time in his life, that the pieces of his life had intersected at this precise moment for a reason.

Drew was meant to be his.

"She's my best mate's sister. Her name is Drew. And she's the most beautiful woman in the world." He tapped his mother's chin. "Save you."

A crack of laughter sounded from his mother—possibly the best sound he'd ever heard. "Well, where is she then?"

"She's at home. And I need to tell her what I've learned. About Wesley and about myself." Reid had believed himself incapable of loving or trusting anyone. He'd believed that his running into Tate was a premonition of danger; a warning to turn back. He'd reasoned that he was leaving for Drew because she deserved to be with someone who wasn't a train wreck waiting to happen.

But as these two weeks had passed he'd realized the train wreck had already happened and Drew hadn't hesitated to sift through the wreckage and find the surviving parts of his heart. Of his very *soul*.

She'd been everything to him before he'd been brave enough to admit it, and now that his life was more unstable than ever, he knew she was his port in the storm.

She was his home.

"I hope she'll take me back," he said to his parents, but mostly to himself. His eyes on his empty breakfast plate he added, "And I hope she believes me when I tell her how much I love her."

Twenty-Six

Drew helped Christina unload her bags from the trunk. Her flight left in an hour, so she needed to hustle. "Have a safe—*oof*!"

Christina hugged Drew tightly, practically choking her in the process. "I'm a horrible, awful, terrible person!"

"Can't...breathe." Drew tapped her roommate's shoulders insistently, half kidding, half needing Chris to release the boa constrictor hold on her neck.

"Oh. Sorry."

Drew inhaled melodramatically before offering her friend a wink. "You're a wonderful, sweet, loving person."

"You shouldn't be consoling me! I'm taking a job in Chicago with almost no notice and leaving you here to fend for yourself at the worst possible time."

"You're taking your dream job," Drew corrected, ignoring the "worst possible time" thing. It'd been over two weeks since she'd heard from Reid, which had sucked her soul into an emotionless vacuum, but she couldn't pin that on Christina. "You paid me rent for the remainder of this month and next, what more could I ask of you? I'm planning on paying you back, by the way—"

"No, you're not. My signing bonus was huge. I want you to have it because I love you." Christina grinned. "I'm going to miss you." They hugged again.

"You're also going to miss your dream flight to your dream job if you don't get going."

Christina dragged her wheeled suitcase behind her and blew Drew a kiss. "I'll call you when I'm settled!"

"You'd better!"

Christina vanished behind the reflective glass doors of the airport terminal, and Drew buckled herself up in the driver's seat. It was the end of an era. Christina hadn't been shy about telling Drew she'd had an eye on Downey Design for her entire adult life. Every time she'd consider applying, though, she'd reasoned her way out of it. Chris didn't know anything about Chicago, didn't want to make new friends, blah, blah, blah. Then that day she'd lain on the sofa while Drew was sharing her first drink with Reid in California, Christina had been brave enough to upload her portfolio.

They'd responded last week and asked her to start right away.

Drew was happy for her friend. Almost as happy for her as she was miserable for herself.

Lately, Gage and Andy had stuck to Drew like a dryer sheet. She could scarcely find a moment to herself if she wasn't at work. Either Andy wanted to take her to lunch or out shopping, or Gage was fussing over repairs in her apartment. He'd come over to change light bulbs for her yesterday—as if she couldn't have done that herself?

She appreciated his doting, though. It showed that Gage loved her, and Andy did, too. So did Christina.

Everyone loves me except the man I want to love me most of all.

What a miserable reminder that was. *Thanks a lot, Brain.*

No problem.

Sundays used to be her favorite day, but now Drew resented the spare time. Gage and Andy weren't hovering since they knew Drew was driving Christina to the airport, and with both of them working full-time jobs, they had to make the most of the weekends. And what more could they do for Drew? She was sad, and there wasn't any fixing it.

Except for...

She cut that thought off at the knees.

The grill marks on the halibut were perfection. The red and green sauces the perfect yin-yang design on the square white plate. Drew rested the piece of fish in the center, sprinkled it with smoked, flaked sea salt and then balanced a small tuft of microgreens atop the fish.

She'd been trying to perfect this dish for quite some time, and now the dish was as pleasing to the eye as she knew it tasted. But just to make sure...

She grabbed a fork and lifted a bite to her lips. A sharp knock came from her front door and, her mouth watering, she sent a forlorn look at the fish.

"I knew you couldn't stay away," she called to what had to be Andy or Gage—or both of them. She turned the knob and pulled, then froze solid at the sight of the man standing in her doorway with a bouquet of roses.

Red roses.

"My brother's alive," Reid said.

Drew blinked as she processed that news. "I don't understand."

"I know. Can I come in?"

"I don't think that's a good idea." As wonderful as it was to see Reid's ridiculously handsome face, she was also feeling pretty damned protective over her own heart. How could she and Reid ever make it if he didn't trust her enough to tell her what was happening in his life? "I ran into him the day before my birthday," Reid continued from the entryway. "At Brewdog's. I bought him a cup of coffee and then blurted out that his name wasn't Tate Duncan like he thought it was. I told him he was Wesley Singleton and scared the life out of him. He thought I was scamming him or something. Anyway. I found him. He remembers being kidnapped. Not much around it or after it, but he remembers the birthday party. He remembers our childhood home in London. And he remembers me."

It was a lot of information to take in, but while Reid talked, her broken heart took a back seat to the miracle that had occurred.

She couldn't hide her awe. "That's incredible."

"He's living outside of Seattle. On an island you have to take the ferry to get to. We're having dinner this Friday, and I'm almost as sick over it as I am excited."

"It's the best news." She found herself returning Reid's infectious smile.

"It is. It truly is. And I didn't share it with you." His smile fell. "I have more I want to say if I could give you these—" he held up the flowers "— and come inside. If you want me gone, I'll leave. If after you hear me out you can't forgive me and have nothing left for me, I will leave,

Drew. I promise. But if what I say changes everything…
it'd be worth it to both of us for you to hear me out."

She watched him for several seconds. He was in dark
gray jeans and a weathered T-shirt. He was holding six
red roses, and the expression on his face was as sincere
as she'd ever seen. As much as he'd hurt her—as much as
she'd been hurting—she couldn't deny herself the chance
to hear what he'd come here to tell her.

She stepped aside and he walked in, resting the roses
on the kitchen table. "I've interrupted your dinner. It's a
work of art."

"It's perfect," she said. "And probably the only perfect
thing left in my life. That's your fault."

"I know it is. And finding Wes—Tate…" He pinched
the bridge of his nose, and she felt for him, she really did.
He had to be struggling with finding his brother, with
adjusting to him being alive and potentially a part of his
life again. She wondered how his parents had reacted.
They had to be overjoyed. After decades, their family was
whole again.

But you're not, she reminded herself.

As great as the news was that Reid's twin brother was
alive, there was unfinished business between Reid and
her. She deserved an apology. Thankfully, he knew just
where to start.

"I'm sorry I shut you out, Drew. I'm absolute shit at
sharing with the people in my life. I could argue it was
because of losing my brother at such an early age. I could
explain that being a twin feels like you're half of a whole,
and I haven't been whole in a long time. But I should've
trusted you. I should've come to you. I should never have
stood you up without a word of explanation." He sighed, his
eyebrows bending in remorse. "I never should have been

so cruel to you when you came to my apartment. You were concerned and I… I was a complete wreck."

He stepped closer but didn't touch her. She wasn't sure if she wanted him to or not. She had no idea if he'd simply come here to make reparations and then leave things as is, or if there was more. Then he cleared that up for her, too.

"I want you, Drew Fleming. Not only in my bed, but in my life. You have a way of pushing me into realms I'd have never discovered on my own. You're healing the deepest part of me. The part that has never been whole. I tried handling this on my own. I tried to clean up the mess and not involve you, but…"

He paused as if gathering his courage, and then started again. "I need you. I have long prided myself on never needing anyone, but you…you're different. I love you in a way I've never loved anyone before. I don't want you at arm's length. I want to come home to you and I want to be held by you when I've had a shit day. I've never thought myself a family man, but when I picture our lives —our marriage and our children—with my family, with my brother, I can hardly breathe because the joy is too great."

Her eyes filled with tears. The picture he painted bloomed to life inside her head with hardly any effort. Marriage, a beautiful baby boy in her arms, celebrating Christmas in London…

"I screwed up. I have no excuse for being a complete wanker. But I can absolutely promise you that I won't do it again. I won't shut you out of my life, and I won't ever keep secrets. I love you too much to risk losing you again." He swallowed thickly, his Adam's apple bobbing. "If you can accept my apology and let me try again, I promise I'm worth loving. If you can let yourself love me."

"I already let myself love you, Reid. It's what I was going to tell you on your birthday. I was planning on telling you how I felt that night." She felt the loss of that night fresh. "I thought once you saw what I'd planned for you, once you were there with the gold and black streamers and the perfect steak dinner…" It sounded so foolish now that she said it out loud. "I don't know what I was thinking. I should've just told you how I felt."

"Streamers?" Realization dawned on Reid's face. "That night…there wasn't a soft opening, was there?" he asked miserably.

"It was a birthday dinner for you. A private one. I borrowed the Fig & Truffle and hired a server, bartender and chef. I wanted you to have a good birthday memory to add to the bad ones. I knew it wouldn't make up for what you'd lost, but I thought it might soften the blow."

Reid stood stock-still and simply stared. "Wow. I really don't deserve you."

"No. Probably not."

"I'm sorry. For all of it." His mouth turned down at the corners. "That was my piece. I've said it. Have I earned my second chance?"

She rested one hand on his cheek and peered up at the beautiful, lost dope of a man who couldn't trust his own heart or himself when he'd finally found true love. "You're still on your *first* chance. I'm completely and totally in love with you. I want marriage and kids and I want to go to London."

His smile emerged, followed by a laugh that sounded suspiciously emotional.

"You're the man for me, and I knew it from the first second I laid eyes on your gorgeous face. It just took us both time to find ourselves. To grow into the people who were right for each other."

"Please, Drew. Can I kiss you and make it all right?"

She looped her arms around his neck and breathed in

the leather scent of his cologne. She was home in his arms and he in hers. They would get through this the way they were meant to go through everything in life: *together*.

Against his lips, she whispered, "You'd better do more than kiss me, Reid Singleton."

* * * * *

COMING SOON!

LET'S TALK
Romance

For exclusive extracts, competitions
and special offers, find us online:

- facebook.com/millsandboon
- @MillsandBoon
- @MillsandBoonUK

Get in touch on 01413 063232

For all the latest titles coming soon, visit
millsandboon.co.uk/nextmonth